C000088743

HIGH KING
BOOK I

THE WEST RISES

S. M. DAVIES

The West Rises Copyright © S. M. Davies

First published in the United Kingdom by Sylfa Press, 2022

The right of S.M. Davies to be identified as the author of this work has
been asserted under the Copyright, Designs and Patents Act 1988.

All rights reserved.

No part of this publication may be reproduced, stored
in a retrieval system, or transmitted, in any form or by any means,
without the prior written permission of the publisher.

The West Rises is a work of fiction. All characters are the
product of the author's imagination, and any resemblance
to persons living or dead is entirely coincidental.

ISBN: 978-1-7396726-2-1

Requests to publish work from this book should be sent to:
smdavies@sylfapress.com

Cover and Interior Design: JD Smith

Preface

Early in the 5th Century AD, Britain faced destruction. The Romans, masters of the province for over 400 years, had withdrawn their forces to protect their overseas possessions and Rome itself. The de facto king, Roman general Constantine, had been murdered by his own mercenaries. Abandoned by the Empire, Britain was leaderless, divided and broken. Its frightened people faced invasion on all sides. The warlike Picts, warriors so formidable that even the Romans could not subdue them, were ravaging the North. The Irish, enemies for decades, had been contained but threatened to join forces with their old Pictish allies. Saxon raids were a constant and growing menace. Appeals for help from Rome had been bluntly rejected. Powerful British warlords, politicians and priests were too obsessed with their own disputes to confront the danger themselves.

'Out of these conflicts came Vortigern', says John Morris, in his history of the British Isles from 350-650; and 'this Vortigern came from Wales,' according to Anglo-Norman poet Wace, writing in the 11th century. We may never know precisely who Vortigern was, or where he called home; but for a while in the early 5th century, a man of the West known as the High King took power and held it against all odds.

He raised armies and battled invaders for a generation, ensuring that there was a country left to fight for when the torch passed to other hands. This is his story, seen through the eyes of the young warrior who has become his devoted companion.

Characters

Those marked * are recorded in history or legend

Cambria

* Vortigern, Lord of Cambria and the West

* Vortimer, known as Rufus, his oldest son

* Katigern, his second son

* Paschent, his youngest son

* Sevira, his late wife, daughter of Roman emperor *Magnus Maximus

Kerin Brightspear, his warrior and confidant

Lud, Vortigern's chief warrior

Macsen, Lud's oldest son

Custennin, Lud's second son

Elir, Lud's youngest son

Mora, Lud's wife

Bened, Lud's nephew

Cynfawr, Vortigern's bard

Hefydd, warlord, Vortigern's ally

Hefin, Hefydd's younger brother

Cenydd, Vortigern's principal servant

Idris, young warrior, ally of Rufus

Brwyn, Idris's father

Mabli, daughter of Vortigern's silversmith

Londinium

Severus Maximus, the praetor

Publius Luca, commander of the city garrison, formerly of the Second Augusta

Marcellus *magister*, the praetor's physician and soothsayer

Alberius, his acolyte

Cheldric, his Saxon cook

Lupinus, his principal servant

Plicius, head of the praetorian guard

Lucius Arrius, member of the guard, friend to Kerin

Livius, junior guardsman

Tertius, older guardsman

Faria, one of the praetor's Phoenician slaves

Sha'ara, her cousin

Aidée, her cousin

Gallus, wealthy merchant

Maximian Galba, praetor of Venta Belgarum, Vortigern's sworn enemy

Marcus Tarpeius, cousin to the Galbas

Manius, a fisherman

Glevum

* Eldof, Lord of Glevum

Varro, his chief warrior

Bertil Redknife, his kinsman and rival

Gael, Bertil's daughter

Gadlyn, Gael's husband

Balin, Bertil's chief warrior

Brennan, Balin's twin brother

Malan, elderly headman of a village in Eldof's territory

Flora, Malan's granddaughter

Berget, Malan's daughter

Morvid, Bertil's subject, an ancient healer

Marc, Morvid's grandson

Other warlords and their associates

* Gorlois of Kernow, Vortigern's loyal supporter

* Garagon of Kent

Brennius, Garagon's friend and warrior

Edlym, Garagon's uncle

Priests and monks

* Constans, monk, oldest son of the late * Constantine, de facto king of the Britons

Father Paulinus, his abbot, brother of Maximian Galba

Brother Padarn, of the same monastery, man of the North

Father Iustig, abbot of Caerwenn, near
Vortigern's citadel

* Bishop Eldadus of Glevum, brother of Eldof

Father Septimus of Glevum, loyal friend of Gael

Father Giraldus of St Alban's chapel in Londinium

Caradog, Chief Druid of Henfelin, Vortigern's capital

Glossary of place names

Armorica - Brittany
Caerwynt - Winchester
Calleva (Atrebatum) - Silchester
Corinium - Cirencester
Durobrivae - Rochester, Kent
Durovernum - Canterbury
Eburacum - York
Gallia - Gaul, France
Glevum - Gloucester
Glywysing* - The Glamorgans
Hafren - Severn
Isca (Silurum) - Caerleon
Kernow - Cornwall
Leucarum - Loughor, Llwchwr
Venta Belgarum - Winchester
Venta (Silurum) - Caerwent

*Glywysing was the name of the ancient Welsh kingdom which included all the Glamorgans; its boundaries changed over time, but it generally extended from the Tywi in the west to the Wye, or at times the Severn.

To Sian and Gareth

1

Spring came late that year. The Romans had known what they were doing when they named the month after their war god. Beneath the swaying branches of the wind-bent elms, the men waited. Their limbs were cold and cramped from squatting in the damp hollow, but they were men of the West, used to harsh conditions, and did not complain. They just pulled their cloaks tight against the bone-chilling wind, stared past the trees at the bleak plains of Sarum and waited. Their horses, trained for silence, stood with heads dropped, reins looped over the elder bushes.

The men were on edge. There was no other way to be in such dangerous times. In the wild country between the walled towns, the air was thick with premonitions of death and everyone kept his sword sharpened. No-one had expected the report the messengers brought at midwinter. The king, butchered by his own mercenaries in some foreign backwater! A dumbstruck officer had brought the severed head home in a bag to prove it. Constantine might only have been another military man, raised to glory by his soldiers like Magnus Maximus before him; but at least for a while the Britons had had a leader. Not the strong-arm they'd hoped for, not everyone's choice, but a figurehead at least. A rallying-point. Now there was no-one. The soothsayers were predicting oceans of blood. The legions were a memory and Rome's empire was falling apart. The islands of Britain were alone.

Men of the West didn't frighten easily. Blooded in the Irish wars, they had spent their lives following a man who feared nothing, and some of that lunatic courage had rubbed off on them. They didn't care much about dead kings, or even about the rumours of invasion which were spreading like the pestilence. But for all that, they understood that the thing they were about to do was unusual. Unsettling, even. They needed a touchstone. Kerin Brightspear would have an opinion. They would seek it, as they always did.

He had left them in the hollow, and was watching the Roman road which ran like an arrow's flight towards the eastern horizon. No-one mad enough to be out on that road in the middle of the night would have seen him, invisible in a cleft of the rocky outcrop at the fringe of the wood. He had taken up his position without reference to the others. No-one had commented. He was the lowest-born of the bunch, one of the youngest; and yet with the exception of Lud, chief warrior for thirty years, they deferred to him without question. Kerin flexed his cold fingers and tucked them inside his cloak. He owed Vortigern his life, and saw no sacrifice in numbing his limbs against a freezing rock while he waited for the man to come back.

A shadow moved and came towards him. His friend, Macsen. It was furtive. Someone had put him up to it. 'Kerin, why are we here?' he whispered.

'The king's dead,' Kerin said, watching the deserted road. 'We're going to look for another one.'

Macsen raised his eyebrows. 'In a monastery?' he asked.

Kerin shrugged but did not reply. Macsen sighed and trudged back towards the trees. He knew when he was battering his head against a wall. Kerin remained where he was, watching the road vanish and reappear as the high clouds drifted across the moon. It was, in fact, nothing unusual for Vortigern to go riding around alone in the unholy hours of the night, when most sane men were sleeping or making love to their wives; but this time they were miles from their home in Cambria, with a warband of only ten men. Kerin could hear the men muttering in the hollow amidst the trees. His hearing was keener than theirs, keen as a hunting dog's, but that was something he had never chosen to tell them. They thought him enough of an oddity as it was.

'Did he say anything?' a deep voice murmured. Lud, Macsen's father.

'No,' Macsen whispered. 'Blood out of a stone. Do you think it's one of those dreams of his?'

'Dreams? That horse-dung?' Custennin, the younger brother, scoffing and sneering as usual.

'Shut your mouth,' Lud growled. 'They're the gods' work.'

Kerin sensed the dark scowl. Custennin had always resented him. His fighting skills, his knack with girls, the way he was with Vortigern, strolling into the chieftains' hall with a smile on his face when other men feared to tap the door. He stretched his cramped limbs and tested the edge of his sword, just in case. His large grey eyes travelled over road and plain with an animal's alertness. He knew that it would have been pointless, trying to explain the situation to the others. Most of the warriors in the warband could see no further than the bottom of their tankards. And so only Kerin knew what they were doing here in the middle of nowhere, on their way to visit a monk – of all things! Only he knew why the monk mattered. The others neither knew nor cared much about the dead king's oldest boy, this skinny string bean of a lad called Constans, who had been in holy orders since the age of fifteen. They were there because they were Vortigern's men, and would probably have butchered their own mothers, if he had told them that it was a good idea.

'Alright, lad?' This time it was Lud who had come out of the wood to try his luck.

'Yes,' Kerin said.

'The boys said you'd had one of those funny dreams,' Lud said tentatively. 'Anything to do with this monk business?'

'No,' Kerin said. 'Tell Macsen I dreamed that there'd be twenty naked women waiting for him behind the chapel.'

Lud grinned and ruffled Kerin's hair. He went back to his warriors and shared Kerin's lie amongst them. They laughed, stifling the sound with their hands. Kerin envied them their good humour, but could not share it. He saw things; or so men thought. Not creatures of the Otherworld, or the spirits of the dead, like the druids sometimes claimed they could see; but things which had not even happened yet. The gift, some people called it. Kerin was not amongst them.

He could barely remember when the nonsense began. In a time beyond the reach of accurate memory, when he was a little child sleeping in a cupboard in Lud's house, he had dreamed a dream about Lud's hunting dog, Migwyn. In the morning he went straight out to the lean-to where the dog slept, to make sure that he was still alive and not stretched out stiff and cold on his bed of straw, as he had been in the vivid, disturbing dream from which Kerin had just surfaced. Naturally, he told Lud's wife Mora – he had to explain away those tears, after all. She pooh-poohed the idea, because Migwyn was fit and strong, even if getting on in years. Two days later, the dog was dead. Then Mora told Lud, and Lud told Vortigern, and the next thing Kerin knew, he was living in luxury in the chieftains' hall. He was not old enough to reason it out. He was simply overjoyed with his new life. He was sleeping in a comfortable bed in a room of his own, instead of being bundled into a cupboard like an afterthought. He was well fed. He could spend his days playing with Rufus, the firstborn son, and his evenings curled up in front of a fire listening to stories. Rufus's mother was kindness itself. Vortigern taught him to ride a horse. No-one said a word about nightmares or prophecies, until one day – around his eleventh birthday, Kerin thought – Lud took him to one side and asked him if he'd had any of those dreams lately. Kerin's blank look must have been sufficient answer, because Lud marched him into the stable, sat him down on a sack of oats and told him that he'd better have some soon, before Vortigern's patience ran out.

'He's a man of power, not a nursemaid,' Lud said,

shaking his finger in the child's face. 'Do you know what his name means? *Vortigern?* High King, that's what. And men like that need prophets, to smooth their way. Why else do you think you're living in the chieftains' hall, like a rich man's son?'

Kerin could not answer Lud's question. He had always supposed that it must be because someone liked him. Hadn't Sevira told him that he was alive only because of an impulsive act of kindness on Vortigern's part; that there was more to Rufus's father than most people understood? Now, Kerin realised, it was not that at all. He was in Vortigern's household on sufferance. Until then, the only pain he had experienced was the sort that happened when you got stung by a bee or cracked your head on a branch. Now he realised that there was another kind, and that it was slowly and methodically cutting away everything he had thought was his; the warmth, the secure home, the family life, the love. It was unthinkable to cry in front of the chief warrior, though, so instead he asked Lud what he should do. 'Give him a reason to keep you,' Lud said, taking him by the shoulders and giving him a shake. 'And it had better be a good one, because there's not much sense or patience in him since Rufus's mother went to the gods.'

And so, as Kerin grew, that was what he did. He practised and punished himself until he was as skilled a warrior and horseman as anyone in Vortigern's company. He trained his powers of observation until he could second-guess almost anyone. He could evaluate situations and, quite often, predict the outcome. Sometimes, when the other warriors asked him how on earth he'd known what was going to happen, he would claim to have dreamed it all. No-one ever argued with that. He was good enough at it for people to speculate about his gift. They took to wondering out loud whether it was a matter of chance, or inherited from the mother or father Kerin had never known. They believed that the gift was real, and that he saw things which other men could not see, just as he detected sounds before most people's ears could pick them up. His hearing was acute, it was true; but he was also far better at listening. He heard the thudding footsteps seconds before any of the men in the hollow. The moon had gone in. Kerin tensed and gripped his sword.

The old man came stumbling out of the darkness, sobbing for breath and dragging the girl behind him. 'Oh, the gods!' he squealed, as Kerin stepped from the shadow of the rock. The warriors were on their feet, drawing weapons; not because of the ragged old man and the girl, but because no-one ran like that in the middle of the night unless something hideous was after them.

'Don't hurt my grandfather!' the girl gasped. She was tall and slender, with a deer's soft eyes and dark, wild hair. As the cloud thinned, Kerin could see the way she was holding herself; tense, on her toes, like a fawn poised for flight. She's terrified of me, he thought, as her eyes darted over his fine clothes. Heavy grey cloak and tunic, dark breeches tucked into supple doeskin riding boots. Silver armlets, silver belt-buckle, thick brown hair cut just to the nape in the style all the young bloods favoured. She had taken him for a patrician, of course, although he was no such thing.

'I'm not going to hurt anyone,' Kerin said. He was about to ask her what she was running from, but then the sound came, growing out of the still night; the drumming of hooves over parched ground. He pushed the girl and the old man behind the rock, calculating that he and his small warband were outnumbered by three to one. 'Macsen, the horses!' he shouted, but it was too late for that. A spear flashed past his ear and embedded itself in the soft earth. The riders came crashing through the underbrush. In the lead Kerin glimpsed a dark man with powerful shoulders, a thick black beard and tiny, gleaming eyes. At his shoulder was a fair, long-haired youngster whirling a sword around his head. Kerin wrenched the spear from the ground and hurled it. The point tore into the younger man's throat and he pitched from his horse with a horrible, gurgling cry. His sword came spinning through the air. Kerin caught it deftly, slashed the bearded warrior's mare across the hind legs and leapt aside as she stumbled and fell. The rest of the men, surrounded in the hollow, were frantically hacking their way out. Kerin glimpsed big, flame-haired Macsen with blood streaming from his forearm; Lud alongside him, red droplets flying from his beard. Kerin lunged towards them, then stopped short. Five warriors barred his way. All of them had swords and axes. One was the dark, pig-eyed man. Someone had slashed off his right ear, and it was pouring blood.

'Kill my horse would you, you young bastard?' he panted.

'Fast death or slow, Brennan?' one of the others crowed. Kerin felt the sweat running down his back.

He would take most of them with him when they killed him. And then came the sound. Muted thunder. He realised that the five warriors were no longer looking at him. Something had frozen them all where they stood. They were staring at a point somewhere behind Kerin's right shoulder.

'Oh, Jesus help me,' one of them whispered. The axe dropped from Brennan's hand and his face drained of colour.

'Run!' he howled.

The black mare came out of the dark like a gust of wind, bronze bridle-rings jingling. Her rider was an extension of her blackness; an apparition in a hooded cloak, but with the hood thrown back, as if he scorned its protection. Sword swinging, he tore through Brennan's men and into the scattering horsemen. The mare's head was down, snaking like a stallion's. She charged into a tall roan gelding, crushing his head under her hooves as he fell. Her big yellow teeth seized his screaming rider by the shoulder. There was a crunch of breaking bones. A shower of blood hit Kerin in the face. He glimpsed Brennan running in blind panic towards the open ground. A brief thudding of hooves and booted feet, then silence. The dark rider reined in and dropped lightly to the ground. The mare shook herself and blew through her nostrils. The men came out of the hollow as if drawn by a supernatural force. Only Kerin remained behind, leaning against a tree trunk as he wiped the blood from his face and caught his breath. Without saying a word the horseman detached himself from the group and strode briskly towards him. Kerin stepped forward. Vortigern always wore black, and in the pitch darkness of the wood he was all but invisible except for the wink of a gold medallion caught by a sudden ray of moonlight, and a flash of teeth in a scant, dark beard which told Kerin that he had smiled.

'You bunch of incompetents,' he said. 'I can't leave you alone for a moment. Who the hell were they?'

'I don't know,' Kerin said, looking around him at the litter of broken bodies. 'One of them was called Brennan. He's missing his right ear.' He looked up through the tracery of branches. The wind had suddenly dispersed the clouds and the moon sailed above them like a white globe, illuminating the wood and the bare plain surrounding it. 'We could do without that,' he said. Vortigern shrugged.

'The same light shines on everyone,' he said. 'You couldn't hide a field-mouse out there, let alone an army the size of Eldof's.'

'He'll find out,' Kerin said. 'Those ruffians might be his. You know they've been ranging further than ever lately.'

'Of course he'll find out,' Vortigern said, then frowned. 'What's the matter with you, for God's sake? You can't be afraid of Eldof.'

Kerin scowled and spat on the leaf mould. 'That's how much I fear Eldof of Glevum,' he said. Vortigern nodded.

'That's what I thought,' he said. An owl hooted somewhere. The men were moving about, dragging the bodies into the hollow and talking quietly amongst themselves. Lud came across the clearing and handed Vortigern a water-skin. Vortigern sluiced the blood from his arms and gave him a wry smile.

'They caught us by surprise,' Lud protested. Vortigern chuckled.

'I could see,' he said. Lud, who had a proud reputation to defend, looked disgusted with his part in things. He was still chief warrior, even if his eyes were a little less keen these days, and his thick red hair and beard were heavily streaked with grey. 'Did we lose anyone?' Vortigern asked.

'No,' Lud said. 'A few cuts and bruises, that's all.'

'Good,' Vortigern said. 'Go and make a fire, and skin that deer Macsen killed.'

Lud coughed uneasily. 'Lord, you shouldn't have gone riding about on your own in country like this. One day, someone's going to put a spear through you.'

Kerin suppressed a smile. The two men had been having this disagreement for as long as he could remember, and it was unlikely to be resolved at this stage of their lives.

'Lud, you're my chief warrior, not my mother,' Vortigern said. Lud gave a snort of disapproval. He spoke quickly to the men and a group of them dispersed amongst the trees, gathering brushwood for the fire. His youngest boy, wiry, dark-haired Elir, set about skinning and gutting the carcass. Vortigern watched them work.

'Lud's like a bastard old hen,' he said. Kerin chuckled.

'He's only thinking of your safety. He'd die for you, and you know it.'

'I know,' Vortigern said. 'But I don't think he'll have to die for me here, and neither do you, or you'd have made a fuss long ago. Eldof's safe at home in bed with his fat ugly wife, and anyway, we could beat his cripples with one hand tied behind our backs. So why don't you think we should be going to see Brother Constans?'

He looked directly at Kerin. The wind ruffled his shaggy black hair. The moonlight gleamed in a pair of dark eyes which could bewitch the unwary or freeze an enemy's blood. Kerin took a deep breath.

'Because I think it'll make trouble for us all, one way or another,' he said. Vortigern regarded him curiously. He didn't believe in anything much, people said; but he did appear to trust Kerin's powers of foresight, or at least his perception of the elusive details that other men missed. He rarely mentioned dreams or prophecies, but he had taken to seeking Kerin's opinion more often since some barbarian butchered Constantine, snapping the last threads of authority. On that day in the stable with Lud, Kerin had realised that his own life hung on getting things right, but now there was more at stake. The country was overrun with leaderless, well-armed men who would start killing each other soon if someone didn't take command.

'I can't see a bunch of monks causing us much trouble,' Vortigern said.

'Neither can I,' Kerin said, feeling the sweat prickle on his forehead. 'But that's not the point. It's not the monks. It's what might come afterwards. And we don't know that, do we? We're here in the middle of nowhere with a warband of ten men, about to remove a monk from his monastery to force a few people's hands, and we don't know what will happen next.'

They both looked up as something moved at the edge of the wood. Kerin had completely forgotten about the old man and his granddaughter. They came creeping through the trees, looking as petrified as a couple of doomed lambs in the butcher's pen.

'They were running away from those cut-throats,' Kerin said. 'There wasn't time to ask why.'

'Because they're murdering bastards, that's why,' the old man said angrily. 'We can't even gather kindling in our own wood these days.'

'Who are you?' Kerin asked.

'My name's Malan,' the old man said. 'I'm the headman of a village just north of here. Beside the old Roman road, the Via Legionis. And this is my grand-daughter, Flora.' The girl's dark eyes met Kerin's and were lowered. A smile and a trace of colour flickered across her pale face. She was wearing a frail blue dress which could have given her no protection from the cold. 'We've seen better days,' Malan said defensively. 'It was a rich village once, but not now, with robbing louts like that about.'

'But this is Eldof of Glevum's land,' Vortigern said. 'Can't he control his dogs better than that?'

'Not when they're Bertil Redknife's dogs,' Malan said sourly. Vortigern nodded slightly, as if the name had stirred some old memory. The girl was watching him, Kerin noticed. He felt as if he himself had become invisible.

'Get back to your village, then,' Vortigern said. 'They won't trouble you again tonight.'

'Lord, can't we send someone with them?' Kerin asked.

'No. We can't spare anyone, and you know it.' Vortigern picked up a discarded sword and tossed it to Malan. 'Here. If you can't use this, you shouldn't be out alone. Keep to the roads, and if anyone crosses you, tell him I'll behead him.'

Malan glanced at the mangled bodies with a nervous smile. Arms linked, he and his granddaughter turned away. As they reached the Roman road, Flora paused and looked over her shoulder.

'Thank you,' she mouthed silently. Kerin nodded an acknowledgement. Vortigern, to whom the thanks had been directed, did not respond; his eyes were distant, his thoughts far from the straggling wood and the girl and the bodies. They sat down on a log beside the fire which the men had lit. The meat, jointed for speed, was starting to sizzle. Someone had set a pot to heat. A pleasant brew made from herbs and honey; it was that or water, when the warband was on the march. As the cups were passed round, Vortigern's oldest son came out of the darkness and sat down beside his father. Vortimer was the name he had been given at his baptism, but no-one here used it. His mother had called him Rufus from his cradle because he had been born with a mop of copper hair, and Rufus meant 'red' in Latin, her native tongue. In time the boy's hair had turned black as night, like both his parents', but the name had clung at home in Cambria, to Vortigern's disgust. He had not wanted his sons to grow up with Roman names.

Rufus was Kerin's age, give or take a few days. He was a babe in arms on the night, twenty-five winters gone, when Vortigern came in out of a raging blizzard with a frozen scrap of humanity wrapped in his cloak. The scrap had been put out in the woods for wolf's meat, and Vortigern could have left it where it was, but instead he brought it home and tossed it to Lud's wife. The scrap had survived, to most people's surprise, and now it was sitting beside the fire with Vortigern and his son, drinking herbal brew.

'How many dead?' Kerin asked.

'Ten,' Rufus said. 'We've laid them out over there. I'd have preferred to bury them, personally, but Lud said that their own would probably come back for them. God knows why they wasted their time chasing those two poor devils.'

'Men like that don't need a reason,' Vortigern said. 'They do it for sport, or for no reason at all. Suppose a beetle crawled across the path in front of you. Would you crush it?'

'I don't know,' Rufus said. 'Possibly. Or perhaps I'd let it go. If I was in a bad mood, I'd probably squash it flat.'

'Yes,' Vortigern said. 'Simply for crossing your path. And thugs like that are just the same. If we hadn't been here, they'd have knifed the old man and raped the girl to death, then gone home to drink ale and enjoy their dinner. So don't waste your Christian charity on them.'

Rufus gave his father a resentful look but did not reply. The fine-drawn features were his mother's. Kerin remembered her clearly, although he couldn't have been more than eight years old when she died, bearing her youngest son. Rufus was wearing a heavy gold crucifix which had surprised Kerin when it made its first appearance. It was the size of a man's fist, and no-one wore a thing like that unless he intended it to be noticed.

'What's the matter?' Vortigern asked, as his oldest

son gazed sleepily at the fire. 'Are you sick, or have I ridden the skin off you?'

Rufus looked round. 'I've got a good new horse at home. I'll race that bone-bag of yours, if you like. A fair race, though. Equal weights, checked in a balance.'

Vortigern raised an eyebrow. 'You'd better take that crucifix off first, then,' he said. Rufus frowned. Kerin shifted uneasily as if he were sitting next to something which might boil over and scald him. For as long as he could remember, Rufus had been his closest friend. Brothers in all but name, since the day they nicked their thin white children's wrists and slammed them together so that the blood mingled and dribbled down their forearms. Rufus had been happy enough to spend his time with a no-account, sharing what all the lads shared; pranks, hunting, horses, the village girls who lifted their skirts for them behind the carpenter's workshop. Kerin couldn't quite remember when things had started to change. Rufus looked directly at his father.

'You know we shouldn't be here,' he said.

'And why not?' Vortigern enquired. 'You're a Christian, or so you keep telling me, so why disapprove when I go to visit an abbot? You'd have enough to say if you thought I'd sold my soul to the druids.'

'You're not going to see the abbot,' Rufus said impatiently. 'You're going to see Constans. I don't care if he is the king's son. Constans is a monk. He's taken his vows and he's God's man now. I know we need a leader, but for God's sake, it can't be him.'

'Then who would you like to have?' Vortigern asked. 'One of his little brothers? Ambrosius, a skinny lad, or Uther, who probably still sucks his nurse's paps? And please, don't give me any nonsense about divine grace. God hasn't stopped the North getting ravaged. Soon people will be butchering each other in the streets, and the Picts will be marching towards Londinium, slaughtering everything they find.'

'And you think a monk can stop them?' Rufus said scornfully.

'No,' Vortigern said. 'But someone must.' He turned as Lud came to the fireside. The chief warrior threw himself down beside the flames, smiling and wiping blood from his hands on the skirts of his tunic.

'A feast fit for a king, lord,' he said cheerily. Kerin caught Rufus's eye, and saw the bitter, disapproving look that burned there.

'You had better put it back where it came from, then, Lud,' Rufus said coolly, 'because there are no kings here.'

Lud looked utterly mystified. 'All right,' he conceded. 'We're not kings. But there's no reason not to eat like them, is there?'

'Probably not, for you,' Rufus said. 'But I have no stomach for it.'

He got up and stalked off towards the bushes where the horses were tied. Lud picked up a chunk of wood, drew a short-bladed dagger from his belt and began whittling.

'It's this Christian nonsense, if you ask me,' he said. 'Father Iustig's a good man, but he's got a lot to answer for where Rufus is concerned.'

Vortigern drew his dagger and examined the blade. 'A good man? All I asked Iustig to do was teach my sons to read and write.' He grabbed a stone and hurled it at the flames. A shower of sparks went spiralling up into the quiet air.

'Lord, exactly why are we going to Caerwynt?' Lud asked. Vortigern slid from the log and lay looking up into the darkness.

'To talk to Abbot Paulinus,' he said. 'The people who made Constantine king will be looking for a replacement. Paulinus has Constantine's son, Constans, in his care. And, monk or not, he's still his father's oldest son.'

'So you think he should be king?' Lud said dubiously. 'A monk, who has never been a leader or a warrior? Who would have to break his vows to take the crown?'

Vortigern sat up, drew his knees to his chest and rested his chin on them, his eyes dark and hollowed by the dancing flames. 'You're missing the point, Lud,' he said softly. Lud shrugged and went back to his whittling. It was the warrior he loved in Vortigern. The rest confounded him. His brain could not cope with a man who had despised the Romans but wore a Roman medallion around his neck; one of those things they called *clipeum*, after their round bronze shields.

'Lord,' he said, 'do you think that a man can learn to be a king?'

Vortigern looked up. 'Do you think that a man can learn to be a warrior?' he asked. Lud thought about it for a moment.

'You can teach him a warrior's skills,' he said, 'but they won't do him much good if he's not a warrior in his heart.'

Vortigern nodded. 'Well, I expect that being a king is much the same. Why do you ask?'

'You know,' Lud said, concentrating hard as he

chipped away, 'if you ask me, Constantine himself was just another Roman soldier who went sailing off with his army when we needed him most. Kings should protect their people, not run away and leave them to the carrion crows. They should make their enemies sweat with fear, like you do.'

Vortigern chuckled. Kerin looked up and caught his eye. He knew Vortigern in all his moods, and knew that when he laughed like that, he was at his most dangerous. Lud beamed with the satisfaction of a man who had made a good joke, no more concerned about the purpose of their journey than he was about the pile of corpses laid out to rot in the hollow behind them. Men of the West didn't lose sleep about things like that, any more than they worried about the tide coming in, or the sun warming the earth with its beneficent light. Men of the West carried their own light with them; and now they were taking it to Caerwynt, to shine upon the unsuspecting son of Britain's dead king.

2

They came to Caerwynt at dawn. The first streaks of light were licking up across the sky to the east like tongues of pale fire. Vortigern reined in on a ridge overlooking the town and his warriors fell in beside him. The horses stamped and whickered, their breath smoking in the frosty air. Kerin shivered and pulled his cloak tight. At home in Henfelin, far away on the south coast of Cambria, the women would be lighting fires and the smell of fresh bread would soon be drifting from the houses, mingling with the tang of sea salt and bracken. Kerin's mare moved restlessly and he reached forward to stroke her neck. Eryr, the eagle, his companion throughout eight years of hunting and fighting. She was a big, lean chestnut with the grace of a running deer. It was almost impossible to believe that she was the daughter of Vortigern's ugly black mare.

They had made good time; only three days from Glywysing to this remote place on its bleak plain. Three days of relentless slog along the good cobbled roads which had once carried the marching legions, and through forest and heath on tracks which had been ancient long before the Romans came, at a gruelling pace which would have killed most men and their animals. Kerin gave it no thought, because he had ridden with Vortigern since he was old enough to straddle a horse, and knew no other way.

'Venta Belgarum!' Vortigern said, with a little twitch of the lips, as if the grandeur of the Roman name amused him. Kerin stretched his limbs and looked down across the barren cornfields at the town, wondering how many women it might contain. He thought for a moment about Flora, the girl in the wood. Some deep, unbidden instinct told him that their paths would probably cross again one day. All in all, he hoped that he was wrong, at least for her sake.

Two riders came up the hill from the town. In the lead, Hefin; big, brown-haired, just turned forty; the sort of man you'd want with you in a scrape. On his tail Lud's nephew Bened, a broad-shouldered ox with huge hands and woolly dark hair. The other warriors called him Dull Bened, accurately but never to his face, because he could have lifted any of them clear of the ground with one hand. 'It's quiet,' Hefin said. 'If there's a city garrison, they're either pissed or asleep.'

They rode through the sprawl of wooden houses at the edge of the Roman town. Grubby children scattered and people peered nervously from their doors. Bands of mounted warriors were usually bad news for a village with women to rape and animals to steal. Kerin read the fear in the faces which stared up at him, and wondered how many times they had suffered it all. The clatter of the horses' hooves echoed between the high, windowless walls of the houses on either side of the deserted main street. A ragged boy perched on the balustrade of a spacious, empty villa while his goats wandered through the ruined gardens, fouling the ornate mosaics beneath their feet. The small procession halted halfway down the street. The men at the front were bickering amongst themselves. Lud rode back, looking unusually ill at ease.

'Lord,' he said, 'the men won't ride through the town. They fear the spirits.'

Vortigern's eyes narrowed. 'The spirits?' he said incredulously.

'Yes, lord,' Lud said reluctantly. Vortigern's breath escaped in a long sigh. He rode slowly up to the head of the line and turned to face his men.

'Look,' he said, 'I'm going to ride to the end of the street. You have that long to decide which you fear most; me, or the spirits of a few dead Romans.'

The men chuckled nervously amongst themselves. Vortigern nodded, knowing that he had won, and rode away from them without a backward glance.

The monastery was nothing much; a group of huts clustered about a pool, a larger wooden building thatched with reeds, and beyond that a simple stone chapel. A black-robed monk was kneeling beside the pool, scrubbing clothes on a flat stone. Vortigern raised his hand, bringing the warband to a halt. He dismounted, tossing his reins to Kerin, and strode towards the pool. Lud stifled a chuckle. The young monk froze as the dark reflection rose before him in the limpid water. He spun round, gabbling and clutching his crucifix, then turned and fled towards the chapel.

'This is madness, Kerin,' Rufus hissed. They waited. There was a movement in the doorway of the chapel and the frightened young monk reappeared, followed by a diminutive grey-haired priest with piercing eyes and skin as brown and wrinkled as an oak-apple. Vortigern regarded him with amused curiosity and folded his arms.

'Do you know who I am?' he asked. The abbot looked up at him without a blink.

'I know who you are, my lord,' he said politely, 'but I was about God's business. I am God's servant, and I acknowledge no master but him.' He braced himself, his little hawk's eyes glaring defiance.

'Well!' Vortigern said softly. 'The little mouse roars like a dragon.'

The abbot folded his hands on his chest. 'You are far from your home in Cambria, Lord Vortigern, and if you'll pardon me for saying so, you don't look like a man who has come to offer himself in the service of God.'

Vortigern gave him a wounded look. He unclasped his sword-belt and let it fall to the ground. 'Your pardon, Father Abbot,' he said respectfully. 'I promise you that I do come in peace.' Paulinus glanced down at the sword-belt and then at Vortigern's warriors, granite-faced and armed to the teeth. He raised a sceptical eyebrow. Vortigern smiled benignly. 'However it may look,' he said. Paulinus gave a grudging nod.

'Alright,' he said. 'I know that no-one can travel unarmed in these times.' He nodded to the nervous young monk. 'Go, find Brother Padarn, and bring a table and benches out here.'

They waited while the monks hurried back and forth, bringing rough-hewn seats and a big scrubbed table. Lud left the warband and moved across to join them.

'Lord,' he said, 'all the men are hungry.'

'We are poor monks, lord.' Paulinus gave a wry smile. 'You are welcome to the bread and cheese we eat ourselves, but that's all we have to offer.'

'Feed them whatever you have,' Vortigern said. 'Bread and water if you like. It's as much as they're used to when they ride with me, whatever they may tell you.' He sat down at the table, motioning to Rufus and Kerin to join him. Paulinus sat opposite them with Brother Padarn, a big, grey-haired man with rough hands and a visible scar across the top of his tonsured head. Padarn probably wasn't as old as he looked, Kerin suspected. His dark eyes were bright and observant, and the skin on his powerful neck was curiously unlined. Perhaps it was trouble that had turned his hair grey and furrowed his forehead. The younger monk came with bread, slabs of cheese and pitchers of water.

'You have come to see Constans, I suppose,' Paulinus said. Vortigern's eyebrows rose.

'You're very direct, Father Abbot,' he said. 'I like that.'

Paulinus poured water into rough wooden bowls. 'I'm not a fool, Lord Vortigern. I may be a monk, but my father served in the Twentieth Valeria Victrix, and I can use a sword on God's behalf if necessary. And my younger brother is Maximian Galba, praetor of Venta Belgarum, so not much happens here without my knowledge.' He broke bread and handed it to his guests. 'What news from the West?' he asked. 'Everyone says you've seen off the Irish invaders.'

Vortigern nodded. 'We have stopped them, at least for now. I have allowed a few to remain as settlers, and they cause no trouble, but we remain vigilant. Always vigilant. You have had reports from the North too, I imagine?'

'Yes,' Paulinus said. 'Hordes of savages with wild hair and painted bodies, coming over the Emperor's Wall, burning the cornfields and slaughtering everything they find. It's nothing new, of course. Hadrian didn't build a defence like that to keep out a flock of sheep, and it was garrisoned to the teeth in my father's day. But a friend of Maximian's has come back from there, a merchant called Tegid. My brother sent for me because he hoped that I might be able to help him.'

'Battle-shock,' Brother Padarn said knowingly, giving his scarred head a tap. 'Had it myself a few years ago.'

Kerin looked curiously at the scar. Padarn spoke with an accent he had never come across, far removed from the cultivated tones of Paulinus. 'Where did you get that?' he asked.

'Same place as Tegid,' Padarn said. 'I'm from the North myself.' He broke off a piece of bread and shoved it into his mouth. 'Ever seen a Pict, young fellow?'

'No,' Kerin said. Padarn snorted.

'Painted bastards,' he mumbled through his bread.

'My brother's on his way to Londinium, to address the ordo,' Paulinus said. 'He's taking poor Tegid with him. Maximian fears that the men of power won't want to fight an enemy they can't see, but Tegid can tell them what it's like up there. Burned villages, whole populations butchered. The fate of Tegid's brother, I do not even wish to speak of.' Brother Padarn made a growling sound deep in his throat and turned away, blinking tears. 'Brother Padarn's family were also slaughtered by Picts,' Paulinus said. 'We must – we *must* – raise arms and march to the North. I am not a man of blood, but it cannot be God's will that we let our people suffer as Padarn and Tegid have suffered.' He broke off abruptly. There was a wild tremor in his clenched hands, and Kerin thought how remarkable it was that so much passion should be boiling away inside so tiny a man, and what a waste it was to devote it all to God, instead of just picking up a sword and getting on with things.

'Paulinus, I don't have much time,' Vortigern said. 'We both want to keep the Picts behind Hadrian's Wall. There are men in Londinium who think that anything from the West is the devil's spawn, and I need Constans to make them listen to me.'

'So what do you think he should do?' Paulinus demanded. 'Break his holy vows? Turn his back on God?'

'My concern is to stop the Picts,' Vortigern said. 'You and Constans must look after your own consciences.' He smiled with a sudden brilliance. 'It cannot be God's will that we let our people suffer as Padarn and Tegid have suffered, all the same.'

Paulinus, who had opened his mouth, closed it abruptly. Vortigern raised his eyebrows expectantly.

'Alright,' the abbot said grudgingly. 'Brother Constans will come to you in the speech house. But when the sun rises above the top of that tall elm tree over there, he must return to his devotions.'

'I will speak with him alone,' Vortigern said. It was a warning, and this time Paulinus did not argue. He leapt to his feet and hurried away across the clearing.

Padarn followed him, glancing behind as he went. Kerin watched them go with a feeling of apprehension which he found hard to justify.

Vortigern rose to his feet. 'Well?' he asked his son. 'Do you want to hear this?'

Rufus remained seated, fists clenched on the table. 'I want no part of it,' he said.

'Come on, for the love of God,' Kerin said. 'Do you want to see the Picts hang our people up for the crows, as well as Tegid's?'

Rufus ignored the question. His eyes met Vortigern's like dark water meeting fire. 'I want no part of it. And if you want to make a king of that monk, you'll have to do it without my help.' He got up from the bench without another word and marched off towards the pool where the warriors were sitting. Vortigern watched his son go.

'He'll never accept it, will he,' he said.

'No,' Kerin said. 'You know what men are like when the faith gets hold of them. They put it before everything else.'

'So be it,' Vortigern said coolly. 'I have until next spring to raise an army, and God isn't going to do it for me, whatever Rufus thinks.' The sound of the monks' prayers came drifting on the light wind. At the door of the speech house Vortigern paused.

'Kerin, you're the only one who dares speak the truth to my face. You're not happy about this.'

'No, lord,' Kerin said. 'But I can see that it might be useful, and I don't have any better ideas, unfortunately.'

Vortigern gave him a quick smile. 'The faith won't trap you, then,' he said. Kerin knew exactly what he was being asked. He thought of a bleak night many years ago, beyond the reach of his memory; of a newborn child lying naked on a frozen rock, and of a man who chose not to pass by.

'No, lord,' he said. 'There's no danger of that.'

*　*　*

The interior of the hut was heavy with the smell of damp earth. A single tallow lamp burned in an earthenware pot. The only other source of light was a tiny window high in the east wall. Kerin sat on the narrow bench beside Vortigern, blinking to accustom his eyes to the murk. Vortigern rested his chin on his hands and stared at the pale young monk who sat, fidgeting uneasily, on the other side of the table.

'Brother Constans,' he said, 'I understand that when the sun rises above the top of the tall elm tree, you must return to your devotions.'

'It is so, lord,' Constans said. He was as slender as a willow-wand, with skin like milk, nervous eyes and a woman's white, fine-boned hands. The light from the window gleamed oddly on the crown of his shaven head.

'And do you like your devotions, Brother Constans?' Vortigern enquired. The young monk looked at him anxiously.

'My vows, lord. It is not for us to like or dislike, simply to keep the faith and serve God as we have promised.'

Vortigern smiled. 'Come on now, Constans. Your dear father – may God preserve his soul – thought that he could serve God best by protecting his people. Don't you think he served God better than Abbot Paulinus does, locked up here in his dark hovel?'

Constans smiled nervously and lowered his eyes. 'You had better not let the abbot hear you say that, lord.'

'Are you afraid of him, then?' Kerin asked. Constans glanced up at him, then back at his hands, which were playing with a simple wooden crucifix.

'Yes, lord,' he admitted. 'Terrified, in fact.'

Kerin grinned. Lord! No-one had ever called him that before, whatever respect he enjoyed amongst the warriors.

'You shouldn't be,' he said. 'What can he do to you?'

Constans's pale eyes widened. 'Lord, he beats monks who transgress,' he whispered. 'He locks us up alone in our cells, with only one cup of water and one crust of bread to keep us alive every day.'

'Have you ever broken your vows?' Kerin asked. Constans's pale face expressed horror.

'No, lord, I have not!' he exclaimed.

'And have you ever wished to?' Vortigern asked, leaning forward slightly. 'What did you do before you entered the cloister, Constans? Did you enjoy a haunch of venison, or a pitcher of wine? Did you wear fine clothes, and take girls to your bed?' A scarlet wave rose slowly from Constans's cheeks to the roots of his shorn hair, so vivid that it was clearly visible, even in the flickering light of the tallow lamp.

'Lord, even the thought of such pleasures is forbidden to us,' he murmured. Vortigern shook his head sadly. He slipped a hand inside his cloak and removed the clipeum. It was an old commemorative coin, polished to brightness and set in gold by a craftsman, bearing the image of a mounted warrior with the buildings of a fine city spread before his feet. There was a Latin inscription around the edge of the coin which Kerin could not read. Constans stared, spellbound by its beauty. Vortigern twisted his fingers so that the medallion spun slowly, winking brilliantly in the single fine beam of sunlight from the tiny window. Timidly Constans reached out to touch it. As he did so Vortigern tossed it in the air, caught it and replaced it around his neck.

'Shame, Brother Constans!' he said. 'Such playthings are not for monks. Now of course, if you were to come to Londinium with me, and do what your father would have wished –'

'But it was my father who made me a monk!' Constans protested.

'Your father was not a prophet,' Vortigern said. 'He put you here because he feared for your safety when he went away to fight. If he had survived, he would have been the first to take you away from this pig-pen.' Constans closed his eyes and mumbled an almost inaudible prayer. Vortigern gritted his teeth with impatience. 'Brother Constans, time is short. If you want to rot here for the rest of your life, then so be it. But come to Londinium with me and I'll make you king over these islands, as your father's rightful heir.' He turned to Kerin and gripped his shoulder. 'Kerin Brightspear, my warrior. He wears fine clothes. He eats good food. He rides one of the best horses in the kingdom, and he's not even of noble blood. But you, a king's son, eat dry bread and go barefoot in the cold. Is that fair?'

Constans sank to his knees, his pale face taut with anxiety. 'I am afraid, Lord Vortigern!' he whispered. 'I know nothing at all about being a king, and besides, what will Abbot Paulinus do to me?'

Vortigern raised Constans to his feet. 'You have nothing to fear from that old buzzard,' he said gently. 'And you may depend on us. We are leaving now, Kerin and I. Come to Londinium with us. We'll soon persuade the people that you should be allowed to renounce your vows.'

Constans smiled nervously. 'I suppose that wouldn't mean renouncing the faith, would it.'

'Of course not,' Vortigern said. 'When all this is over, and the kingdom is safe, you can return to a life of contemplation if that's what you want.'

'You could be a bishop,' Kerin suggested.

'A bishop!' Constans exclaimed. His long fingers moved hesitantly over his rough brown habit, as if transforming it into an elegant purple vestment. Very slowly, he smiled. Vortigern looked at Kerin with un-spoken admiration.

'Kerin, where does the sun stand?' he asked. Kerin stood on the bench and peered through the high window.

'It's just rising above the elm tree, lord,' he said. 'And Paulinus is coming across the clearing,' he added, jumping down from the bench, as the abbot came out of the chapel bristling like a little hunting dog. Vortigern turned to Constans.

'Choose,' he said. The monk closed his eyes.

'All right,' he said, with a tremor in his voice. 'I will come with you.' He spun round as the door of the speech house was wrenched open. Paulinus stood planted in the doorway, framed against the growing light.

'Constans is coming with us,' Vortigern said, with a knowing smile. Paulinus stared up at him impotently.

'Then may God have mercy on all your souls,' he breathed. Kerin stood with Vortigern at the door of the speech house and watched the abbot go. Brother Padarn hurried from one of the huts with a shabby cloak, which he put around Constans's shoulders.

'Go easy on him,' he murmured to Kerin. 'He hasn't got a clue.'

Paulinus had gathered the rest of his monks outside the chapel. He was throwing his hands in the air and calling on God. Vortigern caught Kerin's eye.

'Look after that monk,' he said. 'He'll be no good to us dead.' Kerin looked at Constans, in a huddle with Brother Padarn and the young monk who had brought the bread and cheese. Perhaps they were praying. You are an instrument, he thought; as I am. But there the similarity ended. Poor Constans was helpless, like a hogtied lamb. For Kerin a door had creaked open, just a little, and a tiny gleam of light was beginning to seep through the crack. He thought of the night before they left home, sitting in the library in the chieftains' hall, the holy of holies, as Vortigern explained what they were about to do.

'We're going to Caerwynt,' he said. 'The place the Romans called Venta Belgarum. We're going to remove Constantine's son from the monastery there, and take him to Londinium. And then we're going to make him king.'

'A monk, king?' Kerin said, taken aback.

'Yes,' Vortigern said. 'He won't be king for long, of course.' As brusque as that. And then he gave Kerin that disarming smile which could make you do anything. It could make you kill and starve and freeze and shed your blood for him. It could even make you believe that you held a special place in his heart. Kerin had been trying to fight his way in there ever since that distant day when Lud took him out to the stable and told him the brutal truth. Smooth the way, he had said. Give him a reason to keep you. Of course Kerin would do it, if it could win him the place he craved. If it would bring him half of what Rufus possessed as of right. But all his powers of foresight could not predict the cost, for the monk or for himself. Far less for this man he had loved and revered from his first conscious moment, who was about to walk open-eyed into a furnace of danger and grief. There was probably no-one else who could save the kingdom from everything that was coming to it, but he would never think of saving himself. Someone else would have to do that.

'I hope you're pleased with yourself.' Rufus's voice cut like a blade.

'I'm doing what I have to do,' Kerin said.

'And I too,' Rufus said. 'Think, if you still can.' He gave a nod of the head, sharp like a bird's peck, the sort of thing Kerin had seen him do when parting company with someone he didn't much like. Moments later, he was deep in conversation with Paulinus. It was muttered, it was secretive, even Kerin's sharp hearing couldn't pick it up. Lud was readying the warband for the road. Elir had settled Constans aboard a well-mannered brown gelding, brought along for the purpose.

Kerin mounted up, glad that he was not really the prophet people made him out to be. It was enough to know that this was the most dangerous thing he had done in his life. He didn't want to know, yet, where it ended or who would still be with him when it did.

3

The walls of Londinium loomed out of the morning haze like a cliff face. Massive round towers flanked the gates. Uniformed soldiers could be seen patrolling the battlements, the watery sun gleaming on spearheads and brazen helmets.

'Is it true that the Lord Vortigern doesn't get on with the bishops?' Constans asked anxiously. 'Do you think he might lose patience with me, and – well, leave me by the side of the road? Or send me back?'

Kerin looked down at the white face and frightened eyes, peering from beneath the close-drawn black hood. 'Don't look so worried. He's not going to do that, after taking the trouble to go and get you.'

The monk grimaced. 'Father Paulinus said that he'd eat me alive and spit out the bones,' he said. Kerin chuckled, but privately he was uneasy. There was no knowing how things would go here. The walls were very close now, and behind them lay a city stuffed with rich men; politicians and petty officials, moneylenders and merchants, retired soldiers and well-heeled landowners with villas on the outskirts. Men who had grown fat under the Romans by keeping their heads down and their palms open. Men who still spoke nostalgically about the Empire, even now, when the emperor was too busy mopping up blood on his own doorstep to fret about a backwater like Britain. But these men held the power in Londinium, and most of them despised Vortigern. Despised and feared him, because he would not defer to them, had forged his power in spite of it, and never spoke about the Empire; only about the occupation. Men like these had laughed, years ago, when he cast off his birth name and adopted the only one most people had ever known. 'High King', the nerve of it, when he was a cocky lad and nothing of the sort. But they were not laughing now.

A sharply-dressed man who described himself as an envoy from the praetor, Severus Maximus, met them at the city gates. He was around forty years of age, bland-featured and clean-shaven, riding an elegant, unblemished white horse which had never been anywhere near a fight. The envoy introduced himself as Alberius, and was careful to add that the praetor's house had been built just over a hundred years earlier for the Emperor Allectus; an usurper in some men's eyes, Kerin recalled. They rode into the city through streets crowded with people. Everyone seemed to know who they were, if not precisely why they had come. Children shrieked and danced along the road while men and women cheered, chanted and threw flowers at the horses' feet. Alberius caught Kerin's look of astonishment.

'Everyone knows what Vortigern has done to the Irish invaders in the West,' he explained. 'The poor souls all think he's come to save them from the Picts.'

Kerin kept his counsel. A comely girl in a clinging green dress ran from the crowd and reached up to thrust a laurel branch into his hand. Kerin bent down from the saddle and kissed her hungrily before tearing a twig from the branch and fastening it to Eryr's bridle. A singing, dancing band formed behind them, winding along the cobbled streets between tall Roman buildings interspersed with more modest houses of timber and thatch. The place was swarming with people and dogs. Traders were leading donkeys laden with huge bales of cloth, or wickerwork panniers packed with amphorae full of wine. Down a side road Kerin glimpsed a market, its open tables piled high with jars and bowls, saddles and blankets, cages full of squawking chickens. The place stank of excrement and stale urine, sweat, wood smoke, and the inescapable river smell of dank water and rotting detritus. Macsen and his brothers were singing rowdily as they downed jugs of ale, their eyes almost bulging out of their heads at the sight of so much female flesh. Constans – poor Constans – had jammed a woollen hat on top of his head to hide his gleaming bald pate, huddling into his saddle as if he wished it would swallow him up. Only Vortigern remained impassive, aloof and silent on his stalking black mare.

'This is the house,' Alberius said with obvious pride, flinging out an arm to indicate an opening in a towering wall of yellowish stone. 'It's the finest house in all of Londinium,' he burbled happily. 'You'd think Allectus had only left it yesterday, the way Severus has kept things up. Fountains in the courtyards – they all work, you know – and good bath water, all piped up from the river. And steaming hot, by Jupiter. Even Severus's chariot horses have heating in their stalls; no wonder he has to keep two boys just to sweep out the hypocausts.'

He paused just long enough to draw breath, with a beaming smile. Vortigern gave him a look of bottomless contempt and allowed him to lead the procession into the courtyard. Heavy wooden gates studded and barred with iron swung shut behind them. The silence was almost a physical presence after the racket outside. Ahead was the main house with its steps and soaring columns. There were the fountains, surrounding a towering statue of Minerva, the Roman goddess of wisdom, borne on a chariot drawn by prancing horses. To the right a company of the praetorian guard stood to rigid attention. The pale cold light gleamed on their burnished helmets. The short red cloaks which they wore over their mail shirts fluttered in the light wind. Kerin's practised eye examined their short-handled spears, which looked sharp and well-balanced. He wondered if they could fight as well as they looked. Alberius jumped down from his handsome horse and ran lightly up the steps to the main doorway. He was soon back, bringing with him a shorter, older man whose portly figure was swathed in a rippling white robe edged in purple and gold. A clutch of heavy jewelled rings glinted on the older man's fingers.

'That's the praetor, Severus Maximus,' Vortigern said as he approached them.

'Do you know him?' Kerin asked.

'We met years ago,' Vortigern said. 'I had to come to Londinium with my father, to please the administration, and we stayed at their house. Severus's father had a British wife, but he was a true Roman from a merchant family. I don't think he was very happy to have us under his roof, but he could see that there was money to be made in trading with the West, so Severus had to swallow his tongue and be pleasant to us.'

Severus had arrived in front of them now, wearing a smile which seemed to contain a certain reserve. 'Lord Vortigern, it has been so many years!' he exclaimed, with expertly feigned delight. Vortigern chuckled and slipped to the ground. His mare dropped her ugly head between her knees. The praetor made a little sound of sympathy. 'Your horse looks tired,' he said. 'Alberius, take the poor beast to the stables and tell the lads to rub her down and give her a good thick bed of straw.'

Alberius stepped forward, his broad face still set in that mindless happy smile, and reached for the mare's reins.

'I wouldn't do that if I were you,' Vortigern said.

'Oh, I'm used to horses, lord,' Alberius said jovially. 'She looks as if she could do with a good rest and a bit of feeding up, eh?'

'Alberius!' Rufus exclaimed. But the envoy ignored him. As his fingers closed around the reins, the mare jerked her head back, baring her yellow teeth. She rose on her hind legs with a fearsome screech and struck out viciously with her forefeet. Alberius dived sideways with a yelp of terror, too late to prevent one of her hooves from crashing down on his shoulder, splitting flesh and bone with a ghastly crack. Alberius rolled away, howling in pain. Four of the guards pounded across the courtyard, picked him up and carried him, writhing and screaming, into the house. Severus Maximus ran after them, wringing his hands and shouting for bandages and physicians. Vortigern watched them go and caught the mare's reins. She blew through her nostrils and nuzzled his neck.

'For god's sake,' one of the guards said coldly. 'He could die of that wound.'

Vortigern looked round. 'These are warhorses,' he said. 'If that fool had listened to me, nothing would have happened.'

Severus was soon back. He had the ashen look of someone not accustomed to too much blood and agony. 'My physician is with him,' he said shakily. 'Lord Vortigern, perhaps one of your own men should see to your horse.'

The warriors dismounted, stretching tired limbs, and led the animals off across the courtyard, directed by one of the servants. Constans pattered after them with a nervous glance over his shoulder. Rufus went too, looking like a guard dog.

'I'm sorry about your envoy,' Vortigern said, as he and Kerin walked with Severus towards the house. 'But he should have listened to me. These horses aren't taught to be gentle. They're fighting horses, trained killers. The mare Annwn is worth ten good warriors to me in a battle. She can kill a man or bring down a charging horse with no help from me.'

'Annwn!' Severus said, with a wry smile. '*Hades* in Latin, I believe.'

They mounted the steps and passed through an entrance with massive oak doors, their panels carved with images of hunting. Kerin wondered at the fluid grace of the deer and the pursuing horsemen, so alive that he could almost have expected them to jump out of the doors at him. A pair of guards fell in behind them. Kerin wondered if it was customary, or if Severus Maximus didn't entirely trust his visitors from the West. The praetor led the way down an echoing passage, at the end of which they found themselves in a small room. Severus closed the door behind them. The guards could be heard shuffling their feet in the passage outside. The room was unfurnished except for a table, polished bright with beeswax, and a number of chairs. A bust of one of the emperors glowed, startlingly white, on a plinth in the corner. Everyone sat. A pale light flooded in from the courtyard outside the single window. Kerin thought how tired Severus looked, with his pale lined skin and listless eyes, and how much older than Vortigern, although there could hardly have been more than a few years between them.

'I am glad you have come,' the praetor said, with patent relief. Kerin understood that this was the truth; that this small, weary-looking man had probably been struggling for years with burdens which were too heavy for him, and that he was more than ready to share them, even with men of the West. 'Lord Vortigern, this must be your son Vortimer,' he said, giving Kerin a welcoming pat on the arm. Kerin coloured slightly. In the West, where everyone knew him, no-one had ever made that mistake. Vortigern seemed amused by his confusion.

'No, Severus. Vortimer is returning home to see to my business, so there would be no point in making him party to our conversation. This is my warrior, Kerin Brightspear, and he will do for now.'

Kerin was filled with a disturbing mixture of pride and trepidation. He had ridden with Vortigern since boyhood, and they shared the sort of mutual trust which could only exist between men who had guarded each other's lives. But for all that, he had not expected such an honour. He steadied himself, knowing how stupid it would be to make too much of it.

'I will speak openly, then,' the praetor said. 'You are men of the West. I don't flatter myself that you have come all this way just to save me and my city from the Picts. And it has not escaped the notice of my people that you have brought a monk with you, whom I understand to be Constans, the oldest son of our greatly lamented leader, Constantine.'

Vortigern snorted. 'Well, you can lament him if you like, Severus. But your spies are right, of course; we have got his son with us. You know that I have stopped the invaders in the West. You also know that we now have to stop the Picts. But not all men are as far-sighted as you, Severus.'

The praetor raised his hands in a gesture of resignation. 'I am a practical man, Lord Vortigern. Thousands of people depend upon me for their safety. I know what's going on in the North, and my own men sighted Pictish galleys off our coast last week. That's how bold they have become. Now, if I thought that I could raise ten thousand good, hardened legionaries – '

'Those days have gone, Severus,' Vortigern said softly. 'The legions have gone. The only man who can stop those murdering bastards is me, and you know it. So help me do it.'

'How?' Severus said hopelessly.

'Help me make the monk king,' Vortigern said. Severus blinked.

'*What?*' he said.

'Help me make the monk king,' Vortigern said.

'There are plenty of people who'd support a mangy donkey, if they thought it was Constantine's son.'

Severus Maximus had turned even paler than usual. 'You can't,' he said, aghast. 'You can't make a monk king. What about his vows? What about the bishops?'

'What about the bishops?' Vortigern said witheringly. 'Are they going to ride off and beat the Picts for you?'

'No!' Severus said. 'But they'll whip up anyone who even pretends to be a Christian, not to mention people like Garagon of Kent and Gorlois of Kernow, who have their own little axes to grind. They'll lop the monk's head off, and yours too, probably.'

Vortigern placed his elbows on the table, folded his hands and rested his chin on them. 'I don't think so,' he said. 'Have you seen the people outside your gate?'

Severus avoided his eyes. A muscle in his neck worked nervously. 'What can a monk do, anyway?' he asked. 'Lead the people? Raise an army? They say this Constans is a mouse. Can he do these things?'

'No,' Vortigern said. 'But I can.' He sat, looking steadily at Severus, until the praetor's eyes were drawn back to his as if compelled by some physical force. Severus shivered.

'All right,' he said unsteadily. 'What do you want me to do?'

'Three things. First, let us stay here in your house, as your guests. Second, guard the monk night and day. Don't let anyone near him.'

'Not even the fathers of the Holy Church?' Severus said apprehensively.

'Especially not the fathers of the Holy Church,' Vortigern said sourly. 'No-one goes near him without my permission, except this man here. Do you under-stand me?'

'Yes, lord,' said Severus, who seemed to be physically shrinking by the minute. 'And the third thing?'

'I want a meeting,' Vortigern said. 'An assembly in the curia. Not just people like Garagon of Kent and Eldof of Glevum, although they must be there, of course. I want representatives from every town that still has an ordo, anyone who owns land or commands a hill fort, anyone who leads anything that could possibly call itself an army. And I want the bishops. Can you do that for me?'

Severus smiled half-heartedly. 'Yes. It will take time, because we no longer have anything to compare with the *cursus publicus*. Twenty years ago – '

Vortigern's fist slammed down on the table. 'For the love of God, I'm not interested in the Imperial Post,' he said savagely. 'Can you do it or not?'

'Yes,' Severus said meekly. 'If anyone can do it, I can.'

'Can you do it by midsummer?'

'Yes. I have lists, you see. All the men of influence, the members of the old Roman administration, the owners of land. Every town had them once. Some have been lost, but I have managed to preserve most of them. Come, they are in here. And also the items your messenger asked me to provide.'

He led them through an archway into an adjoining room whose walls were lined with shelves. They were packed tight with leather-bound books and furled parchment scrolls, some old and dust-laden, others new and hardly touched. On the table was a wooden chest, around the length of a man's arm. It was beautifully made from olive wood, carved with an intricate pattern of birds and vine leaves, and had a solid-looking brass lock. The praetor opened the lid of the chest for Vortigern to inspect the contents. Kerin moved closer so that he could see inside too. There were rolls of papyrus, pens, stoppered bottles of ink, a leather-bound folder with an elaborately tooled design on the cover. Vortigern nodded.

'Good. That'll do for now. Have someone take it to my chambers. I imagine you have access to good quality ink, if I should happen to run out?'

Severus Maximus looked a little disconcerted. 'There's a fair amount in the box, lord.'

'I do a fair amount of writing,' Vortigern said. The praetor seemed to have passed beyond the point of disagreement. He simply bowed his head and closed the chest, then took one of the newer scrolls from his shelves and unrolled it in front of them. Kerin found himself wishing, not for the first time, that he had paid attention when he was sent to the monks to learn how to read and write. Vortigern examined the scroll minutely.

'The ordo of Venta Belgarum,' he said speculatively. 'This Maximian Galba, the praetor. His brother Paulinus told us that he was on his way here.'

'Yes,' Severus said. 'He arrived just ahead of you. He's a good man, lord. Very honest, very upright. He's got a merchant with him, a sad-looking little man called Tegid. He lost his brother up in the North, it seems.'

'Yes,' Kerin intervened. 'We know about that. But why is Maximian doing this?'

Severus raised a cautious eyebrow. 'Well, some

people say that he'd like to see Constantine's younger son crowned king.'

Vortigern sighed. 'Are these the same people who'd complain if the monk was made king?' he asked.

'Probably,' Severus conceded. 'Of course, they only need the boy to make the whole business legitimate. They'd soon set up a council to rule on his behalf.' He smiled half-heartedly. 'Much the same thing as you want, I suppose.'

Vortigern looked up from the scroll. 'Severus, that's not what I want at all,' he said.

The praetor's smile faded. 'I'll start sending messengers,' he said. 'You'll have your meeting. In the meantime, I have commanded a feast. I don't have much stomach for it after what happened to poor Alberius, but I'm sure you and your warriors must be ready for it.' He called for one of his guards. 'Plicius, tell Lupinus to conduct the lords of the West to their chambers. My lords, tonight we have deer from my forests, swans from the river and wine from Rome herself.' He bowed his head to them and swept out. His quick, light footsteps tapped away down the long stone-flagged passage. Vortigern replaced the scroll on the shelf.

'Well,' he said, 'what did you make of that?'

'He's terrified of you,' Kerin said. 'He'll do whatever you tell him.'

Vortigern nodded. 'He'll be very useful to us.' He looked at the guard Plicius, hovering uncertainly in the doorway. 'Well, Plicius, how long have you served your master the praetor?' he asked. Plicius stood stiffly to attention.

'Since I was a lad of sixteen, lord,' he barked. 'Twenty-two years and six months.'

Vortigern grimaced. 'Well, he'll be no good to us,' he murmured, as they followed Plicius down the passage.

Kerin winked. 'Don't worry,' he said. 'Once they've shown us where we're going to sleep, I'll go and find the kitchen. Big houses like this are all the same. There's nothing they don't know about in the kitchen.'

'I have another task for you, too,' Vortigern said. 'The monk. If I'm going to make a king of him, someone has to keep him alive. You've got him as far as this, so it may as well be you.'

Kerin took a long, measured breath. 'Not Rufus?' he asked. 'He's the Christian.'

'I'm sending him back to Cambria,' Vortigern said. 'I didn't say that for the praetor's benefit. Someone must go, and if the truth be told, I want Rufus out of the way. He's no help at all to me at the moment.'

Kerin stopped walking, aware of Plicius, who had slowed his pace to match theirs. The guard was listening with half an ear whilst pretending to examine a marble bust of Julius Caesar, which he must have walked past at least twice a day for the past twenty-two years and six months. Kerin caught his eye.

'Leave us now,' he said. 'We'll find our own way.' Plicius gave him a look of fierce resentment and tramped off down the passage. 'Rufus is your son,' Kerin said. 'My brother, in all but name.'

'Yes,' Vortigern said. 'And I'd trust him with my life. But not in this. We're better off without him, for our sakes and his. I'll send him by way of Venta and Isca. He can stay a while there and talk to my estate managers about wholesome things like growing corn and breeding cattle. Perhaps he'll cool his head a little, if there are no interfering priests stirring the pot.'

'Perhaps,' Kerin said, without conviction. Vortigern looked round but did not reply. He could not have missed the inference, but perhaps he needed to believe what he had said. Kerin wanted to believe it with all his heart. He supposed that some men would slaughter and maim for faith, just as they did for land and power; but he had loved Rufus for too long to think that he could ever be one of them. All the sunlit visions of his youth cried out against it; the horses and the hunting, the girls and the sea, and a household full of warmth and light, poetry, ferocious argument and laughter. But this was not an argument. Throughout Kerin's life, even the most heated disputes between father and son had ended with an affectionate cuff and a jar of ale. This time, he knew, it would not end like that.

'The chest,' he said, thinking of another vaguely disturbing unknown quantity. 'What's that about?'

'I intend to keep a record of everything we do,' Vortigern said. 'When Julius Caesar carried out his military campaigns, he recorded everything. That's why people remember him in the way that they do. Any educated man will have a copy of his *de Bello Gallico* and *de Bello Civili*. And there it is; Julius Caesar exactly as he wanted to be remembered. Military genius, politician and one of the worst blood-letting butchers the world has ever seen. But no-one will ever forget him, because his writings will always be there as a reminder. If he'd written nothing, there'd be fifty different versions of his life by now, and in two hundred years' time no-one would even remember that he existed. And that is precisely what will happen to us, if we don't keep a record. So that's what the chest is for. From tomorrow, everything will be written down. Where we go, what we do, how many we kill, how many we lose. You can understand now, why I might run out of ink.'

Kerin met his eyes. He would have liked to say, please God that you will live to write the final chapter, and that I will be there to see it; but, not wishing to sound like a prophet of doom, he said nothing, and simply made a silent vow to find someone who could teach him to read.

4

As things turned out, Kerin did not go in search of the kitchen. The servant Lupinus, who had conducted him through a maze of windowless, lamplit passages, showed him into a big, light room overlooking the central courtyard. There was a bed-chamber to the left, he explained, and another room to the right where a boy would attend him if he wished to disrobe or take a bath. The servant gave Kerin a knowing smile whilst imparting this last piece of information. Kerin sent him packing and sat down on the bed. He wondered where Rufus was, and whether he himself would have sported a large gold crucifix in a house crammed with statues of the Roman gods and goddesses. Perhaps it didn't matter, if your father had Vortigern's power. Kerin took off his own crucifix and turned it round and round in his fingers. Silver and about the size of a quail's egg, it could have passed as an ordinary circular medal. Rufus's mother, Sevira, had given it to him not long before she died. He loved it so much that he wanted to honour the gift. He went out into the forest and laid it on a flat stone alongside the hunting knife Vortigern had given to him. The knife was razor-sharp, but small enough for a child to carry on his belt. Drawing it from its sheath, he nicked his little white wrist and smeared the blood along the blade and over the crucifix. As he did it, he swore to serve Vortigern and protect Sevira for as long as there was breath in his body. Within weeks Sevira was gone, but all these years on, the oath remained. Because of it the crucifix was precious to Kerin, but like most young warriors, he rarely wasted his time pondering religion when it could be better spent thinking about women and drinking. He laid the crucifix down on the bed and set off to explore.

The room to the right contained a long, low couch and a round wooden tub. Spotless white robes hung from hooks on the wall. Kerin ran his hand over the material. It slid easily between his fingers, as smooth and shiny as a woman's hair. A low table held an assortment of jars with rags stuffed into the necks. Kerin removed one of them and sniffed the contents. A sweet, pungent smell invaded his nostrils. Cautiously, he tipped the bottle and allowed a few drops of its oil to drip into the palm of his hand. The oil was light and quickly vanished into his skin when he rubbed his hands together, leaving only its fragrance behind. A slight rustling at the doorway made him turn.

A girl was watching him. She was tall and olive-skinned, with a small, straight nose and the greenest eyes Kerin had ever seen. Her heavy dark hair fell in a waterfall about her strong shoulders. She was wearing a long white gown which rippled about her bare feet and draped fluidly over a pair of full breasts from which Kerin found it impossible to remove his eyes. The girl smiled. The look was generous and without disguise.

'You would like to try?' she asked, taking up one of the jars. She spoke in Kerin's own tongue, but with a foreigner's accent. Kerin wondered where Severus had found her.

'No,' he said. 'Not yet.'

The girl put down the jar and came close to him. 'You have travelled many days,' she said, reaching up to unfasten the chain which secured his cloak.

'Yes,' Kerin said. He knew he should be asking her who she was, what she knew about Severus Maximus, whether she knew Maximian; but his mind refused to frame the questions, and his body was developing intentions of its own. He did not resist as she removed the cloak and hung it on the wall beside the white robes.

'I am Faria,' she said, coming back to him. 'I belong to Severus.'

'Belong?' Kerin said vaguely.

'There were twenty of us,' Faria said, loosening his sword-belt. 'The Roman soldiers took us from our home and sold us as slaves in Ostia. Severus's men bought us for British silver.' She smiled to herself. 'Not very much British silver. Phoenician slaves are cheap, they say.'

Kerin gathered her mane of hair in his hands and drew it back from her face. 'Too cheap,' he said. The luminous green eyes regarded him dispassionately. She felt nothing at all for him, he realised, or for what was about to happen between them. As she had said, she belonged to Severus Maximus, and it was probably all the same to her whether Severus asked her to carry water or lie with his guests. Perhaps she had cared once, but not any more. 'Do you serve the praetor?' he asked. Faria understood and smiled.

'No,' she said, laying the sword-belt on the floor.

'Severus likes his boys. And you?' She slipped her arms around his waist and moulded her body to his, pliant as a willow. An artful smile parted her lips. 'I think not,' she said. Kerin looked down as her strong, practised fingers began to undo the thongs which secured his breeches. Still smiling, she sank to her knees, running the tip of her tongue across her full lips.

'No,' Kerin said quietly.

'No?' Faria said, her eyebrows arched in surprise. 'What, then?'

A little gasp broke from her as she found herself swept from the ground, landing on the couch with a force which almost crushed the breath from her.

'This,' Kerin said, in the half-second before speech became impossible.

* * *

Night fell early, hastened by gathering clouds. The pattering sound of a drum, accompanied by a chorus of reed pipes, grew gradually louder as Kerin hurried down the long, echoing corridor trying to keep pace with Plicius. For a small man, he could move remarkably fast.

'You are late, lord!' he kept repeating, in an increasingly anguished tone. 'All the guests are at table, and the meat is about to be brought in. Severus Maximus will not be happy.'

Kerin smiled to himself. He was ravenous, after a day in the saddle and the past few hours' exertions.

There was pandemonium in the dining hall. Scores

of servants were rushing around dispensing wine, all dressed like Lupinus in short white silken tunics. The room was splendid, with towering columns of blue-veined marble and vivid murals depicting chariot races and mammoth figures of the Roman gods and goddesses enjoying a little drunkenness and debauchery. At the back of the room, a long table on a raised dais had been reserved for the guests of honour. Severus was sitting at the centre with Vortigern on his right hand and Constans on his left. Rufus was sitting beside Constans. The chair to Vortigern's right was empty. Kerin hurried to occupy it.

'You're late,' Vortigern said; then his lip curled. 'And you stink. What is it?'

Kerin grinned. 'Oil of lavender, I believe, lord.'

'Oil of lavender,' Vortigern said in disgust. 'Did you tell her anything?'

'Lord?' Kerin said blankly. Vortigern gave him a baleful glare.

'When were you born?' he asked. 'Severus has sent a woman to pleasure you and find out what we're up to. Did you tell her anything?'

Kerin coloured slightly. He had not seen it like that at all. 'No, lord,' he said, avoiding Vortigern's eyes. 'There wasn't much conversation.'

'See that it remains so,' Vortigern said. His eyes had moved to Rufus, who was attempting to talk to Constans. The monk, swathed in a startling purple cloak, was struck dumb by the rolling tide of alcohol, meat and human flesh. His nervous eyes were darting everywhere, pausing only when they encountered some particularly notable instance of excess; the platters of roast fowl, set on racks which required four men to carry them, or the goings-on at a corner table where members of the praetorian guard had waylaid a serving girl and were removing her clothes.

'I'm sure Severus sent girls to everyone else as well,' Kerin said indignantly.

'Of course he did,' Vortigern said. 'It's hospitality, not to mention common sense. I don't have to tell you what men are like, after two weeks' battle training and a week's hard riding. But the others have less to tell, and Severus knows it. He will have saved his best for us. And before you ask, I sent her away.'

It was the truth, probably. To all appearances, Vortigern had observed something approaching a vow of chastity since Sevira died. 'There's a man sitting to Rufus's left, between him and Lud,' he said. 'Don't look now, I want to eat before I have to suffer him.'

Kerin turned his attention to a steaming platter which had just arrived in front of them. It contained the largest roasted fowl he had ever seen in his life; one of the swans from the river, he supposed. He allowed his eyes to stray casually to the left. The man Vortigern had mentioned was talking to Lud. They looked jovial and at ease, like two soldiers talking. The man was probably Vortigern's age, big and broad-shouldered with thick hair, woolly and dark like a black sheep's. His bushy beard was almost all grey, and his big hands moved as he spoke, beating the air or thumping the table to emphasise what he was saying, of which there was a great deal.

'That's Gorlois of Kernow,' Vortigern said. 'There's no point in letting him know that we're interested; he's too full of nonsense as it is.'

Kerin inspected the swan. 'He seems to have enough to say,' he said, tearing off one of the legs.

'More than enough,' Vortigern said. 'But he's brave and a good fighter, and he leads the best bunch of warriors I've seen, apart from our own. We need him on our side.'

Kerin munched at his meat. It was dry and stringy. 'This is terrible. You'd think it would taste like a goose, but it doesn't.'

'Try the venison,' said a thin, reedy voice to his right. 'Severus Maximus insists on eating swan because it was the custom of the consuls, but it never turns out as well as you think it should.'

Kerin turned. The man who had spoken was small and old. His thin iron-grey hair was drawn back from a high forehead and looked as if it had been brushed through with oil. His skin was sallow, and his sharp, dark eyes were set deeply on each side of a huge beak of a nose.

'I am Marcellus,' he said. 'I am from Ravenna, and I am Severus's physician.' He glanced around, as if to make sure that no-one who mattered was listening. 'I am also Severus's soothsayer, but I am not allowed to make too much of that. Londinium's full of Christians these days, and Severus has to keep the peace with them, whatever gods he worships within his own walls.'

'You are a haruspex,' Vortigern said. Kerin had no idea what a haruspex was, but Vortigern's tone was not complimentary. Marcellus blinked, as if surprised to be found out.

'It is an honourable tradition,' he said indignantly. Vortigern regarded him with distaste.

'Amongst the Romans, possibly,' he said. Marcellus, who would probably not have come up to Kerin's shoulder if he stood upright, puffed himself up in his chair like a belligerent little cockerel.

'Lord, what's a haruspex?' Kerin murmured.

'A priest, of sorts,' Vortigern said. 'They cut animals open and examine their entrails to predict the future. I think I'll settle for you and your dreams.'

Marcellus was still irate. Kerin found it hard to imagine such a small old man butchering a live animal. All in all, he supposed that it must be good practice for being a physician.

'Did you treat Alberius?' he asked.

'Yes,' Marcellus said. 'I might have to take his arm away, I don't know yet.' He picked up a small knife from the table and expertly excised a lump of flesh from the nearest haunch of venison. 'Here, try this. It's better than the swan.' Kerin half-heartedly accepted the meat, finding that he had rather lost his appetite. 'If you want to know,' Marcellus said, catching Vortigern's eye, 'the omens are excellent. If you have important business here in Londinium, good fortune will attend you.'

'I make my own good fortune,' Vortigern said. Marcellus gave him a pitying smile and went back to his food. Kerin tore off another chunk of venison.

'You're right,' he said, acknowledging Marcellus's triumphant little nod. 'It's much better than the swan.'

'Good,' Marcellus said. 'I thought you might have been put off by thoughts about my occupation. Did I hear the Lord Vortigern say something about dreams, by the way?'

'Dreams?' Kerin said vaguely. 'No, I don't think so.'

'Well, as you wish,' Marcellus said. 'But if it had been so, I thought it might be interesting to talk about it; as one professional to another, if you like. It's always interesting to compare different ways of doing things.' He smiled politely.

'It's not so,' Kerin said. 'I don't dream any more than the next man. What's that over there, Marcellus? Is it as good as this venison?'

'It's a sucking pig,' Marcellus said, with a trace of impatience, 'a fact which I would have thought was obvious, if I might venture to say so.' He reached over and hacked off a large piece of pork. 'Here, take it. And let me know if you change your mind.' Kerin accepted the meat. Marcellus nodded towards the door of the dining hall. 'Well, you weren't the last to arrive after all.'

A tall man was sweeping up the aisle between the loaded tables. He was dressed almost exactly like Severus Maximus, in the spotless white purple-bordered robe of a high-ranking Roman dignitary. Kerin had never seen him before, but he recognised the fierce, hawk-like eyes of Abbot Paulinus gazing out from the lean pale face.

'Maximian Galba, praetor of Venta Belgarum,' Marcellus said, with affected grandeur. 'He calls himself a true Roman, but of course he's not. His father was a foot soldier, but his mother was as British as that beast you're eating.'

Severus Maximus was on his feet now, wringing Maximian's hand, encouraging Gorlois and Lud to move up and make room for him. Maximian, for all his civility, looked less than enthusiastic.

'Maximian, my old friend, you must already have

met the Lord Vortigern,' Severus said, beaming and patting Vortigern's shoulder.

'Indeed,' Maximian said curtly. 'More than once.' His glittering eyes met Vortigern's. 'I have just had word from my brother Paulinus. He was concerned enough to send a man on a fast horse. What is that monk doing here?'

Vortigern remained seated. 'A little respect wouldn't hurt, Maximian,' he said. 'That monk, as you call him, is the oldest son of Constantine. I realise that you have no respect for me, of course, because I come from the wrong side of the river.'

Maximian gave a hiss of impatience and turned on Constans. The monk coloured violently and squirmed in his seat. 'You are wearing a splendid cloak, Brother Constans,' Maximian said. 'And I trust that you are enjoying the praetor's excellent wine.'

'The cloak was a gift from the praetor,' Constans whispered. 'And I could not insult his hospitality by refusing the wine.'

'Maximian,' Severus Maximus implored, 'perhaps we can discuss this tomorrow. In the meantime, please join us for the feast. There is room for you next to the Lord of Kernow.'

Maximian bowed his head. 'Out of respect for you, Severus, I shall keep my counsel and join the feast. But I should prefer to sit at that table over there, with the members of your ordo. I cannot share a table with a faithless monk, Constantine's son or not.'

Severus raised his manicured hands in a gesture of resignation. 'As you wish,' he said, 'but please, let us not bring our disagreements to dinner. These are dangerous times, and we have enough to do, without killing each other at the dining table.'

'For once I agree with him,' Vortigern said, as Maximian strode regally away and Severus sank back into his seat with a rueful sigh. 'We can fight the Picts or we can fight each other, and there an end of it.'

Kerin looked up as a shadow fell across them. It was the big, woolly-haired man to whom Vortigern had drawn his attention earlier. Gorlois was beaming, and his broad-featured face was flushed with merriment and wine, several drops of which were sparkling in his beard.

'Vortigern, by the gods!' he exclaimed. 'It's been years!'

Vortigern smiled, with some reluctance. 'Hello, Gorlois. Yes, it has been some time, hasn't it.'

Gorlois grabbed a bench and sat himself down opposite Vortigern and Kerin. 'By the gods!' He reached across the table to grip Kerin's arm. 'I know you're not Vortimer; you must be the younger one. What's your name? Katigern, isn't it? He looks a fine strong lad, Vortigern. I hope he can use a sword as well as he can preen himself; by the gods, lad, you'll have all the women in Londinium after you smelling like that. Not to mention all the dogs.'

'It's oil of lavender,' Kerin said. 'And I'm not Katigern.' Gorlois's heavy black eyebrows rose. 'I'm Kerin Brightspear,' Kerin added, trying not to smile at his confusion.

'Kerin?' Gorlois's brow creased, then a spark ignited. 'The young whelp that came home in the Lord Vortigern's saddlebag! By the gods, Vortigern, this isn't the skinny little runt that used to run around with your boys, is it?'

'Yes,' Vortigern said dryly. 'If I'd known that he'd ever smell like this, I'd have left him for the wolves.'

Gorlois chortled merrily and thumped the table. 'Are we going to fight the Picts, then?'

'Yes,' Vortigern said. 'We're going to fight them.'

Gorlois leaned forward over the table, spreading his arms so that he, Vortigern and Kerin were enclosed in a little private enclave. 'These pansies aren't going to be much good to us,' he murmured. 'Most of them couldn't strangle a chicken.'

'No,' Vortigern agreed. 'But Severus does have influence. Men like him control the garrisons of all the cities, now that Constantine is dead. We need those fighting men, Gorlois.'

'Who's the monk?' Gorlois asked curiously.

'Constantine's oldest son, Constans,' Vortigern said.

'By the gods!' Gorlois exclaimed. Vortigern pressed a finger to his lips. 'All right,' Gorlois said, trying hard to whisper. 'But what's he doing here? And all dressed up like the Roman Emperor?'

Vortigern leaned forward. 'Who would you have for king, Gorlois?' he asked. Gorlois's eyebrows rose into the roots of his woolly hair. He jabbed a finger towards the monk and mouthed an incredulous question. Vortigern grinned. 'Well, they won't have you or me, will they?'

'No,' Gorlois said, wide-eyed. 'But there are plenty of people who'd choose the monk's little brother. Garagon of Kent, for one.'

'Garagon!' Vortigern said speculatively. Gorlois nodded and emptied the pitcher down his throat.

'That's why I'm here, really. Garagon sent a rider to me at Tintagel. There are galleys in and out of the Kentish ports all the time, so he was one of the first to know when Constantine was killed.'

'How strong is he?' Vortigern asked.

'Well,' Gorlois said cautiously, 'in numbers, he probably commands as many fighting men as I do. They all love him because he throws whores and good horses at them, but as for protecting your back in a battle – ' he blew his cheeks out and shook his woolly head.

'They'll learn soon enough, if they come to fight the Picts with us,' Vortigern said. Gorlois roared.

'Vortigern, if you can get Garagon to fight on the same side as you, I'll eat my sword-belt. He despises anything that comes out of Cambria. He'd fight for the Picts first.'

'I don't think so,' Vortigern said. 'Not if he values his cornfields. And he must, because they pay for all those whores and good horses. Where can he be found?'

'Drunk or screwing at this time of night,' Gorlois said. 'He's borrowed a house just down the river from here. It's owned by a merchant called Gallus. They say he has a huge fleet, more than a hundred galleys with thirty crew apiece, and the prows gilded like an emperor's throne, and –'

Vortigern closed his eyes. 'Gorlois, I am not going to Garagon. When you see him, tell him that I'm in Severus's house. That should do the trick.' Gorlois heaved himself to his feet, beaming and belching loudly. Vortigern looked up. 'Gorlois,' he said earnestly, 'say nothing to him about the monk. I should like to do that myself.' For a moment their eyes held. Kerin had wondered whether anything short of death could silence Gorlois, but at that point, something did. He nodded and shambled off to resume his conversation with Lud.

'God,' Kerin said, rubbing his eyes, 'if he can fight as well as he can talk, we won't need to raise an army.' He looked up at the sound of brisk footsteps. Maximian Galba, perhaps emboldened by a few cups of the praetor's wine, was standing in front of Vortigern. He looked ready to explode with pent-up fury.

'I don't know what that monk's doing here,' he said, 'but I swear on Christ's blood that if he comes to any harm, you'll answer to Rome.' His eyes gleamed dangerously. If there were worse things he might have said, Kerin couldn't think of them. Vortigern stood up. Kerin stood too, and moved to his shoulder. Severus tottered over, clasping a brimming jug.

'My finest wine, lords,' he babbled happily. 'I saved it until the other pigs were full.'

'Keep it,' Maximian spat. 'I'm not drinking with these barbarians.' He nodded to a gaggle of white-robed companions who had crowded in behind him. They turned as one and stalked off, elbowing guests and servants aside. Vortigern watched him go.

'That's why you want the child,' he said softly.

'Lord?' Severus said with a nervous blink.

'That's why he wants Ambrosius. The younger brother. The boy who's being raised by Constantine's kinsmen. It's not about God, or apostate monks. It's about Rome. About the Empire. He believes that, if they make Ambrosius king, some future emperor might consider raking up a few legions to put us back in our place. All under the pretext of protecting us from invasion, of course.'

'But, lord,' Severus said anxiously. 'I do have it on good authority that there are not, and will never be, any spare legions.'

'You're probably right, Severus Maximus,' Vortigern said. 'But you're a pragmatist. And a Briton at heart, whatever you may say in public. Men like Maximian and his friends are wedded to the Empire. Whatever disasters befall Rome, they'll go on believing that things will change. That in the end, Rome will rise again in all her glory. It's like feeding a dying fire, one stick at a time. You can keep it going for quite a while.'

The praetor sat down hard. 'Do you think they will send for that boy?' he asked. 'That child?'

'I don't know,' Vortigern said. 'All I know is that we have, at most, a year to raise the forces we need to break the Picts. Any longer and it'll come to the point where we can't stop them. Maximian believes that, if he has the boy, his friends in Rome will see a way back. That they may think Britain is worth one more effort. It's an illusion. Someone should tell him, before he does something stupid.'

Severus Maximus gave him a look of utter misery and emptied the contents of the wine jug down his throat. Kerin drew Vortigern aside.

'Those men in Rome,' he said. 'The consuls, or whatever they are. If they'd see Ambrosius as a way back, how will they see Constans?'

'They won't see him at all,' Vortigern said, watching Maximian leave. 'They'll look straight past him and see me, and the death of all their hopes.'

5

The passage was cold and barely lit. As Kerin walked, a man hurried past him carrying a sack of cornmeal on his shoulder. Another followed, bearing the whole skinned carcass of a sheep. At least I'm going the right way, Kerin thought, shivering as the dank air eddied about him. It was almost midday, but it was impossible to judge time down here in the damp, dark bowels of Severus Maximus's house, far from the sumptuous reception rooms and courtyards, the only area most of the praetor's guests ever set eyes on.

Kerin had been careful to dress in the clothes he wore for his last day on the march. For the moment he had no desire to look like a patrician, or to smell of anything like oil of lavender. A little sweat would arouse less suspicion. As he rounded a bend in the passage, a delicious and familiar smell invaded his nostrils. Someone not far away was baking bread. Kerin followed his nose until he encountered a solid-looking oak door. He pushed it gently and it creaked open to reveal a large room lit by barred windows high up in the far wall. An array of knives and other kitchen implements hung below them, as sinister as an armoury. The room was full of steam, which was billowing out of a large iron pot set over a roaring fire. A big man, about Kerin's height but twice as wide, was stirring it vigorously with a long-handled wooden spoon. Sweat streamed down his round face, which was cherry-red from the heat, and dripped from the ends of his long straw-coloured hair. He was wearing a ragged pair of breeches and a tunic encrusted with the remnants of last night's feast. Suddenly the contents of the pot boiled furiously up over the rim and spilled, spitting, into the fire beneath. The cook cursed volubly in a language which Kerin couldn't understand at all, but the general meaning was abundantly plain. Kerin stifled a laugh. The cook spun round.

'You think is funny?' he roared. Kerin spread his hands apologetically.

'I'm sorry,' he said. 'It smells very good.' He approached cautiously and peered into the pot. 'Who's it for?' he asked.

'The guards,' said the cook, and spat into the fire.

'You don't like cooking for them?' Kerin asked.

'For those pigs? How would I like cooking for Roman bastards?' He spat into the pot for good measure.

'What's your name?' Kerin asked.

'Cheldric,' said the cook. He mopped his brow and sat down on a bag of cornmeal.

'Cheldric,' Kerin said. 'That's a Saxon name, isn't it?'

'Of course is Saxon name, *unwita*,' Cheldric said sourly. 'I am Saxon, so I have a Saxon name. It is not so strange.'

Kerin found himself a bag of cornmeal and sat down too.

'Who are you?' Cheldric asked suspiciously. 'Why are you coming to the kitchen?'

'I'm Kerin Brightspear,' Kerin said. 'And I'm starving. That bread smells marvellous.'

Cheldric rose to his feet with a grunt and picked up a wooden implement which looked as if it might have come in handy for paddling a boat. He opened one of the bread ovens, thrust the broad end of the paddle inside and came out with a golden loaf. Kerin sniffed appreciatively. Cheldric flicked the end of the paddle and sent the loaf somersaulting through the air towards him. Kerin caught it and dropped it immediately with a yelp of pain. Cheldric grinned and sat down again.

'Is hot,' he said. 'You burn your mouth out.'

Kerin gingerly retrieved the loaf from the floor and broke it in half. 'I'll let it cool down,' he said. 'How did you get here?' He had never met a Saxon, and knew nothing about them beyond hearsay; good fighters, born seafarers, men said. The cook's temper seemed to have subsided. He was watching with some amusement as Kerin nibbled his way carefully round the edge of the bread.

'We come in our boats,' he said. 'At home we have too many people.' His arms described a swollen belly, and he winked. 'Many, many babies. But not enough land. Not enough food. We cross the sea to look for a bit of land that no-one wants. And then we find Kent.'

Kerin laughed out loud. 'I think there are already plenty of people who want Kent,' he said. Cheldric shrugged.

'We look only for some poor land,' he said. 'Saxons can make poor land grow. The boys kill pigs, and I am cooking them on a fire. Then some riders come. They say the pigs belong to their master, Garagon. We run to the boats, but I am hurt with a spear. Just here.' He pressed his hand to his side, just above the waistline, and winced as if the wound still pained him.

'What about the others?' Kerin asked. 'Why didn't they take you with them?'

Cheldric looked down at his hands. Kerin noticed that his left thumb was missing. 'Maybe they think I am dead,' he said, but Kerin saw that his eyes burned with grief and rage, even now. He felt sorry for him, Saxon or not.

'Why didn't Garagon's men kill you?' he asked. Cheldric smiled.

'They smell how I am cooking the pig. They say, cook for us like that, and we let you live. I think maybe it is better to cook than die. First I cook for Garagon, then for Severus. Is no better here.' He looked Kerin up and down. 'You are not cook. You are warrior?'

'Yes,' Kerin said. 'Just an ordinary one, though. Not a guard, or anything like that.'

'You are not Roman,' Cheldric observed. He winked. 'I think you do not like Roman bastards either.'

'Why do you say that?' Kerin asked. Cheldric slapped his belly and guffawed loudly.

'I see you smile when I spit in pot,' he said. 'You are – what is the word?'

'Celt,' Kerin said. 'I'm from the West. From Cambria.'

'Ah!' Cheldric said. 'Lupinus – you know Lupinus? – he says that all the people from Cambria are crazy. He says you all drink blood and eat your own babies.'

Kerin grinned. 'What do you think?' he asked. Cheldric shrugged.

'All the Romans are crazy too,' he said. 'You know

Marcellus? You know he thinks he can look in a goat's stomach and tell you what is happening next week? Is crazy. Only Odin knows what comes tomorrow.'

'Who is Odin?' Kerin asked. Cheldric's eyebrows rose.

'Who is Odin?' he spluttered. 'Odin is the great father of all the gods.' He nodded his head emphatically and folded his arms, as if challenging Kerin to disagree with him. Kerin inclined his head in silent acknowledgement, wondering why on earth this fat, rough, short-tempered man made him feel so profoundly uneasy. Cheldric took a chicken bone from the floor and began to pick his teeth with it. 'The Lord Vortigern has a priest with him, Constantine's son,' he said.

'A monk,' Kerin said. 'Yes, he is Constantine's son.'

'Vortigern wants to make this priest king, yes?' Cheldric raised his hand as Kerin hesitated. 'Alright, maybe you cannot say. But if he does, people try to kill him. Vortigern first, then the priest.'

'Why are you telling me this?' Kerin asked. Cheldric grimaced.

'I hate Roman bastards. Maybe you are no better, but you do not look at me like you look at a mangy dog.'

'Why should I?' Kerin said. 'You're not a bad cook. Did you cook for the feast last night?'

'Yes. You enjoy?'

'Very good,' Kerin said, munching steadily. 'Except for the swan. The swan was disgusting. Goose is far better.'

'Ah!' Cheldric said, with a blissful smile. 'I cook

goose fit for Odin. Severus says goose is for servants, but I say goose is for kings. The Roman bastards, they don't know much.'

Kerin grinned. 'They have some pretty slaves, though,' he said. Cheldric snorted.

'You think? You should see Saxon girls.' He nodded sagely. 'Maybe soon they come to you. Warriors. Families. Many ships. Many girls.' His pale blue eyes regarded Kerin expectantly. Kerin felt his uneasiness compound itself.

'I suppose that would please you,' he said.

'Please me?' Cheldric's face darkened, and the fearsome anger returned to his pale eyes. 'They leave me here to die. Why would it please me?'

'They're your people,' Kerin reasoned. Cheldric's eyes brimmed with tears.

'Kerin Brightspear, I have no people,' he said savagely. Kerin looked at him sitting there in the middle of the kitchen in his filthy tunic, shaking with rage and grief, and felt sorry for him all over again. But he also felt something else.

'Cheldric, would you like to get away from here?' he asked.

'Odin's blood, yes,' Cheldric sniffed. 'But how?'

'Suppose I paid Severus to let you go,' Kerin said. 'It would be like a deal, between two merchants. He could just go and buy himself another cook.'

Cheldric shook his head, his eyes blank. 'Why you do that?' he asked. Kerin smiled.

'Because I want to eat goose fit for Odin' he said. Cheldric leaned forward.

'No,' he said. 'Is something else.'

'Alright,' Kerin said. 'I won't lie to you. You say the Saxons will come back. If that's right, and if they want to take our land, I want to know how they fight, how they think. I want to learn your tongue, so that I can understand what they're saying to each other. I want you to teach me all that. And then,' he smiled faintly, 'then you can cook me goose fit for Odin.'

Cheldric stretched his head out so that his little pale eyes were within a hand-span of Kerin's wide grey ones. 'And if I say no?' he asked. The movement was so lightning-quick that it left Cheldric rooted. One second he was nose to nose with Kerin, the next his arms were pinioned behind his back and the ice-cold blade of one of his own kitchen knives was pressed flat against his throat, hard enough to choke the life out of him.

'If you say no,' Kerin murmured, 'I'll slit your throat now, this moment. And then I'll cut you up with that meat cleaver over there, and throw you in the pot bit by bit for the Roman bastards to eat for their supper.'

Cheldric's eyes closed. Sweat streamed down his face and dripped off his chin onto the knife blade. 'Please,' he whispered, his voice a hoarse squeak. 'I only joke, alright?'

'Swear,' Kerin said, gritting his teeth. The blade pressed tighter and a tiny ribbon of blood trickled down Cheldric's neck.

'I swear!' he choked. 'I swear on Odin's head!'

Kerin released him and he rolled gasping onto the floor amongst the bones and the spilt cornmeal. Kerin prodded him with the toe of his boot. 'Get up,' he said mercilessly. Cheldric scrabbled away out of reach, hauled himself to his feet and stood, panting.

'I think you are good man,' he roared bitterly. 'But you are bastard, like the rest.'

'No,' Kerin said, 'I'm not. But you'll have to learn that. In the meantime, don't forget that I'm quicker than you. Do you still want to get away from here?'

Cheldric looked down at the floor. 'Yes,' he said sullenly.

'Good. I'll speak to Severus later. And, Cheldric.'

The Saxon looked up. Kerin winked, spat into the cooking pot and went quickly from the kitchen.

6

The chapel, sacred to the memory of the martyr Alban, stood in a narrow side-street running between Severus Maximus's house and the wharf. It was a small, draughty building whose austere interior contained nothing but a simple altar and ranks of comfortless benches. Kerin would have described himself as a Christian if pressed, but this afternoon, he had not come to church to pray or to do penance. He had come as a nursemaid. He sat at the back of the building, flexing fingers and toes against the creeping paralysis of the cold, and waited for Constans to finish talking to God.

The monk was kneeling on the bare slabs in front of the altar, flanked by two black-robed clerics. There was a modest house adjoining the chapel, home to an abbot and twenty or so lesser brothers who made a profession of caring for the sick. Kerin had seen several hopeless-looking examples arrive; a skeletal man carried on a board by two others, a blind man led by a flea-ridden child, a woman cradling a baby with no arms. They had all been welcomed by the abbot, Father Giraldus, a tall, stooping old man with a patient face and haunted brown eyes.

'*In nomine Patris et Filii et Spiritus Sancti,*' Constans intoned, rising to his feet and bowing to the altar. He looked entirely incongruous, standing beside the sober monks in his silk robe and purple ermine-trimmed cloak. He was wearing a bright red hat shaped like an upturned pot, all the rage amongst Faria's countrymen. It looked ridiculous on Constans, but he was insistent on covering his bald crown. He came tripping down the aisle, flouncing along in his fine clothes.

'Come, come!' he said impatiently, in his high, nasal whine. 'Plicius is waiting to instruct me in the art of sword-play.' Kerin rose stiffly to his feet and followed him out into the street. Macsen, whom he had placed on guard by the door, fell in behind them, trying desperately hard not to laugh. They walked briskly, with the chill wind from the river behind them. Some big galleys had come in earlier and the street was full of merchants' transports loaded with saddlery, garments and bales of brightly-coloured cloth. One of the wagons, drawn by two struggling oxen, was creaking along under a towering statue of Ceres, the Roman goddess of the harvest; or at least Kerin supposed that it was Ceres, because she was holding a sheaf of corn under her right arm. Someone must have paid a great deal of money for the statue, because the wagon was accompanied by a mounted warrior on a costly, high-strung blood horse, and a portly man in a red cloak who was shouting instructions to the driver as the goddess made her stately progress up the street. The warrior, who looked pale and edgy, seemed to have his work cut out controlling his horse as it fidgeted and danced alongside.

'Those poor beasts!' Constans exclaimed as the wagon drew level with them. The oxen came to a shuddering halt and stood, sweating and gasping in the middle of the street. Almost immediately a cacophony of shouts, bangs and braying broke out in the rear as men, wagons and laden donkeys found themselves forced to come to a sudden and unexpected halt and piled up behind the ox-cart.

'Come on,' Kerin said, grabbing Constans's arm. 'There's going to be trouble here.' As he said it, the red-cloaked man roared at the driver of the ox-cart, who raised his whip and brought it down full force across the heads of his animals.

'No!' Constans howled, twisting free. 'They're God's creatures too!' He hurled himself bodily at the ox-cart and grabbed the stock of the whip. The driver let out a screech of rage and surprise and lashed out with his free hand, propelling Constans straight into the rump of the nearest ox. The startled beast gave a moaning bellow and lurched sideways. The crowd which had built up behind the cart surged forward to see what was going on. The warrior drew his sword and began to beat them back.

'God!' Kerin exclaimed. 'Macsen, quick!' Constans's red hat came flying through the air, hung in the wind and dropped in the face of the fretting blood horse. The animal squealed in panic and lashed out with its hind legs, hitting the side of the ox-cart with a splintering crash. Its rider went sailing over its head in a graceful arc, into the middle of what was by now a full-scale fight. Kerin glimpsed Constans's shaven head amongst the thrashing arms and legs and dived forward, seizing him round the neck. At the same time he felt himself caught from behind and dragged backwards.

'It's alright, it's me,' Macsen shouted as they struggled free. The crowd poured towards them again, flinging them back against the wall of the chapel. Pinned there helplessly, Constans's head still clamped in the crook of his arm, Kerin heard a gasp go up from the crowd. As if silenced by some supernatural power, the uproar ceased. The statue of Ceres had broken free of its moorings and was rocking gently on the ox-cart. The red-cloaked man was staring up at it in silent horror. The goddess hung motionless for a long, breathless moment; then, as if some invisible support had been severed, she pitched sideways into the wall on the opposite side of the street. The head split from the body with a deafening crack and tumbled down towards the crowd. A howl of panic went up, and even the moribund oxen began to move. Miraculously, Kerin saw a space open in front of him.

'Run!' he bellowed, dragging Constans behind him. He did not stop until he had put half a Roman mile's distance between himself and the scene of chaos. They were in a dark, stinking street far from the patricians' quarter. Constans sank weakly to the ground. 'Get that off,' Kerin said, grabbing the monk's purple cloak.

'Why?' Constans quavered.

'Do it!' Kerin snapped. His eyes flashed nervously from side to side.

'For the gods' sake, where are we?' Macsen asked.

'God knows,' Kerin said. 'But we can't stay here with him looking like that.'

Footsteps approached. They were accompanied by a voice, singing tunelessly. The sounds had come from a side-street to the left, and they were coming closer. Kerin pressed his finger to his lips and crept to the corner of the building where the two streets met. He flattened himself against the wall. A man came round the corner carrying an axe and a skin bag. Kerin grabbed him from behind and slammed his head into the wall. The man gave a muffled grunt and dropped to the ground in a heap. Kerin tore off his filthy grey tunic and breeches and tossed them to Constans.

'Here,' he said. 'Take your robe off and get these on.'

'What?' Constans said, aghast.

'Do it,' Kerin hissed. 'And these.' A leather cap and belt followed. Constans removed his robe and stood shivering in his loincloth, his alabaster-white skin turning to gooseflesh. His right eye was beginning to swell and discolour where the ox-driver had hit him. He picked up the breeches with the tips of his fingers, his nose wrinkling in disgust. Kerin picked up the axe and the bag, which contained an assortment of tools, and handed them to him as he finished dressing. 'Here,' he said. 'You're a carpenter.'

They walked along the street until it opened out into a square where two old women were selling fish from a stall. 'That looks fresh,' Macsen said. 'We're probably not far from the river.' He glanced up at the sky where a pale sun was beginning to slip towards the horizon. 'This way, for a bet. And if we're not back in Severus's house by sunset, I'll buy the first jug of ale.'

Sundown found them in a crowded alehouse on the waterfront, next to a muddy beach where a slew of shabby boats had been drawn up above the tidemark. Gulls skimmed above the glassy water, crying incessantly.

'You weren't entirely wrong,' Kerin said as Macsen came back to the table with three tankards. 'We did find the river. We're just a bit too far down it, that's all.' Macsen groaned and slumped onto the bench beside him. Through the open doorway they could glimpse the lights of the Roman city, winking enticingly at them from further upstream. 'Don't worry,' Kerin said. 'Once we've drunk this, we'll find someone who knows the way and pay him to take us there. Here,' he thrust a tankard at Constans, 'drink this, and look as if you're enjoying it. But don't say a word.'

Constans gave him a baleful look and began to sip. Kerin looked around the alehouse. It was packed to the walls, steamy with sweat and warm breath, and smoky from the crackling wood fire in the corner. A big, grey-haired man with rough hands and a thick beard sat down opposite them. He stank of fish and the river.

'Haven't seen you round here before,' he said. Kerin shook his head.

'We came in on one of Gallus's boats this morning. The captain sent us to look for a carpenter, and this bag of bones was the best we could find.'

The grey-haired man cackled and pinched Constans's arm. 'Doesn't your mother feed you, boy?' he asked. Constans smiled nervously.

'He's dumb as well as thin,' Kerin said. 'He bedded his father's best friend's wife, and the greybeard cut out his tongue for him.'

The fisherman roared and thumped the table. 'You're lucky it was your fucking tongue, petal.' He drained his tankard at one draught and hailed a small, dark-haired girl who was elbowing her way through the crowd with a jug of ale.

'I'll pay for that,' Kerin said. 'Fill ours as well.'

The fisherman beamed. 'A health to you, boys,' he said, drinking deeply. The ale left a white rim of foam on his beard. 'What were you carrying?' he asked.

'Saddles and harness,' Macsen volunteered. 'Silk. Fine cloaks and leather belts. A couple of good horses. The usual sort of thing.'

'And a very large statue,' Kerin added, nodding sagely. The fisherman shook his head.

'Money turns men's brains to soup,' he said. 'When do you sail?'

'The day after tomorrow.' Kerin gave Constans a prod. 'When the master carpenter's done his work.'

'You should come down and drink with us tomorrow night, then.' The fisherman reached across to grip Kerin's shoulder. 'I'll bet Gallus has got a few nice cloaks and belts to spare, eh?'

'He might have,' Kerin said. 'What's it worth?'

'As much ale as you can drink and as many girls as you can ride,' the fisherman bawled. Heads turned, and the whole room burst into riotous laughter. The fisherman smiled, showing broken teeth. 'Just come here tomorrow night and ask for me. My name's Manius. I know, I know, it's a Roman name – blame my mother, she couldn't keep her hands off the soldiers.'

'You could do us a service tonight,' Kerin said. 'It's worth one of these.' He reached for the pouch at his belt and opened it on the table so that Manius could see the silver coins inside. The fisherman's eyes glinted.

'Well?' he said.

'Take us back to Gallus's wharf in your boat,' Kerin said. 'We don't know our way in the dark, and if we don't get back tonight he'll kill us.'

Manius grinned and ruffled Kerin's hair. 'I'll bet,' he said. 'Most people would go out of their way to avoid crossing Gallus. Alright, I'll take you. But if you don't come back with the goods tomorrow night, I'm going to sail up the river and burn your boats out of the water.'

They drank up, left the alehouse and followed Manius along the beach in the dusk. The air was chill, and Kerin could hear Constans's teeth chattering. Cold, terror, he didn't know.

'Here,' Manius said. 'My boat. Help me push her out, will you?'

They heaved, and the boat slid out into the calm water. Manius held her steady and they climbed aboard, dragging their feet clear of the clinging mud. Manius seized the oars and turned the boat out into the channel. The muscles in his big arms bulged as he pulled against the current and the boat moved steadily upstream, like a tiny pond-skater on the great pale expanse of water. The bank slid by to their left, with its ribbon of wharves and drinking dens and houses where torches were being lit as the darkness drew in. Some large craft with masts and brown reefed sails were tied up at a jetty. They looked sleek and fast.

'What are those?' Kerin asked. 'Fishing boats?'

'Not really,' Manius panted. 'They do a bit of fishing if times are slack, but usually they just run back and forth to Armorica. Rich men wanting to get somewhere in a hurry, bits and bobs that it's not worth Gallus's while to carry. I did hear the bigwigs are going to send one to pick up that boy. What's-his-name? Constantine's son?'

'No idea,' said Kerin, trying to look nonchalant.

Manius nodded towards the bank, where the first buildings of the Roman town were clearly visible. 'We're almost there. Look, that must be your boats.'

The ships were riding at anchor just off the quayside where they had disgorged their cargoes. As Manius's skiff slid silently under their towering sterns, Kerin got his first glimpse of the merchant's house. Unlike the praetorian palace, with its stern impenetrable walls, Gallus's house presented a sociable face to the river. There were windows and there were wide terraces lit by flaring torches, and tonight it looked as if there might be a party of some size going on. The sound of singing and merry conversation drifted out to meet them as Manius guided his boat expertly to the foot of a flight of wooden steps.

'There,' he said, shipping his oars. 'Can't get closer than that, can I?' Kerin smiled and handed him the promised silver coin. 'Now don't you forget our bargain,' Manius said, wagging his finger. He looked up at the ships and shook his head. 'Lovely ladies. But all that wood would make quite a bonfire, you know.'

Kerin and Macsen grabbed Constans under the arms and heaved him up onto the steps. They stood on the quayside and watched Manius's boat slip away into the darkness.

'Hey!' a voice echoed along the wharf. A man was standing at the back entrance of the house. 'You three,' he called. 'What are you up to?'

'Checking the boats,' Kerin called back. 'We saw someone in a rowing-boat nosing around down there, but he's gone now.' The man raised his hand in acknowledgement and went back into the house. Kerin whistled softly. 'Come on,' he said, seizing Constans's arm. 'You've caused us enough trouble for one day.'

They were soon at the praetor's tall gates. Kerin hammered vigorously. A peephole slid open, then slammed shut again, and they heard the sound of heavy bolts being drawn back. The gate swung smoothly open.

'Jupiter's balls, where have you been?' Plicius exclaimed, hurrying to slam the gate shut behind them. 'Vortigern's had search parties out all over the city looking for you. We've had Garagon's people here all afternoon, too, complaining about a statue. I don't know what on earth it's all about, or why they think it's anything to do with us.'

Kerin and Macsen exchanged rueful glances. Constans looked up at them with a nervous smile. Plicius looked curiously at the tool-bag and the axe.

'Come on,' Kerin said, seizing Constans's arm. He frog-marched him across the courtyard, into the house and along the echoing corridor which led to the monk's chambers. The servant Lupinus appeared out of the darkness and pattered along behind them. 'He needs a bath,' Kerin said over his shoulder. 'See to it, please. And find him some clean clothes. You can burn the ones he's got on.' They reached the end of the corridor. Kerin grabbed Constans by the neck of his tunic and slammed him against the door, lifting him clear of the floor. 'Now listen to me,' he hissed. 'I don't care if you're Constantine's son, you're my responsibility, God help me, so you can do what I tell you.'

'Please, put me down!' Constans gasped. 'I can't breathe!'

Kerin lowered him to the ground, but did not slacken

his grip. 'You will say nothing about what happened today. Not a word. Do you understand? Macsen won't talk, so if anyone finds out what happened, I'll know exactly where it came from.'

Constans closed his eyes. 'Alright,' he whispered. 'I won't say anything.'

Kerin released him and walked away. Once in his own quarters, he tore off his cloak and replaced his tunic with one of the collection which Severus's slaves had provided for him. He knew that his clothes must stink incriminatingly of fish and beer. The door of his chamber opened and closed quietly. A pair of slender arms encircled his waist from behind, and the fingers locked on his belt buckle.

'Where have you been?' Faria's husky voice asked reproachfully. 'Everyone thought you were dead.'

Kerin removed her hands from his belt and turned round. 'I got lost,' he said.

'Ah,' Faria said, without curiosity. She picked up his discarded clothes and sniffed, wrinkling her nose. 'You need a bath.'

'Not now,' Kerin said. She looked at him uncertainly, sensing the tension in him. His eyes moved over her and his imagination removed her silk robe, envisaging the warm, supple body beneath. There could hardly be a detail with which he had not become intimately acquainted over the past few days. It was inconvenient, but he desired her intensely. 'I don't have much time,' he said. 'Vortigern's probably ready to hang me, so I must talk to him and get it over with.'

Faria reached up and slipped her arms around his neck. 'You do not need much time for this,' she said.

* * *

The courtyard was deserted. The moon sailed up in a clear sky, illuminating the fountains and colonnades with its deathly white light. Kerin had heard the horses come in. As Faria had predicted, he had not needed much time, and as the firestorm subsided and he became aware of her lying warm and tremulous beneath him, he heard the gates opening below. Hooves clattered on the paving stones. Plicius's voice shouted something as the bolts slammed home.

Two guards stood at the entrance to Vortigern's quarters, barring the door with crossed spears. A single torch burned in an iron bracket on the wall. The guards recognised Kerin and lowered their spears. One of them, not the usual po-faced Roman, gave him a condolent smile. He was a dark-haired lad with olive skin and shining black eyes.

'Are you sure you want to go in there?' he asked.

The door closed at Kerin's back. He stood quite still. He had never been in here before. The room was cool. It was simply an ante-chamber, he realised, with a door leading off at each side. Tallow lamps burned high on the walls. Finding the door directly ahead of him ajar, he opened it cautiously and went inside. There was a couch and a low table, and facing him a window through which the moonlight slanted, pale and cold. There were no signs of life, none of the clutter of discarded clothes, empty goblets and half-eaten fruit which made his quarters look lived-in. The wind moaned far below in the tunnel running between the courtyard and the river terrace. A draught found its way in somewhere, and the door through which Kerin had entered creaked eerily.

'Close it,' a voice said. Kerin shut the door quietly. 'Lock it,' the voice said coldly. Kerin slid the heavy bolt and turned to face the room. Vortigern was standing beside the window. He had come from the adjoining chamber without a sound. The moonlight turned his face pale, the dark face with its darker eyes. 'Come here,' he said. Kerin straightened his shoulders and walked slowly across the room. A few paces from Vortigern he stopped. He tried to keep his gaze steady. He did not really know what he was expecting, or in fact why he feared it so much, since in all of his twenty-five years Vortigern had not once laid a finger on him.

'I'm sorry,' he said. 'You shouldn't have gone to the trouble of looking for me.'

'Half of our men and the entire praetorian guard have been looking for you,' Vortigern said. 'Or should I say looking for Constans. Where have you been?'

'We got lost,' Kerin said. 'There was some trouble in the street outside the church, and we got separated from Constans. It took us a while to find him, and by then we'd taken a wrong turning.'

Vortigern's eyebrows rose. He walked in a slow circle, round behind Kerin and back to where he had been standing. 'You got lost,' he said.

'Yes, lord,' Kerin said, with a hopeful smile. Vortigern stepped forward, his eyes gleaming in the pallid light. His hand moved up to rest gently on the base of Kerin's throat.

'You are lying to me. Or at least, you are only telling me a part of the truth.'

Kerin looked back at him, unblinking. 'Lord, there's nothing worth knowing,' he said.

'I thought you were dead,' Vortigern hissed. 'You and that bastard monk.'

'I'm sorry.' Kerin lowered his eyes. 'I should have been more careful. But I swear on Rufus's life that Constans was never in any danger.'

Vortigern let his hand fall. 'If we lose him, we've done all this for nothing,' he said. 'Maximian will send for his puppy Ambrosius, and they'll march off to fight the Picts with a bunch of incompetents like Alberius, all on their pretty white horses. And Gorlois and all the others will go along for the fun of it, and before they get anywhere near the Picts they'll start fighting each other. I know the monk's a worm. I know you hate the sight of him. But for the love of God, can't you see why we need him?'

'Yes,' Kerin said. 'I can see why we need him.'

'Then don't lose him again!' Vortigern roared. Kerin nodded silently. Vortigern's hands clenched. 'I've trusted you above all the others,' he said reproachfully. 'Keeping that monk safe is the single most important task I could have given you. If you let him get killed, I'll hang you with my own hands. Do you understand me?'

'Yes, lord,' Kerin said quietly. Please God, let that be all, he prayed silently.

'There is something else,' Vortigern said frostily. Kerin looked up. 'Do you know anything about a statue?' Vortigern asked.

'Lord?' Kerin said blankly.

'I've had a creature of Garagon's here this afternoon,' Vortigern said testily. 'A fat, pompous oaf called Edlym. It seems that Garagon spent a great deal of money on a statue of Ceres in the hope that she would bless his corn harvest. Edlym tells me that the statue met with an accident, and is now lying in ruins in the street outside the chapel of St Alban.'

'That's very unfortunate for Garagon, lord,' Kerin said carefully. 'He must be a little upset.'

'Upset?' Vortigern bellowed. 'His blood's boiling. He's beside himself. He sent all the way to Italy for this pestilent statue, and now it's in pieces in the street. And why? Because some fool in a red Phoenician hat picked a fight with the ox-driver, and got dragged away by two other fools whose descriptions just happen to match yours and Macsen's. No —' he raised his hand threateningly, 'don't explain. I don't want to hear it. I've already told Edlym that none of you were anywhere near the chapel of St Alban, God help me.'

'Did he believe you?' Kerin asked, with some apprehension.

'God knows,' Vortigern said sourly. 'At any other time I'd have broken his neck for the sake of some peace, but I need Garagon's fighting men. You heard what Gorlois said. There are plenty of them, even if they aren't much good.'

'Yes,' Kerin said, beginning to wish that he had never got out of bed that morning. 'Will this make a difference?' he asked.

'Probably not, in the end,' Vortigern said. 'But it won't help. Getting people to kill Picts is the easy part. Stopping them from killing each other first is the problem. Garagon hates us enough as it is, without having a headless statue to blame us for.' He rubbed his eyes wearily. 'An expensive headless statue.' Kerin bit his lip and nodded silently. Vortigern spread his hands in a gesture of resignation. 'Well, it's done now. Unlock the door, and send one of those oafs for some wine.'

Kerin unbolted the door and went out through the ante-chamber. The guards stood rigidly to attention.

'You don't have to do that,' Kerin said to the more human-looking of the two. 'But could you get Lupinus or someone to bring us some wine, please?'

The guard inclined his head respectfully. 'Severus has taken delivery of some excellent wine, lord. Straight from the southern provinces. Came in on Gallus's boats today. Very strong, I understand.'

'That sounds most suitable,' Kerin said, with a wry smile. The guard grinned.

'He didn't eat you, then.'

'No,' Kerin said. 'But ask Lupinus to bring some food as well, just in case. And tell him we want tankards, not ladies' goblets. What's your name?'

'Lucius, lord. I'm from the south, like the wine. My grandfather fought with Magnus Maximus. Vortigern married one of his daughters, didn't he?'

'Yes,' Kerin said. He suspected that Lucius had hoped for more of an answer, but there was nothing he could add. Sevira had been dead for almost twenty years, and no-one talked about her, not least because Vortigern wouldn't stand for it. 'Tell Lupinus that he can come straight in,' he said. 'I don't think any of us are going to get eaten tonight.'

* * *

This must be the room which Vortigern used. The first one was simply a barrier. There was a large table with bench seats, where they sat down, and beside the window a smaller one with a single chair. On it was the chest which the praetor had provided. A sheet of papyrus was lying on the table, half-covered with lines of Latin script, most of which Kerin could not read. Just a few words jumped out at him; the ones he had seen written from time to time on milestones or tombstones, or in Vortigern's library. Londinium: the capital. Dux: the leader. Rex: the king. Lupinus and one of his inferiors came in with the food and wine, bowed and slipped out. Vortigern regarded the platter of cold meats, bread and fruit with suspicion.

'I didn't ask for this,' he said.

'I did,' Kerin said. 'I haven't eaten all day, and if this wine's as strong as Lucius says it is, it'll need something to soak it up.'

'Who's Lucius?' Vortigern asked.

'The guard outside the door. The dark one.'

Vortigern shook his head. 'Everywhere we go, you befriend everyone, from the warriors' wives down to the slaves. You even befriend the dogs. Why, for God's sake? They're not worth your time.'

Kerin seized a chunk of meat and devoured it with relish. 'It's useful,' he said. He took the large amphora of wine and filled the tankards, then took a cautious sip and swallowed hard. 'I bought something this morning.' Vortigern shrugged, as if he had no need to know more. 'I bought a cook,' Kerin said. Vortigern's hand halted in mid-air. His eyes narrowed.

'Why?' he asked.

'Mainly because he's a Saxon,' Kerin said. Vortigern blinked.

'Where in God's name did you find a Saxon cook?' he asked.

'Here, in Severus's kitchen. I went down there to have a look around, and I found him. His name's Cheldric. He's not a bad cook, but apart from that, I thought he might be useful to us. He said something which made me think.'

Vortigern snorted. 'How unfortunate that he wasn't with you outside the chapel of St Alban. How did he get here?'

'He landed in Kent with a bunch of warriors looking for land. He cooked for Garagon for a while, and now he's here. But he hates the Romans. In fact I think he hates everybody, the Saxons more than most, for running off and leaving him. That's why I thought he might do us some good.' And I was sorry for him, Kerin thought, but did not say. 'Do you know much about Saxons, lord?' he asked, replenishing both the tankards.

'I've fought them once,' Vortigern said. 'In Kent, about ten years ago. I was visiting Garagon's father, and a ship-load of them landed just down the coast. They'd burned a village and raped the women, so we had to kill them.'

'Good fighters?' Kerin asked.

'As good as any I've met. What did your cook make you think about?'

'He said that the Saxons would come back,' Kerin said. Vortigern shrugged.

'They've been plaguing Kent for years. The Romans didn't build all those shore forts for nothing. But it never comes to much.'

Kerin shook his head. 'No. That's not what Cheldric meant. He thinks his people are coming back. Not just the odd boat-load. Hundreds of them, desperate for land.'

Vortigern put down his tankard. 'When?' he asked.

'Cheldric didn't say. We'll have to talk to him again. But if men are desperate for land and short of food, how long will they wait?'

'Until spring,' Vortigern said, his eyes moving to the window where the moon hung high in the tranquil sky. 'Until the weather's settled, and they can afford to risk a large number of ships and men.'

'How soon will we be ready to fight the Picts?' Kerin asked. Vortigern cupped his tankard in both hands and examined the contents.

'Spring at the earliest,' he said. 'And that's if I can carry all the others with me. If we have to waste time arguing and killing people, it could take longer. And then –' he shrugged. 'Well, what would you do if you were a Saxon?'

Kerin took a deep draught of wine. 'I'd wait until we were halfway to Hadrian's Wall with our armies. And then I'd land in Kent with every man I could find.'

Vortigern smiled resignedly. 'Yes,' he said. 'That's what I'd do, too.' He drained his tankard and set it down beside Kerin's. 'This Lucius. Can you trust him?'

'Probably,' Kerin said. 'He seems straight enough. Why do you ask?'

'Because before long I'll need to replace that weasel Plicius. It'll have to be someone the guards know and trust. How old is Lucius, would you say?'

'Well,' Kerin said, 'his grandfather fought with

Maximus, so he can't be too much older than I am. Twenty-eight or nine, perhaps?'

'With Maximus!' Vortigern said speculatively. 'I might have met the grandfather, I suppose.'

'Well, Lucius knew that you'd married one of Maximus's daughters,' Kerin said, knowing as the words left his mouth that it was something he would not even have considered saying, had he not consumed half the contents of the amphora.

'Do you remember Rufus's mother?' Vortigern asked.

'Yes,' Kerin said. The memory made him smile. 'She was always kind to me. I remember her sitting by the fire in your library, reading us stories. There was one about a fox and a stork. And there was a day when she took me and Rufus down to the edge of the sea – Kat must have been a baby, because she had him tied to the saddle of her pony in a reed basket. Someone else was there too, I think; I can't really remember. It might have been Father Iustig.'

'It was undoubtedly Iustig,' Vortigern said. He spoke quietly, but with a sudden bitterness so intense that it made Kerin start.

'Lord?' he said curiously. Vortigern did not respond. He swallowed the wine in one draught and refilled his tankard to the brim. A cold, hard glaze had come over his eyes, like a door closing; and Kerin, drunk as he was, knew at once that that was that.

7

Kerin remembered almost nothing about the earliest years of his life. The tiny room in Lud's house where he had slept; Mora feeding him gruel from a wooden spoon. Nothing more. He hardly thought about it at all, unless some chance remark jogged his memory. *Do you remember Rufus's mother?* All he knew was that, one winter's night, someone had come to the house and asked for him. Mora, instead of shooing him off to bed as usual, had put a little cape on him and given his hand to this person, who led him out of the warm house through the fine snow and into the biggest building he had ever seen.

He remembered the blaze of light; such a shock, after Lud's dim house. The fire crackling on the hearth, its bright orange flames casting a net of dancing shapes across the dark roof. The torches burning high in their brackets, illuminating brilliant red and gold tapestries, and row upon row of books and furled manuscripts. There was his playmate, Rufus, curled up on the cushions beside the hearth with a big grey dog. There was the chubby toddler called Kat, drowsing under a blanket. There was a smiling, dark-haired woman, smiling with her eyes, too; taking Kerin's hands, settling him down with her children. And then came Vortigern, throwing himself down amongst the cushions, an easy arm around his wife's shoulders. She said something which made him laugh. He reached for a vivid red shawl and wrapped it around her. Rufus gave Kerin a sweet apple he had saved from the dinner table. His mother read the children a story about a fox and a stork. No-one ever came to take Kerin back to Lud's house. He knew that he never wanted to leave this place. And in his heart, he never had.

'Happy to get out of the cloister, then?' Lud asked, digging Kerin in the ribs with the butt of his spear. Behind them Vortigern's men were chatting amicably with Gorlois and the Kernow warriors as they rode home from the hunt. The ox-carts were piled high with deer and boar destined for Cheldric's cooking fires. Kerin groaned aloud.

'Don't start,' he said. 'Do this, Kerin, do that, Kerin. Wipe my royal arse with a perfumed cloth, Kerin.'

The warriors laughed raucously, then broke off and took notice as a group of horsemen passed them at a brisk hand-gallop. Their horses were immaculately groomed, the riders similarly elegant and unblemished, the sort of handsome young men who'd have turned any girl's head. Peacock clothes rippling, gold trinkets winking in the sun. Their leader looked a patrician from his neatly cropped black hair to the toes of his well-made riding boots. His face was olive-skinned like Lucius's, with wide dark eyes set above high cheekbones, a trim black beard and a thin-lipped smile which flashed briefly when he recognised Gorlois of Kernow.

'Well, well!' Gorlois said, waving an acknowledgement. 'Young Garagon, off to the city to spend his inheritance.'

Garagon of Kent, Kerin thought, and watched as the horsemen rattled away towards the city gates. Garagon the young hothead, lord of the corn-lands, purveyor of blood-horses and pretty girls; a man with thin lips and eyes which darted back and forth rather too quickly, meeting Kerin's own eyes for a mere split second, dwelling on his appearance for just long enough to establish that he was a man of the West, and not worth the time of day. Well, Kerin thought; we shall see.

* * *

Darkness came early. A thick bank of cloud rolled in from the west, obscuring the setting sun and bringing with it a fine cold rain which put out the torches in Severus's courtyard, and the fire on which Cheldric had been roasting the meat. Kerin leaned in the window of his bedchamber, watching the kitchen slaves running about below him, and wondered where he was going to get a large quantity of good quality cloaks and belts.

'We could try Gallus's warehouse,' Macsen said, smiling at Faria as she came in with a tray of honeyed figs and sweet pastries.

'It's guarded day and night,' Kerin said irritably. He had noticed the smile. Faria crossed to the window and looked up at Kerin, head on one side like a curious bird.

'Why do you need cloaks and belts?' she asked. 'Surely you have enough already?'

'We promised them to someone,' Kerin said. The prospect of Manius's hospitality seemed less alluring now that she was standing beside him with her cool hands and perfumed hair, but it had occupied his mind for most of the morning, and it was idle to pretend that it would not occupy him again when she had gone. They all looked up as the door opened. Macsen's brother Custennin came in, with Dull Bened and one of the praetor's guards.

'Vortigern's looking for you,' he said.

'Me?' Kerin asked. 'Or both of us?'

'You,' Custennin said sourly. 'Is it ever otherwise?'

Kerin shrugged. Custennin pouted and helped himself to the figs. It was hard to believe that he had been raised at the same hearth as Macsen. The mean streak, all that baseless resentment. Only his flame-red hair and muscular limbs signalled the family connection. Bened parked his ample behind on the couch and gave Faria a wink.

'I'll keep your seat warm, boy,' he said, grabbing a handful of pastries. 'And anything else you like, too.'

'You are going?' Faria asked as Kerin stretched and flung on his cloak. There was a sudden sharpness in her voice.

'Yes,' Kerin said. 'What's the matter?'

'Nothing,' Faria said lightly. She looked up at him and smiled. Well, he thought, whatever it is she won't tell me in front of the others, so it must keep.

'Ask him if he's got any cloaks and belts to spare,' Macsen's voice echoed after him as he tramped off down the cool passage.

Kerin found Vortigern on the terrace overlooking the river. There was a litter of wine goblets and unfinished food on the trestle tables, but the cool drizzle had driven the diners indoors. It did not appear to trouble Vortigern, who was leaning on the stone balustrade, watching the slow passage of small boats up and down the river whilst gulls cried overhead and the rain formed a fine mist on his hair and the shoulders of his black cloak. Kerin found himself a spot on the balustrade. A skiff glided past beneath, laden with open barrels full of salt fish. Kerin picked up a loose pebble from the terrace and aimed it downwards. A yelp of surprise came from the retreating boat as it bounced off the curly head of one of the oarsmen and plopped into the brown water.

'Bastard Roman!' the oarsman bellowed, shaking his fist up at the terrace.

'I'm a Celt!' Kerin roared back.

'Bastard Celt, then,' came the furious reply. Kerin grinned.

'Well,' he said, 'that's closer to the truth than he knows. You sent for me, lord?'

Vortigern nodded. 'Two things. First of all, Garagon of Kent has invited himself to this feast tonight. I'm not asking you to become his best friend, but you will be civil to him.'

Kerin sighed. 'Yes, lord,' he said reluctantly. He watched the skiff disappear amongst the tall prows of the merchant's galleys, and his thoughts turned briefly to the provision of cloaks and belts. 'There was some-thing else?' he asked.

'Yes,' Vortigern said. 'Eldof of Glevum is heading

for Londinium. He has a few hundred well-armed warriors with him, and that loathsome brother of his, Eldadus the Bishop.'

Eldof, Kerin thought. A big man, sitting his heavy white horse with a soldier's erectness. Wide shoulders, thick hair studiously tamed, a ginger beard turning grey. Eldof liked the finer things in life, and lived in a splendid house which had been built some time ago for the Roman provincial governor. He and Vortigern had a history stretching all the way back to childhood, peppered with disputes and bloody skirmishes over land, cattle and boundaries. Eldof was the only man in the West who held anything even approaching Vortigern's power, and Vortigern did not love him for it.

'Will he make trouble for us?' Kerin asked.

'It all depends,' Vortigern said. 'Naturally Eldof doesn't want to see the country go up in flames, but if you gave him a choice between stopping the Picts and seeing me hang, he'd have to think very hard about it.'

'What are we going to do, then?' Kerin asked.

'Well,' Vortigern said, 'we do need him to beat the Picts. Whatever might be said about Eldof, he fights like ten men, and he's got some fine warriors. If we took them on, we'd beat them, but we'd lose half our men doing it. So you and I are going to talk to him.'

Kerin's eyebrows rose. 'Just you and I?' he asked.

'Yes,' Vortigern said. 'Eldof cares about what people think. He won't kill two men arriving on their own until he finds out what their business is.'

Kerin pursed his lips and let his breath escape between them in a long, slow hiss. A curious stillness had enveloped the city at that moment, broken only by the murmur of the river sliding beneath; and as Kerin felt it surround him with its illusory peace he thought how ludicrous it would be, on the face of things, for two men to go riding alone into a hostile camp on the off-chance that they wouldn't get killed before explaining why they had come.

'Are you sure about that?' he asked doubtfully. Vortigern grinned.

'We'll all die sometime, Kerin. But I don't think it'll be at Eldof's hands, and neither do you. Find some fast horses that we can afford to lose, and get ready. We leave straight after we've eaten. Tell no-one.'

'Tonight!' Kerin exclaimed.

'Why not?' Vortigern said impatiently. 'You can bed the woman again when we get back, for Christ's sake.' Kerin shook his head in mute horror. He could not possibly explain about the cloaks and belts.

* * *

The weather changed, as if by act of God, at the very moment when Severus Maximus was out in the courtyard lamenting that the feast would have to be transferred to the great hall.

'Lupinus!' he shouted, waving his arms about as the drizzle stopped and a wan moon swam up through the thinning mist. 'Light the fires! Bring out the tables! By Jupiter, we'll eat under the stars tonight, just like our forefathers!'

'Why's he doing all this?' Kerin asked, keeping his voice low enough to be muffled by the babble of the fountains.

'They say it's to please Vortigern,' Lucius said, staring straight ahead so as not to attract attention. He cut rather a splendid figure in his guard's uniform; the blood-red cape and burnished helmet with its scarlet crest went well with the smooth brown skin and bright dark eyes. Kerin remembered that Sevira's colouring had been just the same. He thought of the brilliant red shawl. Her father Maximus was Hispanic, he knew; perhaps Lucius shared the same blood, if his grandfather had fought alongside the old emperor.

'Why should it please Vortigern to eat outside?' he asked, relaxing as Severus moved away. 'I know the praetor thinks we're all savages, but we do keep a roof over our heads in the West.'

Lucius suppressed a smile. '*I* know that, lord, but I don't think Severus has much idea about what goes on outside the city walls. And it's no secret that Vortigern doesn't like it here. He keeps to himself, doesn't he, and he's turned away every girl Severus has sent him. Goddesses, some of them.' He cast his eyes heavenward with a sigh, as if resigned to the fact that no-one was likely to offer such gifts to the ordinary mortals of the praetorian guard.

'How is Alberius?' Kerin asked.

'Marcellus had to take his arm off. It kills most men, but Alberius seems to be on the mend. He's as strong as an ox, you know.' Lucius grinned. 'And about as bright.'

'Can you ride?' Kerin asked.

'I haven't been on a horse for years,' Lucius said. 'My father was in the cavalry, and we always had a few horses. His unit was attached to the Second Augusta. He died when I was eight years old.'

'In battle?'

'Fighting Picts, yes. The legion's main base was in Cambria, as you'll know, but they sent detachments to the Wall now and then. The commander of the Second was Publius Luca. He's a good man – commander of the city garrison now. He came to tell my mother what had happened. Her family lived in Londinium, so he had us all sent back in a carriage.'

'Have you been here ever since?' Kerin asked.

'Yes. After a while my mother married a merchant, Marcus Arrius. His first wife was British, so between them they had friends all over the city. We live just round the corner from St Alban's chapel; it's quite a big house with iron gates and a bay laurel growing in the courtyard. You should call if you're passing.'

'I will,' Kerin said, feeling an unexpected stab of envy as he considered this unknown family with their pleasant house and their huge circle of friends. It had never really occurred to him that there might be lives other than the one he had lived with Vortigern. He wondered how it might feel to have a wife, or a grand townhouse with a courtyard and a bay laurel; and whether all that would be better than living anyhow on his warhorse, or whether in time he would begin to regard the house as a prison, and long for the kiss of the rain, and a sky full of stars. 'Do you like it in the guard?' he asked.

'It's alright,' Lucius said cautiously. 'The pay's not bad, and we don't even have to do anything dangerous, most of the time.' He smiled wistfully. 'I don't want to spend my whole life in the same city, though. I remember my father telling me about some of the places he'd been with General Stilicho. He fought in Africa, you know, against Gildo the rebel. He said the rocks were the colour of fire, and he fought men on horses that could wheel and turn like swallows in the air.'

Kerin smiled. He liked the way Lucius's eyes lit up when enthusiasm grabbed him. 'Well, in the meantime, if you're not happy in the guard, you should do something about it,' he said. 'Learn to ride properly, for a start. I'll get you the wildest horse I can find.'

He looked up as a stentorian bellow echoed across the courtyard. Cheldric the cook was standing on the steps by the main door. Two kitchen slaves had been carrying the whole roasted carcass of an enormous deer, skewered on an iron rod; but the person at the rear end of the beast had lost his footing, causing the dripping carcass to slide down the rod and flatten him. Cheldric came lumbering down the steps and hurled the hapless slave into the fountain.

'That cook's mad,' Lucius observed.

'Yes, I know,' Kerin said. He knew that he needed both Lucius and Cheldric. Persuading them to get along would have to wait.

The procession heralding the arrival of Garagon of Kent was audible long before it arrived. At first Kerin didn't take much notice of the muffled drumbeats. There was enough of a racket going on as Severus's guests took their seats; warriors and lesser citizens at the long tables beside the fountains, civic dignitaries and leaders on the purple-draped dais before the main entrance. Lupinus was making a performance of showing the late arrivals to their seats. Kerin noted that he had deliberately seated Maximian Galba at the far end of the table, between the haruspex Marcellus and a dark, powerfully-built man dripping with gold. Gallus the merchant, someone said. Next to him sat a clutch of elderly men in Roman garb, then several well-to-do young women; followed by Gorlois, Lud and his sons, and Kerin himself. There were thus around twenty people between Maximian and Vortigern; probably not one too many. To Vortigern's right were Severus and his wife, a small, plump, grey-haired woman who rarely made a public appearance. Constans had been confined to his quarters, in case any of the diners had been outside the chapel of St Alban the day before. The drumbeats were coming closer, now accompanied by a chorus of pipes. Vortigern gave Kerin a curious look.

'What on earth is that?' he asked. In the gateway appeared a small fat man on a tall brown mare, whom Kerin recognised, instantly and with silent dismay, as the guardian of the statue of Ceres. The musicians arrived behind him, all in red and gold, marking time like well-drilled infantrymen. There was a short inter-val – just long enough, Kerin realised, to ensure that everyone in the courtyard was watching – then the rest of the cavalcade swept in behind them. Sword-blades, bridle rings and gold armlets flashed in the torchlight.

'Make way!' the fat man bawled, as servants and sol-diers surged forward to see what was going on. 'Make way for Garagon, mighty lord of Kent!'

'For the love of God,' Vortigern said sourly. Garagon rode right up to the foot of the dais on a prancing white horse. Tossing the reins to an acolyte, he sprang from the saddle and landed lightly on the platform. He was arrayed in the finest clothes his cornfields could possibly have bought for him; a heavy red cloak trimmed with ermine, elaborately stitched doeskin boots which must have taken some craftsman days to make, and a massive gold-buckled sword belt set with gold studs, each with an onyx eye. Well, Kerin thought, one of those studs is probably worth more than I paid for poor Cheldric. Garagon bowed elaborately to Severus Maximus, who rose to greet him. Even as their hands clasped across the table, Garagon's eyes were turning to his right.

'Lord Vortigern,' he said, with a nod of acknowledgement.

'Garagon,' Vortigern said impassively. Garagon's face fell at the muted welcome. He tilted his head back, chin thrust out in an attitude of peevish defiance which Kerin would come to know well.

'I am lord of all my father's lands now, you know,' he said petulantly. Vortigern looked back at him with his basilisk's stare.

'Yes,' he said. 'I had heard.'

Garagon's hands flexed uneasily. 'I thought that perhaps it might have earned me a little more respect,' he said tetchily. Vortigern rested his chin on his hands.

'Because your father died of the plague and left you his fortune?' he said. 'There's no distinction in that, Garagon. Suppose he had had no children, and had left it all to one of his flea-ridden dogs. Would you expect me to respect the dog?'

Severus uttered a small sound of despair. Garagon stood quite still. A crimson flush spread slowly from the close-fitting collar of his black tunic, inflaming his cheeks and seeping up to the roots of his hair. The young women further down the table tittered amongst themselves, and Garagon gave them a portentous glare.

'Lord Vortigern, there are few men here who would compare the Lord of Kent to a flea-ridden dog,' he said stiffly. Another salvo of female laughter came from along the table, and the colour of Garagon's countenance deepened. Kerin, remembering Vortigern's admonitions about civility, wondered where all this was leading.

'I would never make such a comparison, Garagon,' Vortigern said mildly. 'All I am saying is that, if you want my respect, you won't buy it with your father's money. You are welcome at our table, however.'

An expectant silence followed. Garagon shifted uneasily from foot to foot, sensing the eyes of the gathering upon him. 'Very well,' he said haughtily. 'I shall not insult the praetor by spurning his hospitality.' He stalked off along the dais to make his way round to the row of vacant chairs next to the praetor. Severus turned beseeching eyes upon Vortigern.

'Lord, I entreat you, do not upset the young lord of Kent,' he whispered. 'His cornfields are the bread basket of the city.'

Vortigern smiled faintly. 'You should lose no sleep about that, Severus. Now, would you mind moving just a little, please, so that Garagon can sit next to me?'

Severus hesitated. 'Lord, is that wise?' he asked apprehensively.

'It is necessary,' Vortigern said flatly. 'Now, move.'

Severus looked deeply affronted, but lost no time in vacating his chair. Vortigern invited Garagon to sit. As he did so, two men came down the steps behind the dais; the guardian of Ceres and a slim whip of a lad with short-cropped fair hair, a trim beard and a nose as sharp and hooked as a falcon's beak.

'May my companions join us?' Garagon asked. 'You have met my uncle, Edlym, and the other is my friend, Brennius.'

Vortigern nodded his approval, and the two men sat. The servants were moving along the table now, bearing platters of roast pork encrusted with herbs and great steaming bowls of meat broth. Kerin looked up as Lupinus deposited two huge pitchers in front of them. He was glad to see the pitchers, less so Lupinus. Principal servant or not, the boy was far too full of his own importance.

'Mead from the West, lords,' Lupinus said, with a flourish. He raised one of the pitchers and poured three huge goblets full of clear golden liquid. Kerin closed his eyes and took a long, slow draught. The familiar, much-missed taste carried him straight back to Henfelin; to Vortigern's hall in the heart of the citadel, to an ash-log fire and lambs turning on the spit, their fat crackling and spitting as it dripped onto the glowing brands beneath. Shadows dancing, warriors laughing and bragging. *A song!* someone shouted to the bard. *A song, Cynfawr, or a poem!*

'Kerin,' Vortigern's voice said sharply. Kerin sighed as the vision dissipated.

'I'm sorry, lord. But the mead –'

'I know. Give it to someone else. It's the last thing you and I need tonight.'

Kerin passed the pitcher to Garagon, who tasted the contents with experimental caution.

'Not bad,' he conceded. 'You drink a good deal of it in the West, I understand.'

'We do,' Kerin said. 'But it's better than this.' He smiled. 'I would say that, of course.'

'You would probably say that your fields grow better corn than ours, Garagon,' Vortigern said, 'and that your horses are faster, and your women more beautiful.'

Garagon chuckled and swallowed his mead. 'We should put it to the test,' he said. 'My lands are only a day's ride from here. You are welcome at my table with your warriors and your household. What do you say, Brennius? Can we silence these doubts about the quality of our women and our horses?'

Brennius laughed out loud. The sound was nothing less than a shrieking cackle. His blue eyes creased at the corners and his thin, angular face was transformed by a wild, spontaneous merriment. It disconcerted Kerin, because it would, he knew, be far simpler not to like any of the Kentishmen.

'Our horses go like the wind!' Brennius shouted, slamming the table so that the plates and goblets rattled alarmingly. He gave another of his ear-splitting shrieks. 'And by Jupiter, so do our women!' He raised his goblet to everyone in a gesture of indiscriminate hospitality. Severus and his grey wife, sandwiched between Brennius and Garagon, exchanged nervous smiles. Kerin felt a little sorry for the praetor.

'What are you thinking?' Vortigern asked.

'That all this could very soon get out of hand,' Kerin said, staring out over the rows of tables in the court-yard below, where over three hundred well-armed men with barely enough elbow-room to eat were emptying pitchers of mead as quickly as Severus's slaves could fill them. The Cambrian warriors were starting to sing; one of Cynfawr's old battle-hymns, Kerin realised, as the fractured refrain drifted up to him. As if in competition, Garagon's musicians struck up some slow martial air which drew an instant response from the Kentishmen. Brennius howled with delight. He and Garagon joined in, hammering the table with their goblets in time to the sonorous drumbeat. Down below, one of their young warriors leapt onto a table, stumbling over bowls and platters of meat. He was small, sprightly, colourfully dressed and wreathed in gold chains. Whipping out his sword, he spread his arms wide and began bellowing a rival war chant.

We are the men of Kent,
Our swords are sharp and bright;
Our enemies flee before us,
We'll taste their blood tonight…'

The Kentish warriors roared along in unison. The man on the table strutted back and forth, purple cape swirling, sword-blade and gold armlets flashing in the torchlight.

'Our enemies flee before us,
We'll taste their blood tonight!'

he crowed, and shook his sword at the dais. Garagon's song died in mid-breath. He clutched Brennius's arm. Custennin leapt onto his chair, brandishing his sword above his head.

'Our enemies flee before us?' he roared. 'They must be fucking rabbits, you piece of horse shit!'

A massed howl of fury arose from below. A sword hurtled through the air, narrowly missing Custennin's left ear, and clattered onto the steps behind. Everyone on the dais sprang to their feet. Custennin cleared the table in a single bound and hurled himself at the Kentishmen. Lud and Macsen were already up on their chairs, daggers out.

'No!' Vortigern bellowed. He dived headlong at the two men and caught them both round the legs, bringing them crashing down onto the steps. Kerin's eye caught a glint of metal. Garagon was glancing manically around, no idea what to do with the dagger he had drawn. Kerin grabbed his wrist and twisted until he dropped the weapon with a yelp, then threw him backwards onto his chair, landing on top of him with full force.

'Garagon!' he gasped. 'I don't want to fight you.' He glanced sideways at Brennius, whose lean face looked more frightened than hostile. 'We've got to stop this. Keep him here. It's for his own good.'

Brennius grabbed Garagon by the arms. Vortigern had vanished. Severus and his entourage were cowering in the doorway of the great house. Plicius and his troop formed a tight circle around them, spears braced. Kerin overturned the table, sending bowls of broth and amphorae raining down onto the melee beneath, and leapt from the dais. The whole courtyard had dissolved into a massive, formless brawl. Straight ahead, through a tangle of flailing arms and legs, Kerin glimpsed the stupid little peacock who had set it all off. Dropping his shoulder he charged through the mob, seized the fool round the neck and wrestled him back to the fringe of the fight. The heaving mass spewed out Lucius, bruised and dishevelled, and without the red-crested helmet which had made him look so distinguished such a short time ago.

'Here,' Kerin panted. 'Hold on to this idiot for me.'

'My pleasure,' Lucius said grimly. He seized the peacock by the hair and wrenched his right arm up behind his back. Kerin turned back towards the fray and stopped short. Vortigern was up on the single table which the fight had left standing. He had Custennin on his knees in front of him, one hand grasping a handful of red hair, the other holding a dagger to the throat of Lud's second son.

'Stop!' he roared. 'Or on my mother's grave, I'll slit every throat in the place.' The sound carried like a thunder-clap. The pandemonium subsided. The warriors broke off their fights and stood, eyeing each other uneasily. The cold dagger lay flat against Custennin's throat, cutting edge to his windpipe. Vortigern's gaze moved over the silent crowd and rested on Lucius. 'Bring that thing up here.'

'Lord,' Lucius said eagerly. He booted the peacock up onto the table, scrambled after him and forced him to kneel beside Custennin, sword-point to the back of his neck.

'What about it, then?' Vortigern asked. 'Shall we kill these animals now?' Custennin's eyes rolled upwards in a chalk-white face. The peacock shivered and wept. The warriors fidgeted nervously, afraid to speak. 'I cannot hear you, mighty warriors,' Vortigern said softly. The silence thickened. Kerin edged forward. 'Now, hear me,' Vortigern said. 'I'd love to feed these two worthless bastards to the ravens. But you don't need the gods' wisdom to work out that we can't fight invaders and fight each other. If we don't stop the Picts soon, Londinium will burn. The cornfields of Kent will burn. They'll rape our women and children and hang them up for the buzzards. Is that what you want?'

'Lord Vortigern,' Severus's thin voice quavered, 'that cannot be what any sane man wants.'

'No,' Vortigern said, savagely jerking Custennin's head backwards. 'And here we are, wasting our time on petty quarrels.' He nodded to Lucius. 'Take his clothes off.' Lucius put up his sword. Off came the purple cloak, the jewelled sword-belt, the gold neck-chains, the fine tunic of soft black wool. 'Alright,' Vortigern said. 'That'll do.' The Kentishman stood on the table and shivered in his boots and breeches. His face burned scarlet. The skin on his narrow, hairless chest was as white as swan's down. Vortigern looked back out over the silent crowd. 'Fine clothes do not make a warrior, men of Kent,' he said softly. The Cambrian warriors murmured their approval. Vortigern's eyes blazed. 'And neither do loud voices and an old man's songs, you garrulous fools,' he shouted. The warriors, to a man, shut their mouths abruptly. In the frozen silence which followed, Vortigern looked up at Garagon. 'What shall we do with these two, then?' he asked. Garagon started, as if that were the last thing he had expected anyone to say to him.

'Either kill them both or spare them both,' he said. 'We must be even-handed in all things.'

Vortigern's eyebrows rose. 'You have spoken wisely, Garagon,' he said. Garagon scowled.

'There's no need to look so surprised,' he said sullenly. Vortigern chuckled.

'Which is it to be, then?' he asked. Kerin saw Custennin's eyes roll upwards, his face a mask of rage and incomprehension. He had not expected to have his life placed in the gift of a Kentishman.

'Spare them,' Garagon said. 'If we're going to fight the Picts together, we shouldn't start by killing our own, however stupid they are.'

Vortigern nodded his approval. 'Well spoken. Now, let's get back to the feast, if it's the praetor's pleasure.'

Kerin moved forward to the table.

'We were lucky there,' a voice said at his elbow. Kerin turned to find Brennius beside him.

'It wasn't luck,' Kerin said.

'No,' Brennius conceded. He hauled the crestfallen little warrior down off the table and booted him in the buttocks. 'Come on, you numbskull, get dressed and keep your mouth shut.'

Vortigern arrived beside them, still with an iron grip on Custennin's arm. 'Tell Garagon I want to speak to him alone,' he said. Brennius seized his compatriot by the shoulder and propelled him away through the crowd.

'Lord, am I free to go now?' Custennin hissed between gritted teeth. Vortigern released him with a sharp upward movement of the arm which sent him staggering into one of the upturned tables. Custennin recovered himself and stalked off towards the dais, his eyes burning with mute resentment. The kitchen slaves scurried back and forth, trying to raise the semblance of a feast from the ruins. Severus Maximus came picking his way across the courtyard, treading with extreme care on the grease-filmed paving slabs.

'Do you really think we should go on with this tonight?' he asked.

'Yes,' Vortigern said. 'There'll be no more trouble, I can tell you.'

Garagon arrived, looking less full of his own importance than he had done after making his triumphal entry. Vortigern poured wine and handed it to him. Severus hovered uncertainly, as if wondering where his share had gone.

'Leave us,' Vortigern said. 'This is between ourselves.'

Severus turned and marched off across the courtyard with as much frayed dignity as he could muster.

'He's praetor of Londinium,' Garagon said incredulously. 'Do you have no respect for him?'

'We have already discussed respect, as I recall,' Vortigern said. Garagon coloured slightly.

'Alright. I know you have none for me.'

Kerin could not help feeling a little sorry for him. Arrogant and self-regarding though he was, he had conducted himself well when it mattered.

' I have more for you now than when you rode in pretending to be the King of all the Britons,' Vortigern said. 'Will you come with us in the spring?'

'Yes,' Garagon said without hesitation. 'There's much to discuss, but as to the purpose, you have my agreement.'

'There's something else you should know, then,' Vortigern said. 'We have a monk with us. Constans, the oldest son of Constantine.'

Garagon's eyes narrowed. 'Constans? They say that Constantine only packed him off to the monastery because he knew he'd never make a man of him.' He grinned. 'Send him to us, and we'll give him a pretty whore and a jug of ale. That'll tell you how much of a man he is.' He waved to Brennius and started to thread his way back towards the dais. Kerin watched him go; brash, insouciant, gathering his warriors like moths to his bright flame.

'Well, Kerin,' Vortigern said, 'what have we gained so far, apart from the Cornishmen? A monk, a Saxon cook and a thousand Kentish warriors who've never seen a fight.'

'And that could have been a bloodbath,' Kerin said. 'We were within a hand's breadth.'

Vortigern looked out over the courtyard, where Garagon and his men were settling down again, mopping their cuts and bruises and straightening out their fancy clothes. 'I've been within a hand's breadth all my life,' he said.

8

A glimmer of pale light appeared on the horizon to the east, turning the sky to a deep sea-green, as the wagon rumbled towards Londinium. The ox-driver and his companion, a balding man on a fat pony, were far too busy arguing to notice the two riders approaching until it was too late to pull over and hide in the hazel thickets alongside the road. The younger of the two men, senior in rank if not in years, wore a good blue cloak and a jaunty grey hat with a silver pin. His older companion, sitting hunched in the saddle as if he couldn't stand being on a horse, kept the hood of his cloak drawn well forward about his face.

'Go on,' Vortigern said grudgingly. 'You're the patrician this morning.'

Kerin chuckled, adjusted his cap and trotted off towards the wagon on the smart grey horse which he had borrowed from the praetor's stables without asking. The ox-driver touched his cap respectfully.

'What have you got in there?' Kerin asked.

'Hides from the tannery down the road, sir,' said the driver. 'Best quality pure white cow, bound for Rome.'

'On Gallus's ships,' Kerin said, using the tip of his sword to lift a corner of the sheet which covered the wagon's contents. 'What's your name, driver?'

'Mab!' the driver said indignantly. 'I wouldn't lie to you, sir!'

'Probably not,' Kerin said, 'but I'm a merchant myself, and I might need some white cowhide one day. Are the roads peaceful today? Have you seen any warriors on the march?'

Mab gave a rueful smile. 'They're everywhere these days, sir, but no. There's been some talk, though. We drank with a couple of horse-dealers. They said they'd sold some animals to Eldof of Glevum. According to them, Eldof is riding for Londinium with five hundred fighting men –'

'And a baggage train,' his companion butted in eagerly. 'That's why they wanted the horses, I'll be bound. There were tales of lameness and sickness, you know. Give me a good, strong ox any day.'

Mab closed his eyes briefly before continuing. 'As I said, five hundred fighting men. And a baggage train, naturally. The dealers said that Eldof has his brother the bishop with him. They're marching down the Via Legionis – that's the old military road from Viroconium. It joins this road further west. Less than half a day on horses like yours.'

Kerin touched his cap, wheeled his horse in the road and tossed a coin to Mab.

'Thank you, sir!' a shocked voice echoed back to him as he and Vortigern rode away. The coin was a silver denarius, and would buy Mab and his family a princely supper, as well as paying to repair the cart which had been damaged in that regrettable incident outside the chapel of St Alban.

Further down the road, out of sight of anyone except the kites wheeling above the rippling grassland, Vortigern straightened in the saddle and threw back the hood of his cloak.

'If I'd known you were ever going to put on airs and graces like that, I'd have let you die,' he said. Kerin grinned.

'I was afraid that the driver might recognise me. But he must have had his mind on his oxen the other day.'

'The statue,' Vortigern said sourly. 'I might have known.'

They rode on across gently rolling countryside where herds of sleek white cattle grazed beside shallow pools, switching the flies which buzzed in clouds above swathes of meadowsweet and water-mint as the sun got up. At the edge of a rivulet fringed with yellow flag, two ragged farm boys were playing knuckle-bones on a smooth rock. Kerin found it easy to wish himself inside the threadbare tunic of one of the boys. They looked well-fed, and could have had no responsibilities beyond driving their charges back to the safety of a village compound before darkness brought the wolves from the woods. They did not have to worry about Eldof of Glevum, or wonder whether a halfwit like Macsen had managed to get hold of a quantity of cloaks and belts. And they did not have to hope that Lucius Arrius was doing what he had promised to do; following Constans like a shadow, and guarding the door of his apartments whenever he was inside.

* * *

There was a wood beside the disused Roman road. First came the smell of smoke and roasting meat, then the sound of men's voices, still some way distant. The two riders turned off the road onto a narrow deer-path. The delicate trees of the outskirts gave way to oak, with a dense understorey of hazel and elder, wreathed in brambles. They tethered their horses deep in the thicket and crept forward. By now they could hear fires crackling, horses munching their fodder, a woman calling her children. The sun's rays filtered through the leaf-cover, casting a dappled light across the underbrush. Crouching low, they peered through a tangled screen of brambles and honeysuckle. There was an abandoned village, taken over by a company so large that it overflowed the village and seeped out into the trees. There were scores of armed warriors and a handful of dignitaries in Roman garb. There were also laden carts, baggage animals, servants, craftsmen, priests, camp-followers and hunting dogs. A tall, well-made man whom Kerin recognised at once as Eldof of Glevum was standing outside the largest of the ruined dwellings. His white tunic and opulent red cloak, fastened at the shoulder by a gold spread-eagle brooch, were pure Roman. Only the thick, flowing hair spoke of his British parentage, and it had been diligently brushed, as if in a gesture of respect to Roman orderliness. An old man came to speak to him.

'Look!' Kerin hissed. 'It's that old goat we saved in the woods.'

Vortigern pressed his finger to his lips. Eldof was haranguing Malan, making expansive gestures, and looked rather proud of the entourage he had managed to drag all the way from Glevum. He was joined before long by two other men, who came out of the house stretching and smiling, as if they had just enjoyed refreshment. One was tall, with slightly stooped shoulders and thinning hair. Even without his long black clerical robe and the heavy silver crucifix he could have been identified as the Bishop of Glevum, for he closely resembled his brother; Eldof grown older, with less flesh on the bones. He was followed by a rather younger man, Vortigern's age, perhaps. He was neatly dressed all in dark grey. Lean, clean-shaven, his thick grey-flecked hair cropped short. His face, probably once handsome, was ravaged by the plague. Unlike Eldof, who was well tricked-out with gold armbands, neck-chains and a ceremonial sword-belt, this man wore not a single ornament. Kerin knew, at once and for no reason he could name, that the man was trouble. Vortigern touched his arm.

'Come on,' he murmured. 'We'll wait until the sun goes a little.' They wormed their way back to the place where they had tied the horses and stretched out on a mossy bank, waiting for dusk. 'It's like a Roman circus,' Vortigern said, wrinkling his lip with distaste.

'Who's the man with the pock-marked face?' Kerin asked. 'The one who came out of the house with the bishop?'

'That,' Vortigern said, 'is Bertil Redknife.'

Kerin remembered what Malan had said. *Not if they're Bertil Redknife's dogs.* 'Who is he?' he asked.

'An ally of Eldof's,' Vortigern said. 'Not a friend. Rich and powerful enough to be a nuisance to him.'

'What's he doing here, then?' Kerin asked.

'Bertil's a time-server,' Vortigern said. 'He must see some advantage in it. He's a fighter, though; I'll grant him that.' He rolled onto his back and lay staring up through the rustling canopy. 'He and Eldof fought the Irish with us – years ago, not in the last invasion. We captured a settlement they'd built, far down on the west coast. The ones we didn't kill were taken prisoner, and Bertil married one of the women. They had two children, but the woman died in the plague that killed your people. The children too, I believe. Bertil paid the price of surviving it, as you can see. And before you say that all that's enough to turn a man bad, let me tell you that he's no more or less evil now than when he was a babe at his mother's breast. It was ever so.'

Kerin thought over what Vortigern had said and wondered why, out of all the men he had met since leaving home, it was this one who had made him stop short. All of the others he could take or leave – the wistful Severus; garrulous, well-meaning Gorlois; proud, self-regarding Garagon of Kent. But Bertil Redknife chilled him to the bone.

'What's the matter?' Vortigern asked, rising on one elbow. 'You look as if someone had drained the blood out of you.'

'Nothing,' Kerin said brightly, feigning bewilderment. It would have been impossible to say, even though he knew it to be the truth, that he and Bertil would one day try to kill each other. They waited without speaking further until the light grew dim and the sounds of evening began to drift in the air; men laughing and singing as they gathered around the fires, some of Eldof's musicians playing a soft melody on their pipes, the hooting of the first owls. They crept from the thicket and round the perimeter of the settlement, to a point from which it was possible to see the nearest fires burning. A woman was sitting on the ground mending clothes. There was a long, low building which might have been a byre, a pen containing a few listless ponies. Vortigern gripped Kerin's arm.

'What do you suppose they were doing there, then?' the voice said, startlingly close.

'I don't know,' came the reply, 'but we'll find out tomorrow, when Tullius gets back.'

The men who had spoken were no more than a few paces away, hidden from view by a low bank on which a thick stand of hazel saplings rose from a sea of lady's lace. Vortigern and Kerin edged on their bellies to the top of the bank. The men who had spoken were Eldof and his brother the bishop. There was sweat on their horses' necks. Beside them, in the act of dismounting, were Bertil Redknife and a big, broad-chested man with a florid face and short grizzled beard. He wore a soldier's leather jerkin over his tunic, and was armed with sword, spear and twin daggers. A nasty livid scar ran down his right cheek and across his neck, disappearing under his collar. The four men began to unsaddle their horses.

'Well?' Bertil said. 'What did he say?'

'I was right,' Eldof said. 'They did go to Venta Belgarum. I've sent my son to find out why.'

'It could be nothing,' Eldadus said soothingly. Eldof grimaced.

'It's not nothing. I've known Vortigern since we were both lads, and I know when he's up to no good.'

'You shouldn't be too hasty about all this, brother,' the bishop remonstrated. 'There are many reasons for going to see a churchman, so don't condemn a man out of hand until you know the facts. The grace of God moves in strange ways from time to time.'

Eldof snorted. 'You've been too long in the cloister, Eldadus,' he said. 'I've no idea why Vortigern went to see Father Paulinus, but I can promise you that it had nothing to do with the grace of God.' He looked up as a troupe of servants arrived to take charge of the horses and saddlery. 'Come on; the meat will be ready by now. We'll speak when Tullius gets back.'

They moved away. Kerin sat up, shaking flowers and insects from his hair. Rather to his surprise, Vortigern appeared to be on the verge of laughter. 'Do you still think it's a good idea to talk to Eldof?' he asked.

'Yes,' Vortigern said. 'We must tell him about the monk before his idiot son does.' He sprang to his feet and marched off towards the village. 'Take off your sword-belt,' he said, as Kerin caught up with him. 'We go unarmed. Daggers too. Here,' he took the weapons from Kerin and thrust everything under a spindle bush. They walked on. Ahead of them rush lamps glimmered in the gathering dusk and cooking fires blazed. As they passed the horse pens, a dark figure leapt from the shadows, wearing rough breeches and a blue tunic with a white cross on the front. They found themselves on the point of his spear.

'Who the devil are you ?' he barked.

'I'm Vortigern of Glywysing,' Vortigern said cheerily. 'And this is my warrior, Kerin Brightspear.'

The guard laughed raucously. 'And I'm the Emperor

of Rome, you lying hound,' he hooted, prodding Vortigern's chest with his spear. He glanced to his left and bellowed at the shadows. 'Marcus! Come here, Marcus, and bring a light.' Another guard appeared, similarly dressed. He raised his flaring torch to illuminate the faces of the two strangers.

'Oh, Mother of God!' the first man whispered, and turned pale with terror. Vortigern chuckled maliciously, took the spear from him and buried its point in the earth.

'Now, take us to Eldof before I break your head,' he said.

'Lords,' the guard stammered, glancing fearfully over his shoulder as if some tide of flame were about to overtake him from behind. As they reached the big ruined house, Eldof emerged from the low doorway, flanked by Bertil Redknife and the silent, grey-bearded warrior who had accompanied him earlier. Eldof looked Vortigern up and down, a slow grin spreading across his face as he observed the plain brown tunic and breeches and the threadbare woollen cloak.

'Well,' he said, folding his arms. 'Are times so hard on the other side of the river?'

Vortigern smiled. 'I am not one for display, as you know, Eldof,' he said courteously. 'And besides, what can a man do when his face is known in every corner of the country? Sometimes it's good for him to travel privately, without every little prince and landowner running to spread garlands at his horse's feet.'

Eldof's smile turned brittle. 'You'll get no garlands from me, Vortigern,' he said.

'None are required,' Vortigern said. 'A haunch of venison would be pleasant, though.'

Eldof nodded to Marcus the torch-bearer, who was hovering nervously in the background. 'Tell the cooks to see to it,' he said, a little grudgingly, Kerin thought. 'And tell the servants to make beds ready, and see to their horses. Let no man say that Eldof lacks hospitality.'

He led the way to the cooking fire, and indicated a place on his right hand where Vortigern could sit, between him and the silent warrior. The air sang with the smell of roasted meat, the scent of burning ash wood and another smell which Kerin could not place, heavily sweet and yet shot through with the sharp fragrance of herbs, like some of Faria's aromatic oils. A dozen or more men were there already, sitting or sprawling on blankets and luxurious cushions; a few old hands and some cocky-looking youngsters. Kerin found himself a space to Eldof's left. Old Malan, who had been feeding the fire, greeted him cordially and sat down close behind him. Bertil Redknife sat opposite, next to a squat, dark-haired man with powerful shoulders, a thick black beard and small, pin-sharp eyes. If the man had not had two healthy, unblemished ears, Kerin would have sworn that he was looking at Brennan, who had come close to ending his life on the way to the monastery. Eldof lowered himself to the ground with a grunt.

'You will have met my chief warrior, Varro,' he said.

'Indeed,' Vortigern said, with a respectful nod. 'We fought together against the Irish.'

The big man smiled and extended his hand. Vortigern clasped it warmly and they fell into conversation. Despite his size and fearsome appearance,

Varro spoke in a husky, barely audible whisper. Kerin wondered whether it was something to do with the old neck wound. He became aware that Eldof was watching him intently.

'It seems strange,' Eldof said, 'that he did not bring one of his sons.' Kerin shrugged. He supposed that Eldof had a point, but it was not the man's business to know why Rufus had been sent home to Cambria, far less that Kerin's own position was less secure than it appeared. 'I've seen you before, though, haven't I,' Eldof said curiously.

'Yes,' Kerin said. 'In Glevum last spring, perhaps, or at the feast you held in your house at Eastertide. The bath was wonderful.'

Eldof's eyes narrowed. 'Yes, I thought I knew you. You're that robber's bastard he raised in his own household.'

Kerin grinned. 'That's right,' he said equably. He was so well used to such remarks that they hardly offended him, but he felt that Eldof could have put it better.

'Were you at Venta Belgarum with him?' Eldof enquired.

'Venta Belgarum?' Kerin said vaguely, but loudly enough for the words to carry. Vortigern laid a hand on Varro's arm and turned.

'You seem quite interested in what I've been doing, Eldof,' he said mildly.

'Not really,' Eldof said, prodding the fire with a stray stick. 'I'd heard some rumour about Venta Belgarum, that's all. It seemed like an odd place for a man to pass through on his way to Londinium. Particularly a man who doesn't make a habit of calling on priests.'

Vortigern chuckled. 'Well, I wouldn't have gone out of my way to call on that poisonous old toad Paulinus without a good reason. But I don't have to tell you that, do I?'

'No,' Eldof said bluntly. He waited. The servants arrived with tankards and pitchers of ale. One of the kitchen boys hacked a thick slice of meat from the dripping carcass, laid it on a wooden platter and presented it to Eldof with great ceremony. Eldof raised a deferential hand. 'Please,' he said, 'serve the Lord Vortigern first.'

Vortigern accepted the meat with a gracious smile. 'You are too generous, Eldof,' he said. For a moment their eyes met across the platter, with a hostility venomous enough to make the air crackle. Kerin drank half-heartedly, with one eye on Bertil Redknife and his gimlet-eyed companion. Vortigern ate and drank with apparent relish and said not a word. Eldof picked at his meat and drank a judicious amount of ale. Kerin watched the fingers of his large, bristled hand clenching and unclenching on the handle of his tankard, and knew that impatience was eating him alive. Vortigern leaned back against a pile of cushions.

'Do you know, Eldof,' he said, 'that we now have a Saxon cook?'

Eldof put down his tankard. 'Why, for God's sake?' he asked. Kerin realised that everyone else around the cooking fire had fallen silent, and was listening intently.

'Know thine enemy, Eldof,' Vortigern said softly. Eldof's brows knitted in an exasperated frown.

'Come to the point,' he growled.

'The Saxons are coming back, Eldof,' Vortigern said,

sitting up straight. Kerin had never seen the two men close to each other before, and realised that Eldof's gaze was being held against his will, in his own camp and in the midst of his picked men.

'What do you mean, coming back? The Saxons are no more than a nuisance. Never have been. The odd bunch of pirates here and there.'

'No,' Vortigern said. 'Not this time.'

'But the Picts –'

'Are still the immediate threat, of course. But next year, when their ships are ready and the weather's right, the Saxons will look towards the cornfields of Kent. So it must be obvious that we need to beat the Picts soundly and fast, because it will not stop there.'

Eldof sat quite still. He was not the quickest of thinkers, but he did possess an ability to sit, quiet and uncannily motionless, whilst he weighed things before opening his mouth. 'So,' he said. 'This is why we are all meeting in Londinium.'

'Yes,' Vortigern said. 'As soon as the snows melt, we must march north. This is what Constantine would have done, if he had not chosen to go and fight elsewhere.'

Eldof raised his hands. 'He did his best. At least, according to his own lights. Constantine was not a bad man, and I for one always thought that our salvation lay in keeping the Empire whole.' He smiled wryly. 'I know we disagree about this. But at least while Constantine lived, men had someone to call king, or what you will. Now, God knows where anyone's allegiance lies. If Constantine's sons were older, perhaps –'

'Lord, we've been through this,' Varro said, with an air of strained patience. 'Armorica is the safest place for those lads, until they're old enough to decide things for themselves.'

Eldof's eyes met Varro's in an uneasy acquiescence. Kerin suspected that he might have had more to say, if his old adversary had not been listening.

'Varro's right,' Vortigern said. 'The boys have many enemies. The least we can do is protect them, now that their father's dead.'

Eldof's eyes narrowed. 'Vortigern, we've known each other for nearly forty years, and I've never seen you waste one minute of your time on protecting the defenceless unless it benefited you. Why start with the sons of Constantine?'

Vortigern leaned slightly forward. 'Because all I care about at the moment is beating the Picts and the Irish. If someone butchers Constantine's sons now, there'll be civil war, and we can't fight invaders if we're fighting each other. Why do you think I went to Caerwynt? For pleasure?'

'I've no idea why,' Eldof said, looking increasingly bemused.

'Look,' Vortigern said, 'you know as well as I do that Constantine had another son.'

'Constans, yes. The oldest one. But he took holy orders when he was a lad. He's been in that monastery ever since.'

'Well,' Vortigern said, 'I didn't think it wise to leave him there. The sort of men who would kill Ambrosius and Uther would disregard the House of God, if they wanted to do away with Constans too.'

Eldof hesitated. He looked utterly perplexed, and not without resentment, as if he knew quite well that he was being outwitted in some way which he could not quite grasp.

'Lord Vortigern,' Bertil Redknife enquired, 'are you saying that you have removed the monk from his cloister?'

'Yes,' Vortigern said. 'For his own safety. He's under my protection in Londinium, and is of course free to return to his monastery whenever he chooses.'

Varro pressed Eldof's arm. 'Lord, this isn't a bad thing,' he said in his rasping whisper. Eldof looked unconvinced.

'I shall visit Constans when we reach Londinium,' he said, draining his tankard. 'I'd sooner hear this from his lips than yours.'

Vortigern nodded his agreement. More pitchers of ale were brought. A girl appeared out of the darkness with a small flask and a silver goblet. It was Malan's granddaughter, Flora. Smiling shyly she knelt in front of Eldof, filled the goblet with a clear, golden liquid and held it out to him. At once the air was filled with the sweet, unfamiliar smell which Kerin had detected earlier. He wondered how the girl had fared since he saw her last. Eldof took the goblet and sniffed it cautiously.

'What's this?' he asked. 'And who are you?'

'Lord, it is our own metheglin,' Malan croaked. 'Our own secret blend of mead and woodland herbs. And this is my granddaughter, Flora.'

'The goddess of the flowers,' Eldof said jovially. He drained the metheglin, planted a wet kiss on the girl's cheek and slapped the ground at his side. 'Please, my lord,' he said to Vortigern with mock deference, 'move up a little so that the goddess may be seated.'

Vortigern smiled politely and moved up. With a nervous smile, the girl sat down on the blanket between him and Eldof, drew her knees up to her chest and covered her feet demurely with the folds of her blue dress. Her large eyes darted back and forth, met Kerin's and were lowered. Eldof requested more metheglin, gulped it down and raised the girl's chin on the tip of his forefinger. Whatever else he had brought from Glevum, Kerin thought, it could not have been his wife. The girl did not resist – how could she have done? – but her face and body were tense and unyielding, as if she knew what was probably coming, and did not welcome it.

'She's beautiful, isn't she?' Malan said. Kerin smiled.

'Yes,' he said truthfully. 'Your son's daughter?'

'My second daughter's daughter,' the old man corrected him. 'I have six daughters, but no sons. They're good girls, but they all married fools and lazy bastards. And of course it was much easier to tag along with Eldof's crew, pretending to be warriors, than to stay home and do the work. So here we all are, men, women, children and all.' He sighed noisily and lifted the frayed hem of his grey tunic. 'We're no better off, as you can see. We may just as well go all the way to Londinium with them, and see what the pickings are there.'

'Come now, Malan,' Eldof said, reaching across to slap the old man's shoulder. 'Have we done you any harm?'

'Not a great deal,' the old man said grudgingly. 'Unless you count eating and drinking everything we brought with us.'

Eldof chuckled. 'Well,' he said, 'warriors must eat. And never forget, we're the ones who'll defend you when the Picts come calling.'

Malan eyed him balefully, as if he didn't believe a word of it. Bertil Redknife appeared at Eldof's shoulder and bent to murmur something inaudible in his ear. Eldof smiled broadly, elbowed Kerin aside and flung an arm around Malan's shoulders. 'I have a request,' he said. 'My men are intoxicated by the goddess of the flowers. Will your girls share a goblet of metheglin with these brave warriors?'

Malan stared up at the sky and sighed. 'Lord Eldof, you can take my meat and you can take my ale, but if your warriors try to take our women against their will they'll be dead men, if I have to cut their throats myself. Of course, if our women are stupid enough to lie with your warriors of their own free will, as some of them have been doing all the way here, then there's nothing more to be said.' He beckoned to one of the girls who was gathering empty pitchers and platters. 'Dunia, you are free to go when you've finished, you and the rest of the girls. It's your choice whether you go to your beds or bring more metheglin for these brave warriors.'

He spoke with a heavy irony which was not lost on Dunia, judging by the coy little smile she gave as she bent to pick up the last of the platters. Kerin observed the curve of her breasts and the way her thin tunic clung to her buttocks as she walked away. There was a rough, earthy familiarity about Dunia which interested him, after weeks of perfumed sheets and refined pleasures, and he found himself watching the sagging doorway through which she had disappeared. She was ugly, compared to Faria, but her body had the supple strength of a young animal's, and he knew in any case that she would look less ugly after a goblet or two of metheglin.

'Well,' Eldof's voice said, just beside him, 'perhaps there'll even be one to spare for a robber's bastard.'

Kerin smiled and stretched easily. 'I'm only interested in goddesses,' he said. Eldof snorted.

'Goddesses don't lie with peasants,' he said, and turned to reassert his claim to the goddess of the flowers. He stopped short. The space beside him on the blanket was empty. 'Where did she go?' he asked indignantly. There was no reply. No-one, it seemed, had seen Flora leave. The warriors had been too absorbed in watching the serving girls, and if Malan knew where his granddaughter had gone, he was not about to admit it. Kerin had noticed a fierce light flash in his eyes when Eldof made his request. You really would cut a few throats to protect your girls, he thought, if those skinny arms could find the strength.

'To one of the houses, perhaps?' Malan said vaguely, waving his hand towards the trees. Eldof sighed.

'No matter,' he said philosophically. 'Let the young stags chase the hinds tonight. Malan, there's metheglin enough for both of us in this flask, if you would care to share it with me. You too – what's your name? Kerin? – here, drink if you want to. You may as well, if you're only interested in goddesses.'

Kerin smiled broadly and accepted the goblet which Eldof handed to him. He sipped the metheglin with care, knowing how unwise it would be to let it undermine his judgment, and wondered how long it would be before Eldof noticed that Vortigern, too, had vanished.

9

'Kerin, bring me my scrolls, will you, please?' Constans said absently. 'I should like to read for a while. Perhaps it will take my mind off everything which is going to happen tomorrow.'

He was sitting on the low wall which surrounded the pool in the centre of Severus's splendid reception room, admiring his reflection in the limpid water. The fountain was not working, and the surface of the pool was as smooth as a looking-glass. Constans's fine white hands adjusted the gold brooch at his shoulder and moved slowly over his purple robe, as if he found it impossible to recognise the shabby little monk who had fled from Venta Belgarum. At his side was a small low table on which silver wine cups, a decanter and bowls of fruit jostled for space. Kerin remained where he was, stretched out on a couch strewn with velvet cushions which smelt faintly of sandalwood. To his relief, he had returned from his expedition to find Gallus's ships lying serene and undamaged beside the merchant's wharf. Constans seemed none the worse for being under Lucius Arrius's protection for a while, and this confirmed what Kerin had already divined; that Lucius was steady and dependable, and might become a friend.

'Are you frightened?' he asked.

'Yes,' Constans confessed, with a nervous smile.

'Of what?' Kerin asked. 'Of burning in hell because you've broken your vows?'

Constans coloured furiously. 'I'm sure God understands that his servants must sometimes follow strange paths,' he said.

Kerin grinned broadly. 'Well,' he said, 'I hope he was looking the other way when you were getting drunk on the praetor's wine.'

The monk's eyes flashed. 'How dare you?' he spat. 'Don't forget, I'll be King of all the Britons soon, and I shan't forget remarks like that.'

Kerin found it hard to feel more than mildly irritated by this threat. 'It hasn't happened yet,' he said. 'The great men meet tomorrow, as you know, and it's for them to decide.'

Constans laughed deprecatingly. 'You don't understand. The Lord Vortigern has promised me that it will be so.'

Kerin shook his head and walked over to the window. Below him a group of slave girls crossed the courtyard in the bright morning sunlight, chattering like magpies, but Faria was not amongst them. For some reason unexplained, it was her cousin Sha'ara who had been waiting when he returned to Londinium. He had surprised himself by sending Sha'ara away, and was further surprised now to realise how much he desired Faria's company the moment that she was not available to him. This realisation had not, of course, come to him in the village beside the Via Legionis. He thought of the fires and the music, of the potent smell of herbs and honey, and of Dunia writhing dementedly beneath him as they rode to oblivion on a tide of lust and metheglin. He thought of Flora, standing on the bank beside the Roman road with a hood pulled low over her dark hair, watching with her haunted eyes as they rode away into the drifts of morning mist.

'Well,' a voice said behind him, 'can you spare a cup of wine for a poor traveller who's ridden all the way from Cambria?'

'Rufus!' Kerin exclaimed with delight. He sat up and they embraced warmly. Rufus looked well; there was a colour to his countenance and a lively sparkle in his eyes which Kerin suspected that he himself might have lost.

'How are things at home?' he asked.

'Much the same,' Rufus said, stretching out on the couch and kicking off his riding boots. 'The usual petty little fights and pointless arguments. But the water's clear, the ale is good, the mutton is sweet –'

'Don't,' Kerin sighed, raising his hand to silence him. Rufus chuckled, leaned over and helped himself to wine. Constans perched on the end of the couch and gave him a hesitant smile.

'There's no need to look at me like that, Constans,' Rufus said. 'I'm not my father. I won't eat you for dinner.'

'Your father's done me nothing but good,' Constans said blithely. 'Why should I be afraid of him?'

'For the same reason that you'd be afraid of a starving wolf,' Rufus said. Constans's pale face assumed a look of disbelief, stiffened by mortal offence.

'How can you speak like that?' he asked. 'Aren't you

loyal to your father? I wish I still had a father to be loyal to, I can tell you.'

'Any man should be loyal to his father, if he can,' Rufus said. 'But sometimes, other things must come first.'

'But surely, a man's duty,' Constans began. Rufus's dark eyes flashed fire.

'Duty!' he exclaimed. 'You broke your vows to God as easily as if they had been dry twigs. Look to your own conscience, Constans, and don't talk to me about duty.' He jumped up, pulled on his dusty boots and stalked out of the room. His footsteps echoed away down the tiled walkway towards the main courtyard. Kerin ran after him and caught him up beneath the statue of Minerva. Rufus looked agitated, like a man who had just been in a fight.

'For God's sake, come back and finish your wine,' Kerin said. 'I know you don't approve of all this, but why frighten the life out of Constans before tomorrow?'

'Because he ought to be frightened,' Rufus said. 'And because he ought to know the truth, before someone tries to put a crown on his head.'

'The truth?' Kerin was stung to anger. 'What's that, Rufus? One monk's conscience, or ten thousand dead and a country full of burned villages?'

Rufus closed his eyes. 'Look, you know I can't be part of this,' he said.

'I know,' Kerin said. 'And I'm sure your father knows it, too.' He paused, wondering how far he wanted to take it, and found that there was no way to avoid finishing what he had begun. 'In fact, if I were your father, and I thought that my son would refuse to support me, then I think I'd feel betrayed.'

Rufus blinked. It was impossible to judge whether the thought had not occurred to him, or if the shock lay in hearing the words come out of Kerin's mouth. 'Betrayed? Is that how you see it?'

Kerin seized him by the arms. 'Look,' he said, 'you're my dearest friend, and I'll love you like a brother until the day I die. But I'd need to share your faith to see things as you do.'

'You do share it!' Rufus exclaimed. 'It's the faith we learned from my mother. The faith Iustig taught us.'

'No, it's not,' Kerin said. 'Not any more.'

Rufus shook himself free from Kerin's grasp. 'It's not the faith that's changed. It's the way men twist it for their own ends.'

Kerin knew that argument was pointless; his own grasp of the issues was far too shaky. But there was no escaping the feeling that Rufus looked far less confident than he was trying to appear. 'Will you go to the meeting tomorrow?' he asked.

'Yes,' Rufus said. 'Since I'm here, I can't very well refuse to go. But I've got to pray now, and talk to Father Giraldus. Please understand that I have no choice in this.'

Kerin raised his hands in resignation and let him go. Lucius, who was on duty at the main entrance, sized up the situation and gave Kerin an uneasy glance as he opened the gate for Rufus to pass through.

Constans was picking at a plate of dried figs which someone had brought for him. He put it aside and looked up at Kerin with unhappy bewilderment.

'Why is the Lord Vortimer so angry?' he asked.

'Because he can't choose between his father and his conscience,' Kerin said. 'It's really nothing to do with you, whatever he said just now.' Constans lowered his eyes.

'And you?' he asked. Kerin smiled.

'I'm only Vortigern's warrior,' he said, looking out of the window as the slave girls, still without Faria, came back across the courtyard with bales of washed sheets and towels. 'Rufus is his son, so he has a position to keep up. I don't, so what I think doesn't matter.'

'I don't think that's entirely true,' Constans said carefully. 'Everyone seems to think that the Lord Vortigern values your counsel.'

Kerin sat down on the couch. He had no intention of discussing his position with the monk; but much as he disliked Constans, he felt that the poor fool deserved some explanation before he put his head on the block. 'I think that there are some men who will refuse to fight the Picts with Vortigern unless he gives them a king they can accept,' he said. 'Some of them will welcome you, just because you are Constantine's son. Others will condemn you for breaking your vows. And then, of course, there are those who would follow Vortigern anyway, whatever happened about the kingship. Until tomorrow, there's no way of knowing what will happen, or how strong any of these people are.'

'Yes,' Constans said, refusing to be deflected. 'But what do *you* think?'

'I think we have to beat the Picts or get slaughtered,' Kerin said. 'In the end, I suppose that it doesn't much matter how it's done.'

'So you think I should be king?' Constans said hopefully.

'I think you will be king,' Kerin said. 'And I think that Vortigern will get what he wants from it. Whether or not that's good for you, is not for me to say. Do you want it?'

'Yes,' Constans said quietly. He looked down at his white woman's hands and twisted a heavy ring on his left index finger. It was made of gold and silver braided together and set with a large peridot. Kerin wondered where it had come from. Constans smiled wistfully. 'Do you think it's so terrible?' he asked. 'For a monk to want to leave the cloister, and be king?'

Kerin shook his head. 'Not at all,' he said. 'I know which I'd prefer.'

'You're not a Christian, though,' Constans sighed. Kerin was a little surprised by that conclusion.

'I'm not anything else,' he said cautiously. Constans laughed.

'Perhaps not. But you don't lose any sleep worrying about the wrath of hell, do you?'

'No,' Kerin said, smiling, 'particularly since I hope not to have to endure it yet.'

'You'd worry about it if you'd been taught by Abbot Paulinus,' Constans said ruefully. 'Never mind Bishop Germanus. Father Paulinus used to rant about him all the time. He's from Gallia, but he was a soldier in the Roman army before he took orders. He came over here once, do you remember?'

'I've heard the name,' Kerin said. 'Wasn't there a battle, somewhere in Cambria?'

'Yes, yes.' Constans fluttered his slender white hands 'My father used to tell me about it when I was a little lad. He and Germanus fought together. He said that all Germanus had to do was open his mouth and shout "Hallelujah!" and all the enemy ran away or fell down dead.'

Kerin gave a snort of laughter. 'We'd better get him back here, then,' he said. Constans smiled nervously.

'I wouldn't say that too loudly if I were you. Father Paulinus was forever telling us that he was coming back at any moment, to fight the Pelagians.'

Kerin grimaced. It was tricky enough trying to keep monks and druids apart, without the Christians wanting to cut each other's throats. 'I don't understand any of that,' he said. 'If you can explain it to me, in a way that an ordinary man can understand, I'll promise not to tell Father Paulinus about the praetor's wine.'

Constans blushed. 'It's all very simple, really. Pelagius believed that you could win favour with God through your own good works. But now there's a powerful bishop from the Eastern Empire, a man called Augustine, and Bishop Germanus has become a follower of his. They believe that we all come into this life with the sin of Adam in us. That babies are damned at birth unless they receive baptism, and that the rest of us are damned unless we obey the church and take the holy sacrament, no matter how kind we are to the stray dogs and the lepers. Rome has banned the Pelagians, and you can get thrown in prison or even executed, just for being one.'

'Is it about free will?' Kerin asked. 'Rufus seems to think so.'

'Yes, it's all about free will,' said Constans. 'Pelagius believed that we had it, and could make our own fate through the good or bad we did. Augustine believes that there's no such thing, and that our only hope is the grace of God. Is Vortigern a Pelagian? Lupinus seems to think so.'

Kerin thought that he must remember to have a word with the talkative Lupinus. 'You should ask Vortigern,' he said, knowing that Constans never would. A commotion in the courtyard below drew them both to the window. A chariot had arrived, accompanied by a troop of foot-soldiers in green tabards emblazoned with the symbol of a golden cockerel. The men preened, and their tabards and short-bladed swords glinted in the sun. Kerin, scanty though his Latin was, knew that *gallus* could mean a cockerel as well as a man of Gallia. These were the merchant's guards, for a bet. The charioteer handed his animals' reins to one of the foot-soldiers and went inside the house.

'I'm going to find out what's going on down there,' Kerin said.

'But you haven't fetched my scrolls!' Constans whined. Kerin looked over his shoulder.

'Ask Lupinus,' he said, noting the faint flush which coloured the monk's pale cheeks as he considered the suggestion.

10

The foot-soldiers had been joined by several of the praetorian guard, Lucius amongst them. From the cheerful banter, it was clear that they had much in common; family ties, drinking dens and a good few women.

'What's going on?' Kerin asked, running his hand over the fine, muscular neck of the nearest chariot horse.

'Oh,' said Lucius, 'they've come for Gallus, that's all. He's inside somewhere, talking to Severus Maximus and the Lord Vortigern.' He leaned forward and gave Kerin a conspiratorial wink. 'The galleys are still afloat,' he murmured. 'Macsen will tell you the rest.' Kerin grinned and patted him on the shoulder. A troop of servants came bundling out of the house carrying baskets of fruit, cushions and embroidered bed covers. 'Severus has guests arriving this evening,' Lucius said. 'Eldof of Glevum and his party, I believe. A messenger arrived at first light this morning, and the household staff have been running around like ants ever since. They're staying in the castra; it's that large building just over there, on the other side of the street. Built as a prison originally, I think. Allectus used it to house his personal guard, but Severus doesn't do things quite on that scale. The city garrison is quartered there now, but it's far too big for them, so the praetor uses the rest of it for his guests. The less important ones, that is.'

Kerin smiled, glad that Lucius had his priorities in order. 'Alright,' he said. 'Now, I have to leave the house, so I want you to put a guard on Constans. No-one goes near him, apart from myself and the Lord Vortigern, and his personal servant. No exceptions.' He would have liked to add, *especially the Lord Vortimer,* but it was not something he wished to think, far less say out loud. At that moment, Gallus appeared at the front door of the house; a taller man than he had appeared when seated at the praetor's table, dark-eyed and brown-skinned like Faria and her relatives. There was something unusually intent about the way his gaze moved back and forth across the courtyard, appraising its contents. Kerin had no doubt that, if asked days later, he would have been able to provide a list of everything that was in there. Vortigern followed, then Severus, who was smiling wanly and wringing his hands as if something rather worrying might just have happened to him. Gallus and Vortigern shook hands. It was the firm, no-nonsense handshake of two men who had completed a successful business transaction. As the chariot rumbled out of the courtyard and the guards went back to more pressing duties, Vortigern left Severus hovering between the towering columns of the portico and came down the steps to meet Kerin. He had lost, overnight, the spark which had animated him throughout their absence from the city.

'Where's Rufus?' he asked. 'I know he's here some-where, Severus mentioned it earlier.'

'I don't know,' Kerin said, before he had time to think. Vortigern gave him a curious look.

'Why?' he asked. 'There was a time when you and Rufus were like a body with two heads. And he shouldn't even be here. I thought he was still at home in Cambria.' He turned away and started across the courtyard towards the gateway. Kerin followed, feeling guilty for being less than open. It was the day of the cattle market which was held every week on the wide riverbank, and the street was thronged with traders leading horses and oxen, or herding knots of unco-operative goats. The rest of the populace seemed to have decided to go along, to watch if not to buy, or to patronise one of the other stalls which always sprang up around the periphery of the mart peddling pottery, leather goods, clothing, birds both dead and alive and petrified small animals.

'I'm going to the castra, to make sure that the city garrison knows what it's supposed to be doing tomorrow,' Vortigern said. 'You're free to come with me, if you wish.'

'I might go to the market,' Kerin said, surveying the scene. 'I need a horse.'

'A horse?' Vortigern said, in disbelief. 'You can't buy a horse in this place. Look at them, for God's sake.'

'Oh, it's not for me,' Kerin said, 'it's for Lucius Arrius. He'll be no good to us unless he can ride. I want to find him a horse, a good wild one. He'll need a warhorse later on, of course, but at the moment he just needs a beast that hates mankind. What time should I come back?'

'By sunset at the latest,' Vortigern said. 'Severus has

some Roman bigwigs coming here this evening. I want to know what they talked about, and you seem to be uniquely well placed for finding out that sort of thing. If you should happen to come across my oldest son, send him back.'

He turned without waiting for a response and disappeared into the crowd. For a moment Kerin hesitated, wondering whether he should have directed him to the chapel of St Alban, but common sense prevailed. He began whistling cheerily to himself as he imagined the consequences of a shouting argument in a chapel within earshot of the praetor's residence; not the best prelude to choosing a king, however much unintentional entertainment it might provide for the halt and the lame who were queuing up to see the monks. He made his way towards the market place, where things were already in full swing. On the fringes, next to the area where animals were being traded, was a row of stalls selling kitchenware; earthenware jugs and beakers, wooden bowls and dishes, pots and cauldrons of all shapes and sizes. A woman was standing in front of the nearest stall, examining a small cherrywood bowl. As Kerin approached, she turned to speak to the stallholder and stopped short. Flora. She looked as frail as ever, but her grey woollen dress was of far better quality than the worn-out clothes Kerin remembered from the woods.

'Flora,' he said, smiling. 'What are you doing here?'

'Lord Kerin,' she said, with a little bow of the head. He had not expected her to remember his name. 'We followed Lord Eldof's company all the way here. We've made a camp just outside the city walls. My grandfather's there, with the families and the older people. But some of us younger ones have found work within the city. The lads are working down on the wharfs, and the girls are in the laundries or the kitchens. But I'm serving Lord Eldof's wife. He's taken a house just along the river, did you know? And when he realised that you might all be here for some time, he sent for his wife and daughters. It was the day after you came to our camp. The family took a carriage with fast horses, and caught up with us on the road.' She smiled and gave a little shrug, as if to suggest that Eldof might not have had much choice in the matter.

'How does she treat you?' Kerin asked.

'That depends,' Flora said. 'In a good mood, she's not unkind. In a bad one, she shouts and bawls and tries to catch me with her walking stick.'

'Fat and ugly?' Kerin asked, recalling another conversation. Flora's hand stifled a laugh.

'You've met, her, lord, obviously,' she said.

'Not at all,' Kerin said. 'That was someone else's opinion.'

Flora looked up, her smile fading. 'You're still staying at the praetor's house, I understand. You and the Lord Vortigern's company, that is.'

'Yes,' Kerin said. 'We're still there.' He remembered Eldof's camp and the village beside the Via Legionis, and this girl who had stood and watched him and Vortigern ride away, her eyes bleak, as if she believed that some part of her life was leaving with them. All he knew for sure was that she and Vortigern had vanished at the same time, neatly sidestepping Eldof's intentions. Had she offered Vortigern the same helping of casual pleasure? Would he have accepted? Kerin had no idea, but he knew that Flora's eyes were asking him questions which pride and decorum forbade her to put into words. 'We're all well,' he said. 'And we'll be there for a while yet.' His eyes moved to the cherrywood bowl. The stallholder was watching them both hopefully. 'Are you going to buy that, then?' he asked. Flora laughed.

'No, of course not,' she said. 'It's lovely, isn't it, but I'll have to serve Eldof's wife a while longer before I can buy something like that.' Kerin picked the bowl up and handed it to her, and slipped a coin to the stallholder. 'Oh no, I can't!' she exclaimed.

'You can, and you will,' Kerin said. 'Now go and give my regards to your grandfather. But not to Eldof's wife. And next time she tries to catch you with her walking stick, remember that she's fat and ugly, and you are not.'

The animal market was a ferocious place, full of men who looked ready to kill each other over the price of a cow or a good ram. Next to the horse lines were several small pens containing an assortment of goats, one of which was being closely scrutinised by Marcellus the haruspex.

'Hello, my young lord,' Marcellus said, shading his eyes from the brilliant noonday sun. 'It's Kerin Brightspear, the Lord Vortigern's companion, is it not?'

'It surely is,' Kerin said, leaning on the rail of the pen. A small white goat nibbled the sleeve of his tunic and bleated softly. Kerin looked down into the creature's amber eyes, thinking that it might have looked a little less sanguine if it had known what the future might hold for it.

'I have hardly seen you at all since the night of that feast,' Marcellus said, opening the goat's mouth to examine its teeth. 'We were discussing the relative merits of swan and venison, as I recall. Did you come to any conclusions?'

'Well,' Kerin said, 'I shan't complain if I never have to eat another swan. My cook swears by goose; he thinks it's the food of the gods.'

'Ah!' Marcellus said, with interest. 'The cook you purchased from Severus Maximus, I take it. That seems a strange thing for a young man such as yourself to do.' He squinted up at Kerin, his sharp little eyes half closed against the sunlight.

'I suffer from poor digestion,' Kerin said, deciding to repeat the same pack of lies he had told to the praetor. 'Someone told me years ago that the Saxons can work magic with fish, so I thought it would be worth risking a few denarii to find out.'

'I can vouch for the fish,' Marcellus said. 'Alberius has eaten nothing else since his – well, his accident, and it seems to have done him a power of good.'

'That's probably got more to do with the physician's skill,' Kerin said. Marcellus's thin lips formed a surprisingly cordial smile.

'And with the patient's constitution,' he conceded. 'Strong as a bull, you know. And of course he was determined not to miss the meeting tomorrow. There are men coming from the four corners of the islands for this, and they won't go home until they've got what they want. And what they want –' he prodded the goat's nose, causing it to bleat piteously – 'is not simple.'

'It looks simple enough to me,' Kerin said. 'They want a king.'

'Well, that's true,' Marcellus agreed, 'and all the omens suggest that they will get one. Finding one who is any good to them will be the trick.' He looked up as a thin lad passed, leading a prancing bay horse. 'An uncommonly good animal for this market, don't you think?'

'Yes,' Kerin said. 'A friend of mine needs a horse. Will you come with me to look at it? A second opinion is never a bad thing.'

Marcellus looked a little surprised, but his pleasure at being asked for advice by a sceptic like Kerin was palpable. 'Come on, then!' he said, and bustled off after the horse, his fine-spun robe billowing like a sail. The lad was struggling with his animal which was jumping about and snapping irritably as the halter-rope tightened round its nose.

'He's never been into the city before,' the boy said, in defence of the horse. 'I don't think he likes the crowds.'

'Neither do I, very much,' Kerin said, running his hand over the powerful neck. The horse eyed him curiously and blew through its nostrils. 'Why are you selling him?' Kerin asked.

'He threw my brother off and broke his leg,' the boy said. 'They say he'll be lame for the rest of his life. My father won't keep him now.' He grinned. 'The horse, that is, not my brother.'

'What do you think?' Kerin asked.

'It was my brother's fault,' the boy said bluntly. 'He beat the horse and made him wild. He's not a bad horse. My brother's a drunkard,' he added, for good measure.

'Strong legs, powerful shoulders,' Marcellus observed. 'It looks like a chariot horse, boy. Are you sure your brother didn't steal it from the praetor?'

'Of course I'm sure!' the boy said indignantly. 'Would I be stupid enough to sell it here if it belonged to Severus Maximus?'

'Probably not,' Marcellus conceded, squinting at the boy with his beady little bird's eyes.

'My father used to work in the praetor's stables,' the boy said, realising that an explanation was expected of him. 'He had to leave because he was losing his sight, but they let him put his mare to one of the stallions. This is the colt. He's a good horse, lord,' he said hopefully, catching Kerin's eye. Kerin spoke to the horse and rubbed its ears, thinking it was no wonder that the boy was keen to sell it, with a blind father and a crippled brother to worry about.

'Alright,' he said, 'he'll do very well. Here,' he took a denarius from his pouch and handed the money to the boy. 'Take the horse to the praetor's house. Tell the stable-lads that the horse belongs to the Lord Vortigern, and ask them to feed it and put it in a stall until I get back.'

The boy's eyes gleamed as he looked down at the coin winking in his hand. It was a fair price for the horse; perhaps a little more than he had expected in such uncertain times.

'You're not the Lord Vortigern, though, lord,' he said, with a questioning look.

'How do you know that?' Kerin asked. The boy looked at him as if his sanity might have been open to doubt.

'Everyone knows what the Lord Vortigern looks like, lord,' he said scornfully. 'He's older than you, with black hair and eyes as dark as midnight, and he can kill twenty warriors single-handed.' He smiled cheerfully. 'He's going to save us from the Picts. Everyone says so. We can't wait for this meeting that's coming up. He'll be king after that, won't he.'

Kerin looked curiously at the boy. He couldn't have been more than twelve years old. He couldn't, by any stretch of the imagination, have made that up. And besides, it had come out with the unthinking certainty of something learned by rote; perhaps it really was what people were saying, in their homes and in the market places, repeating it like the monks did their litanies, until even the children had it word for word.

'Who's everyone?' he asked.

'Everyone,' the boy said impatiently. 'My father and mother, and my brothers, and my grandfather, and all the men who come to the ale-house in our village, and the carpenter who made our ox-plough, and the weaver in the workshop next door, and all the fishermen from the river, and –'

'Alright,' Kerin said, raising his hand to stem the torrent. 'Go, now, and take the horse. Say that Kerin Brightspear sent you. And if you don't do it, I'll find out where you live and slit all your throats.'

The boy darted him a nervous smile, untied the horse and led it away through the noisy, argumentative crowd which had gathered around the goat pens.

'Well,' Marcellus said. 'It must cheer your heart, to know that your Lord Vortigern is held in such high regard by the ale-drinkers and the carpenters. Not to mention the fishermen from the river.'

'Perhaps,' Kerin said, his voice neutral. Marcellus was a Roman, and the fact that he was Severus's physician did not mean that he shared all Severus's opinions, most of which had, in any case, been formed out of necessity. 'What do you think?' he asked. Marcellus gave a world-weary smile.

'I think that I'm an old fool who should have gone back home to Ravenna years ago,' he said, and waved one slender hand about him, at the tall Roman buildings and the river where Gallus's merchant ships lay. 'Men have given their lives for this. Good men, good Romans. *Civis Romanus sum.* That was a proud claim once, you know, and still is, for some of us. No man who values it could stand by and watch it swept away by a bunch of barbarians. But there is no hope of help from Rome, whatever men like Maximian Galba might think. We must shift for ourselves.' He raised his hands in a gesture of hopelessness. 'Monks, children, what difference does it make? The power will rest with the men who support them, not with their poor wretched puppets.'

'And if you could choose?' Kerin asked. Marcellus smiled faintly.

'If I could choose, Kerin Brightspear, I should have Vortigern to beat the Picts and an able Roman administrator to preserve the fabric of the state. But I don't suppose I can have both, can I? Perhaps that pretty white goat will help me to make up my mind. First of all I must go to that stall over there, though. My wife has set her mind upon a pair of turtle doves, and there will be no peace in my household until she is satisfied. You aren't married, I take it? No, I thought not. When you are, you will learn that the barbarians are a lesser consideration; the worst terrors a man can encounter are the ones which face him across the breakfast table.'

He inclined his head politely and shuffled off towards the purveyors of hens, ducks, geese and other assorted fowls.

Only a short time later, Kerin paused outside the house around the corner from the chapel of St Alban; the one with the tall iron gates, and the bay laurel growing in the middle of the courtyard. In the crook of his arm the small white goat struggled, bleating plaintively, and turned accusing amber eyes upon him.

'Be quiet,' Kerin said tersely. 'You're luckier than you think.' As he peered between the bars of the gate, a young man crossed the paved courtyard; a servant, probably, but a well-dressed one, in a short white tunic and leather sandals. He noticed Kerin and came across to the gate. 'I have something for Lucius,' Kerin said. 'I know he's on duty, but perhaps you could take care of it until he comes home.'

The servant gave Kerin and the goat an appraising look. 'Who should I say called?' he asked.

'Kerin Brightspear,' Kerin said. 'I'm a friend; I'm staying in the praetor's house with the rest of my company. Please can you tell him that I've found a horse for him? And a goat. The horse is in Severus Maximus's stables, but I'll leave the goat with you, if I may.'

The servant eyed him dubiously and unlatched the gate. 'Give it to me, then, lord. Would you care for some refreshment? Perhaps Master Lucius's sister will know something about the goat.'

'No, no,' Kerin said swiftly. 'It's a surprise. Please, put the animal somewhere safe and say nothing until Lucius comes back. And thank you for the offer of refreshment, but I must return to the praetor's house. There's an important meeting this evening.'

'Ah, yes,' the servant said. 'It's something to do with this gathering tomorrow, isn't it? Everyone's talking about it. I'm Petrus, by the way. I've been with Marcus Arrius all my life.'

'Well, thank you, Petrus,' Kerin said, giving the lad a coin. 'Perhaps I'll call and have that refreshment another day.'

He left Petrus cradling the goat and walked back to the praetor's house through crowds of people coming home from the market. Plicius accosted him as he approached the portico.

'The horse,' he barked. 'What's going on with the horse?'

'It's my horse,' Kerin said, without apology. He detested the way Plicius looked at him; as if he were a rather lowly member of a group who were all barbarians in any case. 'What's it to you, anyway?' he asked. 'The stables aren't your responsibility.'

'Well, you're right,' Plicius said grudgingly. 'I like to keep my eye on things, that's all.'

'In that case,' Kerin said, 'you'll be able to tell me if there's a meeting going on here at the moment.'

Plicius eyed him with a degree of suspicion. 'Why do you wish to know?' he asked.

'Because it's my business to know,' Kerin said. 'And please, don't forget that I'm in a position to make trouble for you if you don't tell me.'

Plicius gave an owl-like blink of astonishment. As head of the praetorian guard he was probably not accustomed to hearing that kind of warning, particularly from someone he considered only one or two levels above the gutter. The threat seemed to carry some weight, however, because he cleared his throat and nodded towards the house. 'The praetor is meeting some of the leaders of ordines, and some of the big military men,' he said reluctantly. 'They're preparing the council chamber in there now.'

'Lord,' Kerin said, enjoying himself. As a product of Vortigern's household, he was used to an iron hand, but not to petty officiousness.

'Lord,' Plicius said venomously. Kerin grinned and trotted up the steps. If there was a way to observe the goings-on without being observed oneself, there was no better man to provide the information than Cheldric.

11

The sound of the cook's aggrieved bellow came to greet him as he hurried down the dark passage. The Saxon was standing in the middle of the kitchen, surrounded by steaming pots and racks of small roasted game-birds. Sweat was streaming down his scarlet face and dripping from the rat's tails of his lank fair hair. He was brandishing a meat-cleaver at a cowering kitchen slave, who had crawled under a table to escape from his wrath.

'Ah!' he exclaimed, spotting Kerin through the clouds of steam. 'Here is the lying bastard from Cambria!'

'Not so,' Kerin said, helping himself to a partridge. 'A bastard, yes; but a liar, never.'

'You say you take me away from Londinium,' Cheldric grumbled. 'And I am here, still here. Today they have partridges and fig-peckers.' He looked at the small golden carcasses with disdain.

'They're very good,' Kerin said, through a mouthful of flesh. Cheldric snorted.

'Babies' food,' he said scornfully. 'Small, no meat. And also they eat these. Look, you try.' He held out something which looked like a small leather-bound package. On closer inspection Kerin discovered that it was a vine leaf, skilfully wrapped around a lump of forcemeat. He tasted it cautiously.

'It's better than it looks,' he said, taking another mouthful. 'The meat's as soft as butter.'

Cheldric smiled beneficently. 'Is pigs' balls,' he said. Kerin's hand halted halfway to his mouth. 'Eat!' Cheldric roared, thumping the table. 'Saxons eat. No fruit, no leaves, meat only. Is man's food. You eat, then you fight and make love.'

'At the same time?' Kerin asked, nibbling the morsel with reduced enthusiasm. Cheldric chuckled heartily.

'Sometimes is better like that,' he said. He looked down at the kitchen slave, who had timorously poked his head out from under the table. 'Come out, *hundes tyrdel*,' he growled, hauling the lad out by the sleeve of his grubby tunic. 'You drop birds again, I cut your hands off, yes?'

The slave gave an insane, terrified smile and fled from the kitchen.

'I need to know something,' Kerin said once he and Cheldric were alone. 'Do you take the food in through the door where the big men go in, or is there another entrance?'

'Is back door,' Cheldric said. 'For servants only.'

'Good,' Kerin said. 'And if you go in through this door, is there anywhere you can hide so that the people in the room can't see you?'

Cheldric's little eyes narrowed. 'Why you ask?' he said. Kerin leaned forward.

'Because I don't trust the Roman bastards,' he said. 'I want to hear what they're talking about.'

'Ah!' Cheldric said approvingly. 'There is – I don't know what you say,' he said, struggling to put words to an idea. 'Two babies and a wolf.'

'In the council chamber?' Kerin said, with mild surprise. The situation was resolved by the arrival of the white-clad servants who were to serve the food.

'Julius!' Cheldric exclaimed. 'You tell this man what is in the room where you take the food.'

The servant shrugged. 'A table? Some chairs? Couches, where the praetor and his friends recline?'

'No, *unwita*,' Cheldric said irritably. 'The wolf.'

'Oh!' Julius said. 'The statue, of course. A big statue on a plinth. It's of Romulus and Remus, the founders of Rome, being suckled by the she-wolf who found them abandoned by the Tiber.'

'How big is it?' Kerin asked. Julius shrugged.

'The plinth is about as tall as your shoulder, lord, and the statue about as much again. Why do you need to know, lord?'

'Because when you serve the food I am going to come in behind you and hide behind the statue,' Kerin said. 'And if you or any of the others breathe a word, then I shall tell Cheldric to chop you up into small pieces and put you in the stew he makes for the guards. Do you understand?'

'Yes, lord,' the servant mouthed, although no sound came out.

* * *

When the culinary procession reached the council chamber, Lupinus and his minions were already in attendance, pouring goblets of wine for Severus and a group of five or six companions. Kerin entered behind the slaves, crouching low, and secreted himself behind the plinth. Rising cautiously to his full height, he discovered that the top of the plinth was on a level with his chin. The she-wolf, who was standing on all four legs while the infants suckled beneath her, was flanked by a collection of spurious boulders and logs. Kerin judged that, if he kept perfectly still and peered between this detritus, he stood a good chance of both seeing and hearing everything that took place without being observed. Julius and his companions arranged the feast on the big table to a chorus of appreciative grunts and murmured comments, then followed Lupinus out of the main entrance.

'An excellent meal, Severus,' said the lordly Maximian, who was seated next to the praetor. Kerin observed the other occupants of the table. There was another much younger dignitary, similarly dressed in the standard imperial uniform of snow-white toga and opulent cloak. There was Gallus the merchant, who was probably far too wealthy to omit, and three men of military appearance whom Kerin did not recognise, two around thirty years of age, and one much older. The older man bore himself with unforced dignity, and when he spoke later there was a gentleness in his voice which surprised Kerin, in one who was evidently a soldier of the highest rank. He was handsome in a sober way, with the olive skin of the true Roman, and thick iron-grey hair cut short in a military crop.

'It pains me to say so, gentlemen,' Severus sighed, 'but I fear we must return to our discussion, much as I should like to abandon myself to the food and the wine.'

'You keep too good a table, Severus,' said one of the

diners; a praetor of somewhere-or-other, by the look of him, although he was younger than might have been expected. Severus bowed his head.

'We do our best, Flavius,' he said modestly. 'It is not Rome, but I hope it is as good as anything Eburacum has to offer.'

Kerin recognised the Latin name, and knew that Severus was referring to a city in the North; one which he would undoubtedly see for himself, if they were ever to get anywhere near the Picts.

'Far better, in these times,' Flavius said. 'Wouldn't you say so, Flaccus?'

'Without a doubt,' replied one of the younger soldiers. He smiled wryly at Severus Maximus. 'Unfortunately most of our time, not to mention our blood and money, is spent on keeping the savages at bay.'

'Severus, we must agree something tomorrow,' Flavius said earnestly. 'Our men have done their best, but half of them are dead, and the rest are exhausted. Even the Picts will be driven indoors when winter comes, but if we're not ready for them next spring, it's not only the North that will burn.'

The older soldier laid a hand on Flavius's arm. 'You've struggled long enough,' he said. 'Severus, if I have to take two thirds of all the city garrisons and march them to the North, this can't continue.'

'I know,' Severus said, his face grey with anxiety. 'But we can't leave the cities undefended either. For love of the gods, you must be able to see that.'

'Of course,' the older man conceded. 'But if we do nothing, we may lose the cities anyway. Sometimes it's necessary to take the fight to the enemy.' He had spoken firmly, but with a note of reluctance. He probably understood the praetor's dilemma only too well.

'I know you're right,' Severus said wearily. 'But you see things with a soldier's eyes. I must try to speak for the merchants and the lawyers and the priests and the ordinary people, as well as for your city garrison.'

Kerin realised then that the man Severus was addressing must be Publius Luca, the former commander of the Second Augustan legion and saviour of Lucius's youth.

'We should consider the Lord Vortigern,' the commander said briskly. It sounded like a deliberate attempt to ruffle some feathers and get the stagnant discussion moving.

'The man's a lunatic,' Maximian snapped. 'A blood-letting savage.'

'Have you seen his warriors, though?' the second of the younger soldiers said, with some uneasiness. 'And have you heard the way people are gossiping in the city?'

Maximian hissed with impatience. 'Look, Albinus,' he said, 'I wish everyone would stop talking about this man as if he possessed divine powers. Vortigern's a mad Celt, no more and no less.' He sat up straight and folded his arms. Publius Luca coughed politely.

'With respect,' he said, 'I'd advise you not to discount him. He's had the West eating out of his hand for years, and it didn't happen by accident. He also leads the finest company of mounted warriors in these islands, and can outride or outfight any one of them.'

'That's a sideshow, commander,' Maximian said, smiling tolerantly. 'We're talking about the council chamber, not the battlefield.'

Severus clenched his fists in exasperation. 'Look,' he said, 'you're missing the point. Vortigern hasn't come here to fight.'

Maximian looked up. 'He's brought a few warriors, though,' he said.

'Of course he's brought warriors,' Severus said impatiently. 'Only a fool would travel without them in these times. But it's only a distraction. Everyone knows quite well what Vortigern's fighting men can do, and if the delegates at the curia think they're waiting round the corner, then they'll give Vortigern a hearing.'

'Go on,' Maximian said. The easy smoothness had gone from his face. He's listening now, Kerin thought.

'As I told you, he hasn't come here to fight,' Severus said. 'This man has been stalking the ordines for the last ten years, and I've seen the way he does it. Believe me, he can reduce a room full of strong men to gibbering wrecks without so much as lifting a sword.'

'Severus, the man's a barbarian,' Maximian said, teeth clenched. 'And as for what he's doing dragging that monk here, I have no idea. We should return the young man to my brother Paulinus and let him carry on with his devotions, as his father intended. It's the younger son, Ambrosius, that Constantine saw as his successor. Too young to rule yet, for sure, but brought up in the best Roman traditions by his own kinsmen in Gallia. Surely you can see that the only way for these islands to prosper is to return to Imperial rule, as soon as Rome has dealt with the barbarians at her own gates. We must bring young Ambrosius to Londinium, and set up a council of able administrators to direct the affairs of state until he's old enough to take power on his own account. What clearer message could we send to the Emperor? Troops would be sent as soon as they could be spared. This country would be Britannia Prima again, a proud province of the Empire, instead of the festering backwater it will soon become.'

Publius Luca leaned forward, and when he replied Kerin recognised for the first time a vein of iron running beneath his reasonableness and charity. 'Maximian Galba, as far as Britain is concerned, the Empire is dead,' he said bluntly. 'How many times must the consuls write to explain their position? They didn't choose to abandon these islands, after fighting so hard to get them and keep them. But there are no spare troops. They have told us to look to our own defences. And before we worry about able administrators and the affairs of state, we must deal with the threat of invasion. We don't have a tenth of the good, Roman-trained soldiers we'd need to beat the Picts. The country's crawling with warbands and half-baked armies, all answering to different mad leaders, and would any of them listen to you or me? No. Most of them would probably just as soon cut each other's throats as fight the Picts. But these men are all we have. And if there is anyone who can lead them – all of them, at the same time – even if you think he's a barbarian, even if he spits on Rome and the Empire, then you'd be worse than a fool to ignore him.'

Maximian sat quite still. The colour drained from him, leaving a face as white as that of the statue in Severus's library.

'I'm sorry, Severus,' Publius Luca said, 'but I believe I'm right. And I suspect that you agree with me; you've given Vortigern and his friends the run of your house, and relations between you seem to be civil enough.'

'I do agree with you,' Severus said bleakly. 'And yes, relations between us are civil. I have gone out of my way to make them so. If you were drowning, and a man threw you a rope, would you turn your back on him? I must think of my city and its people. We cannot always do as we would wish.'

Publius Luca did not reply immediately. The silence was so intense, Kerin imagined that every one of the men at the table must have been able to hear him breathing in his hiding place behind the she-wolf and her odd pups.

'Then why are you so unhappy about it?' Publius Luca asked. 'Do you think he'll betray us?'

Severus stared vacantly down at the table. 'No,' he said. 'It's not that. Please, don't ask me to explain. It's got nothing to do with the monk; none of that means anything to me, except insofar as the bishops might stir up trouble. It's something else.'

Gallus the merchant had said nothing up to this point; he had simply sat with a passive expression on his dark face and his large hands folded on the table in front of him. Now he clenched one of these hands into a formidable fist, and brought it down so hard that the untouched partridges, fig-peckers and stuffed vine leaves leapt off their platters. When he spoke, his voice was as powerful and resonant as his appearance suggested.

'Severus, you know that Pictish galleys have been sighted east of Camulodunum,' he said. 'If they've got that far, they can get to Londinium. That puts my ships at risk, and every other merchant's ships too. Do you expect us to sit here and do nothing while you dither? Make your mind up, man, or it'll be made up for you.' He folded his arms. Flavius caught Severus's eye, smiled politely and helped himself to a partridge.

'There is, I suppose, no chance at all of our arranging the return of Ambrosius, as Maximian has suggested?' he enquired.

'The boy?' Gallus scoffed. 'To what purpose?'

'Well, to the purpose of preventing as many people as possible from killing each other, I think,' Flavius said tentatively. 'These are excellent, Severus; your cook must be a man of great skill.'

Severus smiled half-heartedly, probably not eager to discuss the sale of his Saxon cook. 'I have nothing against Ambrosius,' he said. 'But that's for the future, surely. The ones who support him for their own ends will wield the power, and the ones who don't will feed him to the crows at the first opportunity. I know perfectly well that the same could be said of the monk; but at least he's a man in years, if not quite the sort of man any of us might have had in mind.'

'Severus, are you really telling us that this poor fool can lead the country against the Picts?' Flavius said, his arched eyebrows as well as his voice conveying the ridiculousness of the idea.

'What the praetor means,' Publius Luca said patiently, 'is that if you accept the monk, you will get Vortigern too. One to represent the old tradition, the other to forge an army. The assembly must decide, but do remember what the alternatives are. As I have said, for Rome, Britain no longer exists. Don't waste your breath on another appeal to the consuls. There'll be no help. There are no spare legions any more.'

His grave eyes held Flavius's, and the praetor of Eburacum looked away, shaking his head. Perhaps the desperation of the situation had only now come home to him. Kerin felt sorry for Flavius, who looked frightened and bewildered, as if he felt that the familiar world might be about to collapse beneath him.

'What are you saying, then?' the young praetor asked. 'That we should yield to the man who wields the biggest stick? As Severus Maximus said, the Lord Vortigern is lucky enough to have a fine body of fighting men, so naturally the delegates are going to listen to him. But does that mean that we should, too?'

'Luck has nothing to do with it,' Publius Luca said. 'That's the whole point. If you killed every man in his warband and gave him a bunch of beggars, he'd have something almost as good in six months' time. And they'd all have his nerve and confidence and single-mindedness, and every one of them would die for him.'

Flavius looked up with a nervous smile. 'How can that be possible?' he asked.

'Flavius Secundus,' Publius Luca said gravely, 'if I knew that, I'd be Caesar, not the commander of the city garrison.'

Maximian choked back an angry growl. Mouth clamped, he rose stiffly to his feet and swept out of the room. Severus stared up at the vaulted ceiling and muttered imprecations to the gods. He offered wine, and the remaining six men drank and ate in silence. The light from the window began to fade, and Lupinus came in to light the torches on the walls. Kerin crept from his hiding place and slipped silently out of the servants' entrance. The cold air of the courtyard was refreshing and welcome. He thought of the reserved, courteous men whose conversation he had listened to and looked out across the black city where lamps were being lit in homes and ale-houses, little pools of brightness amidst a huge, seething darkness where people were slaving, drinking, killing each other and making love.

'Kerin Brightspear!' A voice accosted him, sharp and hard. Maximian Galba was standing beside the fountain, at the foot of the statue of Minerva. Probably he had been there, cooling his head, since his exit from the council chamber. 'You'll get your come-uppance at that meeting tomorrow,' he said. 'You and your bunch of upstarts.'

Kerin smiled politely. 'I can't wait,' he said. Maximian's cold eyes gleamed.

'You really don't understand, do you,' he said.

'What does that mean?' Kerin asked, affronted. 'What don't I understand?'

'What the kingdom stands to lose,' Maximian burst out. 'Yes, Rome is struggling now, but it won't always be so. Rome will rise again, and we can either rise with her or we can sink back into the bog she dragged us out of. So you can give a message to that cut-throat you serve. Tell him to watch his step. He thinks he can trifle with me, but if he harms a hair on that monk's head, he's a dead man.'

'The same monk that you can't wait to get rid of?' Kerin asked.

'I want to replace him, not get rid of him!' Maximian said. 'I wish him no harm at all. I want him sent back to his monastery where he belongs. And I want the power to pass to men of good sense, not to some crackbrain from the West who's only serving his own ends.'

He turned, pulling his cloak close against the cool night air, and marched towards the gates. Two members of the praetorian guard swung them wide to let him pass. Kerin listened to his sandaled footsteps slapping away down the street until the sound merged into the general noise of the city; Londinium Augusta, the creature of Imperial Rome, filled with ale-drinkers, carpenters, weavers and fishermen from the river, who outnumbered its acolytes a thousand to one.

12

The hours of darkness were few. Under a sky of pale, transparent blue the city stirred and came to life. Gallus's fleet put out from the wharf laden with bales of wool, great drums of salt fish and fine white cowhides, and began its stately progress down the river with clouds of gulls circling in its wake. A thin line of women stood on the wharf and watched the galleys leaving. Some of the younger ones wept and all of them waved to the men who could be seen on the decks of the receding ships, a few of whom would never return. Further up river, the gangs of labourers who were employed by Severus and his council to clean and care for the municipal buildings were putting the finishing touches to the curia.

They had swept and polished the great central floor with its complex mosaic portraits of Jupiter and Juno. The tiers of stone seating which surrounded the hall on three sides had been washed clean of the dust which had drifted in during the last month's dry weather. The massive oak table on the dais occupied by the presiding dignitaries had been polished with beeswax until its smooth surface shone like a mirror, and the twin bay trees which grew in urns on either side of the entrance had been clipped until not an offending leaf disturbed their perfect, symmetrical outline. Severus had made it clear that no effort was to be spared, and the nervous urgency which emanated from him as he spoke about the forthcoming meeting had infected his workmen. Everyone knew what was going on, of course. It had been the talk of the city for weeks. There would be no place inside the curia for the men who had prepared the building with such care, but they would wait at the gates until they found out what had happened inside, and they would not be alone.

In Severus's house, Kerin watched with silent apprehension as the monk made fidgety adjustments to the pin which fastened the neck of his workmanlike cloak. Constans was not happy, but Vortigern had insisted upon this plain brown cloak worn over the simplest of white robes. It was far removed from the regal purple which the monk had taken to wearing, and in fact less impressive than the well-made grey tunic and breeches, topped with a light cape of fine black wool, which Kerin had chosen for the occasion.

'These are a pauper's clothes,' sniffed Constans, who seemed to have forgotten how recently he had acquired any sort of clothes, other than a rough habit and a poor man's sandals.

'There's no point in complaining,' Kerin snapped, rising to his feet and pacing the length of the chamber. Tension had made him impatient. Constans pouted at his reflection.

'How can people choose a king who looks like a beggar?' he said tartly.

Outside the courtyard walls the noise was intensifying. Kerin looked out of the window, from which it was possible to see above the walls to the street outside. Garagon of Kent was passing the gates, accompanied by mounted warriors, strutting musicians and two over-dressed companions; his corpulent uncle Edlym and the lean, beak-nosed Brennius. Garagon was smiling and waving regally. Crowds of ordinary citizens milled along beside the pompous procession, all heading in the same direction and looking happy to have been given an excuse to forget the ordinary details of their lives for a day, whatever the outcome might be. Close behind came the troop of neat, green-uniformed foot-soldiers who had turned up in Severus's courtyard the day before. They preceded their master Gallus, joined in his gilded chariot by a younger man of similar build and colouring; his son, probably. The two were deep in conversation, oblivious to the melee surrounding them.

'What's happening?' Constans asked, peering over Kerin's shoulder.

'The entire city is on its way to the curia,' Kerin said. 'Does that please you?'

'It terrifies me,' Constans said, with a tremor in his voice. Kerin turned.

'You could have stayed where you were, you know,' he said. 'Vortigern would never have dragged you out of the monastery.'

'I know,' Constans said, lowering his eyes. 'And I do want to be king. But I shall be very happy when today is over and done with, whatever it brings.'

'Yes,' Kerin said. 'You're probably not alone in that.'

He looked back at the street as a military trumpeter blasted out a fanfare. A detachment of the city garrison was marching by in perfect, well-drilled step. Publius

Luca rode at its head, magnificent in his ceremonial uniform, with the light breeze swelling the folds of his vermilion cloak and the sun winking on a polished breast-plate and helmet. Kerin had never expected to respect a Roman commander, but Publius Luca had surprised him.

'When shall we leave?' Constans asked nervously.

'When Lud comes for us,' Kerin said. 'I've told you this before. Vortigern doesn't want to arrive at the curia until everyone else is inside. And please, stop looking at yourself as if you were wearing something the dogs had dragged in. There'll be time enough for purple robes if you become king.'

'If?' Constans said apprehensively. 'Do you think I might not?'

Kerin closed his eyes and turned away. He doubted whether Constans remotely understood the enormity of what Vortigern was about to attempt, or how unprecedented it was, or how dangerous. 'There's always doubt until something is settled,' he said. Outside, the uniformed troops moved out of sight and were followed by the livelier-looking band belonging to Gorlois of Kernow. Gorlois himself was in the lead, riding a stocky dun warhorse with a damaged left ear and conspicuous battle-scars on her shoulders. He and his warriors looked as if they might already have shared one or two pitchers of ale, but their joviality did not diminish the impression that this was a body of men who knew how to fight. Their eyes were alert, their weapons polished and well cared for, and their rough-coated horses were hard and fit. All the men watched Gorlois and Gorlois watched everything that was going on within a spear's throw of his warband, like a shepherd keeping a killer's eye open for wolves.

'Lords!' a hoarse and rather high-pitched voice croaked outside the door. The sound was accompanied by an insistent hammering of fists on wood. 'Lords, are you in there?'

'Hefydd!' Kerin exclaimed. He would have known that voice anywhere. It belonged to Hefin's elder brother, who lived with his many relations and a bunch of hot-headed warriors at Carneddlas, a hilltop settlement near Henfelin. In his younger days Hefydd and his 'boys', as he liked to call them, had caused endless trouble for Vortigern. They had raided, pilfered, rustled cattle and picked quarrels for no particular reason until Vortigern lost patience and burned the village to the ground. Hefydd himself was said to have been stripped naked and stuffed into the large family cauldron, but he had taken his beating with equanimity; there had been no further trouble, and Hefydd himself had mellowed into one of Vortigern's staunchest allies. Kerin opened the door to admit him. The older man shambled in, beaming, and gripped him by the shoulders. He looked as if he had just come in off the road. His face was flushed, his cloak was awry and the light morning wind had blown his straggling grey hair into a wild halo. He stood in the middle of the room, panting and chuckling to himself, and brushing road-dust from his ample tunic and breeches. There was a dagger in his riding boot and a sword on his belt, and he was expert with both, although the years had grizzled his beard and expanded his belly. Constans looked at him in consternation.

'Kerin, I had to come, boy,' Hefydd said breathlessly. 'I didn't think we'd be in time, but hell, here we are.'

'It's good to see you, Hefydd,' Kerin said, smiling at the sight of a familiar face, and at Constans's discomfiture. 'We need men like you today. Have many come with you?'

'Hundreds,' Hefydd said gleefully. 'From every corner of Cambria.' He winked and pressed Kerin's arm. 'We may have our little differences, but we're all Vortigern's men when it comes down to it.'

'Even Gwyndaf of Craig Goch?' Kerin said doubtfully, thinking of another old score.

'Gwyndaf?' Hefydd frowned and cleared his throat. 'Hmph. Gwyndaf. Well, perhaps not him, no. But everyone else is here. Go and have a look in the curia, it's nearly splitting at the seams.' He seemed to notice Constans for the first time and raised a suspicious eyebrow. 'Well. Who are you, then?'

'Hefydd, this is Constantine's son, Constans,' Kerin said.

'The monk!' Hefydd said. 'Rufus was telling the truth, then.' He extended his large hand and Constans took it hesitantly, wincing as Hefydd's horny fingers closed around his slender white ones. Hefydd looked at him with some surprise. 'Well,' he said sagely, 'I dare say Vortigern knows what he's doing.'

Constans avoided his eyes. 'You must forgive me,' he said. 'Until the last few months I knew nothing but the cloister, and all this is difficult for me, although Kerin has been very patient with my shortcomings. It's different when the Lord Vortigern is with me, of course.'

Hefydd snorted with laughter. 'Yes, I'll bet it is,' he said. Constans's brow creased with anguish.

'What do you mean by that?' he asked.

'Nothing, my pigeon,' Hefydd said, gently patting the monk's pale cheek. 'Say your prayers, and leave the rest to us. My God, I thought we'd seen the last of those bastards.' His eyes had moved towards the street, where a procession which would have done credit to an imperial triumph was making its stately way past Severus's gates. Chariots rolled by in quick succession, flanked by uniformed outriders and bearing an assortment of dignitaries in splendid ceremonial cloaks.

'Not here,' Kerin said. 'Londinium's almost as Roman as ever. Not true Roman, of course; most of those men down there have British blood. Not all of them would thank you for reminding them, though.'

Hefydd harrumphed. 'Perhaps it'll take the Picts to remind them,' he said, as the procession passed out of sight. 'Guard your head and this fool's. I'm taking my boys to the curia.'

Kerin gripped his shoulder as he turned to go. Below them in the courtyard Severus's retainers had brought up his chariot, and the praetorian guard was standing by. Footsteps echoed in the passage. Lud appeared in the open doorway and nodded to Kerin. Without speaking, Kerin took the monk's arm and they followed Lud out into the echoing darkness, down through the serpentine corridors of the great house, across the cool, tranquil atrium and out at last into the courtyard, where Macsen and Custennin fell in beside them. The sunlight burned and the buildings quivered. The stable boys had brought out the horses. Severus's chariot swept by, raising a pall of fine, blinding dust. Kerin just had time to glimpse the silent, grey-faced figure of the praetor before he disappeared from sight. There was a sudden unholy silence. The streets outside were empty. The dust thinned and settled. Alone in the centre of the courtyard, Vortigern sat his black mare. Kerin left Constans to Lud and his sons, and walked forward until he was standing at the mare's shoulder.

'Lord,' he said, looking up. Vortigern inclined his head, but did not speak. Kerin noticed that he was unarmed. He could not remember ever seeing him so in public. The black tunic, breeches and cloak were well worn, and he had discarded even the simple gold armlet and shoulder-pin which he usually wore. The clipeum remained, shining twice as brightly as usual, it appeared; or perhaps it was the brilliance of the sunlight that made it seem so. He was calm and pale, in the way that he always was before a battle. From a distance he could have been anyone. Only the mesmeric eyes seemed rightly to belong to a man on whose head the Romans had once placed a price above rubies.

'Come on,' he said, drawing in his rein. 'Let's settle this thing.'

The noise from the curia came to meet them. It was not immediately obvious what it was, or where it was coming from. They were moving up the deserted street; Vortigern and Kerin riding abreast, Constans on a white pony flanked by Macsen and Custennin, Lud guarding the monk's back. It came at them like the sullen roar of an advancing flood tide, punctuated by eerie, high-pitched notes which seemed to have no connection to its swelling ground bass. Kerin glanced apprehensively at Vortigern. From the corner of his eye he saw Macsen and Custennin exchange similar looks. They rounded the corner into the huge paved square which fronted the imperial government building, and the tide burst upon them. The square was packed to the walls, as if the whole population of the city had been funnelled into this space and was making as much noise as possible; a shrieking pandemonium of wild, brawling humanity abetted by dogs, bawling donkeys, bands of competing musicians and, somewhere in the middle distance, the straining blasts of the praetorian trumpeters. The troopers of the city garrison were manfully maintaining an open path to the door of the curia, arms linked and shields to the fore as they held back the seething mass behind them.

'Gods,' Lud murmured. 'This is worse than the Circus in Isca. How long before we see the lions and the gladiators?'

'Make way!' bellowed a guardsman, his deference unfortunately not matched by his common sense. 'Make way for the Lord Vortigern!'

A hysterical roar arose from the crowd. It surged forward from both sides. The struggling military barrier stretched and wavered, but held together. Half of the square seemed to be chanting Vortigern's name. Hats were thrown in the air, flowers and bay laurel branches showered onto the paving stones ahead. Constans was shaking like a poplar leaf. Vortigern looked over his shoulder at him.

'Put your hood up,' he said. 'And keep your head down. Now, ride.'

He led the way forward into the delirious crowd. The remaining path was so narrow that it could only be traversed in single file. Amidst the tide of heads, hats and waving hands, Kerin glimpsed Malan and Flora. His right hand clenched on the hilt of his sword. He wished fervently that Vortigern had a weapon, body armour, anything; the crowd could not possibly be on his side to the last man, and any of the hands which reached out to touch them as they passed could have held an assassin's dagger. By the time they reached the railed courtyard in front of the curia his hands were slippery with sweat. The tall iron gates swung shut as they passed through, and the crowd poured up against them. Kerin jumped to the ground and helped Constans down from his pony. The praetorian guardsmen were standing in a neat row on the steps which led up to the entrance. Lucius broke ranks, ignoring an angry bark from Plicius, and hurried towards them.

'Shall I take the horses, lord?' he asked.

'Yes,' Kerin said. 'And have them ready, in case we need them.' Looking around he saw Rufus and Hefin at the corner of the building on their tall warhorses. They had brought a useful number of warriors with them. Kerin and Lud followed Vortigern up the steps. Macsen and Custennin followed, supporting something which looked as inert as a sack of grain. The main entrance led into an antechamber with an inner door, which was standing open. It was guarded by Publius Luca himself, and two other formidable-looking soldiers of advanced rank. The commander nodded respectfully.

'I'd be careful if I were you, sir,' he said calmly. 'It's bedlam in there.'

Vortigern raised an eyebrow and walked past him. Kerin followed, still gripping his sword. They halted on the threshold of the curia. The place was in uproar. The tiered seats which swept from floor to ceiling were packed to bursting point, and scores of ordinary warriors and lesser officials had spilled over onto the central floor, where some sat cross-legged whilst others wandered impatiently back and forth waiting for the proceedings to begin. Quarrels broke out, flared to the very edge of bloodshed and subsided again as one or other of the leading men intervened.

Kerin glanced quickly back and forth, trying to get his bearings in case a hasty escape proved necessary. They had entered by the main door but there was another at the far end of the building, high enough to admit a mounted warrior, if it came to it. This too was guarded by members of the city garrison. Inside and to his right, a flight of stone steps led up to a dais half the height of the room where Severus was sitting at a table with two elderly officials and Eldadus the Bishop of Glevum, surveying the contents of the room with dismay. In the centre of the mosaic floor was a small raised platform, about the height of a man's knee. On it were a gilded chair and a wooden stand, the sort used by men addressing an ordo, if they wished to set out a scroll and read from it. Kerin doubted whether anyone would have much use for it today.

The crowd fell naturally into a number of more or less well-defined groups. Immediately to the left sat the chieftains of Cambria with their sons, wise men, poets, priests and strong-arms; a seething hotbed of flashing eyes, sudden laughter and impassioned argument. Kerin knew most of them by name, and almost all of them by sight. There were men who had fought beside

Vortigern, men whom Vortigern had fought and beaten, men who loved him more than they loved their wives and men who ordinarily hated the ground he stood on, but would fight to the death for him rather than support anyone from the other side of the river. Next to them were the Kernow men, surrounding big, bearded Gorlois. He was talking as much as ever, and appeared to have struck up a cheerful entente with Hefydd and his boys. Some of the Kernow men seemed intent on nettling the warriors and elders attached to Eldof of Glevum, who were sitting to their left. The men of Glevum were resisting the bait, muttering amongst themselves whilst their leader looked out over the curia with a cheerless expression, making occasional comments to the sober Varro and to Bertil Redknife, who was sitting alongside him with his stocky, sharp-eyed chief warrior. A blaze of gaudy colours and winking gold decorated the seats to their left, denoting the presence of the contingent from Kent. Garagon was lording it in the midst of his adoring warriors, as usual; Edlym was holding forth with his customary self-righteous assurance, and Brennius was emitting a shrieking laugh which, to Kerin's astonishment, could be heard above the general uproar. Next came an odd assortment of men whose only common characteristic appeared to be conspicuous wealth. Gallus the merchant was there with his dark-haired son, sharing a bench with several other solid-looking citizens in costly clothes. There were men who might have been retired soldiers, and others who had a look of the prominent landowners Vortigern was often obliged to rub shoulders with. Next to them, in orderly rows, sat the old Roman and

Roman-British administrators; men like Maximian Galba and Flavius Secundus with their colleagues, and a scattering of priestly characters including the haruspex Marcellus, talking earnestly amongst themselves and keeping a wary eye on the rowdy gathering across the hall, as if they were nervous that it might overflow and drown them. Kerin noticed that Maximian had a sad-eyed little man with him; Tegid from the North, he supposed. He had also brought a pair of surly-looking guards, in bright red tabards bearing the image of a golden falcon with outstretched talons. The Roman contingent was soon joined by a group of monks, including the solemn Abbot Giraldus of St Alban's chapel and several black-robed churchmen, possibly minor bishops from the outlying cities. They all greeted each other with surprising cordiality, given their religious disparities. Severus came down from his dais in a flurry of white robes.

'You had better do something before they start killing each other,' Vortigern said. Severus ran a frantic hand through his thinning hair.

'How?' he said. 'What can I do, for love of the gods?'

'That's for you to choose,' Vortigern said. 'Do it, or I will.'

Severus flinched and whispered something to Publius Luca, who accompanied him back up the stairs to the dais, waving energetically to two of the praetorian trumpeters. The musicians raced up the stairs, raised their instruments and blew an arresting fanfare. The uproar continued unabated. Severus gestured to his trumpeters, who blew again, at ear-splitting volume and with such effort that their faces turned purple. Publius

Luca drew his sword and hammered on the table with its brazen hilt. This time, at least half of the gathering took notice. A shout ran round the curia, sleeves were jerked and mouths clamped, and the racket subsided to a querulous muttering. Severus stood up and cleared his throat.

'Gentlemen, *cives Romani*, lords of the Britons!' he shouted, as loudly as his thin voice could manage. 'Constantine is dead, and we his people must choose his successor. Our enemies threaten us by land and sea. They know that our king is dead. They know that a country without a leader is ripe for the taking. I have called you together today to resolve this situation.'

'Not before time, you Roman weasel,' came a sneering shout from the left. There was an eruption of laughter and rowdy cheering, punctuated by the heavy stamping of boots on stone. Publius Luca pounded vainly on the table. Eldof of Glevum sprang to his feet, but was hauled back down by Varro. The noise diminished again.

'Those of us who hoped for Imperial assistance have seen our hopes crushed,' Severus said shakily. 'Rome has told us to look to our own defences. This does not mean that we should abandon all she has taught us, but it does mean that we cannot look to her for a leader, or an army. A king need not be a warrior, any more than an emperor needs to be a military man, but he must command the loyalty of all his people; warriors, governors and ordinary citizens alike. Please remember these things when you make your choice.'

Eldof, unable to contain himself any longer, shook off Varro's restraining hand and rose to a resounding cheer from his entourage. 'Constantine has a son,' he bellowed. 'Ambrosius, a fine young man raised in the best Roman traditions. He is the natural choice to succeed his father.'

'Ambrosius?' Hefydd hooted. 'You'll have to tear him from his mother's teat first.'

'Be quiet, you old fool,' Garagon of Kent bawled, his eyes flashing dangerously. 'He's a growing lad now, and worth a barrel of you and your savages, boy or not.'

'The little snake,' Vortigern murmured. 'He's going to side with Eldof after all.'

Garagon waved gaily to the lord of Glevum and smiled ingratiatingly at the churchmen below him.

'Don't take any notice of him, you God-lovers,' roared Gorlois of Kernow. 'He worships Ceres when his mother's not looking.'

The Kentishmen erupted. If they had been able to get at Gorlois, there would have been a bloodbath there and then. Severus watched helplessly as mayhem reasserted itself.

'Enough of this,' Vortigern said under his breath. He touched Kerin's arm 'You know what to do. Stay here with Constans, and when I give you the sign, bring him out into the hall. He'll never have the nerve to do it on his own.'

The scene in the curia was enough to have terrified a much braver man than Constans, Kerin thought. Swords glinted as tempers flared, and it was impossible to see how a man could make himself heard, let alone avoid getting himself killed by offending one or other of the rival factions.

'I'll come with you, lord,' Lud said.

'You'll stay here,' Vortigern said. 'If I need Rufus and the warriors, I'll raise my hand above my head. Otherwise, stay where you are. And if it comes to a fight, save Constans. I haven't gone to all this trouble to see his throat slit. The rest of us must save our own skins.'

Lud gave him a disapproving glare, but did not argue. For a moment Vortigern stood quite still. His fingers closed tightly around the clipeum. He shut his eyes and pressed it quickly to his lips, then let it fall, squared his shoulders and walked alone into the chaos beyond the antechamber. He walked slowly and deliberately until he reached the open space which still remained in the centre of the hall. There he stepped onto the low platform and stood, arms folded, waiting for someone to take notice. On every side arguments raged on unchecked. Kerin watched, transfixed. He could feel Constans trembling violently beside him. Vortigern waited.

'The gods protect him,' Lud whispered. Kerin could feel the sweat running down his neck. He wondered how long any man's nerve could hold out there, in the middle of that lethal inferno. Severus looked down from the dais, catching Kerin's eye, and raised his hands in a gesture of helpless resignation. Publius Luca came down the steps, sword already in his hand.

'As mad as ever,' he said under his breath. Kerin turned.

'You knew him before this?' he asked.

'Years ago in the West,' the commander said. 'He was no different. I'll do my best, but no-one can protect him out there.'

As they watched, a howl of excitement came from high up on the left. Gorlois of Kernow was on his feet. He clambered across the seats, stepping on his own warriors and some of the Cambrians, shook Hefydd by the shoulder and gestured wildly towards the centre of the hall. Garagon of Kent noticed the movement and waved his arms at Eldof. A shiver of anticipation flew round the hall like wildfire. Quite suddenly the uproar subsided, and was replaced by a silence so intense that Kerin could hear Constans's teeth chattering beside him. The men of the West waited, bright-eyed and taut with expectation. Garagon and Eldof exchanged uneasy glances while Maximian Galba and his allies stared coldly, as if both appalled and fascinated. Vortigern smiled at their confusion and surveyed the dumbfounded gathering as calmly as if he had been addressing a meeting in his own citadel.

'Good,' he said, raising his voice only enough to ensure that it would carry. 'It'll be no good if we can't hear each other.'

Kerin's eyes flicked to the right as the sharp sound of a dagger being whipped from its sheath came from the huddle of men on the tiled floor behind Vortigern's back. Lud tensed and gripped his sword. Vortigern did not even look over his shoulder.

'Put it away,' he said. 'We haven't come here for that.' He loosened his cloak and let it fall, then raised his arms and turned a full circle so that every man in the room could see that he was unarmed. 'You see? I carry no weapon. There will be no bloodshed here. Anyone who has a death wish can fight me later, if he likes.'

The men of the West chuckled amongst themselves.

Vortigern looked up at them expectantly. They fell silent again, and he nodded his approval.

'Well,' he said, looking around him, 'as my honourable friend Severus Maximus has said, we have come here to choose a king. We need to choose a king because we need to beat the Picts. And we need to beat the Picts, because if we do not – ' he paused suddenly and directed an accusing finger at the Roman administrators and the churchmen. 'How many of you have seen a dead man?' he asked. 'And by that I don't mean a man dead of the plague, or in his bed, of old age. I mean a man hung up and butchered like an ox. How many of you?'

The churchmen lowered their eyes and muttered, and the officials eyed each other uneasily. Vortigern nodded.

'None of you,' he said. 'Those of us who have had to fight from our cradles have seen things which would make the rest of you wake in the night and howl to the gods. And if we don't beat the Picts, you will see them too, and you will see them here, in your own streets. You!' He looked directly at Tegid, who was staring silently at him while large tears coursed down his sunken cheeks. 'Yes, you. Tegid the merchant. Come here.'

'No!' Maximian exclaimed, rising to his feet.

'Why not?' Vortigern said. 'I'm unarmed; what do you think I'm going to do to him? Come here, Tegid. These people need to hear you.'

Kerin saw Maximian's face turn livid with rage as he realised how comprehensively Vortigern was about to steal his thunder. Tegid rose hesitantly to his feet and picked his way forward. Vortigern stretched out his hand and helped him onto the platform.

'He's under my protection!' Maximian protested.

'Then come out here and protect him,' Vortigern said. Maximian half-rose, then sank impotently back into his seat. Vortigern took Tegid's arm and sat him down in the gilded chair.

'Tell them what happened to your family,' he said. Tegid whispered something inaudible. The Cambrian warriors guffawed triumphantly at the Romans. 'Be quiet, you savages!' Vortigern roared. His men shut their mouths abruptly. The silence ran back like water. 'Tell them,' Vortigern said. The merchant wept and mumbled. 'Did the Picts burn your town?'

'Yes,' Tegid whispered.

'Did they butcher your wife and children?'

'Every one.'

'And what did they do to your brother?'

Tegid looked up beseechingly.

'Tell them,' Vortigern said brutally.

'Let him be!' Maximian growled, rising to his feet again. Vortigern ignored him.

'Tell them,' he said. 'Don't you think they should know, before they let it happen here too?'

'Yes!' Tegid choked.

'Then tell them,' Vortigern said. He moved round to stand behind Tegid and placed his hands gently on the merchant's quivering shoulders. 'Did they kill him?' he said softly.

'Yes.'

'Mercifully?'

'No.'

'I didn't hear you, Tegid.'

'No!' Tegid howled. 'They slit him from neck to

crotch and let the dogs devour him while he still lived. Now let me go, for the love of God!'

Vortigern looked up and caught the eye of Father Giraldus. Two of the monks hurried forward to lead Tegid away, weeping and retching. Vortigern looked calmly around him at the rows of silent faces.

'Is there any man here who believes that we should not raise arms against the Picts?' he asked. The silence answered him. Vortigern nodded. 'Good. Then the only question is, how it should be done. Does any man here have an idea?'

Maximian leapt to his feet, his face still livid with anger.

'There's only one possible course!' he shouted, throwing his arms about. 'If there really is no prospect of help from the Empire, we must gather the city garrisons and the remaining legionary detachments. We must put them under the command of an experienced Roman-trained general and march north as soon as possible.' He broke off, his eyes wild with temper. When Kerin first saw him at close quarters in the praetor's dining hall, he had looked the model of self-possession; but Vortigern had found the chink in the wall, as usual. High above, Gorlois of Kernow rose to his feet.

'Why?' he asked, his rumbling voice carrying to every corner. 'So that the Picts can have them for a first course? A little plate of sweetmeats? There aren't enough of them, man. In case you hadn't noticed, most of them have gone running back to Rome.'

'Just like Constantine,' came a knowing voice from amongst the Kernow warbands. A collective cheer rose from the ranks of the West.

'Who are you, anyway, old man?' crowed Hefydd, who was easily ten years older than Maximian. The praetor of Venta Belgarum looked up disdainfully.

'Perhaps you had better tell them,' Vortigern said, with a polite but infinitely condescending smile. Maximian looked as if he might be about to suffer an irretrievable loss of control.

'I am Maximian Galba, praetor of Venta Belgarum,' he roared, 'as any man in this room worthy of the name already knows.' He took a deep breath, blinked away desperate tears and recovered his composure. 'Now,' he growled, indicating the civic dignitaries and the churchmen, 'perhaps you should tell these distinguished gentlemen who *you* are.'

Vortigern raised his eyebrows. 'Well, I will if you really want me to,' he said.

'Do it!' Maximian spat. 'They should know what sort of a barbarian they're listening to.' Vortigern chuckled. He walked down the length of the curia, waved the guards aside and marched out into the antechamber, passing within a pace of Kerin and the trembling monk. Then he seized the iron handle of the great outer door and flung it wide open. A deafening roar arose from the crowd outside in the square. Vortigern raised his hands for silence. As the din subsided a little he cupped his hands around his mouth.

'Citizens of Londinium!' he shouted. 'Tell the noble praetor and his friends who I am!'

A wall of sound rolled forward like an ocean breaker. As it crashed from wall to wall it resolved itself into a deep-throated chant and Maximian stood, his face frozen in silent rage, as Vortigern's name echoed around the vast curia. The two soldiers who had stood at the door with Publius Luca elbowed their way past Kerin and slammed the outer door shut.

'We'll have those louts coming over the railings in a minute,' one of them said nervously. Inside, the noise sank back to a simmering murmur. Maximian went dumbly back to his seat. Vortigern, who had regained the platform, looked confidently around him.

'I am Vortigern of Glywysing,' he said, 'Lord of Cambria, Lord of the West, Celt of the Celts. Some of you would call yourselves my people. Some of you, I expect, would call yourselves my enemies. Please understand that I have not come here to fight you. I will do it if I have to, but it is not what I want.' He paused. The silence in the curia intensified. Outside the crowds in the square chanted on, the sound deadened by the barred doors. 'You want a king,' Vortigern said. 'But what sort of a king do you want?' He looked around him. 'A Roman for the Romans? A Christian for the Christians? A Celt for the Celts? A warrior for the warriors, even?'

'Lord Vortigern,' Severus said from his perch on the dais, 'no man can be all of these things.'

'You are right, Severus,' Vortigern said respectfully. 'The best we can hope for is to choose one who is most of them.'

'Then choose Ambrosius!' Eldof exclaimed, on his feet again in spite of Varro's efforts. 'His father was a Roman, his mother was true British, and he was raised a Christian, like his parents.'

Vortigern looked up at him curiously. 'Lord,' he said, 'Lord – I'm sorry, I don't recall your name.'

'Eldof!' the Lord of Glevum roared, crimson with indignation.

'Lord Eldof,' Vortigern continued, 'why are you so eager to see this young lad become king? Surely if he does, the power will lie with his supporters and not with him?'

'Then it is for us to see that he is well-advised,' Eldof said curtly.

'For us?' Vortigern enquired. Sounds of suppressed laughter came from the left.

'There is no alternative,' Maximian said, suddenly recovering his nerve. 'The boy may be young, but he's Constantine's son, after all. Raised by his father's kinsmen, in the finest traditions of Rome. And yes, he will be well-advised; by a council of protectors who have his interests at heart, as well as those of the state.'

'Protectors!' Vortigern said speculatively. 'An interesting use of the term, Maximian.'

'You can mock if you like,' Maximian retorted. 'I still maintain that there is no alternative.' He turned and nodded to the abbot of St Alban's chapel. 'Bring it, please, Giraldus.'

The abbot rose to his feet. Kerin, edging forward, saw that the old man was holding a small pig-skin bag. From it he drew a fine silver band with a sculpted edge.

'Lords,' Maximian cried, 'here is Constantine's crown, left with the brothers of St Alban for safe-keeping. I call upon Eldadus, bishop of Glevum, to consecrate it here before us all and then to go to Gallia and set it on the head of Ambrosius, in the house of his kinsmen.'

The luminaries of Glevum nodded their agreement.

Eldof signalled to his brother, who was still standing beside Severus on the dais, looking, Kerin thought, a little perturbed by the turn events had taken. There was a loud assenting murmur from the dignitaries of Londinium. Vortigern glanced about him, then flung out an arm in the direction of the antechamber.

'Come on,' Kerin said, shoving Constans towards the doorway.

'God, no!' the monk whined. Lud drew his dagger and pressed the point of the blade to Constans's throat.

'Look, do you want him to fry us all?' he growled. Constans closed his eyes, drew the hood of his brown cloak tightly over his head and gripped Kerin's arm. As they reached the door, he froze. Kerin seized him by the shoulders and peered under the hood.

'Do you want to be king?' he asked. Constans's eyes fastened on the gleaming crown, and for a moment his desire for it broke the paralysing spell of fear.

'Yes, I want to be king,' he whispered.

'Then hold your head up and look like a king,' Kerin said. Constans straightened his slender shoulders and they stepped forward, slowly across the mosaic floor into a silence as terrifying as the tumult in the square had been. As they reached the centre of the hall Vortigern stepped forward and flung back the hood of Constans's cloak, revealing his tonsured head. The crowd erupted.

'Silence!' Vortigern roared. 'I set before you Constans, the oldest son of his father Constantine, and rightful heir to the crown. Let him set aside his vows and fulfil his duty to his father, and to the people of his father's kingdom.'

'No!' Maximian thundered. 'It is an offence against God, to touch those who are dedicated to his service. Lords, if we drag this monk from his cloister we'll burn in hell, every one of us.'

'The Lord Vortigern is right!' Gorlois was standing, arms folded, on one of the stone seats. 'Do you really think that God wants us to get slaughtered? I don't think so. God wants to protect his flock, and if that means we have to borrow a monk from him, then so be it.'

'Ambrosius!' came a sharp, rather high-pitched voice from the Kentish quarter. 'Send the monk back to his monastery! Give the crown to Ambrosius!' It was Edlym, Kerin saw; he was astonished that the man had the nerve.

'Eldadus!' Maximian entreated. 'For the love of God, come down and bless the crown, and take it to Ambrosius.'

Vortigern caught Kerin's eye. 'I've got them there,' he murmured. 'Eldadus won't move without his brother's say-so, and Eldof's afraid to cross me, however much noise he makes.' He looked up at the dais, where Severus and Publius Luca were watching silently whilst Eldadus glanced nervously about, like a sheep looking for a way out of the pen at the slaughterhouse. Vortigern's gaze moved slowly around the hall.

'Lords,' he said steadily, 'I ask you to give the crown to this man, Constantine's son. He is all that Ambrosius is – a Roman, a Briton, a Christian. He is not a warrior, but whilst he is king I will fight in his service, and in yours.'

'Give the crown to the monk!' Hefydd bawled. 'We'll fight to the last drop of blood for him!'

The warriors of Cambria and Kernow roared and stamped and brandished swords and daggers until Vortigern raised a hand to silence them. Kerin noticed that the dignitaries had started to mutter uneasily amongst themselves, as if they no longer had any idea of what to do next. Vortigern had seen it too, and now he looked upwards towards the dais again, knowing that if anything could be relied upon to persuade the doubters, it was the opinion of the two men who were standing behind its stone balustrade.

'Severus Maximus,' he said. 'Publius Luca. Who should be king?'

The praetor cleared his throat. 'Lord Vortigern, Publius Luca will speak for us both,' he said. Kerin looked up at the veteran soldier, standing squarely on the dais while a slanting beam of sunlight flashed on his polished breastplate. Everything Kerin had seen of him confirmed a man of clear, unsentimental opinions. He had fought, and dealt with men, and commanded a great legion in hard, dangerous times when imperial strength was no longer the certainty it had once been. Such a man would seek a practical solution; but no degree of admiration for Vortigern guaranteed that he would risk his own position and reputation by supporting him now.

'Lords of the Britons,' Publius Luca said gravely, 'most of you know me as a soldier. I speak to you now as a soldier; and indeed it will fall to us soldiers to deal with the Picts. Sometimes it has fallen to soldiers to make and unmake emperors, although please the gods it will never fall to me. But now you ask me who should be king. In truth I cannot see that there is much to choose between a monk and a boy, although the monk at least is a man in years, and old enough to choose his own path. I know that this will never sit easily with those of you who believe that his vows to his god should take precedence, and so there will always be room for argument. Some of you may say that, as a servant of Mithras, I have no right to judge what a Christian should do. To you I would say that none of this will matter when the invaders are at the city gate. A Pictish sword will not distinguish between Christian and pagan, druid or worshipper of Jupiter. Please remember this as you call on your gods. You have asked me who should be king. Perhaps you have asked me the wrong question. A boy or a monk, what difference does it make? But of one thing I am quite certain. If you asked me to name the man I should most like to have beside me when I march against the Picts, then I should look no further, because he stands before you now.'

He inclined his head respectfully. Vortigern looked up at him with unspoken gratitude.

'Lords,' Severus Maximus said, in a voice which was barely more than a whisper, 'you have your answer.'

'It cannot be!' Maximian bawled in desperation. 'You fools, don't you understand what's happening? Lord Eldadus! Where's the holy bishop?'

'Eldadus has gone,' Hefydd sneered. 'Perhaps he had something important to see to.'

'Then where's the man of God who'll put a stop to this madness?' Maximian shouted, whirling round.

'Now,' Vortigern said, under his breath. He raised his hand high above his head. Kerin saw a swift movement in the antechamber. Almost at once the door at the rear of the hall burst open. It was not Rufus but Hefin who appeared there, astride his big brown warhorse. Heavily-armed riders came crowding in behind him. The men of the West roared with joy, and a feeble, precautionary cry of 'Constans!' went up from the citizens of Londinium.

'What about it, then, men of God?' Vortigern asked. 'Which of you will bless the crown?'

The little group of priests and monks huddled and shrank. Only Abbot Giraldus stood firm, head unbowed.

'Cowards!' Gorlois bellowed. 'Which of you will take the crown and put it where it belongs?'

'We cannot!' the abbot of St Alban's chapel said. 'Whatever the rights and wrongs of the succession, Constans is a monk!'

'You see, Vortigern?' Maximian said triumphantly. 'Not one of them will lift a finger. And a king uncrowned is no king at all.'

Vortigern sighed. 'Well, priests,' he said, turning to confront them. 'Isn't there one of you man enough to do this thing?' The priests lowered their eyes and squirmed in their seats. Vortigern shrugged. 'Then damn your souls, I will do it myself,' he said. As the astounded crowd looked on, he seized the crown from Giraldus's hands and carried it back to the platform in the centre of the hall. Constans stared at him in dismay. Even the men of the West were speechless, for once.

'The devil's in you,' Maximian breathed. Vortigern smiled broadly and raised the crown high.

'Lords of the Britons,' he said, 'I, Vortigern of

Glywysing, will set the crown on the head of our rightful king.'

As Constans bowed his head, there was a sudden scuffle at the back of the hall. Kerin leapt forward. A tiny, black-robed figure burst through the crowd, ran across the open space and stumbled onto the platform, panting for breath. Paulinus of Venta Belgarum threw himself between Vortigern and Constans, his little grey eyes blazing defiance.

'I have come for Brother Constans,' he said, turning to glare at the shrinking figure behind him.

'Your brother no longer,' Vortigern said. The abbot did not flinch.

'Your soul will burn in hell if you do this thing,' he hissed.

'So be it,' Vortigern said. 'My soul is my concern.'

Kerin pinioned the abbot's arms behind his back. Paulinus watched impotently as Vortigern raised the crown again.

'I, Vortigern of Glywysing, will crown the king,' he said. 'On my soul be the sin and the judgment. And if the rest of you can't see that that's a good bargain, God help you all.'

He set the fine silver band firmly on Constans's head. The crowds surged forward, brandishing swords and cheering wildly. Hefin rode up to the platform, grabbed Constans by the scruff of the neck and hoisted him up onto the scarred quarters of his warhorse. Paulinus twisted from Kerin's grasp and stood, shaking, in front of them all.

'The curse of God be on you!' he howled. The platform was besieged by a mob of warriors, both mounted and on foot. Some were shouting the new king's name while others roared their battle hymns, all differences submerged. Constans was seized, raised aloft and swept away towards the open doors of the curia, bobbing around between the shoulders of the jostling horsemen.

Kerin looked up at the dais and saw the praetor of Londinium, standing motionless and quite alone at the stone balustrade. As the chanting procession passed beneath, one of the young riders drew rein; an ordinary warrior of no particular standing, but as his insolent eyes took in the praetor's silken robes and bejewelled fingers, he laughed.

'Slave!' Severus mouthed. The man made a parody of a bow and rode off after his companions. Severus looked down at Kerin with silent apprehension. It was the fearful, cowed look of a man who realised, too late, what he had started. The armies of the West were riding to war, but they were not fighting for the Church, though they carried a Christian on their shoulders. Most of them were probably not even fighting for Britain. They were fighting for Vortigern, and he had made them in his own image.

13

It was past midday, and Kerin's head was still thick with sleep and Phrygian wine, when he noticed an object lying on the marble table beside his bed which confirmed that he had not dreamed the whole thing. It was a fine silver band embossed with intricate designs, its polished surfaces winking in the fine beam of sunlight slanting through the window; and as Kerin lay on his back, watching the play of light on the ceiling above, he vaguely remembered fishing it out of a fountain in Gallus's courtyard the night before. Someone else – Macsen, as he recalled – had rescued the new king. Kerin lay quite still, reliving every moment of the previous day's events; staggering even at the time, but so terrifying in the clear gaze of hindsight that he could feel a film of sweat forming on his brow, even here, in the safe depths of the praetor's house.

It was odd, the way the incident had unfolded. There had been a feast in the evening, arranged by Gallus months beforehand to welcome a delegation from one of the leading Byzantine trading families. A cordial invitation had been extended to the new king and his principal supporters. Kerin had supposed that it would please Vortigern, to celebrate his triumph in a building which had no links with the imperial past; but things had not played out quite as he expected. He remembered standing in Gallus's courtyard, thinking that of all the urban houses he had encountered, this was the only one he would have coveted for himself. There were lush plantings of trees and flowering shrubs which Kerin had never seen before, and the walls were invisible under showers of greenery. On the far side, visible through an archway, was a lawned garden where peacocks strutted and displayed; and beyond that the river, shimmering in the warm evening light.

Lupinus arrived at some point in a state of breathless excitement, complete with a full set of royal regalia. The courtyard filled up with dignitaries, traders, military men, many familiar from earlier in the day. Gallus swept in from the street with four elegant companions, the men's skin smooth and tawny, their almond eyes black as jet. The Byzantines, someone said. They wore soft caps with forward-turning peaks, brilliant red or deep sea-green, all trimmed with gold; their short cloaks covered white tunics and loose trousers cut from material of luminous delicacy, shot through with golden thread. They were talking rapidly and incomprehensibly amongst themselves, and to Gallus, their fine hands moving in animated accompaniment as they swept by, leaving behind the trace of a heavy, disquieting perfume. A troupe of retainers trotted in their wake, followed by a crowd of little ebony-skinned boys.

And then came Lucius, with his message. Kerin was to meet the Lord Vortigern outside the Chapel of St

Alban, please; he was to go without delay, and to tell no-one. Lucius looked mystified. Kerin remembered that much.

Vortigern was leaning against the outer wall of the chapel. His horse's reins were looped over his arm. The street was deserted.

'What about the feast?' Kerin asked. Vortigern shook his head.

'Not tonight,' he said.

'What, then?' Kerin asked. Vortigern looked up.

'Fresh air and some peace,' he said. 'You must give my apologies to Gallus. Tell him anything you think he'll believe, and assure him that I'll meet him and his Byzantines tomorrow. And keep your eyes on the monk. It would be a pity if someone cut his throat after all this.' He stared up at the sky above the roofs of the tall buildings, where a silver crescent moon was rising against the deep luminous blue. 'It's strange,' he said, 'to think that the same moon shines on Henfelin.' The black mare nuzzled his sleeve affectionately, and he reached up to pull her ears. For the first time in Kerin's memory, he looked dog-tired.

'Are you well, lord?' Kerin asked. Vortigern looked round, catching at once the odd note in his voice; a conflict between anxiety and disbelief.

'Yes. I'm well enough. It's not every day that one crowns a monk king, all the same.'

'No, lord,' Kerin said, avoiding his eyes. Vortigern sighed.

'You're not happy about it, I can tell.'

'Not entirely,' Kerin said. 'Not least because of the

risk to you. But it's done now, and there are worse things to think about.'

Vortigern swung onto his mare's back and smiled. 'Yes,' he said. 'But not tonight.'

Kerin stood in the street and watched him ride away. Abbot Giraldus came out of the low doorway of his chapel and peered down the street.

'Where is he going?' he asked.

'I don't know,' Kerin said guardedly. 'Why do you ask?'

The abbot looked at him from beneath his close-drawn hood. His face, unlike Paulinus's, held nothing but sadness and compassion. Kerin supposed that that was to be expected from one who had dedicated his life to the care of the hopeless, but it surprised him to see it now.

'Why do you want to know, Father?' he asked, gently this time. The abbot looked away down the street.

'Because I fear that I have failed him,' he said. Kerin frowned, suddenly uneasy. The abbot merely shook his head at the unspoken question, and crossed himself. 'May God have mercy on him and his house,' he said, as horse and rider vanished into the gathering dusk.

* * *

'Get moving, you idle loafers!' someone bellowed, just under Kerin's window. It was the grating voice of Plicius. The prospect of sleep long departed, Kerin heaved himself out of bed and padded into the bath-house. He knew that someone would have filled the tub with hot, perfumed water for him, as they did every morning; and even though the water had cooled, it was a welcome antidote to the excesses of the night before. He bathed, rubbed himself down and put on one of the white silken robes which hung alongside. It was his intention to spend a pleasant half hour fortifying himself with the bread, smoked meat and dried fruit which was set out daily on the table next to the window, before going in search of Rufus. As he sat down, a movement caught his eye. A woman was crossing the courtyard below him. The fluid, graceful walk and fall of dark hair were unmistakable.

'Faria,' he murmured. She was walking towards the tunnel which led to the slaves' quarters. Kerin blinked vigorously, half expecting the vision to dissipate, but it did not. At that moment the woman turned and looked upwards. She could not have failed to see him. She looked away and quickened her pace, moving as swiftly as she could without breaking into a run. 'Faria!' Kerin shouted at the retreating figure. She did not look back. He flung on tunic and breeches and ran barefoot down the cold passages to the courtyard. The midday sun had heated the paving slabs and they burned the soles of his feet. Halfway down the tunnel two guards, spears crossed, were barring the entrance to the slaves' quarters. Severus was free with the favours of his human chattels, but any services they rendered to his guests were expected to be performed in the guests' own chambers, not down here in the dank rabbit-warren where they lived out the rest of their lives. Kerin stumbled to a halt. His head was pounding ferociously.

'Please,' he panted. 'Let me pass.'

'I'm sorry, lord,' the older of the two guards said respectfully. 'The rules are very strict, you know.'

Kerin closed his eyes, then opened them again as his head began to swim. 'Faria, the Phoenician girl,' he said. 'Did she pass you just now?'

'Yes, lord,' the guard said, staring straight at the wall in front of him. 'She asked us to be sure not to let anyone follow her, lord. And to be truthful, I can quite see why she might not have wanted you to follow her.'

Kerin looked at him uncomprehendingly. He was aware that the other guard had moved closer and had tightened his grip on his spear. Still befuddled with sleep and wounded to fury, he seized the spear-shaft in both hands, wrenched the weapon from the guard's hands and brought it down on the man's bare head with all the force he could summon. The older guard, caught wholly by surprise, bawled out a vain cry for help and went for his sword. Kerin lashed out with his fist, catching him squarely on the chin, and he pitched to the ground. Kerin seized the sword and bolted down the barely lit passage into the slaves' quarters. A doorway opened on his right, revealing a black hole of a room lit by a single rush lamp. There was a couch scattered with sheepskins where two boys lay, idly pleasuring each other. They gave Kerin an uncurious look and went back to what they were doing. Further along the passage a second entrance beckoned. The sound of female chatter came from behind its closed door. Cautiously Kerin raised the latch and peered round the door. He found himself a pace away from Faria's cousin, Sha'ara. She gave a little stifled scream of surprise, which died in her throat when she recognised the intruder. He stepped quickly inside and closed the door behind him. There were four or five other women in the room, all unfamiliar to him. Sha'ara gave him an apprehensive look.

'Faria,' he said, cupping her chin in his hand. 'And don't lie to me.'

'The next door on the left,' she said, backing away from him. 'Lord, don't go to her.'

Kerin had already gone. He found the door locked. 'Faria,' he whispered urgently, rattling the latch. There was no response. 'Faria!' he repeated, more loudly. This time there was, unmistakably, a sound; a long-drawn, shuddering sob. Kerin kicked the door. It resisted. He gritted his teeth and shoulder-charged it, and went crashing into the room. Faria was standing with her back to him, facing the far wall. There was a small table in front of her which held a comb, a small towel, a gilt-framed mirror with its face averted, and an assortment of little bottles and jars with stoppered necks, like the ones which held the oils she had used on him to such effect.

'Faria, why didn't you come when I sent for you?' he asked, unable to keep the pain and confusion out of his voice. She was a slave, and it shouldn't have mattered to him. In the end she had no right to deny herself against Severus's will. And yet for some reason she had not come to him, despite the long hours of what he had taken to be a shared pleasure; and that reason held her still, silent and frozen, while he stood and watched her in helpless bewilderment. Her shoulders trembled slightly. Kerin suspected that she was weeping silently. 'Why?' he repeated. Still she did not speak. He looked again at the table, and at the mirror with its face to the wall, and a half-formed thought disturbed him. He placed his hands carefully on her shoulders and turned her round. She stood as if petrified with tears spilling from her closed eyes. The left-hand side of her face was disfigured by a violent bruise which started under her eye-socket and appeared to extend below the neck of her plain white bed gown. Kerin moved quickly to bolt the door. He picked up the towel and dried her tears, his hands shaking with impotent rage. The injury did not look fresh. Whoever had done it had also split her lower lip, although that too was beginning to heal. Her bare arms were blackened. Gently Kerin undid the drawstring at the neck of her gown and lowered it from her shoulders. She shuddered as it fell to the floor. Her breasts and thighs were covered with bruises and with a mass of ugly red weals which looked deep enough to have been inflicted by the claws of an animal. She buried her face in her hands in an agony of shame. Kerin seized the gown and pulled it up to her neck again, his fingers fumbling clumsily with the drawstring.

'Merciful God, who did this?' he whispered, drawing her into his arms. Faria began to shake.

'No-one you know, lord,' she stammered, sobbing violently. 'A guest of Severus. A stranger.'

Kerin had no reason to suspect that she was not telling the truth. And yet somewhere deep within himself, he knew that she was not. 'Faria, tell me,' he said, holding her at arms' length. She twisted free and retreated trembling to the dark corner of the room. Somewhere in the distance there was a shout, followed by the sound of running footsteps.

'Go!' Faria shrieked, her eyes wide with terror. 'They cannot find you here!'

Kerin threw the bolts and ran out into the passage. The noises were coming down the tunnel. Faria's door slammed behind him and the bolt slid home. He ran down the murky, damp-smelling passage as fast as his bare feet would take him. Other half-open doors flashed by; a grain store, a rudimentary bath house. The passage swung to the left and ended abruptly at a big locked door. Kerin jerked at the latch, but it was obvious that the door was barred from the other side, and that no effort of his was going to shift it. He turned, gasping for breath. Plicius came round the corner at the head of a troop of guards.

'That's him, sir!' cried an aggrieved voice. Kerin recognised the older guardsman whom he had floored at the entrance to the slaves' quarters, elbowing his way forward to Plicius's side. 'Do you know the young ruffian, sir?' he panted, rubbing his chin. Plicius smiled broadly.

'No, Marcus, I've never seen him before in my life,' he said, with unconcealed delight. Kerin stared straight back at him.

'You know who I am, Plicius,' he said.

'He knows your name, sir!' one of the guardsmen said curiously.

'Of course I know his name, you cloth-head,' Kerin shouted, 'I've been living here as Severus's guest for the last three months. I'm Kerin Brightspear, Vortigern's warrior.'

'Vortigern's warrior?' Plicius crowed gleefully. 'Down here, with no boots on? He looks like a common thief off the streets to me, lads.'

Kerin flattened himself against the door. The guards were crowding up behind Plicius. All of them had swords at their belts, some had short-handled spears, and some were carrying stout wooden staves, which they had started to slap meaningfully against their palms.

'Call them off, Plicius,' Kerin said, keeping his voice steady with some effort. 'You know who I am. You know what'll happen if you touch me.'

Plicius chuckled. 'They'll have to find you first,' he said. 'We usually throw dead thieves in the river, don't we, lads?' The guardsmen laughed and edged closer. The smile faded from Plicius's face. 'Do it,' he spat. His troop gave a bloodcurdling howl and charged. Kerin dived at their legs, bringing several to the ground in a tangle of limbs, swords and spear-shafts. Clubs and bodies thudded against the door. Someone seized Kerin by the hair, and he felt something heavy crack down on his shoulder. A vicious pain ran down his arm and across his chest. Blood was streaming down his forehead and into his eyes. Someone had grabbed him round the neck. Through it all he heard the bolts on the other side of the door begin to rattle. For some reason, the grip on his neck slackened.

'What you do, *hundes tyrdel?*' a deafening roar resounded somewhere above his head. Kerin suddenly found himself released. He rolled aside and looked up, blinking the blood away. The big door was open and Cheldric was standing where it had been, holding a huge black pot of steaming liquid. Plicius, livid with rage, was edging forward at the head of his troop.

'Put that down, you oaf,' he hissed.

'You come, I throw,' the Saxon bellowed. 'Is boiling. Hurt you plenty.'

'Throw it and you're a dead man,' Plicius said, gritting his teeth. His guardsmen were backing away. All their eyes were riveted to the sweating cook and his lethal pot. There was a sword lying on the ground only a few paces from Kerin's hand. Slowly, cautiously, he reached for it. Plicius saw the movement. He lunged forward with an angry growl.

'Odin!' Cheldric screamed and hurled the pot. It bounced off the roof of the passage and fell, knocking one man senseless and showering its scalding contents over several others who fled, howling in agony. A meat-cleaver hurtled through the air and hit someone's helmet with a sharp metallic clang. The kitchen door slammed shut in Plicius's face. Kerin fled up the passage towards the tunnel. Footsteps thundered after him. He knew that there were at least six guards left to worry about, and that his only chance of escape lay in reaching the courtyard, where they might be more wary of killing him than in the private darkness of the slaves' quarters. He wiped the blood out of his eyes as he ran. The pain in his shoulder was intensifying. The end of the tunnel lay ahead of him, a square of brilliant light. As he stumbled out into the blinding daylight a hand grabbed him from behind and hurled him face down on the paving stones. A booted foot drove into his injured shoulder and turned him onto his back. Plicius stood over him, framed by the cruel blue sky. He was smiling, and in his hand was one of those thick wooden staves.

'Well, lord?' he said, with mocking emphasis. 'Who's going to help you now?'

He raised the stave above his head. Half-blinded and dizzy with pain, Kerin didn't hear the running footsteps; didn't see or hear the sword until it whistled through the air above him and sliced Plicius's head neatly from his shoulders.

'Odin's blood!' Cheldric's voice said somewhere behind him, with fervent admiration. Kerin struggled to his knees, clutching his shoulder. A few paces away the helmeted head gazed at him with sightless eyes, the body pumping blood while its lifeless extremities twitched grotesquely. The guardsmen stared vacantly at the remains of their commander. Kerin tried to get up. The walls of the courtyard and everything else swam out of focus, and he sank back to his knees. He felt an arm encircle his shoulders, and did not resist as it steadied him. A blessedly cool cloth cleaned the blood from his face, and was held to the wound above his brow. He heard voices, some of them raised, but could not understand what they were saying as they merged into a general darkness.

He did not know how long it took for his head to clear. When it did, the first thing he saw was Cheldric sitting cross-legged on the paving-stones, picking his teeth with a guardsman's knife. The body and its severed head had gone, but a significant pool of blood remained to assure him that he had not imagined it all. He was leaning against something; or rather against someone, because the arm was still supporting his shoulders and the cloth was still pressed to the wound in his head.

'Lord, he wakes!' Cheldric said, with a look of relief.

'About time,' Vortigern said tersely. He rose to his

feet, dragging Kerin with him. Kerin gave a yelp of pain and seized his shoulder. Vortigern snorted. 'You're lucky. It's no more than a bruise. And if that cook of yours hadn't come to get me, Plicius would have spread your brains all over the courtyard.'

Kerin looked at him with trepidation. He knew that he couldn't have been unconscious for long. Vortigern's tunic was spattered with Plicius's blood, and it looked fresh.

'Lord, there's a reason,' he said, knowing as he spoke how inadequate it was going to sound.

'I hope it's a good one,' Vortigern said testily, 'given that I've just beheaded the commander of the praetorian guard in the middle of the praetor's courtyard.' He took Kerin's arm and guided his wandering footsteps in the direction of the atrium. Cheldric trotted beside them, looking well pleased with his part in the drama. A little group of servants who had gathered by the fountain, gossiping frenetically about what had just happened, scattered like a flock of sparrows. Vortigern led Kerin to one of the carved stone benches which lined the colonnaded walkway.

'Sit,' he said. Kerin sank weakly onto the bench. Vortigern sat beside him. Cheldric perched on the low stone wall on the opposite side of the walkway, just a few paces away. He looked uneasily at Vortigern, as if expecting to be dismissed. 'Stay where you are,' Vortigern said. 'He'd be dead meat if not for you. What's your name?'

'Cheldric,' said the cook.

'Alright then, Cheldric. Sit there where I can see you, and keep your mouth shut. Now then.' He looked enquiringly at Kerin.

'Faria,' Kerin said, closing his eyes.

'That slave girl?'

'Yes. The Phoenician girl. Someone's beaten and raped her half to death. You'd think it was a wild animal. She told me a stranger did it, but I think she was lying. I followed her to the slaves' quarters, and Plicius caught me there. If it hadn't been for Cheldric, you'd never have found me. They were going to kill me and throw me in the river.'

Vortigern considered the information. 'Why should she lie to you?' he asked.

'God knows,' Kerin said. 'Because she's afraid of what might happen if I found out who did it?'

'She's a slave,' Vortigern said. 'It's not worth the trouble. And don't delude yourself that she has any feelings for you. It's a transaction. Severus put her there, that's all.'

Kerin avoided his eyes. He suspected that it was no longer as simple as that, even though it must necessarily have been so in the first place; but it embarrassed him to admit it, even to himself.

'Either way, it's happened because of me,' he said. 'The business with Plicius has nothing to do with it, really. He hated me anyway, and I gave him an excuse by being in the wrong place.'

Vortigern drew his sword and examined the blood-stained blade before placing the weapon at his side on the bench. 'Do you know who did this?' he asked the cook. Cheldric shrugged and spat out something which he had extracted from his teeth with Plicius's dagger.

'I find out, I tell you.' He caught Kerin's eye. 'First you take me out of here, like you promise.'

'Alright,' Kerin said. 'I'll arrange something.'

'Today!' Cheldric said emphatically.

'Yes, today. As soon as I can see straight.'

'Why today?' Vortigern asked. 'You can take him with you when we go home.'

'No,' Kerin said. 'He'll be strung up here. Tell him, Cheldric.'

The Saxon chuckled. 'They come with swords and sticks,' he said. 'I throw my pot' – he demonstrated the action – 'and they run, run. Burn like chickens on the spit. He is my friend, so I protect him.' He drove a fist into his palm, and beamed.

'I hope the rest of your friends have more brains than this one,' Vortigern said. Cheldric's smile vanished.

'You call him idiot?' he growled. Kerin's heart sank. Vortigern picked up his sword, extended the blood-stained blade and carefully lifted a lock of Cheldric's greasy hair.

'Don't speak to me like that again,' he said.

Cheldric closed his eyes and a droplet of sweat formed on the end of his large, bulbous nose. 'No, lord,' he said, in a barely audible whisper. 'I remember good.'

Vortigern stood up and put the sword away. 'Come on, then,' he said briskly. 'We're going to talk to Severus Maximus.'

'Now?' Kerin said apprehensively.

'Yes, now, before he hears ten other people's versions of events, before the rest of Londinium finds out. Now get on your feet and move.' He stalked off across the atrium. Cheldric helped Kerin to his feet with a shaky smile and they hurried after him.

The portals of Severus's chambers were protected by, possibly, the only two members of the praetorian guard who had yet to hear about the fate of their commanding officer. One of them was Lucius. The other was a much older man, whose weak chin and amenable eyes suggested that his seniority owed more to long service than to military prowess. Kerin supposed that he and his companions made an unexpected trio; Vortigern with his blood-spattered tunic, he himself with a split head and no boots, and Cheldric with his uncombed locks and filthy apron. The older guard looked them carefully up and down. Lucius shot Kerin an apprehensive glance. Vortigern folded his arms. The senior guard gave him the same look of respectful denial which had met Kerin at the entrance to the slaves' quarters.

'I'm sorry, lord, but you can't take him in there,' he said, nodding towards the Saxon. Kerin laid a restraining hand on Cheldric's arm and waited for something to happen.

'What do you mean, I can't take him in there?' Vortigern said.

'I mean you can't take a kitchen slave into the praetor's private apartments, lord,' the guard said patiently. 'Severus Maximus is very particular about that sort of thing. Only his principal servants and his guests may pass these doors.'

Vortigern looked at the ageing guard with complete incredulity. 'Do you know who I am?' he asked.

'Yes, lord,' the guard said with a deferential nod. 'I should think everyone knows that by now. But with respect, lord, your companions look like a pair of ruffians, and I'd be neglecting my duty to the praetor if I let you take them into his private apartments.'

'Get Severus,' Vortigern said. The guard looked appalled.

'He's the praetor, lord. I can't just get him. I can tell him you're here, if you like.'

'Tertius,' Lucius said, 'I think –'

'Hold your tongue, young pup,' Tertius snapped. 'If I want your opinion, I'll ask for it.'

Vortigern's breath escaped in a long sigh. 'Tertius,' he said, 'you have one last chance to open this door for me. And before you decide what to do, please understand that I have no qualms at all about killing defenceless old men.'

'Tertius, I think you'd be well advised to open the door,' said the pragmatic Lucius. 'The Lord Vortigern can overrule the praetor if he wishes, so it would be pointless to refuse him, don't you think? I'll go and speak to Severus Maximus for you, if you like.'

Tertius gave him a tight-lipped glare. 'Very well,' he said curtly. 'But make sure you tell him that I don't approve. Lord, you and your companions may enter the antechamber.'

He led the way into a cool vestibule where they waited, walled in by frescos of Bacchus and his leopards, until Lucius came back to inform them that the praetor would receive them in his private audience chamber, kitchen slave and all.

It was, Kerin supposed, a room which had seen emperors come and go. The watchful statue of Apollo would have presided over their meetings with military commanders, bishops and the highest-placed members of ordines; but it seemed unlikely that Apollo had ever set his marble eyes upon a Saxon cook. The god could not have been more surprised than Severus looked; and in fact Apollo had an advantage, as he had not been carried senseless from Gallus's feast the night before. The praetor was sitting in a huge, high-backed wooden chair whose intricate carvings echoed the Bacchanalian frieze in the antechamber. Elaborate vine tendrils curled over its back, and its arms were sculpted into smooth, clawless leopards' paws. Severus, chalk-faced and unsteady, rose to his feet as they entered. He placed both hands on his large oak table and stared silently at them all with the despairing air of a man who, having hoped that his troubles had ended with the coronation in the curia, had suddenly seen endless vistas of complication begin to open before him. Kerin wished that, if nothing else, he had had time to find himself some boots.

'Lord Vortigern,' the praetor said wearily, 'why have you brought that – that *thing* in here?'

Cheldric's big fists clenched and an angry flush rose from his neck to the roots of his hair, but fear kept him silent, and he gazed at Severus with mute loathing.

'Severus,' Vortigern said, 'I am standing in front of you covered in blood, and one of my leading warriors has a split head and a broken shoulder. Can you think of nothing better to ask me?'

'I was coming to that, lord,' Severus said, closing his eyes. 'It is not always easy to know where to start.'

'Then let me start,' Vortigern said. 'Plicius is dead.'

'Plicius?' Severus mouthed, and sank into the chair. 'O Jupiter! How? Why?'

'Because he was about to beat this man to death,'

Vortigern said. Severus shook his head uncomprehendingly.

'Is this true?' he asked Kerin.

'Yes,' Kerin said. 'He found me in the slaves' quarters. I admit that I shouldn't have been there, but it could have been settled without blood.'

'Then why?' Severus asked despairingly.

'Because Plicius hated me and saw a chance to get rid of me,' Kerin said. 'He set his troop on me. Cheldric here helped me to get away from them, but they caught me in the courtyard.'

'So you killed him?'

'No,' Vortigern interposed. 'I killed him. It was unavoidable.'

'Unavoidable?' Severus said in horror. 'He was my chief of guards. He had been with me for twenty years. How can it have been unavoidable?'

'He was nothing to me,' Vortigern said brutally. 'Do you encourage your guards to beat unarmed men to death?'

'No!' Severus exclaimed. 'They're here to protect my household and my guests.'

'Then they are failing in their duties,' Vortigern said. 'This man is your guest, and look at him. They can't protect your possessions either. This has only happened because one of your slaves has been flayed alive by some savage. And they can't even protect you.'

'Me?' Severus said nervously. Vortigern grinned. With a lightning movement he whipped out a dagger and hurled it. It lodged quivering in the back of the chair, a hair's breadth from the praetor's head. Severus stared at him, transfixed with terror.

'You, Severus Maximus,' Vortigern said, with a brilliant smile. 'They can't protect you, because most of them are either half-witted brutes like Plicius or poor, brave old fools like the man outside your door. You are quite alone, you know.'

Severus swallowed hard. 'Why are you doing this?' he said hoarsely.

'Because I want you to understand what I am about to do,' Vortigern said. He marched around the table, jerked his dagger from the back of the chair and replaced it at his belt. 'I am taking command of the praetorian guard,' he said.

'You can't do that,' Severus said, his face a blank mask.

'I am doing it,' Vortigern said flatly. 'If you oppose me I shall ask the king to make a decree, and you can try opposing that, if you like.'

Severus looked up at him with a reproachful smile. 'Lord, I have given you hospitality and helped you in every way possible,' he said. 'I did not think it would come to this.'

Vortigern sighed. 'Severus, I want to protect you, whatever you may think,' he said. 'One day soon, when you have a troop of good fighting men instead of those lame ducks, you'll thank me for this.' He looked round as Tertius and Lucius edged cautiously into the doorway. 'Alright. Come here, you two. The praetorian guard is under my command now, so hear me.'

Tertius looked at Severus in disbelief.

'It's true, Tertius,' the praetor said reluctantly. 'For all our sakes, please do as you are told, and serve the Lord Vortigern as you have served me.'

Tertius took a deep breath and bowed to Vortigern with soldierly restraint. Lucius, on the other hand, looked like an eager young dog straining at the leash.

'Tertius, stay here and guard your master the praetor,' Vortigern said. 'You have shown yourself more than worthy of the honour. Lucius, come with me. I have work for you.'

Severus held his head in his hands and watched impotently as the oddly-assorted party swept out of the audience chamber. Tertius laid a consoling hand on his arm before hailing a couple of servants who were loitering outside and sending them for Lupinus, to dispense medication and sympathy.

They had scrubbed Plicius's blood from the paving stones in the courtyard. Lucius stared down at the spot, dark and steaming itself dry in the high sun. He looked astonished but not at all distressed.

'What do you want me to do, lord?' he asked.

'First, I want all the guards here in the courtyard as soon as possible,' Vortigern said. 'Leave Tertius where he is; he's had enough excitement for one day. If you have any trouble with the rest, deal with it as you wish. I shouldn't be asking you to do this if I didn't think you had it in you.'

Lucius straightened up, his eyes glowing with pride. 'Thank you, lord,' he said eagerly, and marched off across the courtyard as fast as military decorum allowed.

'What are you going to do?' Kerin asked.

'Remove any trouble-makers and get Publius Luca to knock some sense into the rest of them,' Vortigern said. 'I might put Lucius in charge, once he's had some proper training. I'll take Publius's opinion on that. I know Lucius is young, but so are you, and you've managed to keep Constans alive after a bad start. Don't get complacent, though. The men who want him dead will be more determined than ever, now the crown is on his head.'

'That's not what you meant when you said that he wouldn't be king for long, though,' Kerin said. Vortigern looked directly at him.

'No,' he said. 'Constans will cease to be king at a moment of my choosing. And the moment is everything. The right conjunction of circumstance and public opinion and opportunity. You're the prophet, or so they tell me. You of all men should be able to see it coming. And I couldn't care less if you have prophetic dreams or if you just keep your eyes open and your ear to the ground. The others can believe what they like. I just need to know what's round the corner. That's your responsibility.'

'Even after what's happened this morning?' Kerin said wryly. Vortigern shrugged.

'In the end it's for the best,' he said. 'I'd have had to kill Plicius sometime. What are you going to do about the slave?'

'I don't know,' Kerin said. 'What do you think I should do?'

'Find yourself another bedfellow and forget it ever happened,' Vortigern said. 'For God's sake, don't we have enough to contend with?'

'Yes, we have, I know,' Kerin said, seeing in his mind's eye Faria's battered body and despairing tears.

'Look,' Vortigern said, 'the first thing you should

do is get your shoulder seen to. Go to that old crow Marcellus. He seems to have saved Alberius against most people's expectations.'

'Alright, lord,' Kerin said, with little enthusiasm.

'And for the love of God get someone to wash that Saxon. He smells like a rotting carcass.'

Cheldric looked mortally affronted, but had enough sense to keep his indignation to himself.

'Come on then, *hundes tyrdel*,' Kerin said severely. Cheldric burst out laughing and clapped his hands.

'There's one more thing,' Vortigern said. Kerin looked at him beseechingly. 'Go back to Henfelin,' Vortigern said. 'Tomorrow, if you're fit to ride. You can take this lunatic with you, out of harm's way.'

'But, lord!' Kerin said, nonplussed. 'After everything you've just said?'

'Someone has to go,' Vortigern said. 'I need to know how things lie there. How the people take all this. How the Christians take it. How the Druids take it. You're no good to me with one fighting arm, so it may as well be you. Just choose someone you trust to guard Constans until you get back. For everything else I've got Lud and our leading men, not to mention Gorlois's people, and Publius Luca's garrison. Take Hefydd and his boys. They'll be some protection for you on the journey. I'll tell them to meet you by the city gate.' He broke off. 'Do you want to go, or not?'

'Yes, lord,' Kerin said fervently.

'Leave at first light, then,' Vortigern said. 'Don't come back until you've healed that shoulder. Hefydd can come with you; you're not to travel alone on this side of the river. We've made too many enemies in this place. You should take Rufus as well, if you can find him. God knows, that's more than I can do.' He nodded abruptly and marched off across the courtyard before further discussion was possible. Kerin looked wonderingly at Cheldric.

'Can you ride a horse?' he asked. Cheldric scowled and spat on the ground.

'Saxons don't ride horses,' he said. 'Horses are for crazy men. You ride horse, I walk.'

Kerin grinned. 'All the way to Cambria?' he said.

Cheldric scratched his large nose. 'You find me mule and wagon, then,' he said. Kerin smiled. It should not be difficult to requisition a wagon, and for once, the prospect of an easy journey on the Roman roads appealed to him more than the usual hard cross-country slog. All too soon there would be forced marches, fighting and blood. For now, all he wanted was his home, some peace and goose fit for Odin.

14

Lupinus came in with a weary expression on his pale face, as if the order to attend Kerin was the last thing he needed after such a dramatically eventful morning.

'You must know that Marcellus *magister* doesn't treat people in their own chambers,' he said in an off-hand sort of way. 'He has rooms down by the gardens where he sees to them. It's more convenient, obviously, because it means that he can keep all his medicines in one place. And his instruments.' He lingered over the last word with a meaningful smile. Kerin shrugged, as nonchalantly as his injured shoulder would allow.

'I thought you might have been with Severus Maximus,' he said, in an equally casual tone.

'I'm on my way back there now,' Lupinus said. 'Marcellus asked me to look for you as I passed.'

'The praetor's not ill, is he?' Kerin asked.

'Ill?' Lupinus said, rather edgily. 'Well, no, not ill, exactly.' He pulled a small phial from the pocket of his tunic and held it up to the light. 'He told me to ask Marcellus for a sleeping draught. I'm not surprised, either, after what happened to Plicius. It's not – ' he broke off suddenly, and his hand crept up to his mouth, which had formed a rather silly little smile.

'Do you think he should have been allowed to club

me to death, then?' Kerin enquired, his humour snuffed out by the pain in his shoulder.

'No, no, lord, of course not,' Lupinus said, his hands performing a gesture of horrified denial. His smooth white brow puckered suddenly. 'Lord, what did the Lord Vortigern do to the praetor?'

'You mean, apart from killing his chief guard to save my skin?'

'It's more than that, lord,' Lupinus said nervously. 'He looks – well, battle-shocked, like soldiers some-times do. But there isn't a mark on him, unless I missed it somehow.'

'There's no mark,' Kerin said. 'At least, not the kind that you can see. You'd better go back to him with that sleeping draught.'

'Yes,' Lupinus said absently. 'Marcellus says it's very strong. Two drops in a goblet of water and no more, or you're a dead man.' He looked up at Kerin, his dark eyes suddenly anguished. 'I don't want things to change, lord. I've served this household since I was a boy. Even Constans is frightened, and he's the king, for the gods' sake.'

Constans? Kerin thought. You are a servant, albeit a high-ranking one, and you have the effrontery to call the king by his first name? But in the end there was nothing presumptuous about it; just the unthinking naturalness which had caught Kerin's attention. You are more than a servant now, he thought.

Kerin had never been in the part of the house where Marcellus held his consultations. There were two rooms, one small and one much larger, which contained several beds. Both overlooked a small, blessedly green garden whose flowers, all white, released a gentle but intoxicating perfume. Somewhere a fountain flowed musically into a pool.

'Sit down,' Marcellus said, indicating a wooden bench. 'I fear I shall have to cut your tunic; a pity, but you don't really want to raise your arms above your head for me to remove it, do you?' He took a small pair of shears and began to snip his way up the sleeve. 'You know,' he said, 'I may be alone in this, but I wasn't much surprised when I heard what had happened to Plicius.'

'Really?' Kerin said, a little taken aback. 'Why do you say that?'

'Because he was a bumptious oaf who had it coming to him,' Marcellus said, snipping away. 'I am not, of course, saying that I would have wished it to come to him in quite the way it did.' He did not smile, but there was a twinkle in his little bird-like eyes. The tunic fell to the floor. Kerin looked uneasily at his shoulder 'An impressive sight,' Marcellus said, scrutinising the damage with a professional's interest. 'This will, of course, hurt a little.' Kerin set his teeth, blinking back tears of agony as the long, elegant fingers of the haruspex probed and manipulated. A flock of doves, as white as the flowers, floated down into the garden. They landed in a huddle beside the fountain, pecking and cooing in incongruous peace and contentment. 'Well,' Marcellus said, 'it is indeed a bruise, if an unpleasant one. Not your sword arm, I hope?'

'No, fortunately not,' Kerin said.

'All the better. I must advise you to rest it, though.

Please drink this,' he offered a small earthenware cup, 'it will lessen the pain. Now I shall make a support for your arm and dress the shoulder with a tincture of arnica for the swelling and inflammation. It all started over a slave girl, I understand?'

'Not really.' Kerin winced as Marcellus applied the ointment. 'It started months ago, when I wouldn't give Plicius the respect he thought I owed him. The slave girl was his excuse. You've probably heard that he'd have killed me if he could.'

'Indeed,' Marcellus said. 'And that a pot of perfectly good meat stew was wasted in the course of your escape.'

'It saved my skin,' Kerin said. ' Even if it scalded a few other people's.'

'Five, to be precise,' Marcellus said. He extracted a broad strip of cloth from a basket and fashioned a sling for Kerin's arm. 'Now, I am going to find you a servant's tunic; you may not like the idea, but you will understand the purpose when you see it.' He shuffled away into the room which contained the beds and returned with a white cotton garment, rather like the ones Lupinus wore when he was not on display. 'You see? It opens at the front and fastens with a sash, like so. Much kinder to your shoulder, you must agree.' Kerin gave a grudging nod, and allowed Marcellus to help him dress. 'Kerin Brightspear,' the haruspex said thoughtfully. 'That's an unusual name, if I may say so.'

'I had an unusual start,' Kerin said. 'No living relatives; no illustrious ancestors to call me after. Lud's wife picked my first name. She remembered it from some old poem the bards used to spout when she was a child. And the warriors named me Brightspear. They found out I could throw one, and that was that.'

Marcellus chuckled as he tied off the sash. 'Well, it could be worse,' he said. 'It could have been Nobody Wolfsdinner, from what I've heard.'

Kerin found himself laughing too. There was far more to this man than he had suspected when they met at the praetor's feast. 'Marcellus,' he said tentatively, as he rose from the couch, 'do you treat slaves?'

The haruspex gave him a searching look. 'You must understand that the occasion does not arise,' he said. 'To men like the praetor, slaves are a commodity. If they become sick, one does not waste too much time or expense on treating them. One replaces them, as one would a broken amphora, or a worn-out chariot horse. But that is not really what you are asking.'

'No,' Kerin admitted.

'Come,' Marcellus said, taking his arm 'Let us walk in the garden for a moment.' They passed through a graceful archway onto a square of springy green turf. The doves rose in a soft rush of cooing and beating wings and flew up to the rooftop. The scent of jasmine and lilies enveloped them like an invisible veil.

'It's lovely here,' Kerin said. 'It reminds me how much I miss greenness and fresh air.'

Marcellus nodded. 'I suppose that most men miss their home, whether or not the absence is of their choosing. There are times when I pine for Ravenna, and the sound of the wind in the olive groves. Shall we sit here beside the pool? I cannot treat your slave girl; Severus Maximus would never allow it. They say she has been beaten?'

'Yes,' Kerin said. 'Her whole body is bruised, and there are other marks – teeth? Nails? God knows, but they must give her pain.'

Marcellus shook his head at the pointlessness of it all. 'Well,' he said, 'if you knew who did it, you would not be sitting here talking to me. No doubt he also beats his dog, and his wife, if he has one.' He looked intently at Kerin's shoulder. 'You know, that really is the most extensive bruise I have seen in a long time. You will need liberal quantities of arnica to dress it, and perhaps also a soothing draught to ease the pain. I shall get them made up this evening. Who knows, if the quantities are generous enough, you might even find that you have a little left over.' He looked up expectantly. Kerin smiled.

'Yes,' he said, with gratitude. 'I think I might.'

'You should sit here for a while,' said the haruspex, 'you will find that the medicine you took just now will make you drowsy. I myself am going to call on the praetor. Perhaps I should not say this, but Severus Maximus was never really suited to high office. An able administrator, but no good in a crisis. And no judge of men whatsoever.'

'Why do you say that?' Kerin asked.

'Because if he had been, he would have seen all this coming months ago,' Marcellus said, rising to his feet. 'I'm not saying that Vortigern had planned to behead Plicius, naturally; he was simply protecting his own. But something of the sort was going to happen, and I didn't need to consult the entrails to see it. It's only the beginning, of course.'

'What do you mean?' Kerin asked apprehensively.

'I mean that I can see a trail of blood stretching from here to a point far beyond the horizon,' Marcellus said. 'And you can see it too, if I'm not much mistaken. Do you remember what I asked you when we met first, at the praetor's feast?'

'About dreams?'

'Yes. You chose not to speak of it, and I respect your silence. But you have a visionary's eyes, and that is something I have never seen in a common warrior. Whatever the ins and outs of it, I suspect that you sometimes find it more of a burden than a blessing. As I do.'

Kerin looked up at the haruspex. In the small dark eyes, which could be so waspish when they chose, there was a compassion which he had not expected to see. 'Yes,' he said, relieved by the admission, and by the knowledge that he was not, after all, quite alone. 'We shall speak of it one day soon. Some men call me a prophet. It's not that at all, really. It's not something I usually talk about, but you're right, it can be a burden. And you're right about the trail of blood, too. I've seen it from the beginning. Not in any way I can explain. But it's as if – ' he hesitated. He had never tried to articulate it, even to Vortigern. 'It's as if the consequences I can foresee, and everything that's happening now, are two threads. Like two strands of the same rope, being woven together. I think a moment will come when they're woven too tightly to be separated. When the one will lead to the other. I don't know if that makes sense.'

Marcellus nodded. He seemed to Kerin to have shrunk, and to be gradually disappearing into a sea of green light, in which white blossoms and white doves swam and receded.

'Rest now, while I attend to that poor fool,' whispered the voice of the haruspex. Anything else he might have said was lost as Kerin sank into a deep and dreamless sleep.

* * *

The sounds insinuated themselves one by one into the warm blankness which Marcellus's potion had induced. The steady trickle of running water; voices talking in the distance, then breaking into laughter. Kerin shook himself awake. It was almost dark, but the garden was bathed in a flickering yellow light. There was no way of telling if this was twilight or dawn. For a moment nothing was in focus. Someone was sitting on the low wall which encircled the fountain. A man; big, broad-shouldered, dressed in white. Kerin blinked, shook his head and looked again.

'Cheldric!' he exclaimed, with an involuntary smile.

'Ah!' the Saxon said with relief. 'At last you wake. I wait and I wait.' He rose to his feet with a grunt. 'You hurt now?' he asked. Kerin investigated with caution.

'Yes,' he said, wincing as he flexed his shoulder. 'But not as much as before. What on earth have they done to you?'

'They bath me!' Cheldric said, with grievous indignation. 'They rub, rub until I have no skin. Now I smell like girl, like pretty flower.' He held out his large hand, redolent of lavender and sandalwood. Kerin grinned.

The Saxon's long hair shone, gleaming and golden in the torchlight. His round face was pink and scrubbed, and they had dressed him in a neat white tunic, brown breeches and well-made brown boots.

'Much better,' Kerin said. 'You might have the women after you now, instead of the dogs. How long have I been asleep?'

'All day and all night,' said Cheldric. 'See, over there, the sun comes. And now we leave. Outside is my cart.'

Kerin sat up straight. 'A cart? Already? Where did you get it?'

Cheldric winked. 'Outside also is Lucius. He tells you. You put on clothes instead of girl's dress, and you come.'

Lucius was standing in the street outside the trades-men's entrance of the praetorian residence, holding the bridle of a big, well-fed grey mule. The animal was harnessed to a solid-looking cart whose contents were covered with an oiled waterproof blanket. Eryr was hitched to the back of the cart, tacked up ready for the journey, with Kerin's weapons slung from the saddle.

'Where did all that come from?' Kerin asked.

'From my father's yard,' said Lucius. 'Don't worry, he approved it. He prefers not to get involved in politics if he can avoid it, but he's completely on your side in all this. And anyway, I owe you for a horse, don't I? Not to mention the prospect of a promotion.' He gave a self-conscious smile. 'I'm truly grateful, lord. You've gone to a lot of trouble.'

'Not really,' Kerin said. 'The promotion wasn't my doing, and you'll be expected to earn it. As for the horse, it's up to you to make it worth my while. By the time I get back, I expect you to be able to stay on it without a saddle.'

'There's something else, too,' Lucius said cautiously. 'The goat. Neither I nor my sister could really understand what it was all about. We appreciate the animal, of course, but –'

'It's an excellent milking strain,' said Kerin, who would have cut his own throat rather than admit to his moment of weakness at the market. 'Goat's milk strengthens the bones, you know.'

Lucius gave him an unblinking polite smile. 'Well, yes, lord. And I suppose we could breed from it. After all, we couldn't very well eat a gift, could we? And please, do call round for a meal and some wine when you get back; we still haven't discussed our evening with Manius.'

Kerin could hardly believe that the incident had happened, so distanced was it by subsequent events. He peered under the blanket to see what was in the cart.

'Some spare clothes and blankets for the journey,' said Lucius. 'I didn't think the praetor would miss them. Your medication, from Marcellus *magister*. And some bits and pieces belonging to the cook.' Cheldric smiled and stared up at the brightening sky. Lucius took Kerin's arm as the Saxon hauled himself up into the driver's seat. 'I saw the Lord Vortimer when I was in the stables just now. He wanted to know what I was doing with your horse. He was saddled up ready to leave, so I took it that he was going with you. But he told me he was off on business of his own, and I shouldn't tell his father. I didn't feel too comfortable about that, lord. I know the Lord Vortimer's a good friend of yours, and I don't mean any disrespect at all, but I don't think he should have asked me to lie to my commanding officer.'

'No, he shouldn't,' Kerin said. 'But with any luck, it won't arise. Vortigern isn't likely to ask you about his son. If he does, though, you'll have to tell him the truth.' He smiled, wishing to make light of it. It had been a harrowing few days, and he needed no reminding of the way in which events were nibbling at the fabric of a friendship he had once thought indestructible. Lucius smiled back, but there was a shadow there which told Kerin that he had understood.

'Is there anything I can do for you while you're away?' he asked.

'Yes,' Kerin said. He delved under the blanket and drew out two bottles from the basket Marcellus had provided. 'Give these to Sha'ara. Tell her that the large one's for pain, and the small one for bruises. Tell no-one else. And guard Constans. Keep him safe. He's my responsibility as a rule. I always escort him when he goes out, and I make sure that there are reliable guards outside his door day and night. Just make it your own responsibility while I'm away, and keep your ears open for any gossip in the city. He's not king by everyone's consent, and you never know what might be going on under the surface.'

'I will,' Lucius said. And then, cautiously, 'I can't help thinking that it would be a good idea for him to have his own bodyguard, lord. We do our best, but sometimes we get called away for ridiculous things, like escorting the praetor's wife when she takes her dog for a walk. You could do with a few good fighting men with nothing else to do except protect the king.'

'Yes,' Kerin said. 'You're probably right. Mention it to the Lord Vortigern. He wouldn't have promoted you if he expected you to stand there with your mouth shut. And there's another thing. Stop calling me lord, take my horse's saddle off, and put it under the blanket with everything else. Then put my spears in the back and the rest of my weapons under the driver's seat. I'm going to ride home on the wagon with my cook, like the low-born bastard that I am.'

They did not see much activity on their way to the city gates. A few ox-drivers harnessing their animals; a baker stoking his fires and pulling out the first loaves, their appetising smell overlaying the pervasive city stench of excrement and decay. Hefydd and twenty of his boys were waiting outside the gates, mounted and heavily armed, ready for the road. They chuckled to see Kerin sitting on the wagon beside Cheldric.

'Where's Kerin Brightspear, then?' Hefydd asked.

'I can't remember where I left him,' Kerin said. 'Lead on, Hefydd; you're in charge today.'

The mounted men moved off, singing one of their old battle-hymns, too drunk on the promise of home-coming to need any liquid assistance. Cheldric chirruped to the mule and drew the wagon in at the tail of the column. Without being asked, four of the warriors reined back and fell in behind them, a reassuring re-arguard. Perhaps they had all been told that their own lives depended on escorting their charges safely home.

Around a third of the way between Londinium and Glevum there was a crossroads where another well-preserved Roman road crossed the main highway, running away to cities north and south. Just beyond it lay the town which the Romans had called Calleva Atrebatum, a big, prosperous place with fine buildings and towering city walls. A warren of travellers' drinking dens had grown up outside the gates. Hefydd dispatched his boys to the first alehouse. The chirpy reception from the serving girls suggested that they were no strangers there.

'Will you come with us?' Hefydd asked.

'No,' Kerin said. 'Get your boys fed and watered. We'll stay here with the wagon. It looks peaceful, and if you sit at those tables outside, you'll see any trouble start.'

In truth, he preferred to avoid the noisy conviviality of the alehouse, the curious looks which would have greeted his cuts and bruises, and the cheerfully tactless explanations which Hefydd's boys could be relied upon to provide. He stretched his aching limbs as they trooped off, and took stock of the surroundings. A short distance away, five horsemen were resting in the shade of a dusty oak on top of the bank beside the road. They had dismounted and were sitting on the ground, sharing bread and salt meat while their animals picked at the sparse turf. Kerin did not recognise them at all, but the fact that they wore smart, identical guards' tunics and had trimmed their beards suggested some organisation. The tunics were red, and bore the image of a golden falcon with talons outstretched. Kerin knew that he had seen it before, but couldn't place it. Londinium was awash with the stuff.

Something was happening. One of the men stood up, and the rest followed, straightening tunics and brushing off the dust. A rider was coming out of the city gates on a fine grey horse. Kerin would have recognised him a mile off, but Rufus paid no heed to the wagon drawn up on the verge or its down-at-heel occupants. He nodded an acknowledgement to the men outside the alehouse, who looked none too pleased to see him, and said something to the guardsmen which made them gather up their belongings and see to their horses.

'Not speaking, then?' Kerin said loudly. Hefydd's boys chortled and supped their ale. Rufus came down from the bank in a frenzy of polished hooves, gilded saddlery and sharp, well-made clothes. You look like a king's son, Kerin thought, and I look like a common ruffian who's just had a scrap. He smiled, without humour. There was an element of truth in both assumptions, probably.

'Jesus' blood,' Rufus exclaimed, staring in consternation at Kerin's bruised face and strapped shoulder. 'What happened? Why didn't you send for me?'

'I would have done if I'd known where to look for you,' Kerin said. He had tried to keep the sting out of it, but after the events of the past two days, that was beyond him. Rufus reined back.

'I couldn't stay under the same roof as my father after that travesty,' he said. 'But I'd have come for you. You must know that.'

Kerin looked up at him and shrugged. 'It doesn't matter,' he said. 'I got away with it.'

'No thanks to me,' Rufus said, avoiding his eyes.

'No,' Kerin said. 'No thanks to you.' He supposed that he was waiting for Rufus to ask him what had happened, but the question didn't come. Rufus's hand moved half consciously to his crucifix. Kerin wondered if he was struggling with some of the things it asked of him.

'Who's going to guard the monk while you're away?' Rufus asked. Kerin shook his head. For God's sake, he thought; I'm sitting here looking like a battle casualty, and that's all you can ask me?

'I've no idea,' he said. 'Why don't you do it? You're the Christian.'

Rufus snorted. 'Even if I didn't have more important things to do, my father wouldn't let me anywhere near him,' he said.

'No,' Kerin conceded. 'You're right about that.' He looked up into Rufus's face – so unhappy, and so racked with uncertainties, for all his righteous anger – and found that, in spite of everything, he wanted nothing more than to mend everything that had broken, and make their life what it once had been. 'Come with me,' he said. 'Come on. Get rid of those oafs, and come home with me. We can get drunk and bed some girls, and forget about all this for a while.'

'I can't,' Rufus said. 'You know I can't. And I know that it's no good asking you to come with me either. You made a choice, when you sold your soul to my father.'

'This isn't about anyone's soul,' Kerin said, keeping his voice calm. 'It's about making an army out of nothing, before we all get slaughtered in our beds.'

'And you think that's all there is to it?' Rufus

demanded. The colour was rising in his face. Kerin knew that he was not equal to an argument.

'No,' he said. 'But at the moment, it's what matters most.'

'Then I'm leaving,' Rufus said crisply. 'What you do next is for you to decide.'

His guards crowded up behind him; Maximian Galba's men, Kerin realised now, as he remembered the pair who had attended their master at the curia. Finding that he had nothing more to say, he raised his hands in resignation. Rufus reined back without another word and turned his horse towards the road. Kerin sat on the cart and watched the thin pall of grey dust recede into the south west. He blinked, and found that his eyes were full of tears. Cheldric looked at him without curiosity or censure.

'Once I tell you that I have no friends, no people,' he said. 'Sometimes, is easier that way.'

Kerin supposed that he was right, but his whole life had been built on other foundations, and he could not acknowledge it. Cheldric, understanding all this, went round to the back of the wagon and lugged out a large wicker basket which he heaved up unto the driver's seat, removing the lid with an extravagant flourish.

'What on earth?' Kerin said.

'Is from the kitchen,' said his beaming cook. 'I make, so I take. Is fair, no?'

Kerin tried to gather his wits. Starvation would serve no purpose, he supposed. 'Yes,' he said. 'Very fair. What have we got?'

'Pigeons stuffed with liver and rosemary,' said Cheldric. 'Figpeckers cooked in honey. Here some cheese from the cow, and here some dates and candied fruit from Master Gallus's boat. Underneath, a leg of the pig. And also in the back, with my knives and my pots, a big jar of *falernum*. Today I am the lord, and I say we waste enough time here. We eat, we drink, and then we go home to Cambria.'

15

The breakers of a rising evening tide roared on the shingle beach at the mouth of the valley. A light wind was blowing in off the sea, raising fine spindrift from the crests of the rolling waves and shivering the grass on the sand dunes above the tide mark. The long beach was quiet, except for a handful of men fishing in the choppy water where the river ran into the sea. Sounds drifted from the settlement in the valley; a smith hammering at his anvil, cattle lowing in the stock pens, the steady clack of the weavers' looms.

Down on the dunes Kerin lay on his back amongst the sea grass, watching the movement of clouds and the soundless passage of gulls overhead. For a long time he lay perfectly still, enjoying the pleasant warmth of the sand beneath his body and the elusive valley smell which came and went with the wind. How he had missed that smell; the sweet, mingled scent of bracken, salt and gorse blossom. The narrow streets and palatial buildings of Londinium seemed of another world. Kerin sat up and flexed his shoulder. It was still painful, although Marcellus's ointment had helped. His young grey horse, hitched to a driftwood log nearby, was watching him attentively. Blaidd, the wolf, four years old, warhorse in training. Kerin whistled softly and the horse blew through his nostrils in reply. If a man came over that sand dune and grabbed me, you'd kill him stone dead, Kerin thought.

Out on the beach Rufus's brothers were racing their mares in the surf, just rounding the foot of Penrhyn Fawr, the towering headland which separated the valley and its sheltered bay from the vast expanse of firm beach to the west. The two riders came flying up over the soft sand and jumped off, leaving their sweating animals to nibble at the bramble bushes. Paschent, the younger of the two, withdrew to a sun-bleached log further along the tide mark and started whittling a piece of driftwood. Katigern, his older brother, flung himself down on the sand beside Kerin. He resembled Vortigern in build, broad-shouldered, supple and powerful; but from somewhere far back in his ancestry he had inherited light brown curly hair and a pair of sparkling pale blue eyes. Unfortunately, the progenitors who had given him his amiable disposition had not provided a lightning intelligence to illuminate it.

'Where have you hidden that cook, then?' he asked.

'He's asleep in my house,' Kerin said. 'Poor Cheldric, it's probably the longest journey he's ever been on in his life. He's cooking a goose for me tonight, though.'

'For you?' Katigern hooted. 'Just for you?'

'Well,' Kerin said, 'for us.'

'I should think so, too,' Katigern said, beaming. 'And I hope you're not running off back to Londinium too soon, either. Life has been rather dull around here lately.'

Kerin could see that it might have been, for a young man whose greatest pleasures were riding, hunting and feasting, and who had been deprived of most of his usual companions-in-arms. 'Not just yet,' he said. 'There's plenty to dislike about Londinium.'

Katigern scratched the side of his nose. 'I did hear that you had rather enjoyed yourself there, though,' he said, with a mischievous smile. 'And that you'd learned a trick or two.'

'I don't know what you're talking about, Kat,' Kerin said airily. Katigern dissolved in mirth.

'You'd better ask Mabli, then,' he said, recovering himself. 'She's still wearing the smile you put on her face last night.'

Kerin found, to his disgust, that he was blushing furiously. He was well aware that Faria had taught him a few subtleties, but to have them mentioned here on home ground was not his idea of sport. In the end he did not really want to say where he had acquired them, far less to admit that he had not known them in the first place.

'Mabli?' he said sourly. 'She's like a bitch on heat. She'd enjoy it with Caradog.'

This set Katigern off again as he visualised pert little Mabli, the silversmith's daughter, rolling around in a sweaty tangle with the ancient druid. 'Oh no,' he said eventually, wiping his eyes. 'She assured me that she's never known such pleasure. You're selling yourself short, Kerin Brightspear. Or should I say Kerin Stiffspear? Oooch!' He yelped as a pebble clipped the side of his head.

'If Londinium had been that wonderful, I'd have stayed there,' Kerin said grumpily, and felt disgusted with himself. Faria deserved better. It was only an accident of fate that had made her a slave. He thought for a moment how pleasant it would have been to have her beside him, and then realised that it would be impossible. She would wither in Henfelin, like a rose in the frost. He drew his knees up and rested his head on them, feeling suddenly bereft.

'It's those portents again,' Katigern said sternly. 'You and Rufus are as bad as each other. You spend so much time worrying about tomorrow that you ruin today's pleasures.' He laughed and slapped Kerin on his injured shoulder. 'Why don't we all go to Londinium, then? Hefydd says it's overflowing with wine and beautiful women. And it's quiet enough here. The people are happy.'

'I know,' Kerin said. 'Our own people won't complain, but others will. Eldof of Glevum for one. He might not be much of a Christian, but he wouldn't have picked a monk for king.'

'And neither would Rufus, if the truth be told,' Paschent said from the sanctuary of his log. The others looked up. It was the first time he had spoken since they left the citadel. Kerin had never been able to get any sense out of Paschent, but all in all he pitied rather than disliked him; an indifferent fighter, hopeless with girls and disdained by both his brothers.

'Enough of your pig shit,' Katigern snapped. 'Are you saying Rufus isn't loyal to our father?'

Paschent did not look up. He remained squatting on the sand, whittling away, a narrow-shouldered lad with lank black hair, a thin, pinched face and close-set dark eyes. There was no question at all that he was Vortigern's son, but Kerin sometimes wondered where

Paschent had come from. Katigern, at least, could ride and fight; he had always hunted and harried and enjoyed a jar of ale, and all those things had forged a deep bond of affection with his father, even though Kat's dim-wittedness often drove Vortigern to distraction. But where to begin with Paschent? He didn't care to hunt. He ducked out of battle training at the flimsiest excuse. No man could help being born smaller and weaker than his brothers; Lud's youngest son would never match Macsen and Custennin for strength, but he had fought to make himself indispensable in other ways. Elir the archer, the horse-handler, was as valuable to the warband as any of its swordsmen. Paschent didn't have that sort of grit. He showed no interest in improving his fighting skills, or even in developing the talents he had. All Vortigern's efforts to encourage the scholar in his youngest son had met with indifference. Paschent didn't give a fig for history or poetry, and never went near his father's vast library of Latin manuscripts, despite being one of the sharpest learners the monks had ever taught.

'Have you lost your tongue, you little worm?' Katigern bawled. 'I said, did you call Rufus a traitor to our father?'

Paschent laid down his knife and examined the driftwood. 'I said that Rufus wouldn't have the monk for king,' he said. 'And if that makes him a traitor, then yes, I suppose that's what I called him.'

Katigern roared and lunged forward. Paschent squealed and fled away down the beach.

'Let him be, Kat,' Kerin said. Katigern turned.

'But he –'

'Let him be,' Kerin said. 'He's right.'

Katigern's eyes narrowed. 'Right? What do you mean, he's right? He calls Rufus a traitor, and you tell me he's *right?*'

Kerin looked up at Katigern, who was staring at him with bemused incredulity. His enquiries had not revealed much concern about a monk's piety amongst Henfelin's half-hearted Christians, most of whom kept one foot in the druids' camp, just in case. The followers of the old gods were simply wondering what all the fuss was about. But Kerin's memory of the confrontation at the crossroads outside Calleva lingered like an unhealed sore.

'I don't understand,' Katigern said blankly, as Kerin got up and unhitched his horse.

'It's very simple,' Kerin said, swinging into the saddle. 'For Rufus, the faith is either everything, or it's nothing. And he thinks your father has sinned against God by making that monk king, without even getting the blessing of a churchman.'

'But what choice was there?' Katigern asked. 'Constantine is dead, and everyone knows that Ambrosius and Uther are only children.'

'Monks, boys, it's all the same,' Kerin said. 'Constans won't make a good king if he lives to be a hundred, and that's got nothing to do with being a monk.'

Katigern picked up a pebble and hurled it at the grass. 'What are you saying, then?' he asked. 'Is my father stupid, for choosing the wrong king?'

'Oh no,' Kerin said. 'Your father knows quite well what he's doing.' He could have added that there was no point in falling out over it, as Constans would not be king for long; but that information was not his to share. Katigern blinked, the logic far beyond him.

'Can you talk to Rufus?' he asked. 'He's your blood brother. You can talk some sense into him, if anyone can.'

'I can't, Kat,' Kerin said. 'Nothing I say will make any difference. His faith is more important to him than anything else. Me, you, your father, anything. He's not a traitor in the way you mean, but his faith comes first. So if you want to help your father – and I'm sure you do – just keep telling everyone here that Vortigern is the only man who can keep the Picts out and stop the Romans coming back to crush us all over again. Tell them that everything your father has done is for that. To keep the kingdom safe.'

'And what if Rufus comes back and argues with me?' Katigern said unhappily. 'He could always tie me up in knots.'

'Just remember that for him, you're much less important than God,' Kerin said. 'And that for your father, nothing's more important than this place, and these people. Tell everyone that. It's all they need to know, for now.'

Katigern scrambled onto his horse and galloped off at full tilt along the beach. Kerin sat on Blaidd as the drumming hoofbeats faded, and watched another pair of fishermen trudging down the beach with their drag net. Paschent came plodding towards him, still clutching the fragment of whitened driftwood. He had hewn it into the shape of a rough crucifix. Looping his horse's reins over his arm, he took the cross and snapped it neatly in two.

'You'd better give this to Rufus,' he said, reaching up to press the pieces into Kerin's hand. 'And tell him not to get into such a lather about that monk. It's a waste of energy. I don't give Constans more than a couple of months, do you?'

Then he gave a wicked smile – the single attribute he seemed to have inherited from his father – and sauntered off along the tideline, whistling to himself.

Kerin rode slowly up from the beach, letting the tranquillity of the evening enfold him. The wind had dropped and a fine mist had come in with the tide, cloaking the countryside in its soft whiteness and obscuring all the landmarks he knew so well. Crib Garw, the long moorland ridge to the north where the deer ran; the flat summit of Penrhyn Fawr, sacred to the druids long before the monks' faith raised its voice. And there was something else up there too, high on the crag to the east of the river, invisible in the mist and yet drawing Kerin with the power of the pole star; Vortigern's citadel, the home of the *uchelwyr*, the high-born, perched like an eyrie on the cool headland.

In the valley, most of the men were home from the fields after the day's work, and there was a convivial buzz about the place as some tended their draught animals while others unloaded wagons. The scent of wood smoke hung heavy in the air as cooking fires were lit, and children careered madly in and out of the houses chasing dogs, chickens and each other. Kerin felt a stab of regret as he saw himself and Rufus in those grubby, carefree faces and wondered where the time had gone.

There was already a noisy, good-humoured crowd

outside the alehouse on the bank of the river. Kerin dismounted and tied Blaidd to the hitching rail. Two men were coming out of the alehouse, tankards in hand. The shorter of the two was the archdruid Caradog, undoubtedly the oldest man Kerin had ever known; the other was his younger cousin Cynfawr, the chief bard. Caradog was wearing a rough brown robe instead of the flowing green garment he wore when performing his official duties, and was leaning on a gnarled oak staff. Cynfawr, who never dressed below his station, was swathed in a voluminous blue cloak over a spotlessly white tunic. He carried himself with a haughty pride which reminded anyone who might have forgotten that he was the scion of a long line of gifted poets.

'Ha! Young Kerin Brightspear!' Caradog hailed him in his cracked, wheezing voice. Kerin smiled. He liked Caradog. Stiffness and aching bones had made the druid crotchety in his old age, but there was a well of compassion beneath, for anyone who knew how to see it. His pale blue eyes seemed to look right into the soul of a man. Kerin bowed his head respectfully to the two venerable men and they all sat down together at one of the beer-stained benches. 'What's this news from Londinium, then?' said the druid, all excitement. 'Has he done it, then? Is it true that he's made that monk king?'

'Yes, it is,' Kerin said.

'Ha!' the druid cackled with vehement delight. 'That's one in the eye for that self-righteous Abbot Iustig. You'll have to write a poem about this, Cynfawr.'

The bard, who shared his cousin's dislike of the

monks but not his lack of subtlety, looked at the druid with a tolerant smile. No one would have guessed that the tall, elegant Cynfawr, with his well-combed grey hair and beard, was related to wiry little Caradog, whose grizzled mop looked like the fleece of a mountain sheep. Unlike his cousin, Cynfawr never had much to say for himself; but it all came out in the poems. He revered Vortigern with a passion which even Kerin found startling, and every drop of it went into the epics he composed for feast nights in the chieftains' hall. Kerin smiled his thanks as a mug of foaming ale arrived in front of him.

'What do you think about it all, then?' the bard asked. 'A monk for king! Who'd have thought it?'

'No-one would have thought it, and some people don't like it,' Kerin said. 'But someone had to be made king, so that we could get on with things. We'll be marching north in spring, and that isn't much time to raise the sort of army we'll need.'

'The Lord will do it,' Cynfawr said, with the sublime confidence of one who had no idea what he was talking about. Like most people here, he usually referred to Vortigern simply as 'the Lord'. It never caused any confusion, since there was no-one else they could possibly have meant.

'Who doesn't like it, then?' said Caradog, with a wheeze and a rattle. 'Eh? Who doesn't like it, Kerin Brightspear?'

'Well, Eldof of Glevum isn't too happy about it,' Kerin said. Caradog screwed his face up.

'A trifle. Who else?'

'Some of the Romans,' Kerin said. 'Or at least, the

people who call themselves Romans. The ones who'd still get the legions back here if they could.'

Caradog's eyes turned cold as a blade. It might have been generations before his time, but everyone knew how the Romans had massacred the druids when they first came to the islands, and no-one in the West had ever forgotten it, least of all those who wore the mantle of the priesthood. 'May the spirits devour them,' Caradog murmured, staring up at the sky. Cynfawr patted his shoulder.

'All in good time,' he said. 'I have ale to drink, and a poem to write. And you, I should imagine, have to burn some sacred branches or whatever else you do, to thank the gods that we have a strong leader like the Lord to hold this poor monk's hand.'

Caradog looked up as Kerin downed his ale and rose to leave. 'I will light the fires,' he said. 'Tonight, when the sun goes. And I'll ask the spirit guardian to watch over the Lord. He may call himself a Christian, but here in his heart –' the druid pressed a hand to his chest and winked one rheumy eye. 'There's some very old gods living in that dark place, Kerin Brightspear.'

* * *

The lamps were being lit in the houses of the *uchelwyr*, the high-born, and the citadel looked as welcoming as ever when Kerin rode through the gap in the stockade. The gates were standing open, as they always did between dawn and nightfall; Irish marauders aside, there had been no threat to Vortigern on his home ground for more than twenty years. It was a mystery to many why he had chosen Henfelin. The family had owned most of Isca Silurum, so the older people said, as well as property in Caerwent, and estates along the whole of the southern coast; and that was before Vortigern got his hands on Magnus Maximus's daughter Sevira, and all the land that came with her. And yet, for reasons never explained, he would not set foot in Isca, and had chosen to make his home on a wild headland, like a common warrior.

The door of Kerin's house faced south and opened onto a central square around which the dwellings of the other leading men were arranged. Most of the houses had a wooden bench outside, where the warriors sometimes drank on fine evenings, or their women gathered to talk, sew, feed children or prepare food. Lud's wife Mora was out there now, mending a woollen tunic and chatting to her servant Elin, who was picking over a basket of herbs. She looked up and gave an affectionate smile, which Kerin returned. He would always be grateful to Mora for finding room in her crowded household for the orphaned baby he once was. Granted, his abiding memories were of getting under her feet and sleeping in that wretched cupboard; but she had fed him and clothed him, and given him a place beside her hearth fire. Mora had not aged gracefully. It was hard to believe the older men, who said that she had once been a lithe beauty who could sit a horse and wield a sword when necessary. Her hair was brindled grey as a badger's coat now. Six children and a well-stocked larder had made her almost as broad as she was tall. But Kerin still had a vague memory of the young woman who had patched up his cuts and bruises, and carried him on her hip; for him her dark eyes and her smile were still beautiful.

'Good to see you back, lad,' she said. 'What's that man of mine up to in the big city?'

'Doing what he always does,' Kerin said. 'Trying to keep Vortigern out of trouble.' Mora laughed and shook her head.

'Those two,' she said.

Kerin's house, gifted to him when its owner was killed in a skirmish, was similar to Lud's. Some people had seen the gift as an honour. Kerin suspected that Vortigern was simply glad to get rid of him, once he was a young man with his own weapons and horse gear and the prospect of marriage and a family somewhere along the track. The houses were sturdily built of local timber and thatched with reeds from the nearby saltmarsh. Only the hall of the chieftains was larger; but that was as imposing as any timber-built house could possibly be, with its great dining-hall, a warren of private chambers and a central lookout tower from which a watchman had a clear view along the coastline and across the hills inland.

A voice hailed Kerin as he dismounted. A small grey-haired man wearing a neat brown tunic and breeches was sitting on the bench outside the chief-tains' hall, mending a fishing rod. He put it aside and ambled over, squat, round-faced, smiling. Cenydd, the chief servant of Vortigern's household, was a little older than Vortigern himself and had known all the young warriors from their cradles.

'Hello, lad,' he said, taking Blaidd's reins. 'Good to be back on home ground, then?'

'Very good,' Kerin said. He drew aside the blanket which screened the doorway of his house and peered inside. 'Has there been any activity in here?'

'Not that I've seen,' Cenydd said curiously. 'Why? Should there be?'

Kerin winked. 'I'll introduce you later,' he said. 'Please could you get one of the boys to rub my horse down and give him a feed? I've got other things to do at the moment.' He went into his house, whistling, leaving Cenydd standing in the square with the horse. Once inside, he tiptoed to one of the small windows and peeked out. Cenydd was in the horse pens with Blaidd, taking the tack off whilst trying to keep his eyes off Kerin's house. He thinks I've got a woman in here, Kerin thought, and by tomorrow morning everyone in the valley will know that I've come home from Londinium with two concubines and an illegitimate child on the way. He chuckled to himself, delighted with his contribution to the village gossip, and slipped out of his house by the back door. It was far too early to eat, and with any luck Mabli might have finished cleaning her father's workshop.

'Kerin Brightspear!' a voice hailed him from the gateway. Kerin groaned aloud. Bouncing around on his jenny donkey, beaming and waving gaily, along came Abbot Iustig. Kerin cursed his bad luck. Unless an invitation had been extended, the monks rarely came up to the citadel except at festive times like Easter and Christmastide. They kept themselves to themselves over at Caerwenn, a wooded cliff beyond the big headland, whose shady depths concealed the caves where they lived. In the stone chapel nearby Abbot Iustig prayed three times a day with his brothers, blessed the marriages of the Lords of Henfelin, and begged for God's mercy on their souls when they transgressed; something which was likely to keep him busy for a while, the way things were going.

'Hello, Father,' Kerin said, trying not to sound too unenthusiastic. His mind was already halfway into Mabli's bed; and besides, it was hard to be entirely amicable towards anyone who had the abbot's uneasy relationship with Vortigern. Kerin had watched them for years, circling each other like a couple of wary, hostile dogs, and he was no nearer than he had ever been to finding out what lay behind it. There was no escape, so he invited the abbot to sit on the bench outside his house. Iustig sat, a sturdy little man with a lined brown face and calloused hands. He could do two men's work in the fields, but was a grown man when Vortigern was a lad at his father's knee, so he must have seen sixty summers, if not more. He had kept his sprightly gait and bird-bright eyes, and the younger monks who lived under his benevolent authority complained that his energy wore them out.

'How is your shoulder?' he enquired.

'Much better, thank you,' Kerin said, raising his arm to demonstrate.

'It happened in a fight, I understand?' said the abbot.

'Not at all,' Kerin said. 'I drank too much wine one night, and fell down one of the praetor's marble staircases.'

Iustig smiled, in a guarded way which suggested

that a lie was suspected. 'I hope someone's taking good care of that poor young monk while you're away. Rufus told me that he was your particular responsibility.'

'Indeed,' Kerin said. 'I have a friend in the praetorian guard, and I left him with strict instructions for guarding Constans at all times.'

'Thank heavens for small mercies,' said Iustig. There was an uncomfortable silence. 'What's really happening?' the abbot asked.

'Well,' Kerin said, 'someone's sure to have told you that Vortigern crowned the monk himself, so I won't waste my breath denying it. But if you've heard that Constans was dragged from the monastery, that's completely untrue. He couldn't wait to get away from Abbot Paulinus.'

Iustig raised his eyebrows. 'That much I can understand. I met Paulinus when we were both young men in training. He didn't want much to do with us poor simpletons from the West. Do you know anything about his friend Germanus, and his war against the Pelagians?'

'As much as I want to know,' Kerin said. 'And quite enough to know which side I'm on.'

Iustig drew back, as if sensing the beginning of an argument he didn't want to have. In a vague way, Kerin was disappointed. He had never set much store by priestly guidance, but for all that, he felt that it should have been offered; or perhaps, after a jar of powerful ale, he just wanted the opportunity to shout it down.

'Idris's father is waiting for me,' the abbot said, rising to his feet. 'He has some concerns about his son. Are you acquainted with him?'

'Idris?' Kerin said. 'I know him, but not well. He's a few years younger than the rest of us – Rufus, Macsen and myself – so we never really bothered with him. I know he tried to talk his way into Vortigern's warband, but Lud wouldn't take him. I don't think he trusted Idris, but I'm not sure why. The lad's a good enough fighter, so it must have been something else.'

Iustig raised his eyebrows, as if he might have had an idea where the rub was. 'Well, I shall go and meet the father, and see what a Christian and a druids' man can find to agree about. When you see Rufus, tell him that he should make things up with Vortigern, if he can.'

Kerin looked up, alarmed rather than reassured. 'You don't agree with him?' he asked.

'It's not a question of agreement,' Iustig said. 'What Vortigern has done is completely wrong, but Rufus won't make it right by running off to Paulinus. The abbot may be a man of God, but he's hand-in-glove with the old Roman faction, and his brother Maximian Galba is a fervent supporter of young Ambrosius. If Vortigern's own son goes to them full of wrath and indignation, there'll be war before you can blink your eyes. Tell Rufus that.' Kerin got up, feeling the ale begin to bite. 'I'll pray for you,' the abbot said.

'Yes please, Father,' Kerin said. 'I'm not the heathen you might think, to hear me talk.'

'I know,' Iustig said, patting his arm. 'And tell Vortigern not to tempt God any further. I shall pray for him, too. It's probably the last thing he wants, but tell him I'm going to do it, anyway.'

'I will,' Kerin said; and thought he caught, before

Iustig had time to disguise it, a look of acute unease which seemed out of place in a man who claimed to be at peace with himself and his god. It could have been for Rufus, but Kerin's instinct told him that its roots lay somewhere older and darker. He tried to dismiss it; there were more urgent matters at hand.

'If Rufus comes back, will you speak to him?' he asked. 'You're probably the only man he'll listen to.'

'I'll do my best, but I don't know how much good it will do,' Iustig said. 'You've met Paulinus. You know how this thing works. Once it gets hold of people – ' he shook his head. Kerin looked at this kindly, troubled man, steeped in the teachings of his own childhood, and wondered where all this was leading. He thought of the peaceable, good-hearted Christians living amiably here alongside the druids and the people of no faith at all, and the thought filled him with dread.

16

Darkness was gathering. A fire of ash logs was crackling on the central hearth in Kerin's house. At the far end of the principal room, a door opened into the main bedchamber, currently in some disarray. There were two further doors, one at each side. Behind one of them Cheldric was still snoring. The goose which he was supposed to be cooking was still dangling from the rafters. Kerin looked at it wistfully. He had refused Cilydd's wife's pigeon stew earlier in the day in anticipation of the promised feast, but the goose didn't look as if it was going to be fit for Odin for some time yet. Mabli sat on the dining table, swinging her bare feet, and gave him an I-told-you-so look.

'Alright,' Kerin said gloomily. 'I know I should have had the stew.'

Mabli tossed her dark curls. 'That's the trouble with you,' she said knowingly.

'The trouble with me? What do you mean?'

'Oh, not just with you. With all of the *uchelwyr*. You're happy enough to share our beds, but you wouldn't lower yourselves to share our tables, would you.'

'That's nonsense, Mabli,' Kerin said, pulling the goose from its hook. 'I only refused the stew because I was expecting to eat this. Your father's a craftsman, anyway; one of the finest in Glywysing. Why should I look down on his family? Me, of all people?'

Mabli glared at him, then lowered her eyes. 'Alright,' she said grudgingly. 'You're not like the others. Custennin – well, you know what went on between us. But would he even look at me when he was with his well-born friends? Not to save his life.'

Kerin shrugged. 'Well, that's Custennin for you,' he said, laying the goose on the table.

'What are you doing?' Mabli asked curiously.

'I'm going to pluck this bird. Something most of the *uchelwyr* wouldn't be seen dead doing, I'll have you know. And then I'm going to kick Cheldric's arse out of bed so that he can cook it. You're welcome to join us, if you like.'

'Us?' Mabli enquired.

'Myself and Cheldric, and Katigern, if he turns up. You may as well. Unless it's beneath you, of course.'

Mabli laughed and her dark eyes sparkled. 'I like goose enough to endure it. What about Rufus and Paschent? Are they coming too?'

'No,' Kerin said. 'Rufus is a hundred miles away praying for his soul. And goodness knows what Paschent's up to, but I'm not about to share my goose with him.'

'Something's happened to Rufus,' Mabli said, frowning.

'What do you mean?' Kerin asked. Mabli batted aside a cloud of white down.

'I don't know, exactly,' she said. 'He used to be one for the girls, like you and Macsen, but now –' she shrugged. 'Even Branwen, Hefydd's daughter, says he won't give her the time of day, and they were all over each other before you went off to Londinium.'

'Yes,' Kerin said, plucking away. 'I know.'

'Branwen thinks he's found a girl in Londinium, but it's not that, is it,' Mabli said.

'No,' Kerin said, 'it's not that.'

Mabli gave him an accusing look. 'Kerin, please leave that goose alone and tell me what's going on. I've had Branwen crying on my shoulder these last two days, and it's all too much.'

Kerin put the goose aside and sat down on the bench alongside the table. 'Is that why you're here? On an errand for Branwen?'

'No, silly,' Mabli said, pouting. 'But she's my best friend, and if Rufus has been putting his sword in someone else's scabbard, I think she ought to know.'

'As you guessed,' Kerin said, 'it isn't that. Perhaps it would be better if it was, even for Branwen; but no. It's his faith. Rufus doesn't have much time for pleasure these days.'

'Unlike you,' Mabli sighed. Kerin looked up. She smiled, without affectation. 'It's alright, Kerin Brightspear,' she said. 'I know what sort of a bargain you and I have. One day you'll find yourself a well-born girl and bring her back here to your house, and father a dozen children on her. And one day I'll find a good brave man who'll think I'm a princess, instead of the silversmith's daughter. But until they come along –' she smiled impishly and ran the tip of her finger down Kerin's chest.

'Until they come along, there are better things to do than pluck a goose,' he said, reaching out for her. As his hands gripped her waist, a crash resounded from the room on the left. Kerin started. Mabli recoiled. The door flew open and Cheldric blundered out into the light, blinking and rubbing his eyes.

'Odin's teeth!' he cried desolately. 'The goose!' His eyes fell on the partially plucked carcass. Mabli giggled nervously. 'You do this?' Cheldric said wonderingly.

'*I* did it,' Kerin said indignantly. Cheldric snorted.

'You lie to me. Warriors do not do this work. This is your woman?'

'No, no,' said the forthright Mabli. 'At least, not in the way I think you mean. We've known each other since we were this tall –' she demonstrated – 'and we are very good friends.'

'Ah!' Cheldric said, with a knowing wink. Mabli grinned good-naturedly. 'You go now,' Cheldric said, rubbing his hands. 'I finish here.'

'Will it take long?' Kerin asked. 'I'm ravenous.'

Cheldric stumped over to the door and looked up at the sky, now the deep luminous blue of twilight. 'When the moon is over there, it will be ready,' he said, pointing to the tall trees on the western rim of the valley. 'This time I cut up small, to cook quickly. Who eats? You and the woman?'

'And Katigern, Vortigern's other son,' Kerin said. 'And you, of course.'

Cheldric blinked. 'I am cook,' he said. 'I am servant. Servants do not eat with warriors.'

'In my house they do,' Kerin said. Cheldric shook his head silently. He seemed to be overcome with emotion.

'In Londinium, we are lower than the dogs,' he said. 'Now I think I have died and gone to the Halls of the Aesir. I can stay here?'

'Yes,' Kerin said. 'Unless we go off to fight. Then

you'll have to come too, to cook for us. I'll get you a bigger cart. And some proper large cauldrons, and a few kitchen boys to do the peeling and chopping for you. Warriors have to eat, to keep their strength up.'

Cheldric clenched his fist. 'I feed you good,' he said. 'I pay back.'

'There's no debt,' Kerin said. 'Just do all the things we've agreed. It's enough.'

Cheldric's eyes brimmed with tears. 'Go!' he shouted fiercely. 'Out of my way! Or no-one eats!'

'I thought he was going to burst out weeping,' Mabli said as they walked, arms linked, away from the house. 'Why have you got him? You don't really need a cook, do you; you've always eaten at the Lord's table.'

'He deserves better than he had in Londinium,' Kerin said, taking a deep draught of the sweet sea air as they reached the open hillside overlooking the valley. He would keep to himself any ideas about the wisdom of befriending Saxons. They sat down on the rough grass with its tufts of sea-pinks and creeping vetch. Below them a sea of little yellow lights flickered warmly as people went indoors and lit their lamps. It was the calmest of evenings, quiet enough to hear the distant cries of sheep grazing inland on the high moors of Crib Garw.

'God, I've missed all this,' Kerin said softly.

'Stay here, then,' said Mabli, with her deathless logic.

'I can't.' Kerin squeezed her hand. 'You know I can't.'

'Why?' Mabli said anxiously. 'What do you think is going to happen?'

'I don't know,' Kerin said. 'But Vortigern's risked a

lot, making that monk king. He's done it for the best, I know; but not everyone sees it like that, and there are some powerful men in Londinium.'

'Not more powerful than the Lord, surely!' Mabli said dismissively.

'Well, no,' Kerin conceded, 'and most of them are terrified of him, without a doubt. But it only takes one knife in the dark.'

'No-one can kill the Lord,' Mabli said scornfully. 'He'd cut them open and hang them up like we hang the deer in the smoke-house.' Kerin grinned, amused by her confidence. 'He should take a wife,' Mabli said, out of the blue. Kerin looked up, astonished.

'Why? What would that solve?'

'Well,' Mabli said, 'if she was worth having, she might keep him at home, then he wouldn't go taking you all off to Londinium. And then you and I could –' Kerin laughed out loud, both at her nerve and at the thought of anyone keeping Vortigern anywhere for very long. 'Why are you laughing at me?' Mabli said indignantly. 'It shouldn't be difficult. He could have any woman he wanted.'

'Well, of course,' Kerin agreed. 'He's the most powerful man in the kingdom now.'

Now it was Mabli's turn to laugh. 'Not because of that,' she said scornfully. Kerin looked at her blankly, which only made her laugh all the more. She was still rolling helplessly around on the wiry grass when Katigern came up the track from the valley, carrying a vast pitcher of mead.

'What's the matter, you mad bitch?' he said, prodding her with his foot. Mabli sat up, giggling, and pulled her skirts over her knees.

'It seems that I said something amusing,' Kerin said stiffly. For reasons which he could barely understand, he felt deeply affronted. Katigern set down his pitcher. He squatted on the grass beside Mabli and began to fiddle idly with the drawstring which fastened her skirt at the waist. Mabli slapped his hand away impatiently.

'I'll bet she wouldn't do that if it was your father's hand,' Kerin said sourly.

'My father's hand?' Katigern said incredulously. 'Do you mean to say –'

'No, you halfwit,' Mabli said acidly. 'The Lord wouldn't look twice at me. But that's not what I said, is it?' She looked at Kerin with an arch little smile.

'No,' Kerin said, seizing the pitcher and gulping a mouthful of mead. It shouldn't have mattered to him, he knew, because there would never be anything more between him and Mabli than the bargain which she had so accurately described. The feeling was hardly jealousy, because nothing so base could come within the compass of his devotion to Vortigern. And yet it pained him. In everything else, like everyone else, he deferred to Vortigern without question; in everything except this small, unregarded area in which he had come to feel secure. The girls loved him. The pleasure was mutual, as far as he could tell. Now he began to wonder if he had imagined it all; if the ground here was as shaky as the rest of his life. He thought suddenly of pretty Flora, in that sad village beside the Via Legionis. Was it the case – could it possibly not be, when you thought about it – that the same force which drew and held the warriors could draw a woman, too? It had never occurred to Kerin, probably because he had so rarely seen Vortigern in a woman's company, unless you counted the older warriors' wives. All in all, Kerin believed the people who swore that he had lived like a monk since Sevira died. Oddly enough, every one of those same people also said that he had betrayed her shamelessly while she lived. Mabli gave Kerin a hesitant little smile, as if well aware that she had said something amiss.

'Do you still want me to help you eat your goose?' she asked.

'Yes,' Kerin said. 'Of course I do.' He got up, pulling Mabli with him. It was as pointless to curse her for telling the truth as it would have been to resent Vortigern for it; it wasn't the candle's fault when the moths got burned alive, after all. 'Go and fetch your sister,' he said, ruffling her hair. 'She can pick the bones.'

Mabli poked her tongue out at him and went skipping off down the track into the valley.

'What was all that about?' Katigern asked, straightening up and reaching for his pitcher.

'She thinks your father should find himself a wife,' Kerin said. 'According to Mabli, if he had a woman to keep him at home, he wouldn't go dragging all the lusty young warriors off to Londinium.'

Katigern snorted and took a draught of mead. 'After twenty years? I'll eat my horse's saddle if he ever does.'

He swallowed another mouthful of mead and handed the pitcher to Kerin. They turned and walked slowly back towards the citadel. An enticing smell was already drifting from the open doorway of Kerin's house. They sat down on the bench outside, leaning against the wall of the house, and waited for the goose to be ready. The pitcher passed back and forth between them, its contents inducing a mood of mellow indolence, beneath whose serene surface all unpleasantness slipped and vanished. A figure swam towards them out of the darkness.

'Good evening, young lords,' said Cenydd. 'Something smells delicious, if I may say so.'

'That,' Kerin said, with a concerted attempt at clarity, 'is goose fit for Odin.'

Cenydd chuckled. 'Well, I don't know who Odin is when he's at home, but it smells fit enough for me,' he said. There was a scuffling sound from inside the house and Cheldric peered round the door-post. There was a wary look on his face, as if he had heard the name of the deity being taken in vain. Kerin staggered to his feet and placed a restraining hand on the arms of both men.

'Cenydd, this is my cook, Cheldric. From now on, he'll be living here, in my house. Cheldric, this is Cenydd. He's the head of the Lord's household, and you must respect him and do as he tells you.'

'Cheldric,' Cenydd said curiously. 'That's a Saxon name. Where did you spring from, then?'

'Cheldric came from Londinium with me,' Kerin said. 'He used to cook for Severus Maximus, the praetor.'

Cenydd's eyebrows rose. 'A great household,' he said admiringly; then could not resist adding, 'as far as the Romans go, that is.' Cheldric was not to know that Cenydd's father had served the Roman governor of Caerwent, and had loathed every minute of it, but he was not slow to catch the note of disapproval.

'Is alright,' he said appreciatively. 'I hate Roman bastards, too.'

Cenydd grinned. There was nothing to beat the discovery of common ground. 'Cheldric,' he said, flinging an arm round the Saxon's brawny shoulders, 'come and show me what you're doing to that goose.' They disappeared inside the house, chatting amicably. Kerin leaned back against the warm wall and stared up at the stars, wishing that he could stay here in Henfelin forever. Then his peace was disturbed by the sound of raised voices. They were coming from the far side of the citadel, where the warriors of lower rank lived.

'I don't give a damn what the abbot told you,' one of them bawled. 'He's as wrong as you are. You and your petty little gods.'

'Petty?' an older voice roared back. 'What, petty like the sun and the rain, you halfwit? Get out of my house, and take this thing with you. You're no son of mine.'

Something banged into the fence of the horse pens. There was a scrabbling sound, then a tall, straight-backed figure marched out of the darkness with a little sack tucked under his arm. Long black hair, intense dark eyes. Idris. The sack was tied at the neck with something red. Over amongst the houses, the older man was trying to pacify a weeping woman. It was all lost on Katigern, who had probably been drinking for most of the day. He leaned across and gripped Kerin's arm.

'Kerin, I'd eat my horse's saddle,' he said earnestly.

17

The early sun had just broken the white veil of mist when Kerin saw the deer. At his back the Hafren gleamed like a silver ribbon, winding away down to Glevum and the estuary far beyond. Ahead of him, the gentle hills and wooded valleys of Eldof's country sparkled with the first frost of autumn. He was alone; the one thing Vortigern had forbidden. Only Hefydd's shamefaced wife had come out when he rode into the citadel on Carneddlas to meet his escort. She promised that she would kick her men out of bed and send them after him. They had not caught up; and so Kerin found himself here, a day from home, balancing the prospect of a succulent meal against the certain knowledge that he should settle for dried meat and ride on.

It did not take long. He was a practised hunter, as well as the finest spearman in Cambria. Hoisting the doe's carcass onto Eryr's back, he secured it with leather thongs and rode for cover. Ahead was a belt of tall beech trees which might provide a quiet nook where he could eat undisturbed. He noticed the first set of tracks at the edge of the wood, small and close-set, made by a pony's hooves. He hesitated, ears straining, but there was no sound apart from the wild calling of rooks overhead. The ground beneath the trees was furrowed and disturbed, probably by pigs. Soon Kerin detected the sweet scent of wood smoke and freshly-made bread. Beyond the wood lay a pleasant green valley. The sides sloped gently upwards towards high ridges clad with bracken. A solitary hut stood beside a stream, a fire burning outside. Further down the valley a herd of pigs moved over the short turf, rooting and wallowing in the mud pools. Kerin reined in outside the hut and listened, but there was no sound, so he slipped from the saddle and tiptoed warily towards the door. Then he froze, feeling between his shoulder-blades the unmistakable cold pressure of a spear point. He turned round slowly, and found himself face to face with a man who looked almost as old as Caradog the druid. He was little and bent with a big nose, runny blue eyes and skin like a horse's hide. His clothes were worn but clean; a simple brown shirt and breeches, with a jerkin of pigskin.

'Stay where you are!' he barked, prodding Kerin's chest with his spear. 'We've had enough of your kind round here.'

'Put your spear away,' Kerin said, smiling. 'I won't hurt you.'

The old man squinted at him from beneath bushy grey brows. 'You aren't from these parts,' he said, detecting an unfamiliar accent. 'Cambrian, aren't you?'

'That's right. I'm Kerin Brightspear, from Henfelin, in Glywysing.'

'And I'm Morvid the swineherd,' the old man said. 'There's not much to add to that, really.'

'Good morning to you, Morvid.' Kerin glanced downwards. 'And please, put away your spear.' The old man's brow puckered. He still seemed unconvinced. 'I'll share my meat with you, if you'll share your fire,' Kerin said. Morvid snorted.

'You may well offer, seeing that it's Eldof's deer,' he said, lowering his spear. 'Alright then; I suppose you'd have slit my throat by now if you'd had a mind to.' He looked towards the doorway of the hut. 'You can come out now,' he called. 'He means no harm.'

The skin which hung across the doorway moved aside and a boy stepped out, gripping a short-bladed knife. He was sturdy and dark-haired, about fourteen years old. His sharp brown eyes glared defiantly at Kerin.

'My grandson, Marc,' Morvid said. 'Come on, boy; this is Kerin Brightspear, a warrior from Cambria. Come out, and skin that deer.'

The boy ventured out of the door, still gripping his knife. He circled warily round the chestnut mare, then cut down the carcass and set to work on it. From time to time his eyes met Kerin's suspiciously.

'You must forgive the lad,' Morvid said, as they settled down beside the fire. 'He's learned mistrust from his cradle.' He fanned the flames with a rough blanket and tossed Kerin a warm piece of bread, then sat back with a grunt to await the meat.

'Why do you live here alone?' Kerin asked. 'I was expecting to find a village.'

'There is a village,' Morvid said. 'Just down the valley. I used to live there with my family. My wife's been dead for years, but the rest of us were contented enough. Then a famine came. Everyone was starving, so one night my son Rud sneaked off and pinched an ox. It was wrong of him, I know, but what's a man to do?'

'What happened?' Kerin asked. Morvid grimaced.

'The lord of these lands round here is a murdering thug called Bertil Redknife,' he said. 'Lord Eldof hates him, really, but he needs Bertil's warriors to help him keep that bastard Vortigern out of his city.'

'Bertil!' Kerin said. Morvid looked up.

'You know him?'

'We've met, yes. But he's no friend of mine.'

Morvid spat into the fire. 'When Bertil found out, he burned the village down. Rud and his wife were killed, and more than half our young men. The rest of the people blamed us, so I ran away with Marc, and here we are.'

'What about Bertil?' Kerin asked. 'Is he back from Londinium?'

'Yes, more's the pity,' Morvid said. 'These swine are my living, and he takes them whenever he feels like it. Last time he even set fire to our house, didn't he, boy?'

But Marc was not listening. He had dropped the carcass. Five riders were coming along the crest of the north ridge.

'Quick!' Morvid hissed, shoving Marc into the hut. Kerin grabbed his spear and followed them. They crouched in the darkness, peering through a small hole between the wattles. The riders came splashing through the stream. Bertil Redknife was in the lead on a rangy white horse, dressed as usual in his sober dark clothes. Two men were following just behind him. Kerin recognised the nearest one immediately as the thickset, pig-eyed warrior who had accompanied Bertil in Eldof's camp, and at the curia. Riding right on his heels was living proof, at last, that Kerin had not entirely lost his wits; the two men were as identical as a pair of cock sparrows on a branch, except that the second one was missing an ear. They were followed, to Kerin's surprise, by a woman. She was small and slender, as far as he could tell under the dull black cloak which enveloped her. A wisp of copper hair had escaped from under the close-drawn hood. At her side rode a fat, wrinkled old man on a gleaming chestnut mare. He looked a little overdressed for the woodlands in his bright red tunic and a heavy black cloak with a flashy gold shoulder pin.

'Who are the others?' Kerin whispered.

'The twin brothers Balin and Brennan,' Morvid whispered back. 'They split heads for Bertil. The man on the fine horse is Gadlyn, a lord of Eldof's following, and the woman is Bertil's daughter Gael. He gave her to Gadlyn in marriage these two months past.'

'But Gadlyn's ancient,' Kerin murmured.

'Yes,' Morvid said, 'and a cruel bastard too, but he's the wealthiest man for miles around. They say his hall is stuffed with golden coins. I expect Bertil's more interested in that, than in his daughter's pleasure.'

Kerin suppressed a sound of disgust. Bertil circled his horse. He observed the fire, the carcass and the strange mare like a hawk sizing up its prey.

'Morvid!' he bellowed. 'Must I smoke you out like I did last time?'

'Stay here and don't move,' Morvid mouthed. He peered through the doorway, blinking at the sudden brightness of the sunlight. Bertil's thin lips formed a predatory smile.

'Why are you hiding from me?' he asked.

'Why?' Morvid echoed him. 'You steal my pigs and

burn my house, and you ask me why I hide from you?'

Bertil shrugged. 'Is it my fault, if God has given me a weakness for pork? Move your arse, old man, and kill me a pig before I decide to kill you instead.'

'Kill me if you must,' Morvid said truculently. 'I'm an old man, and I can't stop you stealing my swine. But I'll slit my own throat before I slit theirs to make you fat.'

Bertil's eyes narrowed. 'You're stupid to call me a thief, Morvid,' he said, drawing his sword and pointing to Eryr. 'Where did you steal this fine horse?'

'I didn't steal her,' Morvid said sullenly.

'Lord,' Balin interrupted, 'this isn't a local horse. Look, the silver-work on the bridle. This is a Cambrian horse.'

'I know it's a Cambrian horse, you simpleton,' Bertil said, scowling. He dropped from the saddle and marched towards Morvid. Inside the hut Kerin tensed, spear gripped tight. 'Where's the rider of this horse?' Bertil demanded.

'I saw no rider,' Morvid said, staring at the ground. 'I found the horse wandering in the forest this morning.'

'Ah!' Bertil said grimly. 'And I suppose the deer came walking down the valley and skewered herself on your spit, eh?' He seized Morvid by the jerkin and pressed his sword-blade to the old man's withered throat.

'No!' Bertil's daughter shouted. She drove her black mare forward. The hood of her cloak flew back, revealing a pale face and a mass of copper-gold hair. Bertil spun round, his pock-marked face livid with anger.

'Stand away, Gael!' he roared. Gadlyn seized Gael's arm and held it tightly. She struggled furiously and bit his hand. 'Control your woman,' Bertil said, with a mocking laugh. He tightened his grip on Morvid's jerkin. 'Now then, you old donkey's turd; for the last time, where's the rider of that horse?'

'I'm here,' Kerin said, stepping from the hut. Bertil stopped short and released Morvid.

'And who the devil are you?' he barked.

'I'm Kerin Brightspear,' Kerin said, meeting Bertil's eyes steadily. His grip on the spear-shaft tightened. Bertil frowned.

'I know you,' he said. 'You're one of Vortigern's cut-throats, aren't you.'

Morvid's jaw dropped. Kerin's blood boiled.

'Yes!' he shouted, 'I ride with Vortigern, and I'll cut your throat any time you like.'

As he spoke, the spear flew from his hand. The iron tip buried itself in Brennan's chest, and the warrior pitched from his horse with a hoarse scream.

'That's my brother, you bastard,' Balin howled. Kerin dived sideways as Bertil's sword came down. Whipping his own sword out he hacked at Balin's leg. Balin bellowed with rage as blood spurted from the gash. Kerin leapt astride Brennan's horse and spun round to face Bertil. From the corner of his eye he saw Morvid wrench the spear from Brennan's chest and hurl it at Gadlyn. It hit the fat man a glancing blow and fell harmlessly to the ground. Morvid fled into the hut with Balin in pursuit, dragging his wounded leg. Kerin lunged at Bertil, wounding him lightly in the forearm. There was a loud, metallic crash from inside the hut. Gadlyn recovered himself and went for his sword. For an instant – an instant too long – Kerin glanced sideways at him. Bertil's sword flashed, and Kerin screamed in pain as the keen blade bit deep into his thigh. His head reeled, but instinct told him to duck. Gadlyn's sword whistled harmlessly over his head.

'Kerin!' a shrill voice cried. He wheeled his horse. 'Catch!' Marc shouted, picking up Kerin's spear and tossing it to him. Gadlyn raised his sword high and came thundering down on them. Kerin caught the spear left-handed and hurled it desperately. The arrow-head tore into Gadlyn's throat. He toppled from his horse with a terrible gurgling cry and sprawled, choking to death, in the embers of the fire. At the same moment Kerin felt his horse go down underneath him. Bertil's sword had sliced across her back legs, severing the hamstrings. Kerin leapt sideways as she crashed to the ground. Blood was pouring from the wound in his leg. Pain swept over him in red-hot waves. He had lost his sword. Bertil advanced slowly, sword in hand. He was grinning broadly. Kerin backed away, barely able to stand. He stumbled against Gadlyn's body and lost his footing. Bertil's sword flashed out and nicked his forehead. The blood ran down Kerin's face. A vicious anger overwhelmed him.

'Kill me, then, mighty warrior!' he gasped. Bertil's ruined face was white with rage. As he raised his sword for the killing blow, Kerin's pain-dimmed eyes saw a quick movement behind him. Marc seized Morvid's little spear and drove it into Bertil's back with all his strength. With a bellow of pain and surprise Bertil turned. The sword dropped from his hand. The spear fell away and he lunged at Marc with his fist, knocking the boy senseless. Gathering all his remaining strength,

Kerin grabbed the sword and staggered to his feet. Bertil backed away. Blood was seeping across the back of his tunic.

'Fight me!' Kerin shouted, limping after him. Bertil's eyes darted back and forth as Kerin advanced. Behind him Morvid burst from the door of the hut with a dagger in his hand. He saw his grandson lying face down on the ground, and an animal shriek burst from somewhere deep in his skinny chest. He lurched forwards, his eyes blazing manically. Kerin wrenched the dagger from his hand and hurled it, striking Bertil in the right shoulder. With a howl of pain Bertil leapt for his horse, seized the reins of his daughter's mare and galloped away down the valley. Kerin leaned against the wall of the hut and watched them go. His senses swam and the sword slipped from his hand. Morvid's voice was speaking to him from a dark distance. Bertil's horse clattered through the stream in a shower of spray. His daughter reined in on the far bank and glanced over her shoulder before following him away up the hillside. Her black cape billowed, and above it her long red-gold hair streamed out in the wind. Like a flame in the dark, Kerin thought idly, as blackness enveloped him and shut the vision out.

There were no dreams; or at least none which committed themselves to memory. When Kerin's eyelids flickered open, he found himself lying on a comfortless wooden bed in the corner of an unfamiliar hut. Stray shafts of sunlight filtered in through the wattle walls. Somewhere outside a blackbird was singing. Marc was staring down at him, white and hollow-cheeked. He was sporting an impressive black eye. As Kerin's eyes opened, the tension left the boy's face.

'Grandad!' he whooped, running from the hut. Kerin struggled into a sitting position. A warning stab of pain from his injured leg restored unwelcome memories. He investigated cautiously. The wound was firmly bound with a strip of cloth which seemed to cover a pad of some sort. The limb was stiff and sore, but as Kerin swung his legs over the edge of the bed and rose gingerly to his feet, he found that he could stand without too much discomfort. He limped to the door of the hut and peered out. The sun was setting behind the beech woods. Eryr and Gadlyn's riding horse were grazing beside the stream alongside Morvid's sturdy pony. Marc was leading his grandfather across the grass towards the hut, chattering eagerly.

'So!' Morvid said, gripping Kerin's arm. 'Awake at last, eh?'

'Yes,' Kerin said, blinking at the bright rose-coloured sky. 'Have I slept all day?'

'All day?' Morvid laughed. 'All day, and all yesterday, and the day before that. You've had a bad fever, my boy.'

Kerin glanced down at his leg. 'How bad is it?' he asked.

'Deep but clean,' Morvid said. 'At least the bastard keeps his weapons sharp. My father taught me to heal wounds with the wild herbs you find in the woodland. Comfrey-root paste, that's what sorted you out. The leg will hurt for a while, of course, but see that you bind it with a clean cloth every day and it shouldn't kill you. Just take your journey in easy stages, and stop for a while if it starts to pain you.'

'Thank you, Morvid,' Kerin said, gripping his bony shoulders. 'I'd be as dead as Brennan and Gadlyn if it wasn't for you.' He frowned, suddenly remembering something. 'What happened to Balin? The last thing I remember, he was chasing you in here.'

'Marc hit him on the head with the cooking pot,' Morvid said cheerily. 'While he was senseless we tied him up, then we got him and Gadlyn and Brennan and put them in my cart. The little one, not the strong old bugger I use for taking pigs to market. They're big men, it was damned hard work. Then we harnessed Balin's horse to the cart and sent it home. I suppose we should have killed Balin, really, but I'd seen enough blood for one day, and I'm not one for sticking a man like a pig when he can't defend himself. Now I've lost my second-best cart, of course. I don't expect Bertil will send it back to me, do you?'

Kerin smiled. He was beginning to feel quite fond of the plucky old man and his enterprising grandson.

'It's the boy you should thank, anyway,' Morvid said. 'Bertil would have lopped your head off in the first place if he hadn't speared him in the back.'

Kerin looked at the boy, standing there with his black eye and eager face, and thought how proud he looked, and how like himself at a younger age. 'I know it,' he said, putting an arm round Marc's shoulders and pulling him in tight.

'The boy won't tell you himself,' Morvid said, 'but he hasn't slept since the moment we carried you into the hut. He's been at your side night and day.'

Kerin looked around him at the pretty valley, the grazing horses and the snuffling contented pigs.

'Morvid, you know you can't stay here,' he said. 'Bertil will be back as soon as his wounds have healed, and you won't get away next time.'

'But where can we go?' Morvid asked miserably. 'Who will shelter us, when they know that it'll bring Bertil down on them? They'll stone us from their doors like dogs.'

'Go to Henfelin, in Cambria,' Kerin said. 'I know it's a long journey, but you have Gadlyn's horse, and your pony is strong.'

'Henfelin?' Morvid said sourly. 'So Vortigern can hang us instead of Bertil? Do me a favour, lad.'

'No,' Kerin said. 'Vortigern won't touch you.'

'He's in Londinium, anyway, isn't he?' Morvid said. 'What about the rest of your people? They'll hang us up for the crows, if the bandits don't do it first. And there's the wolves, you know.'

Kerin ignored the prevarication. 'You'll need to find Vortigern's son, Katigern. Tell him that I sent you, and that you're to lodge in my house with the cook.'

'And if he doesn't believe me?' Morvid said sceptically.

'Give him this.' Kerin slipped a heavy silver band from his wrist. 'Vortigern's silversmith made it for me, and he'll recognise it.'

'Perhaps he'll think I stole it,' Morvid said obdurately.

'Look,' Kerin said, 'you'd have to be a complete crack-brain to steal it and show it to him, wouldn't you?'

The old man sighed. 'You're right, of course,' he said, slipping the silver band up his withered arm.

'I'm the one who'll get butchered when Vortigern finds out about this, anyway,' Kerin said. 'He warned me not to travel alone.'

'Someone might have something to say about that,' Morvid said. Mark giggled impishly.

'What do you mean?' Kerin said uneasily.

'You had a visitor, lad,' Morvid said gleefully. 'We can't let you go without telling you, can we, boy?'

'I suppose not,' Marc said cheerfully. 'I'd rather have a puppy if it was me, though.'

'A puppy?' Kerin said blankly.

'A girl, you halfwit,' Morvid crowed. 'Bertil's daughter. She came back to see if you were alright, didn't she?'

'But I killed her husband!' Kerin said in horror.

'She didn't look too worried about that, lad,' Morvid said. 'More worried about the wound her father gave you, by the look of things.'

'She must be out of her mind,' Kerin said. 'What would her father say, if he knew?'

Morvid pursed his lips. 'Plenty, I expect. But then, Gael was always a fearless child, tearing about on her little pony and chasing deer like a young lad. Her mother and brother died of the plague, you know. You'd have thought her father would care for her, instead of marrying her off to an old brute like that.'

'Well, I've made her a rich woman now,' Kerin said uncomfortably, thinking of Gadlyn gasping his life away in the embers of Morvid's fire. 'And all the more reason for getting away, before Bertil finds out she's been here. I must leave at first light.'

Morvid rose to his feet with a grunt. 'We too, I suppose,' he sighed. 'See to the horses and the saddlery, Marc. I'm going to pack up whatever's worth taking, and pick out the best pigs.' He limped away into the hut. Kerin watched him go, then noticed that Marc was gazing up at him with pleading eyes.

'Let me go to Londinium with you, lord,' he said. 'You have no servant. I'll bind your wound, and tend your horses, and see to your food, and –'

'Marc,' Kerin interrupted him gently, 'you can't come with me.'

'But why?' the boy begged. A suspicion of tears rimmed his eyes and he blinked them back defiantly. 'I'm strong and I can fight, and they'll kill me before they touch you, Lord Kerin, I swear it.'

'I know, I know,' Kerin said, squeezing his shoulder. 'You're worth ten of Bertil's butchers. But you must go to Henfelin with your grandfather. He's an old man, Marc. He needs you more than I do.'

'And when you come back from Londinium?' Marc asked apprehensively. Kerin looked down at the boy's eager face with a sudden, unexpected sadness in his heart. He remembered a clear, cold day high on the ridge of Crib Garw when a small, brown-haired lad of around Marc's age and size had struggled to keep pace with Vortigern as they chased red deer across the bare moorland. Every stride jarred the child's body as the horses galloped on, leaping gullies and bog pools. The spear felt so heavy that he could barely keep hold of it, but by some miracle it had found its mark. Pain and exhaustion became exultant triumph as Lud lashed the dead hind to the baggage mule, and Vortigern, in one of his rare moments of tenderness, smiled as he lifted Kerin in his arms and set him on the back of his chestnut mare Gwennol, mother of the black Annwn.

'Lord?' Marc said anxiously.

'Yes,' Kerin said, looking down at him. 'When I come back you may serve me. But as I've served Vortigern. On a fast horse, with a sword in your hand.'

The boy's eyes widened. For a brief moment he stared up at Kerin, speechless with joy; then he leapt to his feet and bolted away along the bank of the stream into the darkness, dancing round the tussocks of grass and scattering the startled pigs. His howls of delight carried far away into the beech woods on the quiet night air.

* * *

The first red glow of dawn had coloured the sky when Kerin rode from the valley. Strapped to his saddle was Morvid's parting gift, a stout pigskin bag packed with bread and salt pork. He was on the point of deciding that he had made his escape when his mare slowed and whinnied loudly. From amongst the trees another horse answered her. Kerin seized his spear and sat quite still. He could hear the animal's soft tread coming up the far side of a grassy mound. The wound, though healing, had weakened him so much that he was not equal to any sort of a fight. The mist still hung amongst the trees in dense white pockets, any of which could have concealed a warrior. Kerin tensed and raised his spear. But it was Bertil Redknife's daughter who came over the rise. Her black mare balanced on the hillock, knee-deep in a drift of mist. Kerin reined back, spear still at the ready. He glanced agitatedly around him. For God's sake where was her father, or even her dead husband's kinsmen? How could he fight one man, let alone a warband?

'I am alone!' Gael said, recognising his distress. It

was the first time he had heard her speak. Her voice was soft, and pitched lower than he had expected; a complete shock after Mabli's shrill treble. She circled him curiously. She sat her horse like a warrior, easily and with perfect control. He wondered if it was her father who had taught her, and indeed how a man like Bertil could possibly have fathered anything as beautiful as this girl, with her red-gold hair and delicate blue eyes. She had a short-bladed sword at her belt and a spear slung from her saddle. She might be small and fine-boned, but Kerin guessed that she could use the things.

'I knew that you would probably pass this way when you left,' she said. 'I have ridden to this place every day at sunrise.'

'Why?' Kerin asked. 'I killed your husband. I could have killed your father, if I'd been lucky.' A pair of wood pigeons clattered out of the birches behind them. Kerin spun round.

'I told you, I'm alone,' Gael said. 'You'd be dead by now if my father was here. He's sick in bed, as it happens; the wound in his back turned poisonous. The old man must have been sticking his pigs with that spear.'

Kerin stifled a smile. 'Alright,' he said, hooking his spear to the saddle. 'I believe you. So why are you here?'

Gael glanced over her shoulder. 'We can't stay here. Follow me.'

'Into a trap? No, thank you.'

'There's no trap,' Gael said. 'If we ride along this track for a while we'll come to a church. You'll be safe there. The abbot is a friend.' Without waiting for a reply she turned her mare's head and rode off along the track. Kerin followed. The church was there, as she had said; a small building rather like Iustig's chapel, but made of the mellow buff stone peculiar to Glevum and its surroundings. There was a garden alongside where three monks were digging a trench. Another two were picking crab apples from a laden tree close to the church door. It was difficult to see how this peaceful scene could possibly conceal an ambush.

'Lady Gael!' said one of the apple-pickers, with evident pleasure.

'Hello, Brother.' Gael smiled as she slipped from her mare's back. 'Is Father Septimus here?'

'In the chapel, lady.'

'We'll go in, then,' Gael said. 'Can we leave our horses with you, please?'

The monk took the black mare and smiled amenably as Kerin dismounted with extreme care and tied Eryr to the hedge. The interior of the church was dim and cool. The abbot, a well-built man of late middle age, was standing beside the simple altar. If not for his robe and shaven crown, Kerin would probably have taken him for a farm labourer; he had the right weathered complexion and big, rough hands.

'Ah, Gael!' he exclaimed, as they entered. 'Is all well? There was some talk in the market yesterday. A fight, something to do with your father's men?'

Gael turned to Kerin. 'Father, I won't mince words. This man helped me when I was in trouble, but he's no friend of my father's. Is there a place where we can speak for a few moments? I can promise you he's honourable; I wouldn't have brought him here otherwise.'

Septimus looked Kerin up and down. 'Who are you, then?' he asked.

'I'm Kerin Brightspear, a warrior from Cambria,' Kerin said, and left it at that. He was in no hurry to tell the abbot that he had slaughtered Gael's husband, albeit in self-defence.

'He killed Gadlyn,' Gael said, to his horror. Septimus raised his thick eyebrows.

'Well, young fellow,' he said, 'I'm not one to glory in bloodshed, as a rule, but I don't think God will strike me dead for saying that you have done this young woman a valuable service. Gael, you may use the speech house. I'll be in the orchard with the brothers, if you need me.'

Kerin followed Gael out of the church and past the monks' garden to a little stone building alongside. It contained a table and two stark chairs, and was altogether cleaner and more pleasant than Paulinus's hovel in Caerwynt. Gael led the way inside, then turned to face Kerin.

'Septimus has already said what I wished to say,' she said. 'You couldn't have known it, but you saved me from a living death. My father married me to Gadlyn because the old goat was rich and had no heirs. He should thank you too, really, because now it will all come to him sooner than he thought.'

'You're Gadlyn's widow,' Kerin said. 'Shouldn't it come to you?'

Gael spat on the floor of the speech house. 'I wouldn't touch anything that belonged to him. And even if I wanted to, my father would forbid it.'

Kerin shook his head. He would have liked to ask her to explain, but he knew how dangerous this was already, and how much more dangerous it could undoubtedly become. He looked down at Gael. A flush had risen across her pale face. Her eyes, which looked a deeper blue in this light, were hurt and defiant. He wondered exactly what had happened, and for how much longer he could have managed to keep his distance if she had not been Bertil Redknife's daughter.

'What makes you think that I'm honourable?' he asked, thinking how pleasant it would have been if he had not felt compelled to be.

'You risked your life to save an old man and a boy,' Gael said. 'Scoundrels don't do that sort of thing.'

'Your father would have killed me anyway, given the chance,' Kerin said. 'He despises anything that comes out of Cambria.' He could have added other reasons, but there would have been no point. He would probably never see this woman again after today.

'If you're still here when he gets out of his sick bed, he'll kill you.' Gael turned her back to him. 'Please, go. Wherever you're going, go now, and go quickly. You must never come back.' She broke off, a little suddenly. Kerin wondered if he had imagined a slight trembling of her shoulders.

'Yes, I'll go,' he said. 'But I can't promise you that I'll never come back.'

'You must,' Gael whispered. Kerin stared impotently at her back, at the slender shoulders and bowed red-gold head. He wanted nothing more than to gather her up in his arms and protect her from whatever her father had in store for her, although he doubted whether her pride would have permitted it.

'What will you do?' he asked. Gael turned.

'It cannot be your concern,' she said. The words sounded harsh, but the voice was otherwise. Kerin suspected that she had been fighting tears, but she had composed herself now. She was holding something in her hands, twisting it back and forth.

'What's that?' Kerin asked. Gael smiled and tossed the object to him. He caught it mechanically. It was a silver ring, a delicate tracery of leaves and intertwined tendrils.

'We shall never meet again,' she said, 'but please keep this, and think of me sometimes. I shall never forget you, or what you did for me.' She placed her hands on Kerin's shoulders and, standing on tiptoe, kissed him lightly on the cheek; then, before he had time to respond, she ran from the speech house. Kerin stood, looking down at the ring nestling in the palm of his hand, and listened to her mare's hooves drumming away down the forest track.

'Are you alright, lad?' Abbot Septimus was standing in the doorway. Kerin's fingers closed around the ring.

'Yes, Father. Thank you for letting us use your house.'

'I have known Gael since she was a babe in arms,' Septimus said. 'Her mother was better than Bertil deserved, and so is she.'

'What will happen to her now that Gadlyn's dead?' Kerin asked.

'Who knows? Perhaps her father will find some other wealthy old cretin to marry her off to. She may refuse; but then she refused Gadlyn until Bertil flayed the skin off her. I tried to speak up for Gael, but of course her father would have no qualms about killing a priest, and in the end I thought that I would be more help to her alive than dead. I did refuse to conduct the marriage, though. Eldadus the bishop did that. He's a relation of some sort, I gather.'

'That old fool,' Kerin said tartly.

'You know him?' Septimus said, with some surprise.

'Not exactly, but I've been in his company. I'm a warrior of Vortigern's following.'

'Ah,' Septimus said. That small syllable conveyed more than Kerin would have thought possible; a subtle blend of surprise, grudging respect and disapproval. 'You should not come back here,' the abbot said firmly. 'But if you are foolish enough to ignore my advice, please remember that all men are welcome in the House of God.'

Once out of sight of the church, Kerin reined in and examined the ring. It was so small that it would not even fit on the tip of his little finger. Carefully he removed the crucifix Sevira had given him. Its silver chain was fastened by a bar on one end passing through an enlarged link on the other. Kerin eased the ring over the bar and let it slide down the chain until it rested against the crucifix; then he hung the chain round his neck again. He knew that he must get back to Londinium as quickly as his damaged leg would allow, but the prospect filled him with dread. He had disobeyed the one command given to him, and his reward was a blood feud dangerous enough to wreck the fragile consensus Vortigern was struggling to build. The tiny ring, caught by the sun, winked brightly against his dark grey tunic. A little spark of white heat; so fierce, so potent, it could break every constraint that had bound his life until now.

18

'I'm glad you're back!' Lud said fervently as Kerin clattered into the courtyard of Severus Maximus's house. Night was falling under drifts of sleet. Lud called Elir to see to the sweating mare.

'Trouble?' Kerin asked, with some apprehension.

'You could say.' Lud scowled. 'The men are homesick. Maximian Galba and his cronies are ranting at every street corner. Pictish galleys have been sighted just off the mouth of the river.' He clenched his fists and stared up at the darkening sky, as if it might somehow provide him with a solution. Four members of the praetorian guard were standing by at the main entrance, looking particularly alert and well turned out. Lupinus was hovering behind them. He gave Kerin a hasty bow and scuttled off. 'You're wounded!' Lud said suddenly.

'It's nothing,' Kerin said. 'A bit of a scrap on the journey, that's all.'

Lud glanced towards the interior of the house. 'You'd better get in there, then. And be careful.'

Voices were echoing in the atrium. Lupinus was coming back with Publius Luca. He must have been under orders; it was no servant's business to summon the highest-ranking officer in the city.

'Kerin Brightspear!' the commander said, with

patent relief. 'The gods be thanked.' He gave Kerin a nod. 'Come with me. This can't be said here.'

The room in which Kerin found himself was the one where Vortigern had conducted his first meeting with the praetor. The polished table, the shelves packed with books and scrolls. Many things had changed in the interim, but not this room. The scent of beeswax and dusty manuscripts hung in the air. There was the bust; luminous white Caesar, or whoever he was, giving Kerin the evil eye. Only one thing was different; the large stack of documents on the table. Sheets of fine material, probably papyrus, enclosed within leather covers and secured with gold silken ties. Not Vortigern's private writings; these were official papers of some sort.

'This house is full of flapping ears,' Publius Luca said. He closed the door and slid the bolt. Kerin wondered what on earth was coming. He had not spoken to Publius Luca since the day Vortigern crowned Constans. 'I'll be brief,' the commander said. 'I know you've had a long journey. But there have been difficulties. The king has acquired a taste for power.'

The king! How odd it sounded, even now. To Publius Luca too, Kerin suspected; he had spoken the word as if referring to a household cat which had suddenly started masquerading as a lion. Some obvious solutions flashed through Kerin's mind, all involving violence and repercussions. 'What difficulties?' he asked. Publius Luca picked up one of the new documents and handed it to him. 'I can't read much,' Kerin said, passing it back. 'You'll have to tell me what it is, I'm afraid.'

Publius Luca tossed the document onto the pile.

'The detail isn't important,' he said. 'These are royal decrees, authorising the imposition of a tax to finance a defensive battle fleet. One for every city which still has a functioning ordo. There's also a sheaf of letters, addressed to landowners and men of power throughout the kingdom, requesting men and equipment for the campaign in the North. Naturally, as royal documents, they require the king's signature. And will the king sign the documents? No, he won't sign the documents.'

'He won't?' Kerin said, incredulous. 'He'll defy Vortigern? That little mouse? Loving God, I wouldn't do it.'

Publius Luca laughed out loud. 'No, even I wouldn't do it, and I've commanded a legion of five thousand men. But of course, weak as Constans is, he's far from stupid. At the moment, Vortigern's power depends upon him, and he knows it. Add to this the fact that Maximian Galba and his friends have been feeding him dung about his kingly rights –' he gritted his teeth, and Kerin realised that the solid, disciplined commander of the city garrison might have liked to rip the king's head off and feed it to his dogs.

'And Vortigern?' he asked. Publius Luca raised his eyebrows.

'Well, I'm sure you know that he didn't come here to sit on his hands while that monk's arse stays parked on the throne of the kingdom. But this is taking too long. The threats grow every day. The Picts are gathering strength, and may yet ally themselves with the Irish. Constans must see reason. I'm hoping that you might be the man to make him.'

Kerin blinked. 'Me? Why?'

'Why?' Publius Luca said. 'Because anyone who's survived twenty-five years with Vortigern could probably talk sense into a donkey. And because we both know that Vortigern is the only man who can save the kingdom. The least we can do is help him.'

He extended his hand, and Kerin shook it. He didn't know whether Publius Luca had seen something in him, or whether his confidence was simply the fruit of other men's good opinion; but it didn't matter. He knew that he had found a true ally in this unforgiving city.

'When you saw that I'd come back, you said "the gods be thanked",' he said. 'Why? Vortigern has any number of good warriors.'

Publius Luca gave an odd little grimace. 'Warriors don't have all the answers,' he said. 'Now go to him, before he eats himself alive.'

* * *

Lupinus pointed out a large door at the end of the passage. Although he had only ever been into this room by the servants' entrance, Kerin was fairly sure that it was the council chamber where he had spied on Severus and his allies.

'I am not going in there,' Lupinus said firmly.

'Alright, then,' Kerin said. 'Off you go.'

The servant bowed obsequiously and withdrew. Kerin wondered what had happened during the past few weeks to silence his prattling tongue. A thought, previously put aside, came back to him. 'Lupinus!' he said sharply. The servant padded back. 'You and the king are good friends, aren't you,' Kerin said, lingering over the words to make sure that he was understood. Lupinus gave him an anxious look.

'Yes, lord,' he said. 'I'm assigned to be his personal servant, as you know. But yes, we have become good friends.'

'And are you also a good friend of Maximian Galba?' Kerin enquired. Lupinus swallowed hard.

'No, lord,' he said. 'I can't stand the man, actually. Why do you wish to know?'

'Because it's my business to know,' Kerin said, tilting Lupinus's chin. 'And understand this. I don't give a damn what you and Constans get up to in the privacy of his chambers. But there are things which only three men are entitled to know; the king, the Lord Vortigern and myself. If I find any of those things flying around where they shouldn't be, I will cut out your tongue. Without a moment's hesitation.'

He removed his hand, and found that it was moist with Lupinus's sweat. The servant gave a gulp of terror and fled. In reality, Kerin supposed, he would probably lock the boy up in the castra; but there was something about the threat of cutting out a tongue. The slicing blade; the mouthful of pouring blood. Kerin had never cut out anyone's tongue, of course, but he was learning the value of a good threat.

The door eased open with a faint creak. Kerin recognised the room at once; the overblown statue, the sumptuous couches, the lamps burning in their ornate silver holders and, at the far end, the table on its dais. Vortigern was sitting at the table, chin resting on his hands. In front of him lay the chest containing his writing materials, a goblet and a silver jug. His thoughts preoccupied him utterly. Kerin waited. Vortigern noticed the motionless figure at the door. His eyes narrowed.

'Where in God's name have you been? Hefydd's boys got here days ago, and they said you left well before them.' He came down the room. Two paces from Kerin, he halted. His finger traced the scar on Kerin's forehead. 'Who did this?' he asked.

'It doesn't matter who did it,' Kerin said. 'The quarrel is mine.'

'There are no private quarrels where you and I are concerned,' Vortigern said. 'Who did it?'

'Bertil Redknife,' Kerin said reluctantly. Vortigern stared up at the ceiling.

'Eldof's minion? For the love of God, couldn't you have picked someone who didn't matter?'

'I didn't pick him,' Kerin protested. 'He picked me.'

'Either way,' Vortigern said, 'you disregarded the one command I gave you. Would this argument have happened if Hefydd and his men had been with you?'

'No,' Kerin said guiltily. They walked slowly up the length of the room.

'Your leg,' Vortigern said, looking down. 'Another wound?'

'Yes,' Kerin admitted; he had hoped that Vortigern would not notice, but his leg was stiff from riding, and it was impossible not to limp. 'It's healing,' he said quickly.

'Show me,' Vortigern said. Kerin glared mutinously at him. Vortigern folded his arms and waited. Kerin unhitched his belt and lowered his breeches to the knee. Vortigern loosened the dressing and examined the scar. It was healing well, but there was no disguising the ferocity of the original wound. 'Who treated this for you?' he asked. 'I've seen men lose their legs with wounds like this.'

'An old man, Morvid,' Kerin said, rearranging himself. 'He's a healer. Comfrey-root paste. You have to put it on every day when you change the bandage.'

Vortigern gave him a sceptical look. They sat down at the table. Vortigern put his pen and papyrus to one side and pushed the jug towards Kerin. He had not touched the wine it contained. 'Tell me what happened,' he said. Kerin filled the goblet and drained it thankfully.

'The old man and his grandson gave me hospitality,' he said. 'Bertil came with his warriors to steal their pigs. Years ago he killed Morvid's son for taking one of his cattle in a famine. We all hid in Morvid's hut; there wasn't any point in fighting four well-armed men if it could be avoided. But Bertil spotted my horse. Morvid went out and lied to him about it, and Bertil was going to kill him, so I had to stop it. I killed a couple of them, with the boy's help. Bertil ran away. I couldn't follow him. The reason's obvious.'

'I'll see to it,' Vortigern said. 'You don't deserve it; this has only happened because you disobeyed a command. But I can't have Eldof's people throwing their weight about, even if you brought it on yourself. For God's sake, do you think I need a dispute with them, on top of everything else? We need these men on our side. And you know where Eldof stands. You've seen the house and the baths and the statues and the formal bastard gardens. For a couple of sesterces he'd throw in his lot with Maximian Galba, and invite the Romans back. So what have you done? Kept the peace with them? No. You've started a feud which I will have to stop, because everyone here sees you as one of my household, and soon enough someone will stand up in the ordo and say, look what this barbarian did, we told you so.' He broke off, white with temper.

'Lord, I'm sorry,' Kerin said. 'I can't undo what's done. But I give you my word, it won't happen again.'

'If it does, you'll be across the road in the castra with Hefydd and the common warriors,' Vortigern said. 'In the meantime, don't go near Eldof or any of his people. The one saving grace is that he can't stand Bertil. Probably they've fallen out over something, and that's why Bertil has gone home. I'll smooth it over with Eldof if I can.'

'*I'll* see to it,' Kerin said. 'The quarrel's mine.'

Vortigern retrieved the silver jug and took a gulp of wine. 'Look, if someone had done this to me, then what would you do about it?'

Kerin refilled the goblet and drained it at one draught. 'You know quite well what I'd do,' he said. 'But it's not the same.'

'What do you mean, it's not the same?' Vortigern demanded.

'It's not the same,' Kerin repeated, keeping his voice steady. 'I know we've saved each other's necks in battle, more times than I can remember. But this is different. Every man should settle his own account. And besides, I already owe you my life. Once is enough.'

'Leave it,' Vortigern said sharply. 'Just let it rest.'

Kerin stopped short, the goblet halfway to his lips. He had no idea what nerve he had touched, but he was afraid to touch it again. He suddenly remembered the tiny silver ring, sitting in the middle of his chest along-side his crucifix. The gift bestowed by Bertil Redknife's daughter, of all people. He felt as if he had an enormous boulder hanging round his neck, and wondered why he hadn't had the sense to slip it inside his tunic out of sight. There was a silence.

'How are things in Henfelin?' Vortigern asked.

'Peaceful,' Kerin said, and poured himself the remainder of the wine. This was not the time to talk about Iustig and his warnings of bloody strife. 'Lud said things were going to hell here. Maximian's people. Pictish galleys.'

Vortigern stared at the ceiling. 'Gallus wants a war fleet to protect the merchant ships. The ordo wants a fleet tax to pay for it. They can't authorise the tax unless the king proposes it, and Constans won't propose it because Maximian has told him that the king shouldn't answer to anyone. God preserve me from politics; if we were at home, we'd behead the lot of them, and that would be the end of it.'

'Well, we can't behead them here,' Kerin said, blink-ing as the wine began to work.

'I think,' Vortigern said carefully, 'that Constans needs to be frightened a little. Not harmed, of course; that would defeat the object. Just shaken. He has to give me command of all the city garrisons. And then,' he nodded, 'we can begin to do what we came here to do.'

There was a tap at the door. Lupinus peered timidly

around it. 'Lord, the Praetor of Londinium for you,' he said. Kerin wondered what else had occurred in his absence, if things had come to the point where the praetor had to request admission to his own council chamber. Severus Maximus came in, followed by a slave carrying another ornate jug and goblet. He sat down on the other side of the table, waved the slave away, and gave Kerin a relieved smile.

'I've just received an envoy from Maximian Galba,' he said, filling his goblet to the brim. 'It seems that he and his supporters are coming here tomorrow, to petition the king.'

'What about?' Vortigern asked.

'I've no idea. But according to my people, the news has spread. My fear is that every little malcontent for miles around will come along to air his grievances. We could end up with half of the city in the courtyard.'

'Well, so be it,' Vortigern said. 'This has been brewing for weeks. Tell Lucius Arrius to have the guard on alert. I'll speak to Publius Luca about the deployment of the city garrison. We're going to settle this tomorrow, whatever it takes.'

The praetor gave a nervous smile and swallowed some wine. 'Lord, I'd much prefer it if this could be done without blood.'

'So would I,' said Vortigern. 'Only fools and savages kill for fun. You don't think I'm either of those, I hope?'

'No, of course not,' Severus Maximus said. He replenished his goblet and held out the jug.

'No, thank you,' Vortigern said. The praetor looked affronted.

'This is my best wine, lord. Is it not to your taste?'

'Nothing in this pestilent city is to my taste,' Vortigern said. Severus stood up.

'It seems that I cannot win,' he said stiffly. 'The hospitality I have given you is the best I can provide. And to be truthful, I should have thought that all this was very fine, compared with what you are used to in the West.'

Vortigern picked up one of the goblets and examined the semi-precious stones on its bowl. 'Londinium is very fine, Severus. But it's like taking a woman to your bed. The body is easily satisfied; the soul, less so.'

Severus raised his eyebrows. He had nothing to add. 'I'm for my bath, lords,' he said. 'I trust that you can keep the peace tomorrow. It would be a great shame if anyone were to get killed.'

Vortigern looked up at him. 'No-one's going to get killed, Severus,' he said with a trace of impatience.

'No?' Severus said. 'Marcellus sees blood on the streets before the year's end, and I have never known him to be wrong. Lords, I hope you sleep better than I am likely to do.'

He gave a quick nod of the head and swept out. Voices echoed in the passage outside. Severus was protesting vehemently about something. He also sounded frightened. There was a loud knock at the door. Lud appeared, spear in hand, and cleared his throat.

'Macsen and Custennin are back from Camulodunum, lord,' he said. 'They have prisoners.'

'Prisoners?' Vortigern said. 'I sent them to frighten the ordo, not to take prisoners.'

'You should see these men, lord,' Lud said. 'They're Picts.'

Vortigern's eyes narrowed. 'Picts? From those galleys we were talking about?'

'Yes, lord. Their leader speaks some British. They were sent down here to spy on us, but they were ship-wrecked on the sandbanks last night.'

Vortigern looked hard at Lud for a moment. 'Alright,' he said. 'Bring them in here.'

Lud marched quickly out of the room. There was a commotion outside the door. Lud burst back in with Custennin and a handful of well-armed warriors. They were herding a string of ten prisoners at spear-point; lanky men, long-haired and bare-legged. They were dressed in rough, sleeveless tunics and their muscular arms were laced with strange red and blue tattoos. They reeked of fish and seaweed. Lud bellowed at them and they staggered clumsily across the room, manacled together by heavy iron chains. Vortigern came down from the dais and studied them.

'Kneel, you mangy dogs!' Lud bawled. Vortigern raised his hand.

'Leave us, Lud,' he said.

'But, lord, they're savages!' Lud protested.

'No more than you or I, probably,' Vortigern said. He glanced up as Lud hesitated. 'They're chained, man, they can't possibly harm me. Now go, and take the others with you.' Lud led his men out, with a look of some misgiving. Vortigern walked slowly up and down the line of prisoners and paused in front of a pale-skinned man with straggling red-brown hair and a long, drooping moustache. His keen eyes and erect bearing marked him out from his companions. 'What's your name?' Vortigern asked.

'I am Bridei,' the man said, speaking clearly but with an odd, clipped accent. 'I am named for a great king of our people. I come with my brothers to learn your fighting plans.'

'I know why you've come,' Vortigern said. 'Where did you learn the British tongue?'

'I learn it from a prisoner,' the Pict said. 'This man is spy. He says his fathers build the Wall, many, many years ago.'

'A Roman,' Vortigern said speculatively.

'Roman, yes. I can see it is good to know how the British speak, so I make friends with this man.' Bridei gave a broad, bloodthirsty grin. 'I learn his words, then I cut his throat.'

Vortigern raised his eyebrows. 'For shame, Bridei!' he said mildly. He drew his sword and examined the gleaming blade. 'A fine sword, Bridei. A fine sword, and a sharp one. Well suited for cutting off Pictish heads.'

The Pict glanced nervously at the blade. 'Don't kill me, lord!' he whispered hoarsely. 'You might do such things, if someone killed your people and took your land.'

'I'd do that and worse,' Vortigern said, but did not put the sword away. Kerin caught Bridei's eye. Not a coward's eye, but not open. A knife in the dark. Bridei clutched Vortigern's arm.

'Spare us and the gods will smile on you, lord,' he whispered. Vortigern detached the Pict's hand.

'I need eyes and ears in the North. Deliver your leaders to me next spring, and I'll give you more gold than you've ever dreamed of.'

Bridei's eyes gleamed hungrily. He turned to his

companions and a noisy parley followed. It ended in as wild a display of enthusiasm as a bunch of men in manacles could possibly have mustered.

'Lord, we are yours,' Bridei said, with a reverence. Vortigern laid his sword down on the table.

'Until we ride north, you will live here at the king's court as free warriors,' he said. 'Duties will be assigned to you. Abuse my trust and you're dead men. Do you understand this?'

'Yes, lord.'

'Kerin Brightspear here will see that you have meat to eat and good ale to drink.'

Bridei fell on his knees. 'Lord,' he cried, 'I –'

'Get up,' Vortigern said. 'First, you must swear to be loyal to me. To me only. Swear on something you hold dear.'

Bridei's hand moved to his belt and he grimaced. 'Lord, I would swear on my father's knife. But your warriors take our weapons.'

Vortigern nodded to Kerin. 'Get him his knife,' he said. 'Let's do this properly.'

Kerin's head was swimming after two jugs of wine on an empty stomach, but nothing could blunt his sense of danger. The air was bristling with it.

'What's going on?' Lud asked as he went outside.

'If I tell you, you won't believe me,' Kerin said. 'He wants the leader's knife.'

'He wants *what?* Is he drunk, or something?'

'Not even slightly,' Kerin said. 'Please, Lud, I need it now. I can't leave him alone in there. Now, where is it?'

Custennin sighed and removed the knife from his belt with a murderous scowl. It was easy to see why he had wanted it; the weapon was beautifully crafted, with a carved bone handle in the likeness of a dolphin and a long, razor-sharp blade. Kerin took it and went back into the council chamber.

'Good,' Vortigern said. He took the knife and held it out to Bridei. The Pict bent his head and kissed the blade.

'Lord, I swear for myself and for my brothers,' he said. 'We will serve you until the day we go to our gods.' The other Picts watched him, wincing as the heavy chains chafed their limbs. Vortigern sat down at the table again.

'Lud!' he shouted. Bridei and his companions glanced nervously at the door. Lud marched in with the disgruntled-looking Custennin. 'Take these men,' Vortigern said. 'Get these chains off them, and give them something to eat and drink. They've sworn to serve me faithfully.'

'But, lord!' Lud protested.

'Don't argue,' Vortigern said. 'Take them.' He beckoned to Bridei, who shuffled forward as far as his chain would allow. 'Lud's my chief warrior. If you don't obey him, he'll kill you as surely as I would. Do you understand this?'

'Yes, lord,' Bridei said meekly. Vortigern watched as Lud and his son herded the Picts away. The silence outside was shattered as the prisoners cheered and broke into a raucous song. The sound echoed far away down empty passages with the rattle of their chains. Vortigern picked up his sword and examined the blade.

'Well?' he said.

'I didn't speak, lord,' Kerin said, sitting down beside him.

'I know you didn't speak,' Vortigern said, 'but one of your silences says more than a month of most men's chattering. You think I should have killed them, don't you.'

'Yes, I do,' Kerin said. 'Bridei serves you for money; he'll sell himself to the first man who pays him more than you do. At the very least, you shouldn't trust them.'

'I don't trust them,' Vortigern said. 'But they'll serve a purpose. You will see. And in the meantime, resume your responsibility for Constans. The longer this goes on, the greater the danger to him. And so, as your friend Lucius suggested, I'm going to appoint an official bodyguard. Bridei and his friends will do nicely.'

'What?' Kerin said, astounded.

'Think about it,' Vortigern said. 'They have no possible political interest in any of this. To them, it'll simply be paid work. Well-paid work. They'll frighten the daylights out of Constans without so much as opening their mouths, and Maximian will go berserk. Just right.'

Kerin closed his eyes. 'And my task?' he asked.

'As I told you. Keep Constans alive. And do something with those Picts. They need to look and smell like a royal bodyguard, not some fisherman's by-catch. They need quarters. Find out if there's room in the castra. They need to understand that they're subordinate to the city garrison and the praetorian guard, as well as to us. And they need to know exactly what's expected of them, what they can and can't do, where they can and can't go.'

'Do I arm them?' Kerin asked.

'Yes,' Vortigern said. 'You have to arm them. When did you ever see an unarmed royal bodyguard?'

'I've never seen any sort of a royal bodyguard, lord,' Kerin said. 'Far less have I trained and equipped one.'

Vortigern gave him a benevolent smile. 'Look on it as practice, then,' he said.

19

The next day, dawn came up with the grey bleakness of winter. The big clouds rolling in from the south-east with their dirty yellow underbellies held premonitions of snow, and the men who had gathered in the court-yard of the praetor's residence were grateful for the protection which its solid walls afforded as the wind rose and the darkness thickened.

'It's too early in the year for all this,' Macsen gasped, shivering as he wrapped his heavy winter cloak tightly around his shoulders.

'I know,' Kerin said gloomily. 'It's nothing like this in the West. Three weeks ago
I was riding around in a shirt and breeches.'

A rattle of hailstones slewed across the rooftops and bounced off the paving stones. The wine Kerin had drunk the night before had dulled his head, and his wounded leg was aching viciously in the bitter cold. He envied Macsen's warm and stylish blue cloak, which he had not seen before.

'Where did you get that?' he asked.

'Gallus's warehouse,' Macsen mouthed, behind his hand. 'Manius's deal, remember? Neither of us could think of a better idea, so we paid Sha'ara and Aidée to get the guards drunk and threw everything we needed on Lucius's father's wagon. And in case you're feeling guilty about Gallus, don't. He'd already sold the stuff to Garagon.'

Kerin stifled a laugh, although in truth he was not sure whether that made things better or worse. His deliberations were soon interrupted by a succession of sounds which he had come to loathe; a strident braying of trumpets followed by trapping hooves and the dull rumble of chariot wheels. Someone self-important was about to arrive. It was Maximian Galba, muffled up against the cold in a fur-lined cloak and attended by a sour-faced squad of guards. He cast a critical eye over the contents of the courtyard before alighting from his chariot.

'Where is Constans?' he said impatiently. 'Where is Severus? And where is Vortigern?'

'All in good time,' Kerin said mildly. 'Severus Maximus has not long risen from his bed, and the king is bathing.' And Vortigern? He neither knew, nor wished to guess.

'They all knew I was coming here at midday,' Maximian said testily. 'Are they doing this on purpose? Or is this the measure of the praetor's hospitality, now that the barbarians are counted amongst his household?'

Kerin suppressed a smile. He found Maximian's pomposity amusing, but the trouble with amusement was the way it could make you forget what a man was capable of. He was glad to see Lucius approaching, and hoped that he was on his way to deal with Maximian, but Lucius marched straight past the praetor of Venta Belgarum and greeted Kerin with a smile and a stiff salute.

'Good morning, lord,' he said cheerfully. 'How was your journey?'

'Pleasant and uneventful,' Kerin said; there was little more he could say, under the circumstances.

'I have a visitor for you,' Lucius said. 'Perhaps you'd like to come with me?'

Kerin glanced at Macsen and shrugged, then followed Lucius off across the courtyard.

'It's a monk, lord,' Lucius said, as they walked. Kerin looked at him with unspoken dread. Please God, if you are a God of love, don't let it be Father Septimus, he thought.

'Who is he?' he asked. 'What does he want?'

'He says his name's Padarn. I'm not sure what he's doing here, but I think he's got something to do with the king.'

'Padarn!' Kerin frowned. 'Yes, I know him. He was at the monastery when we went to get Constans. Has Paulinus sent him?'

'I don't think so,' Lucius said, 'but I thought I'd better not say anything in front of Maximian Galba, just to be on the safe side.'

They had reached the mouth of the passage which led down to the slaves' quarters. Kerin remembered, with a guilty start, what had happened last time he was here. Poor Faria; he had hardly given her a thought since leaving Henfelin. 'The Phoenician girl,' he said. 'The one who used to serve me.'

'Faria,' Lucius agreed. There was nothing he wouldn't know about it, of course; no fragment of gossip which the maw of this pestilent house would not have sucked in, fermented and spewed out. 'She's well, as far as I know. And Sha'ara said thank you for the medication. Very effective, as you must know.'

'You never heard who did it, then?'

'No, lord, I'd have told you straight away. No-one seems to know except Faria, and she won't even tell her cousins. Now, the monk. I put him in the guards' mess; it's the first door on your left here.'

'Was it actually me he asked for?' Kerin was both puzzled and intrigued.

'Oh yes,' Lucius said. 'The Lord Kerin Brightspear, chief warrior to the Lord Vortigern of Glywysing. He was quite exact about it.'

Kerin sighed. 'I'm not the chief warrior, Lucius. You must know that.'

'Well, perhaps not,' Lucius said carefully. 'But everyone seems to think that you have an important position of some sort. It's obviously what this monk thinks, anyway, so I didn't tell him anything different.'

He gave a respectful nod and marched off towards the main gates, where Maximian Galba had been joined by Garagon of Kent and some colourful companions. Publius Luca had appeared too. He seemed to be remonstrating with the two men in a way which, although polite and restrained, did not allow for much disagreement. Kerin opened the door of the mess. Brother Padarn was sitting at one of the bare tables in the middle of the deserted room. On the floor by his feet was a bundle tied up in rough brown cloth. Kerin wondered if it contained all his worldly possessions.

'You were looking for me, Brother?' He sat down opposite the monk, who looked tired and in need of a scrub.

'That's right,' said Padarn, in the heavy northern accent Kerin remembered.

'Why me?' Kerin asked. 'We never spoke much, as I recall.'

'No,' Padarn said, 'but I couldn't ask for the Lord Vortigern, and from what your friend Vortimer said, you're keeping an eye on Brother Constans. Or should I say King Constans now? Sounds a bit strange, doesn't it.'

'Yes,' Kerin conceded. He looked curiously at Padarn, who seemed to be itching to tell him something, but didn't quite know where to start. 'Has Abbot Paulinus sent you, Brother?' Padarn gave a little snort. 'Does he know you're here?' Kerin asked.

'No,' Padarn said. 'He's away, so I left while the going was good.' He chuckled. 'I don't think he'd have been keen to give me his blessing.'

'Why did you come?' Kerin asked. 'It's safer in Caerwynt, surely.'

'Oh, it's safer, alright. But sometimes there are things a man has to do. Someone should be looking after Constans, for a start. I don't mean guarding him like you do; I mean looking after him spiritually. And anyway, when you march north to fight the Picts, I want to go with you. As Father Paulinus told you, I lost my family up there. Some soldiers like to have a priest along, and my father was a wheelwright, so I can turn my hand to mending a broken wagon if needs be.' He hesitated, as if searching for the right words to frame some deeply worrying thoughts. 'I don't like what's happening in Caerwynt. You know the Lord Vortimer's been there, I suppose. It'll end in blood, you mark my words, and I don't want to be part of it.'

'Not even to please God?' Kerin asked. Padarn spat on the floor.

'If you believe that, you worship a different God from me. The God I pray to wouldn't want to see a slaughter, and if you think Vortigern's the man to stop it, I'll be happy to throw in my lot with you until it's over.'

Kerin felt a sudden surge of admiration for Padarn. He had abandoned as safe a refuge as it was possible to find for the promise of danger, hardship and even bloody retribution, were Paulinus to catch up with him.

'You're welcome in our company, Brother,' he said, reaching across the table to grasp the monk's big, rough hand. 'Most of us don't like to admit it, but a priest wouldn't go amiss in Vortigern's army. I'll take you to the kitchen now, you look as if you could do with a good feed.'

Padarn shouldered his bundle with a grunt and turned away, perhaps to hide tears. Kerin doubted whether he had experienced much kindness in the latter years of his troubled life. As they left the mess, Lucius came hot-footing it across the courtyard.

'Lord, there's someone else for you,' he said, slightly breathless. 'Manius the fisherman. I think it's important. He wants to meet you outside in the street, so the people in the courtyard can't see.'

'Manius?' Kerin said, aghast. 'How on earth does he know who I am? The last time I was talking to him, he thought I was one of Gallus's crewmen.'

'We – er, had to tell him who we were,' Lucius said. 'Unfortunately he recognised my step-father's horse and cart from the wharf. You shouldn't worry about it, though. We told him that there might be a reward if he brought us any interesting gossip from the river.'

'Alright,' Kerin said, raising a hand. 'Now, take Brother Padarn to the kitchen and ask the cooks to feed him, then give him directions for the chapel of St Alban. I'm sure Father Giraldus will give him a bed for the night.'

A glance across the courtyard revealed that the gathering by the gates now included Eldof of Glevum, his chief warrior Varro and Flavius, the smooth-faced young praetor of Eburacum. Kerin slipped out through the tradesmen's door and walked briskly along below the perimeter wall.

'Psst!' A sharp hiss came from a pitch-dark alley-way on the far side of the street. Kerin crossed over and leaned against the wall. A potent stench of fish emanated from the alley. 'Come on,' Manius's voice murmured. 'Down here.'

The alley emerged opposite a tavern packed with poor, ragged and down-at-heel drinkers, whose poverty had nonetheless allowed them to scrape together the price of a jug of weak ale.

'That young Lucius Arrius said you pay well for gossip,' Manius whispered.

'The city's full of gossip,' Kerin said. 'I'm not paying for what I can hear in the marketplace.'

'You won't hear this in the marketplace, boy.' Manius gave a knowing nod. Kerin sighed and pressed a sesterce into the fisherman's hand. Manius's eyes glittered.

'My cousin's got a boat,' he whispered. 'One of those fast, pretty boats you were looking at when I took you up the river. Maximian Galba and his brother the abbot have offered him a purse of gold to fetch young Ambrosius. They're saying that the new king's doing nothing about the Picts, and that it's time he was replaced.'

'But there's nothing to be done at this time of year!' Kerin protested. 'The roads will be impassable soon, if they aren't already. Even the Picts won't be able to move. The best we can possibly do is raise a big enough army to fight them in the spring.'

'Well, *I* know that,' Manius said. 'But some people are stupid, aren't they. Stupid and impatient. They want something done now. And the Galbas know all that. They'll use it as an excuse to get their boy over here. If they manage it there's going to be all kinds of trouble, and it's no good telling my cousin not to do it; they'd only chop his hands off and find somebody else.'

Kerin lowered his eyes and tried to think. 'Alright, Manius,' he said, emptying a handful of coins out of his purse and slipping them into the fisherman's hand. 'If you hear anything else, I want to know about it straight away.'

Manius winked and elbowed his way into the tavern, shouting for ale. The wind was gusting wildly up the streets from the river. Flurries of sleet stung Kerin's face as he hurried, bent low, towards the gates of the praetor's residence. The crowd had swelled to occupy most of the courtyard. It seemed that every soldier, landowner and petty official with any possible interest in the proceedings had got wind of what was going on and had come along to add his few grains of corn to the heap. The merchants were there in force too, led by Gallus, to whom they seemed to defer as naturally as warriors did to their battle commanders. Severus appeared at the top of the steps, took a furtive look around and hurried back inside.

The two guardsmen at the door of the king's quarters stood to attention and moved aside. Kerin found Constans sitting on the bed in his undershirt. Lupinus was fussing around, laying out a choice of robes, cloaks and footwear.

'Out,' Kerin said briskly. 'And don't forget what I told you.' Constans looked up as the servant's footsteps skittered away down the passage to the atrium.

'If you ever cut out his tongue, I'll have you hanged,' he said. Kerin sat down on the end of the bed.

'Do you really think the Lord Vortigern would hang me to please you?' he asked. Constans played with the corner of one of the silken robes.

'That depends,' he said.

'Oh?' Kerin said. 'On what?'

Constans looked up with a sly, unpleasant smile. 'On which he values most. You or the power.'

Kerin hardly knew which shocked him more; the brazen nerve, or the assumption. He didn't look shocked. He was smiling. He wondered whether someone had put the question in Constans's mind, or if the monk had got there by himself. He thought he knew the answer; then something prickled inside him, and he realised that he did not. 'Well,' he said, 'if you're interested in power, hear this. Your good friend Maximian Galba and his brother Paulinus have hired a boat to bring your brother Ambrosius over from Armorica.'

Constans stared at him, eyes wide as an owl's. 'You're lying.'

'No. I learned this just now, and you're the first person I've told. I know Maximian's been bending your ear, but that was just to make things difficult for Vortigern. If Maximian gave a damn about you, do you think he'd bring your brother over here to replace you?'

'No,' Constans whispered.

'No,' Kerin said. He took Constans by his skinny shoulders and raised him to his feet. 'Look, I honestly don't want to hurt either of you. I only threatened Lupinus because he's such a gossip, I was afraid he might repeat things that you talk about in private. His tongue is in no danger unless you tell him things he shouldn't know.'

'We don't talk about things like that,' Constans said, looking down at the floor. 'Armies and taxes and government and invasions. Don't you think I have enough of that every day? It's pleasant sometimes, just to talk about ordinary things. And Lupinus doesn't want anything from me. He doesn't expect anything. He's just there, doing kind things for me. Can't you understand why a man might like that?'

'Yes,' Kerin sighed, sitting Constans down on the bed again. 'I can understand that quite well. But now, there's something you should know. The Lord Vortigern has decided to provide a bodyguard for you. Just to protect you, in case anyone wants to harm you.'

'Oh!' Constans said. 'Well, that can only be a good thing, can't it?'

'Yes,' Kerin said, 'it can only be a good thing.'

'Then why have you sat me down to tell me about

it, as if you were about to break some dreadful news?'
Constans asked. Kerin couldn't help smiling. He had
not realised that his misgivings were so obvious.

'Because you may be surprised to know that the
men who will be guarding you are Picts,' he said. 'But
don't be alarmed. They've sworn loyalty to the Lord
Vortigern, and in fact they're going to help us when
we go to fight their people. I suppose it's rather like
the Romans paying barbarian troops to fight for them.'

Constans gave a rueful smile. 'I'd probably be happi-
er to have some members of the praetorian guard. But
on the other hand, I've yet to encounter anything as
frightening as Father Paulinus on a bad day.'

'I'll bring them to you after this meeting, then,'
Kerin said. 'Their leader speaks some British, so you'll
be able to understand each other. Now get dressed.
Warm clothes, it's freezing. And don't forget what I've
said about Maximian and his friends. All they care
about is Rome and the Empire. If it was up to them,
you'd be back with Father Paulinus by tonight if they
didn't kill you first. I don't have to be a prophet to know
that.'

He left Constans shivering in his undershirt. A faint
mumbling sound followed him through the antechamber. He thought the monk was praying.

Hefin and the elderly Tertius were on guard at the door
of Vortigern's private quarters, an unlikely pairing.

'I've got to go in,' Kerin said. Hefin pursed his lips
and nodded. Tertius coughed politely and stared at
the ceiling. The door leading from the antechamber
was open. Vortigern was standing at the window,

looking out over the courtyard where the petitioners had gathered, flinging their arms about and stamping their feet in an effort to ward off the cold. He was wearing a short-sleeved dark tunic over a pair of light breeches; the sort of thing he might have worn on a summer's day in Henfelin. Not even an undershirt. One of his warmest cloaks lay on the couch beside him, a garment woven of heavy black wool and lined with sheepskin.

'You'll need that,' Kerin said, shivering as an icy draught invaded the room. Vortigern looked down at the cloak.

'Oh no,' he said, without concern. 'That's for Constans.'

Kerin's eyebrows rose. 'Lord, it's like winter out there.'

Vortigern chuckled. 'You're like the Romans, grown soft on the praetor's heating.'

'It's sleeting,' Kerin said pointedly. Vortigern shrugged.

'No matter,' he said. 'Most of them think I'm a lunatic in any case, don't they.'

'Some of them do,' Kerin said. 'A lunatic and a blood-drinking Celt. The rest believe that you're either God or the devil, so they probably think you're immune to pain and the cold.'

Vortigern looked down at the swelling crowd. 'Good,' he said. 'Let them think it.'

Kerin joined him at the window. 'Lord, there's some news,' he said reluctantly. 'It's not good. Maximian and Paulinus have hired a boat to fetch Ambrosius. It's ready to sail as soon as the weather calms down.'

'Oh merciful God,' Vortigern murmured, closing his eyes. 'That's what's behind all this.'

'I've told Constans,' Kerin said. 'He's frightened to death, so he isn't going to come out unless we go and get him. Where are we going to do this?'

'In the courtyard,' Vortigern said, picking up the cloak. 'The more uncomfortable they are, the sooner they'll give up.'

The two guards bowed deferentially and stood aside for Vortigern and Kerin to enter. As the door slammed shut there was a scuffling sound from within. They reached the principle room just in time to glimpse Lupinus scuttling away through the doorway which led to the baths and dressing rooms. Constans, blushing furiously, was making fumbling adjustments to his belt. Vortigern threw the cloak at him.

'Put this on,' he said roughly. Constans wrapped himself in the cloak, nearly drowning in its heavy folds. Vortigern steadied himself and adjusted the crown, which had slipped sideways as the king struggled with the cloak. 'Now hear me, Constans. I don't know what Maximian Galba is going to do today, so I can't prepare you for it. You must trust me, and please, don't look surprised at anything I say or do.'

'Of course I trust you, lord,' Constans quavered, shivering inside the cloak. He looked down at its opulent folds. 'Lord – this is your cloak, isn't it?'

'Yes,' Vortigern said. 'What of it?'

Constans looked at his lightweight tunic in dismay. 'You'll freeze, lord,' he said timidly. Vortigern smiled faintly.

'Gods and devils don't feel the cold,' he said. 'You're the ecclesiastic, so I'll leave it to you to decide which is appropriate. Come on; they're waiting for us.'

Severus met them at the door which led out onto the portico. Lud and his sons were in attendance.

'Thank the gods!' the praetor said fervently. 'Maximian Galba is on fire with impatience. We have made the dining-hall ready for you.'

'No,' Vortigern said. 'I'm going to talk to them out there.'

'But they're already frozen!' Severus closed his amenable eyes. 'They'll never stand for it.'

Vortigern's eyebrows rose. 'You don't think so?' he said, and opened the door. An icy gust streamed in, showering them with sleet. Vortigern chuckled and propelled Constans out onto the steps. Severus glanced nervously at Kerin and tapped his right temple with his forefinger. Kerin shrugged, inclined to agree with him, and followed Vortigern outside. Publius Luca was waiting there with a detachment of the city garrison. Maximian was already at the foot of the steps, flanked by Flavius the praetor and Garagon of Kent. Close behind were big, thick-necked Eldof of Glevum and a handful of his menacing youngsters. Vortigern met them halfway down the steps.

'It's that monk I've come to see,' Maximian gasped, teeth chattering. The wind shrieked around the courtyard.

'The king,' Vortigern corrected him.

'He's a monk, and king by your hand alone,' Maximian spat, pulling his cloak tight as the wind swelled ominously under his toga. Vortigern smiled.

'Cold, Maximian?' he enquired.

'Of course I'm cold, you madman,' Maximian bellowed. 'Everyone's cold. God knows, you've kept us waiting out here long enough. Now, can we continue this business inside?'

'No,' Vortigern said. 'There isn't room inside. The king will address his subjects here, in the courtyard. And if you're minded to leave these people outside and conduct your own private audience within, then think again. Every man in this courtyard has as much right to the king's ear as you do.'

'I speak for every man in this courtyard!' Maximian retorted, flexing his frozen hands. He had noticed how Vortigern was dressed, of course; Kerin could see the way his sharp eyes were moving over the thin garments and bare arms in sullen disbelief.

'You exaggerate, surely,' Vortigern said mildly. Garagon of Kent stamped his well-booted feet and thrust out his sharp, bearded chin.

'Well, I'll speak for myself, Maximian, thank you very much,' he said indignantly. 'The day when the praetor of Venta Belgarum speaks for Kent is far off.'

Maximian stared up at the lowering sky, as if imploring God to deliver him from such rank idiocy.

'Let's get on with this,' Vortigern said, twitching impatiently. 'If you've got anything to say, Maximian, get up there on top of the steps and say it. The same goes for you, Garagon, and you, Eldof. The king will answer when you're done.'

Maximian shot him a murderous glance, marched up to the top of the steps and braced himself against the cutting wind. 'Citizens of Londinium!' he shouted.

'The Picts are at the mouth of the river, and our leaders are still here within the city, trying to cobble together an army out of a mish-mash of undisciplined warriors and tired old soldiers.'

A murmur of agreement arose from at least part of the crowd. Flavius and his bodyguard clapped their hands. Eldof strode up to the top step and hammered the hilt of his sword against a pillar.

'He speaks the truth, monk,' he roared. 'We've come to tell you that if you can't deal with the Picts, we'll find someone who can.'

The crowd fell silent.

'Please!' Constans whined. 'Is this how you address your king?'

Maximian leaned forward. 'Lord Constans, we have delayed far too long as it is. I implore you to send messengers to Rome, to beg the Emperor's assistance in crushing this invasion once and for all.'

'No,' Vortigern breathed. He had been standing silently beside Constans, head bowed, but as Maximian spoke he turned on him. 'There'll be no message to the Emperor.'

'That isn't for you to decide,' Maximian said bluntly. 'We have a king. You put him there. Now, let him decide.'

Constans blinked nervously as Eldof's young bloods moved up behind him. Publius Luca gave Vortigern a look; a slight shake of the head. Kerin knew that none of them could afford to speak or raise a hand. Maximian and Eldof needed no excuse to call the king an impotent puppet. Constans took a sharp breath and raised his head.

'No,' he said. 'I will not send to Rome. Lords, you all lead mighty bands of warriors. Every city has its own garrison. We have fighting men enough, if they would unite to serve their king.'

'And who will unite them?' Maximian demanded. 'You, monk?'

'No,' Constans said, meeting his eyes. 'I have known only the life of the cloister, as you are at pains to remind me. I know nothing about warfare, and I don't pretend otherwise. I know the warriors call me a worm. Perhaps you call me worse, behind my back. But at least I'm not a hypocrite.' He took a deep breath, closed his eyes and summoned the loudest bellow he could raise. 'Only one man is fit for this task. I am giving command of all my defence forces to Vortigern, Lord of the West. He will be my representative in all things. A decree will go out this day, to tell the ordines and the garrison commanders what I have decided.'

A roar went up from the courtyard. It sounded triumphant or appalled, depending on which portion of the crowd it emanated from. Constans glanced fearfully at the livid faces of Maximian and his companions. 'Lords,' he added in a hoarse whisper, 'please lend your strength to the Lord Vortigern, because in opposing him you will oppose me, your rightful king.'

Maximian's fingers clenched, probably the only way he could keep them away from Constans's throat. Kerin turned, feeling a hand on his arm.

'My God, I wasn't expecting that,' Vortigern murmured as Publius Luca and his men moved up to protect Constans. 'Stay here and guard that poor fool. I can't talk to them from here.' Pausing only to flash a brilliant smile to Maximian, he dived headlong down the steps and vanished into the crowd. The warriors just below the portico stumbled forward and Gorlois emerged, shaking sleet from his bearskin cloak.

'By the gods!' he exclaimed, elbowing his way upwards. 'What a turn-up! I didn't think the little runt had it in him! Where's Vortigern?'

'Down there somewhere,' Kerin said, waving towards the courtyard. 'God knows what'll happen now. No-one expected this.'

A great collective bawl arose from below. Kerin glanced apprehensively at Gorlois and they pushed forward to the edge of the steps. Everyone beneath them seemed to be gazing upwards at the towering statue of Minerva. The reason became immediately apparent. Vortigern had climbed the statue and was standing high on the goddess's chariot, looking down over the courtyard. He raised his hands and an eerie silence fell, broken only by the moan of the freezing wind.

'You've heard Maximian Galba complain that we have not marched against the Picts,' he shouted. 'Don't forget, this is the complaint of a man who has never led an army. Who has probably never raised a sword in earnest. Am I right, Maximian?'

The crowd turned bodily towards the portico. Maximian flung his arms wide.

'What does that matter?' he protested. 'Must a man be a poet to appreciate Virgil, or a carpenter to recognise a good table?'

Vortigern laughed; quietly at first, then so loudly and raucously that the sound bounced back and forth around the courtyard, multiplying his derision. 'Of course not, you fool,' he mocked. 'But he must know what makes a good poem, or a good table. And do you know what makes a good warrior? If you think you do, then take off that warm cloak and your fine robes and come up here with me!' He tore off his tunic and flung it down. Even from his perch at the top of the steps, Kerin could see the purple tracery of battle scars. 'This is what makes a warrior!' Vortigern bellowed. 'Blood and death and grief. You think this is cold, Maximian Galba? In the North, it's ten times colder than this. Even now, it would be impossible to march much further than Eburacum. The wagons would get bogged down in the drifts. Our horses and men would die of cold and starvation. Am I right, Flavius, praetor of Eburacum?' He waited. *Am I right?'*

'Yes,' Flavius said grudgingly. 'You are right.'

'Yes,' Vortigern said, looking back down over the crowd. 'In your hearts, you all know that I am right. And yet some of you want me to take good, brave men like Publius Luca and Lucius Arrius – like the warriors of Kent, and Kernow, and Glevum – and march them up there to die for your sakes in some frozen hell-hole while you huddle down there in your warm winter clothes. Now hear me, you shivering field-mice. The king has granted me command of his defence forces. Eldof! Garagon! You'd sooner die than serve under me. Some of you hate me with good reason. But I am asking all of you to put that aside until we have beaten the Picts. Fight me afterwards, if you must, but help me to beat them first.' A vicious gust whirled around the courtyard, scattering hail. Vortigern braced himself against the front of the chariot. 'We have the winter to build an army,' he gasped, the wind whipping his breath away. 'The day the roads open, that army will march north to meet the invaders. For the love of God, let's bury our differences and fight them together. If we can do that, we'll beat them so soundly that they'll never trouble us again. But on my mother's grave, I'll fight them on my own, if I must.'

'Never, by the gods!' Gorlois roared. 'Kernow's with you to the death!'

As if that were a signal, the near-silent crowd erupted in pandemonium; whether in approval or dismay, it was impossible to judge. Across the sea of waving fists and swords, Kerin glimpsed Vortigern springing from the chariot to the plinth; he looked down, as if someone had shouted to him from below, then disappeared from sight. Lud and Publius Luca were shepherding Constans away, while Severus was attempting to pacify the apoplectic Maximian. Kerin felt a hand on his shoulder. To his surprise, it belonged to Eldof of Glevum.

'I hate the air he breathes, Kerin Brightspear,' Eldof said. 'But as God's my witness, I couldn't have done what he did out there just now. And he spoke the truth, for once. I'll meet him in the castra this afternoon, if he wishes it.'

'I shall tell him,' Kerin said, extending his hand. Eldof shook it firmly. Garagon hailed him, all excitement, and they hurried away. The crowd parted and Vortigern stumbled up the steps and through the open doorway. Kerin caught up with him in the passage leading to his private quarters.

'Lord!' he exclaimed. Vortigern turned and stopped dead. It was as if, once he ceased to move, the cold petrified him. He had retrieved his tunic but it was dripping melted sleet. Kerin took off his own cloak and put it around Vortigern's shoulders. 'Not God or the devil, then?' he said. Vortigern's numbed lips formed a lop-sided smile.

'Not quite,' he whispered, shaking. 'But keep it to yourself.'

'Well, either way, you convinced Eldof,' Kerin said. 'He'll be waiting for you in the castra this afternoon. Garagon too, I shouldn't be surprised.'

Vortigern's fists clenched and he nodded; a small gesture of triumph. The sound of footsteps came towards them; sharp, hard, a guardsman's boots. Lucius rounded the corner at the double and greeted Vortigern with a respectful bow instead of his customary smart salute.

'I'm sorry, lord, but it's Maximian Galba. Severus Maximus tried to get rid of him, but he's insisting on seeing you before he goes.'

'Very well,' Vortigern said curtly. He took a breath and straightened his shoulders. 'Put him in the room next to the council chamber and tell him to wait for me.'

'Yes, lord,' Lucius said. 'I shan't make him too comfortable.'

Vortigern leaned on Kerin's shoulder as Lucius hurried away. 'Alright. Find Lud, and tell him to have those Picts waiting outside the servants' door. Then get Constans, and meet me in the council chamber.'

'What are you going to do?' Kerin asked.

'I don't know,' Vortigern said. 'We'll see what happens. But I'll tell you this. I am within a hair's breadth of Eldof's allegiance, and Garagon's, and no-one is going to prevent me from securing it.' He removed Kerin's cloak, pulled on his sodden tunic and handed the cloak back. 'Here, take it. It spoils the illusion.'

In the council chamber, eerily silent after the uproar in the courtyard, the king awaited his tormentor. The table on the dais had been moved back and a heavy carved chair set in front of it. Constans sat alone, motionless except for the quivering of his lower lip. His hands gripped the arms of the chair so tightly that his sharp little knuckles looked as if they might burst through the fragile skin. Kerin waited, hand on hilt, while Lud guarded the servants' entrance. Vortigern stood at the foot of the dais; his face pale, composed, hard as flint.

'Don't be afraid, lord king,' he said softly, as footsteps approached the door. 'I am your servant in all things.'

Maximian swept into the room with Flavius pattering at his side. Close behind them the two young soldiers, Flaccus and Albinus, marched side by side. Both were armed to the teeth, but of the four men only Maximian seemed to be on fire with resolve.

'My friends,' Vortigern said politely, 'it is customary to bow in the presence of the king.'

'In the presence of the king,' Maximian barked, 'but not in the presence of an upstart monk, who should go back to his monastery.'

'I am king by right of blood!' Constans blurted indignantly. 'I am the oldest son of my father Constantine, and –'

'And promised to the service of God,' Maximian snapped. Constans gave him a petulant little smile.

'And how may I best serve God?' he asked. 'By locking myself up in a hovel? You had enough to say about my kingly rights when you were trying to shut me up, didn't you?'

Maximian snorted. 'I wish my brother were here. He'd soon whip the Pelagian out of you. So what are you going to do about the Picts, mighty king? Hold a party for them when they come sailing up the river?'

'No!' Constans retorted, his voice rising to a squeak of fury. 'We're going to beat the daylights out of them in the spring.'

'How?' Maximian sneered. 'With Vortigern's ragbag army? I think you are sadly misled. They're a bunch of barbarians, cut-throats and two-faced crooks, and they won't get further than the city walls without slitting each other's throats.'

Kerin tensed. For a moment he almost expected Maximian's head to go the same way as Plicius's. Vortigern did not move.

'Lud,' he said, without turning. 'Summon the royal bodyguard.'

Maximian looked at him curiously. 'The royal bodyguard? Is the praetorian guard no longer sufficient?'

Vortigern smiled cheerily. 'Not in these times of barbarians, cut-throats and two-faced crooks,' he said. Behind him the servants' door slammed open and Lud marched stone-faced into the council chamber followed by Bridei and three of his kin. The Picts were transformed. Kerin had exchanged their rancid clothes for short white tunics and swirling red capes.

Their short-handled spears had been borrowed from Severus's arsenal. It all looked peculiarly at odds with their wild hair and the vivid blue and red tattoos, all the more colourful now that their owners had scrubbed themselves. Bridei grinned toothily at Maximian as he passed and planted himself at the foot of the dais. Kerin instinctively eased his sword in its sheath. The Pict had shown him nothing but respect so far, but there was something mad in those pale blue eyes. Maximian stared at Bridei in disbelief.

'What insanity is this?' he asked.

'This is no insanity,' Vortigern said. 'These are the men who are guarding the king against those who would like to steal his crown.'

'But they're Picts!' Maximian protested.

'What of it?' Vortigern said. 'In the spring they're going to sell their leaders to my ragbag army. And until then they've sworn on their lives to guard the king, and guard him they will. Eh, Bridei?'

The Pict beamed. 'We are yours, lord,' he said. Vortigern raised his eyebrows. 'And the king's,' Bridei added hastily. Maximian turned to his companions.

'Come,' he said curtly. 'The praetor's house has become a den of savages.' He rounded on Vortigern. 'This isn't the end, you know. I don't care how many fools you managed to hoodwink in the courtyard. I've already sent a messenger to the consul Aetius in Gallia, asking him to send as many troops as he can spare. They'll be here within weeks. And then we'll see where the power lies, Lord of the West, Celt of the Celts.'

Without waiting for a response, he turned and swept out of the council chamber with Flavius and the young soldiers on his heels. Vortigern stepped up onto the dais and raised Constans to his feet.

'Come on,' he said gently. 'You've done well today, and now you must rest. Bridei and his friends will keep guard while you sleep. Go with them, Lud, then see to our own men.' He nodded to the Picts and sat down on the edge of the dais. Constans hesitated, trembling still.

'Lord, I'm frightened!' he whispered. Vortigern shook his head sadly.

'Constans,' he said, 'haven't I told you that I am your servant until death?'

'Oh –oh yes,' Constans stammered. 'And I know you'll do your best to protect me. But Maximian –'

Vortigern looked up at him with a smile which could have melted the winter snow on the peaks of the Eryri. 'Sleep, little friend,' he said softly, 'and leave Maximian to me.'

Kerin's breath escaped in a sharp hiss as Constans padded away, flanked by his guards.

'What?' Vortigern said. Kerin shook his head evasively; he could not entirely explain the chill of apprehension, even to himself. Any sane man would have worried about Bridei, but deep within himself, Kerin knew that there was more to it than that. Vortigern looked hard at him and let it pass. 'Alright,' he said, rising to his feet. 'Find Gallus, and tell him to come to me tonight. There's something I want him to do for me.'

Kerin felt aggrieved. 'Lord, there's nothing I wouldn't do for you,' he said. Vortigern smiled and shook his head.

'I know that,' he said, embracing him. 'But tonight

I need a man who knows how the world works. And there are some things I wouldn't ask you to do, anyway.'

Kerin had no idea what he meant until late the following morning, when Lupinus came running in from the street, ashen-faced and breathless, to tell him that Maximian Galba's body had been found floating in the river, without its head.

20

The horses whickered and stamped impatiently. Kerin shivered and stirred the embers of the driftwood fire. A bitter wind was driving straight up the river from the sea; the awful, howling grey expanse which the Romans had called Oceanus Germanicus, and which Kerin had not even heard of, until fate took him to Londinium. The wind must be coming from some even worse frozen wilderness, he thought, shaking a thin layer of wet snow from his cloak. He wondered what might be out there, and whether he needed to worry about it. Everyone knew that the Saxons came from somewhere beyond that sea, although no raids had been reported for a while. Kerin tried to dismiss the thought. He knew that there were more immediate matters to worry about, at least until the spring. Bridei squatted on the shingle beside him, picking at a half-cooked fish. He seemed completely oblivious of the weather.

'Don't you savages feel the cold?' Kerin grumbled, pulling his thick, fur-lined cloak tightly around his shoulders. Bridei grinned.

'I am a Pict,' he said, chewing noisily. 'We are a strong people.'

'I can see,' Kerin said dismally, looking at the other

man's bare arms and legs. Three of Bridei's compatriots were wading waist deep in the murky river, trawling for fish. Kerin could understand why they missed their wild country and the sea, but it was beyond him why anyone should have begged to trade warmth and a certain meal for the opportunity to struggle around in a freezing river. The snow thickened, collecting on the roofs of the fishermen's huts, and on the decks and reefed sails of the boats beached on the mud-banks upstream. Beyond that, barely visible through the veil of drifting white, was the shabby alehouse where Kerin had first encountered Manius. At the water's edge Vortigern was deep in conversation with two fishermen. The snow formed a white crust on the shoulders of his cloak. Bridei finished his fish and helped himself to another.

'Last night there was no ale for us,' he complained.

'I'm not surprised,' Kerin said. 'You drink it like water.'

Bridei tore at his fish. 'The Lord Vortigern, he promised us good ale,' he said moodily. 'He promised us more gold than we ever saw. Well, we do not see it yet.'

'Look, you ungrateful bastard,' Kerin said, 'if it hadn't been for the Lord Vortigern, the praetor would have hanged you the day you were captured.'

'I know,' Bridei sighed. 'He is a good man. You are lucky, you and the Cambrian warriors. But as for that little baby king –' he spat out a mouthful of bones.

Kerin shrugged. 'He does you no harm. And it's your duty to guard him. You swore to do it, on your own father's knife. You keep your promises, don't you?'

Bridei glanced up. 'I do,' he said. 'We have guarded him well, have we not?'

'Yes,' Kerin conceded. 'You have. And I'll see to the ale. If it's run short, that's the fault of the praetor's household. I told the kitchen to keep you in food and drink. But don't forget your oaths. If anything happens to the king, it's my responsibility. We'll all have to answer for it.'

Bridei looked up. 'I told you. I keep my promise. My father teaches me that. Unless the other man breaks his side first, of course. Then there is no promise. But our leaders are right. The Britons are a stupid people. It is Vortigern who should be your king, not that thing.' He patted his chest. 'Then Bridei would be a great man, with many servants of his own.'

Kerin knew better than to dispel the Pict's illusions. As he watched, Vortigern took a leather pouch from his belt and placed it in the older fisherman's hand. Bridei muttered something in his own tongue. Vortigern trudged back up the beach.

'Lord,' the Pict complained, 'there is no gold for us, but you have something for this old man.'

Vortigern looked credibly affronted. 'Bridei, do you question my honesty?'

'No, lord!' Bridei protested. 'But –'

'Get up,' Vortigern snapped, kicking him in the thigh. Bridei yelped and picked himself up. 'I was a wealthy man once, but I've spent all my money serving the king,' Vortigern said. 'And I know he'll never repay me.' He raised a threatening finger as Bridei opened his mouth to speak. 'I'm like you, Bridei. A man of my word. When the weather changes, this old man will sail to my home with a message for my sons. When they come back, they'll bring gold enough for us all.' He paused, with a look of patent distress. 'God willing, I'll live to see the day. These are dangerous times for a man who can't afford to pay his warriors. I hope they all remain as loyal as you have been.'

Bridei fell on one knee. 'Forgive me, lord,' he whispered, clasping Vortigern's hand. Kerin did not know which astonished him more; the magnitude of the lie, or Bridei's ability to believe it.

'Come on, get up,' Vortigern said. 'You've had your breath of fresh air. I don't care if the king turns your stomach. You're here to guard him, so get back to the praetor's house and do it. If anyone harms him, it's on your head.'

Bridei leapt to his feet and bawled some curt orders. The other Picts waded out of the water and rolled up their net, then off they marched towards the city, singing cheerfully and carrying the net between them. Vortigern grimaced and shook his hand in the wind to dispel the odour of fish.

'What did he say?' Kerin asked, as they rode back towards the city.

'Your Manius was right,' Vortigern said. 'Maximian and Paulinus did pay the old man to sail to Armorica for the boy.' He broke off suddenly and raised his hand. Kerin drew rein. Some blurred shapes were coming towards them through the snow. As they drew nearer, they became recognisable. Eldof and Varro were in the lead, followed by Garagon of Kent and the irrepressible Brennius. There was also a riderless horse, which

Brennius was leading by a rope attached to its head-collar. Kerin whistled softly. It was the most beautiful animal he had ever seen. Brennius was talking to the horse, chirruping and offering words of encouragement as it trotted beside him, moving like a dancer on tip-toes. The horse was not happy; anyone could have seen that. It was shivering violently, blinking and snorting as the snow invaded its eyes and wide-open nostrils and settled on its silken bay coat. It lacked completely the harsh layer of shaggy hair which British horses grew to protect them against winter's savagery. Eldof hailed them jovially. It was hard to believe that this was the same man who had stood up in the curia and demanded Ambrosius for king.

'You're as mad as we are, out in this weather,' Vortigern observed. Garagon cleared his throat and puffed out his chest.

'A racehorse needs its exercise,' he said.

'It won't need much when it's dead of frostbite,' Kerin said, slipping from his mare's back. The horse eyed him nervously and backed away. Kerin spoke to it softly, wondering what language it understood.

'You see?' Brennius said. 'I told you it was too cold for it. It should be at home in one of those heated stables, like Severus's chariot horses have got.'

Garagon looked crestfallen. It was bad enough having a low-bred bastard from Cambria implying that he was an idiot, without his own right-hand man agreeing. 'It's ridiculous,' he said grumpily. 'They tell you a horse has got legs like iron, then you find it can't stand the cold.'

'Well, it's hot where the poor beast comes from,'

Brennius said sympathetically. He nodded to Kerin. 'Hot as the flames of hell. No grass, just rocks and sand. The horses must really have iron legs if they can gallop all day on that.'

Kerin looked down at the slender black legs and wondered. The horse stretched out its elegant head and nibbled hesitantly at the sleeve of his tunic.

'He's a beautiful horse, Garagon,' Kerin conceded, too filled with admiration to sound grudging.

'Well, I'll happily challenge any of your bone-shakers to a race when the weather clears,' Garagon said with a patronising smile. Kerin sighed, wishing that the compliment could have been accepted in the same spirit with which he offered it.

'I was speaking to Gallus down by the wharf this morning,' Eldof said. 'He's still talking about war-galleys, you know.'

'Well, he shall have them,' Vortigern said. 'It'll do none of us any good if Gallus becomes disaffected or loses his trade; especially those of us with money to waste on racehorses.'

'Do you really think it was money wasted?' Garagon asked.

'Well, perhaps not,' Vortigern said. 'But I hope you aren't going to squeal too loudly when the king's tax collectors come to ask you for money to protect the merchant fleet.'

Garagon's expression – one of silent dismay – conveyed that this prospect had not previously occurred to him.

'Come now, Garagon,' Eldof said soothingly. 'Everyone knows that the revenue from your cornfields keeps you well provided. And if the merchant fleet fails, you'll lose your markets in the Empire, won't you.'

'Thank you, Eldof,' Vortigern said. 'An impeccable argument. Now, can you please think of an equally convincing one for me to present to the sheep-breeders and cattle-raisers in the West?'

Eldof's smile faded abruptly. 'In truth, I can think of none,' he said stonily. Vortigern smiled blithely. Garagon turned away, choking on the sleeve of his tunic. Brennius threw his head back and brayed at the whirling snowflakes. Eldof wagged a threatening finger.

'Only if you and Gorlois pay too,' he said.

'Well, of course we shall,' Vortigern said. 'Everyone will pay, from the greatest landowners down to the men with a few cows and a donkey, in proportion to their wealth.'

Eldof snorted. 'I never thought I'd say this, but you're starting to sound like a Roman governor. What happens if they refuse?'

'We burn their houses down and break their legs,' Vortigern said. 'Roman law is like the will of God. Sometimes it needs a push.'

Kerin followed him into the driving snow. 'Do you think they'll pay up?' he asked, as they rode towards the outskirts of the city.

'Certainly they'll pay up. We already have enough of an army to guarantee that. And in the spring, I hope, they'll give up their young men for that army. What do you think? Can we count on Eldof and Garagon, would you say?'

'Yes,' Kerin said, 'at the moment, I think we can.

And there's another thing I should tell you. I'm going to have that horse one day.'

'Garagon's racehorse?'Vortigern said scornfully.'He'd never sell it. And you could never afford it, anyway; it must have cost him most of last year's harvest.'

'Oh, I know all that. But one way or another, the horse will come to me. And that *is* a prediction.'

'You're mad,'Vortigern said. Kerin laughed out loud.

'Would you like to climb back up on Minerva's chariot and tell me that?' he asked. Vortigern shrugged.

'It worked, didn't it?'

'Oh yes, lord,' Kerin said. 'It worked very well. But it reminded me of something Iustig said to me. He said that I should tell you not to tempt God any further. He also said that he'd pray for you, whether you wanted it or not.'

Vortigern gave him that odd, bitter look, a reminder of the night when they had got drunk on Gallus's wine. 'You've said nothing about Rufus,' he said suddenly, drawing rein as they reached the first of the great Roman houses. Kerin avoided his eyes. He had been dreading this moment. 'Look,' Vortigern leaned towards him, 'I know he's not in Henfelin because Hefydd told me so, and he's not in Londinium. If you know where he is, then I think you had better tell me.'

Kerin stared down at the street below his horse's hooves where the snow was collecting in wet drifts, stained brown by mud and excrement. 'Lord, he went to Paulinus in Caerwynt,' he said. 'I've no idea if he's still there, or what either of them are doing now.'

Vortigern looked up at the leaden sky and closed his eyes to the snow. 'Well, I can see why you were in no hurry to tell me that.'

'Perhaps I should have done,' Kerin said.

'Perhaps,' Vortigern said. 'But no-one wants to bear the poison chalice, do they?' Above their heads gulls wheeled and screamed, driven upriver by the rising gale.

'Rufus wants to be loyal to you,' Kerin said. 'But once the faith really gets hold of people, there's not much to be done, is there.' They rode on down the narrow street towards the heart of the city. 'Are you a Pelagian?' Kerin asked. Vortigern slowed his mare.

'What's it to you?' he asked.

'Nothing, in itself. I had no clear idea what Pelagius stood for until Constans explained it to me. He was ranting about a bishop called Germanus. He came over here when Rufus and I were little lads, didn't he?'

'Yes, Vortigern said. 'He was a former general, a real fighter. There was a battle up near Segontium, where Magnus Maximus used to have his base. I didn't take part. I was in the south, pushing the Irish back into Dyfed. Further north, they'd made an alliance with the Picts, as they always have from time to time. Germanus rode out with our commanders and trounced them. I remember drinking with him afterwards, and thinking he was a man I could do business with. But things have changed since then. The Church has changed.'

'Constans told me that the Pelagians have been banned in Rome,' Kerin said. 'You can get locked up or executed, just for being one.'

Vortigern sighed. 'That's politics, not religion. If all the idiots believe they'll burn in hell unless they obey the priests, and the Emperor's hand in glove with the Pope –' he grimaced. 'I don't have to elaborate, surely.

But it won't be happening here. If the priests cause trouble I'll start turning the screw on them, and if that makes me a Pelagian, so be it. The fallacy in their argument, of course, is that you have to die to go to hell. It's not essential, as they'll find out if they're not careful.'

'Have you ever spoken to Rufus about this, lord?' Kerin asked.

'I wouldn't waste my breath,' Vortigern said. 'I know what he thinks. And if you're ever in any doubt about the consequences of it all, try asking yourself if you'd sooner be locked in a room with Paulinus or Brother Padarn.' They had reached the tall gates of Gallus's house. The guards recognised the two horsemen and bowed from the waist. 'Well,' Vortigern said, 'I shall tell Gallus about the fleet tax, and then no doubt he will command a feast and break open a cask of his finest. You're welcome to join us if you wish, but it's not a command.'

'It has no need to be,' Kerin said. 'I'll join you later, but I have things to see to in the praetor's house first.' Two things, in fact, he thought; one involving Lucius and a horse. The other, which he had been putting off, involving Faria.

'Very well,' Vortigern said as the great gates swung open for him, 'see to your business. But may I, as a man of experience, offer you some advice? Don't wear that ring dangling from your neck whilst you are seeing to it.'

Kerin's hand flew to his crucifix as quickly as the colour to his face. The silver ring was so tiny, he had convinced himself that no-one would notice it. As he kicked his mare into a trot and rode for Severus's house, he could hear Vortigern chuckling as the gates of Gallus's house closed after him.

As Kerin approached the praetor's house, the gates opened and a horseman came out at a brisk trot. Eyes on the street, he didn't give Kerin a second glance. Idris. Well-dressed and well-armed. Kerin hadn't thought about him at all since overhearing that argument in the citadel. He had had far too much to occupy his mind. Now it all came back to him. The father, Brwyn, was not amongst the wealthiest of Vortigern's following, but he was a frugal man; he had a patch of corn ground and a few good cattle, all well tended, and so his family had never had to struggle. Idris was like him in that sense. His share of the profits couldn't have been large, but he always had a good horse, and a well-crafted sword on his belt. He wasn't like Katigern, who spent his father's money on girls and drinking. Kerin had always admired Idris for that. But now here were that good horse and that well-crafted sword where they had no business to be. Kerin cupped his hands around his mouth. 'Idris!' he shouted. The young warrior dragged on his mare's mouth and spun her round. 'What are you doing here?' Kerin asked. Idris threw his head back, in the way horses did when they were about to try facing you down.

'It's not forbidden, is it?' he asked. Kerin didn't like his tone. Idris had never disrespected him, but there was always something guarded about it; something qualified. Kerin knew that if he hadn't had the dumb luck to land in Vortigern's household, Idris wouldn't have given him the time of day.

'No, it's not forbidden,' he said. 'Not in so many words. But you know quite well what the Lord said before we left. Anyone not commanded to ride to Londinium was expected to stay at home, in case of trouble from the Irish. So what are you doing here?'

'I had matters to attend to,' Idris said, without a blink. 'That's any man's right.'

'Yes,' Kerin said. 'As long as it doesn't interfere with his obligations to his lord.'

Idris gave him a look of utter disdain, gathered his reins and took off. Kerin watched him go. If he had had his spear with him, he might have dropped the boy right there, in the middle of the street. He wouldn't have killed him, of course, but he was good enough to deal the sort of glancing blow which could knock a man out of the saddle. Elir had come to the gate, as he always did when he heard a familiar horse approaching.

'What was all that about?' he asked. Kerin supposed that he looked as surprised as he felt.

'I don't know,' he said. 'Look, I'll see to my horse. I want you to follow Idris. He's heading for the western gate. I want to know where he goes and what he does. Take a horse he won't recognise, and keep out of his sight. Whatever he's up to, I doubt if he'll want the rest of us to know about it.'

'Done,' Elir said, and scurried off to make ready.

Lucius was waiting in the stable block. The bay horse stretched his head out over the half- door and nibbled his shoulder. Kerin looked on with a feeling of vague disappointment. 'He likes you, doesn't he,' he said. 'I was hoping he'd hate you enough to throw you off.'

'Oh, we've done all that,' Lucius said. 'I was black and blue for the first couple of weeks, but we're used to each other now.'

'Good,' Kerin said. 'Next time you're off duty, we could ride out into the open country.'

'I'm off tomorrow,' Lucius said. 'But it's All Souls' Day, isn't it? It doesn't mean much to me, to be truthful, but I usually go along with it to avoid upsetting my parents. Still, if they're down on their knees praying, they may not notice that I'm missing.'

'Tomorrow it is, then,' Kerin said. 'And wear two pairs of breeches, because I'm going to ride the arse off you.' He was about to set off towards the courtyard when something made him turn. Lucius was looking at him with distinct uneasiness. 'What?' Kerin asked.

'It's probably nothing,' Lucius said. 'None of my business really, in any case.'

'What?' Kerin repeated.

'It's those Picts. I know what I said about a body-guard, but do you think those barbarians should be guarding the king? They're a bunch of heathen savages, lord. I wouldn't let them guard a barrel full of rats, never mind the king. Why can't some of the city garrison do it?'

'That's not for me to say, Lucius,' Kerin said in a measured way. 'Has Publius Luca mentioned anything about it?'

'Not a thing,' Lucius said. 'Could you speak to the Lord Vortigern? Lud says he's using the Picts to frighten Constans, and I could see some point in that, because he's been a proper puffed-up little peacock lately. But frightening him is one thing, isn't it.'

'What do you mean?' Kerin asked.

'I've seen these men drunk,' Lucius said. 'They'd knife you as good as look at you. And the king is nothing to them. Why should they defend him?'

'Because they're paid to?' Kerin suggested. 'Because they've sworn an oath to do it?'

'Perhaps,' Lucius said, without conviction. 'I'm not questioning the Lord Vortigern's judgment, of course, but if he really does realise how dangerous the Picts are —' he hesitated and looked down at his boots, as if he scarcely wanted to think the thing, let alone give it words. 'I hardly like to say this, lord, but I can't help wondering how much he cares about the king's safety.'

Kerin, to whom the only surprising thing about all this was that Lucius should have come out with it, reached up to caress the ears of the bay horse. He looked at the animal's coat, grown lustrous with grooming, and wished that he too had nothing to concern him other than the arrival of the next bundle of hay.

'We have to beat the invaders,' he said. 'Perhaps Vortigern's not too concerned about how it's done.'

Lucius looked up, his coal-black eyes shining. Whatever his misgivings, the situation seemed to hold some shiver of excitement for him; whether founded in dread or anticipation, it was impossible to judge. 'Are you saying that the king should be replaced?' he asked.

'No, Lucius,' Kerin said. 'It's not my place to make those decisions, thank God.'

They walked together out of the stables. Kerin was tempted to put off his visit to the slaves' quarters. Faria still held his affection, and deserved his honesty; but how could he tell her that it was now impossible for him to look at a woman, any woman, without finding her image supplanted by a ghost with copper hair and harebell-blue eyes? He would want her, too, when it came to it; that was the worst part. Faria would come to him with her sinuous body and perfumed hair, and he would want her, even if it was Gael's body he imagined beneath him as he gave in to it all.

'Have you got a girl, Lucius?' he asked.

'Well, one or two.' Lucius smiled. 'Not a special one, though. I'm sure my parents think it's high time I found one and settled down, but you've got to find the right one, haven't you?'

'Yes,' Kerin said despondently, wondering whether years of searching could have found him anyone less suitable than the daughter of Bertil Redknife.

Kerin parted company with Lucius at the door of the guards' mess and walked slowly on down the tunnel towards the slaves' quarters. As he approached the entrance to that dank maze, Sha'ara came tripping towards him carrying an armful of silk bath robes.

'Lord Kerin!' she exclaimed, in her low, throaty voice; so like Faria's, really, and yet lacking that engaging warmth.

'Are you well?' Kerin asked.

'Yes, lord.' Sha'ara bowed her head respectfully. 'We are all well,' she added, with a pointed little smile.

'I've been home to Cambria,' Kerin said. He supposed that she knew this, and it was in any case ridiculous to feel that he should have to explain himself to a slave, but there it was. Sha'ara looked up at him quizzically.

'Oh yes, lord. We know that. And we know also that you have been back here for some time, because Lupinus told us.'

That loose-tongued little snake, Kerin thought irritably. He was wondering what to tell Sha'ara when there was a noise at the end of the tunnel adjoining the courtyard; the sort which could only have been made by a group of men who were well on the way to being drunk, although it was the middle of the afternoon. Kerin looked up, expecting to see Bridei and his mob, but in fact the noise had been made by Lud, his three sons and Dull Bened, assisted by Hefydd and a bunch of his boys. Hefydd was carrying a pitcher.

'Kerin, you dog!' Macsen roared, weaving unsteadily down the tunnel and flinging an arm around his friend's shoulders.

'Macsen,' Kerin said, grinning, as Lud and the others caught up. They were reeking of the praetor's poor quality mead.

'We found it in the kitchens, boy,' Hefydd chortled, swinging the pitcher. 'Me and the boys. We went looking for meat, but we found this instead. It isn't all that good, but by God, it reminds you of home.' He held the pitcher up to Kerin's nose. He was right, but Kerin knew that he had to keep his head clear. Hefydd shrugged and passed the pitcher to Lud. The act of putting his thoughts into words seemed to have released some great emotional flood-tide within him, and he looked up at Kerin with tears rolling slowly down his face to lodge, shining, in his straggly grey beard. 'Oh God,' he whispered. 'Oh God. How much more of this pestilent place?'

'Hefydd, Hefydd!' Kerin cried, seizing the older man by the shoulders. 'We've got to make the best of it, haven't we; and at least you and I have had a taste of home to keep us sane. Believe me, we'll be back in Cambria the moment it's possible.' He looked round as a chorus of riotous laughter burst from the other members of the drinking party. Lud, of all people, had poured most of the contents of the pitcher over Bened's head. Lucius poked his head round the door of the guards' mess and winked at Kerin.

'I'll get them all in here,' he said. 'Then I'll fetch some more of that stuff, whatever it is. They'll drink themselves stupid and go to sleep, before they do any harm to themselves or anyone else.' He glanced at Hefydd, who had sunk down on the floor in a quivering heap.

'I'll look after him, ' Kerin said. 'You see to the others.' Then he noticed Sha'ara, who was hovering nearby, as if hoping that he might do or say something. 'Sha'ara,' he said quietly, 'I want to talk to Faria. Please ask her to come to me in my chambers. I'll need to see to this old fool first, but it shouldn't take long.'

Sha'ara nodded silently and hurried away with her bath robes clutched to her chest. Kerin dragged Hefydd to his feet. Lucius had flung open the door of the mess and was smiling and waving the pitcher, which he had managed to prise from Lud's grasp. The warriors poured after him with a roar of approval.

'Come on, you miserable sods,' Macsen bellowed, pulling Elir and Custennin along with him. Kerin hoisted Hefydd onto his shoulders and carried him off across the courtyard. Whatever Vortigern's opinion, he knew that he had been right about the wisdom of making friends. He was heartily glad that Lucius could now be counted amongst them.

Towards evening, as the darkness drew in, the wind dropped and the snow stopped falling. The moon came out from the thinning clouds and cast its ghostly white light across the deserted courtyard. Kerin sat on the window ledge, listening to the faint sounds of the city beyond the walls and the much louder sounds of Hefydd snoring in his dressing room, as evening slipped into night and still Faria did not come. He could not understand it. Sha'ara would have delivered his summons however much she resented him, and Faria would have obeyed whatever her feelings, because they were slaves, and had had obedience beaten into them. It was possible that Faria had already been promised to some high-ranking guest, but it seemed unthinkable that she would not have sent someone to tell him so.

'It *is* unthinkable,' he said, out loud, to the moonlit courtyard and the unconscious snoring body on his couch. A nameless dread filled him, black and suffocating. He leapt to his feet, buckled on his sword belt and rushed out into the night.

The courtyard was deserted except for the usual pair of guards standing at the main gate. Kerin ran towards the tunnel, ignoring their curious glances. A sliver of yellow light leaked under the door of the guards' mess. He wrenched the door open, and the stench of sweat and mead and burning tallow came out to meet him. The room was littered with empty pitchers and the bodies of senseless, snoring warriors.

'Are they alright?' Lucius asked, touching Kerin's arm. His hand was freezing; he must have come from outside. 'I've been inspecting the guard on the gates and the walls,' he whispered. 'I thought your boys would be safe enough here. There was a bit of a fight before, but we soon sorted it out.'

'I don't think they're in a hurry to go anywhere,' Kerin said, glancing over his shoulder.

'Lord?' Lucius said, sensing his uneasiness.

'Have you seen any of the slave girls?' Kerin asked, closing the mess room door.

'Not since Sha'ara left us. Why do you ask?'

'Because there's something wrong,' Kerin said, peering down the tunnel. 'Lucius, there's no-one down there. Who's supposed to be guarding the slaves' quarters?'

'Tertius and young Livius,' Lucius said. 'They were there when I went out, alright. Come on; let's ask the boys on the gate if they've seen them.'

The courtyard was empty, the thin film of snow freezing on the paving slabs. Kerin and Lucius were passing the archway which led to the atrium when they heard the commotion behind them. Running footsteps, a woman's hysterical shrieks; a man's voice trying vainly to silence her.

'What in God's name is that?' Kerin said. At the entrance to the tunnel, Tertius and a nonplussed younger guard were trying to calm and control a howling rabble of slaves, both male and female. Sha'ara's sister Aidée was in the midst of it. As Kerin arrived she broke free and hurled herself at his feet, weeping and babbling incoherently. Kerin seized her by the arms and hauled her up. It was impossible to understand a word of what she was trying to say.

'Aidée, please!' he exclaimed.

'Lord, come,' she gulped, clasping his hand. She ran, sobbing, her breath catching in her throat, and Kerin followed; down the tunnel, past the mess room and its oblivious inhabitants, down into the festering dark hole where Plicius tried to do away with him. Aidée's nails dug into his palm. Sha'ara was leaning against the wall outside Faria's door, staring at the floor. Kerin felt Aidée's grip slacken.

'Sha'ara?' he said uncertainly; then he turned and, with all his force, kicked the door open. A flood of yellow light poured out; there seemed to be torches everywhere. Marcellus met him halfway across the room.

'Wait,' he said firmly, placing his thin hands on Kerin's chest.

'Marcellus, why –'

'Kerin, Kerin Brightspear, please hear me,' the haruspex said gently. 'You must come in with me now, but please, my young friend, prepare yourself for what you will see.'

Taking Kerin's arm, he led him into the room. On the narrow bed, illuminated by the torchlight, Faria lay rigid and cold. Her huge eyes, sightless in death, stared vacantly up at Kerin. Marcellus closed them gently.

'How?' Kerin said hoarsely. Marcellus raised his hand.

'I shall come to that,' he said, drawing back the sheet which covered the body to the neck. Kerin's hand flew to his mouth, stifling an exclamation of horror and dismay. 'It has happened again, as you can see,'

Marcellus said calmly, replacing the sheet. 'That is not what killed her, however.'

'No?' Kerin said blankly.

'No,' Marcellus said, taking a tiny cup from the table beside the bed and holding it out to him. 'This is the cause. It is the sleeping draught I prepared for Severus Maximus, and how she came by it, only the gods know.'

Kerin took the cup and smelt it. A strong, bitter smell burned his nostrils and made him catch his breath. 'Are you sure it's the same?' he asked.

'Completely,' Marcellus said. 'No other physician in the city knows how to mix that particular remedy, and the phial I prepared for Severus Maximus is the only one I have prescribed in a year. The physic is so strong, and so dangerous in the wrong hands, that I only ever give it *in extremis;* and then only to men of good sense.' He shook his grey head sadly. 'How right I was, Kerin Brightspear; how right.'

Kerin closed his eyes. Marcellus's voice sounded as if it were coming to him across a vast, echoing space, although the old man was standing close enough to touch him.

'So you think –' he began, but was unable to continue. A great constricting hand seemed to have closed around his neck, choking the words in his throat.

'She has been beaten and violated, probably by the man who did it last time,' Marcellus said. 'I think that she was already in possession of the sleeping draught, perhaps fearing just such an event, and that when her worst fears were realised she took it without hesitation. All this has happened within the last few hours, you know.'

Kerin stared at the little cup. 'The draught,' he whispered. 'Is it painless?'

'Completely,' Marcellus said, his voice soft as a healing balm.

'Unlike her life,' Kerin said bitterly. He felt a hand on his arm; or rather two hands, one on each arm, gripping him from behind.

'Come on,' Lucius said. 'No; come with me. Marcellus will see to this.'

Kerin allowed himself to be guided, out of the lit room and blindly up the dark tunnels into the cruel, frozen brightness of the moonlit night.

'You can come back to our house,' Lucius said as they walked. 'My parents have got enough guest-rooms to house the Valeria Victrix.' They had reached the main gates. Kerin stopped, freeing himself from Lucius's grip, and slid to the ground with his back against the courtyard wall.

'The guards,' he said. 'Tertius and the other boy. Were they on that entrance all night?'

Lucius closed his eyes. 'That fight in the mess room,' he said. 'Some of your warriors fell out and started brawling and throwing the tables around. Tertius and Livius came to help me break it up. We had to knock a couple of them out cold and lock them in the guard room. It didn't take us all that long, but yes, the slaves' quarters would have been unguarded while we were doing it.'

'Long enough for someone to get in there and do what was done?' Kerin said, staring up at the bright sky.

'Yes,' Lucius said, in despair. Kerin struggled to his feet. He felt cold and sick, but his head had stopped swimming.

'Don't blame yourself,' he said. 'Just find out who did it, and thank Marcellus for me.'

He elbowed his way past the two curious guards who were standing in the centre of the gateway. Once out in the street he walked as fast as he could until he had turned the corner out of their sight, and then broke into a run. He ran until his breath gave out and sweat was streaming down his back, and by then he was out amongst the poor men's houses. There was a rickety pen alongside one of the buildings, occupied by a donkey and two goats. The animals retreated to the far corner and stared at the well-dressed stranger who was leaning on their wooden rail, sobbing for breath and shivering violently as the night air froze his sweaty clothes. The scene in the slaves' quarters came back to him as vividly as if it were being played out in front of his eyes; the blinding light, Faria's beaten body and her vacant, sightless eyes. Gael had eclipsed her, and yet now that she had been so cruelly taken, he ached for her selfless warmth. She had been there when he was friendless and lonely in an alien city, and would probably have been there by choice, even if not commanded; but it had benefited her not at all. He had rewarded her with indifference, and she had died horribly and alone, with no-one to protect her from her assailant or, in the end, from herself. He could have wept for the pity of it, but warriors did not weep. He leaned on the rotten railing and stared at the stinking animal pen, consumed with grief and rage and guilt.

The tall gates of the merchant's house were closed and guarded. Kerin realised that his boots and breeches were caked in foul-smelling mud. He braced himself, then hailed the guards. They must have recognised him, because they opened the gates without hesitation. The senior man looked him up and down.

'Are you alright, lord?' he asked doubtfully.

'No,' Kerin said truthfully, 'but I need to see the Lord Vortigern. I'm invited to join him and your master, but I can't go in there like this.'

'I'll speak to him for you,' the guard said, sliding the heavy bolt on the gates. He nodded to his companion. 'Stay here with him. And whatever happens, don't let anyone else in.'

He suspected problems, of course, Kerin thought, watching the guard as he marched smartly away along the tree-lined path; problems, violence and consequences.

'Trouble, lord?' the younger guard asked tentatively.

'Someone killed a slave,' Kerin said, watching the main door. The guard looked at him curiously. The door opened and Vortigern appeared, framed in the square of yellow light. Kerin met him halfway along the path, under the acacia trees. 'Faria's dead,' he said, without waiting for Vortigern to speak. 'Someone beat and raped her, like last time, and then she took poison. Well, it was a sleeping draught that Marcellus mixed for Severus, but it's so strong that if you take too much it kills you; two drops in a goblet of water, Lupinus said, and –'

'Stop,' Vortigern said, taking him by the shoulders. Kerin closed his eyes. He supposed that he had been gabbling like a youngster after drink. He was shaking with cold or misery, or both. It appalled him, that he should have allowed Vortigern to see him in such a condition.

'I'm sorry, lord,' he said unsteadily. Vortigern's hands held him firmly. Gallus had come from the house, sweeping towards them in a luxuriant red and gold robe.

'What's passed?' he asked brusquely. He looked Kerin up and down. 'What's the matter with you, man?'

'One of Severus's slaves is dead,' Vortigern said. 'A particular favourite of his. Someone had beaten and violated her. It had happened before. This time she took poison.'

Gallus frowned. 'Come,' he said, taking Kerin's arm. They went quickly up the paved path, up a flight of steps and in through the main door to an interior which was as vibrant and ablaze with colour and light as the praetor's house was cool and restrained. Inside they were met by a servant, a lithe young man with smooth, light brown skin, dark eyes and shiny black hair. Gallus spoke softly to him in a language which Kerin could not understand.

'Hani will bring you hot water and clean clothes,' the merchant said. 'After that, he will bring you to my chambers. The feast is over, but there is still some wine. Go, and when you come back, we shall speak of what has happened.'

Kerin mumbled his thanks and followed the servant. After a long trudge down passages which glowed with red, terracotta and gold, they arrived in a bathroom where two small brown boys in white loincloths were topping up the water in a huge wooden tub. Hani waved them imperiously away.

'Your bath, lord,' he said respectfully. 'If you would care to undress, I shall take your clothes to be washed and bring you something clean.'

Kerin tore off his clothes and flung them away; it was almost as if they were tainted with Faria's blood. 'You can burn those, Hani,' he said, sliding down into the silken hot water. 'I never want to see them again.'

'As you wish, lord,' the servant said. 'Now, if you don't mind, I shall add something to the water; you will find that it relaxes body and mind.'

Before Kerin had time to express an opinion, he took a small flask from a side table and poured most of its contents into the steaming water. Kerin closed his eyes while his whole being emitted a silent howl of despair. Inevitably, damningly, it was oil of lavender.

21

'It is All Souls' Day,' Constans said, admiring his reflection in the mirror-like pool. 'Tonight I must go to the chapel with the holy brothers of St Alban to pray for the souls of the dead.'

'The dead are dead, lord king,' Brother Padarn said patiently. 'Why not pray for the souls of the living?'

'For misguided heretics?' Constans enquired, with a supercilious smile.

'For holy men who have forsaken their vows, Mr Monk,' Padarn said bluntly.

On the far side of the atrium, Kerin sat on one of the stone benches with his head buried in his hands and wished that they would be quiet. The only vow he was interested in was one which involved lifelong abstention from Phrygian wine.

'Would you care to try some of this, my young friend?'

Kerin turned to find Marcellus standing behind him, his hands cupping an earthenware bowl from which some hot, sweet-smelling concoction was sending up a little spiral of steam.

'What is it?' Kerin asked weakly.

'It is good for anything from over-indulgence to toothache.' Marcellus sat down beside him on the bench. 'It has even been known to sweeten the tongue of a nagging wife. In short, it is my antidote for the trials of life.'

'Then I had better have some,' Kerin said. He raised the bowl to his lips and took a cautious sip. The fiery liquid burned down his throat like a tongue of flame. 'Gods!' he exclaimed, catching his breath. Marcellus chuckled.

'You see? It has taken your mind off things already, and when it has had a chance to work you will find that it also lessens the pain in your head. That wine of Gallus's is notorious, you know.'

'How did you know about that?' Kerin asked.

'The merchant himself sent a man to enquire after you,' Marcellus said. 'You probably don't know that his own mother was a slave. Most people have forgotten, but a few of us older men remember it well, and the trouble it caused at the time. Gallus could never be indifferent to a man who had got himself into a fix on a beautiful slave's account. He is a ruthless man in many respects, but some of his redeeming features are surprising.'

Kerin closed his eyes, letting the potion do its work. 'What did you do with Faria?' he asked.

'We burned her remains, after the custom of her people. The ashes were given to her cousins, and they were instructed to take them to Severus Maximus's burial ground outside the city walls. Gallus and I went along to ensure fair play. This cemetery is usually reserved for the family's chief servants and guardsmen, so it is something of an honour on the praetor's part, if you like. Most men have less respect for their dead slaves than they have for their dead dogs.'

'Why should he bother?' Kerin asked.

'Out of respect for you, I would have to say,' Marcellus said. 'Although I suspect that your Lord Vortigern might have had a hand in it somewhere. Severus Maximus does seem to be unusually wary of him since he did away with Plicius, and now that Maximian Galba has lost his head into the bargain –' he spread his hands and smiled sagely.

'You don't think we did that, do you?' Kerin asked.

'Well, I'm sure that none of you did it in person,' Marcellus said. 'But equally I'm sure that not one of you could put his hand on his heart and swear that he was not delighted, so I can see why Severus Maximus might be a little nervous about becoming the third member of the triumvirate, as it were.'

'But why should we do anything to the praetor?' Kerin protested.

'Because he had outlived his usefulness, perhaps?' Marcellus said. 'If I were in his position, I think I should be careful. I have seen the way your Lord Vortigern works.'

'And what does that mean?' Kerin said indignantly.

'You know quite well what it means,' Marcellus said, peering into the bowl to see how much had gone. 'He tolerates no-one who is not of some use to him, especially silly weak men like Severus Maximus. Be careful.'

'Be careful?' Kerin said blankly. 'Me?'

'Yes, Kerin Brightspear,' Marcellus said. 'He is the most dangerous man I have ever set eyes on, and I am not saying this because of anything I have seen him do. It is something I know, in the same way that we both know which way all this is going.'

'The trail of blood,' Kerin said, looking down at the half-empty bowl.

'The dreams, if that's what they are,' Marcellus agreed. Kerin looked up.

'Marcellus, you know he saved my life when I was a child,' he said. 'At no possible advantage to himself. Even men who dislike him agree about that.'

Marcellus reached out and rested his thin hand on Kerin's arm. 'Then perhaps you should ask yourself why,' he said. 'I'm not saying that your life's in danger, of course. Vortigern would kill a hundred men to save your neck. But there is something else. You may well decide to hate me for telling you this, but you are an honest and brave young man, and I feel that it is my duty to warn you. Even if Vortigern's intentions are as pure as the virgin snow, he is trouble. Remember that the flame cannot choose who it burns.'

Kerin closed his eyes and emptied the contents of the bowl down his throat. He wondered if Marcellus might know something that he did not. Over by the pool Constans was still preening himself. Lupinus had arrived and was hovering around, his intentions probably thwarted by Brother Padarn's presence.

'Could I have some more of this, please?' Kerin asked, holding up the bowl.

'No,' Marcellus said, rising to his feet. 'I am sorry, but as with the wine, the trick is knowing when to stop. If you are no better by tonight, it will be safe to take some more. I shall be in my garden, if you still wish to have anything to do with an interfering old fool who tells you such unwelcome truths.' He nodded and took the bowl before setting off across the atrium. His head

361

and shoulders were bowed, and Kerin suspected that
it had been hard for him to say the things he had said.

'Marcellus!' he said sharply. The haruspex turned.

'No-one can decide who to hate,' Kerin said. The
old man smiled and inclined his head before going on
his way. One day soon, I will tell you everything, Kerin
thought.

The horse came in shortly afterwards. Kerin heard it,
but he was still too hungover, too stunned by events
and by Marcellus's warning, to take much notice. Elir's
arrival soon put paid to that. He was dishevelled and
hollow-eyed, and looked as if he'd come a long way in
a short time.

'I lost Idris in Calleva,' he said miserably. 'And I'd
had the bastard in sight all the way. There were plenty
of travellers on the road, it was easy enough to go
unnoticed. But you know what that town's like. Full
of merchants and beggars and riders –' he threw his
hands up in frustration. 'I did find his horse, though.
He'd sold it to an innkeeper down by the market.
Couldn't have been long before I got there, the beast
was still sweating. He told the innkeeper he'd bought
a better one, and couldn't ride the two. Then two lads
turned up outside with a fresh horse for him, and they
all rode away together. The innkeeper said he'd never
seen them before, but they were well turned out. Good
weapons. Good, fast-looking horses.' He paused, anxious. 'What's this about? I mean, Idris is one of ours,
isn't he?'

'I don't know,' Kerin said. 'What it's about, or
whether he's still one of ours. But just for now, don't

mention this to any of the others. I expect I'll know if you do.'

Elir gave him a half-hearted smile. Unlike Macsen, he'd always had a healthy respect for Kerin's gift. 'I won't say a word,' he said. And, as he trudged away, 'I always thought Idris was a prick, anyway.'

Kerin got up, rubbing his eyes. A bout of energetic horse-riding with Lucius was the last thing his throbbing head needed. He heard a quiet laugh a short distance behind him and turned.

'Lord,' he said stiffly. Vortigern regarded him curiously.

'What's the matter?' he asked.

'The wine,' Kerin said, turning back towards the atrium.

'The wine?' Vortigern said, as if he knew quite well that it was more than that. Kerin shrugged. There was nothing he felt he could say, after what Marcellus had told him. He thought about what Constans had said, and wondered whether he was more or less important than the pursuit of power. 'There's something you should know,' Vortigern said. 'Messengers arrived in the city this morning, sent by the ordo of Eburacum. Flavius has had spies north of the Wall for months; men of Pictish blood, who can pass as natives. The Picts expect an attack next spring. They've been bringing men down from the mountains to prepare for it. They expect to win, of course. It won't occur to them that we could beat them if the Romans couldn't. And once they've crushed us, they plan to join forces with the Irish under Niall and attack our western coasts. We're even less prepared for that than we are for fighting in the North, so leave the wine alone and keep a clear head. And tell no-one else. Publius intercepted the messengers at the city gate, so only he and I know about this.'

'We'll need ships,' Kerin said. 'Armoured transports at the least.'

'I've commissioned them already,' Vortigern said. 'We have less time than we thought. This is more dangerous, and more urgent, than we anticipated. So I've done it, and now I've come to tell the king.'

'Well, there he is,' Kerin nodded towards the pool. 'Arguing about the nature of grace.'

Vortigern sighed. 'You'd think they could manage to agree with each other on All Souls' Day.' The disputants caught the sound of his voice and looked up. 'Come here, Constans,' Vortigern said. The king gave Lupinus a nervous glance and came flouncing over. Padarn stomped resolutely behind him like a guard dog. 'Brother Padarn,' Vortigern said, 'the king's spiritual welfare is your domain. We don't need your help to discuss the affairs of state.'

'Oh, I don't mind Padarn being here,' Constans said lightly.

'It's alright, Brother,' Padarn said soothingly, as he caught Vortigern's eye. 'I'll be going back to the chapel now, anyway.'

'I'll see you there later, Brother.' Constans's voice faded out as Padarn strode away. Vortigern undid the gold shoulder-pin of Constans's purple cloak, rearranged the garment to his satisfaction and refastened the pin.

'What did you want me for, lord?' Constans asked apprehensively.

'In good time,' Vortigern said, gazing across the atrium towards the pool where Lupinus was still lingering, watching their every movement. 'Do you talk to him, Constans?' he asked, his finger stroking the monk's pale cheek.

'Lord?' Constans quavered.

'Your maidservant over there. Do you talk to him when he shares your bed, or is it only your bodies that hold secret communion?'

'Lord, I tell him nothing you would not wish me to,' Constans stammered. 'More often than not we talk about religion, as it happens. He has taken the faith, you know. He's renounced the Roman gods and committed his life to Christ, in front of Abbot Giraldus in the chapel of St Alban.'

'Then please,' Vortigern said, 'ask him to take himself off to the chapel and pray, instead of lurking around here trying to listen to conversations which don't concern him.' He had raised his voice just sufficiently for the words to carry across the atrium. Lupinus gave Constans an uneasy glance, bowed hurriedly and slunk away. 'The armoured galleys,' Vortigern said.

'Yes, lord?'

'The last time we discussed them you were not too happy about the idea, as I recall,' Vortigern said. Constans cleared his throat.

'I was a little concerned about paying for them, lord. Maximian – God rest his soul, the poor man – told me that we couldn't really afford them without levying taxes, and that it would probably upset the rich men if we did that. I thought it might not be prudent to upset the rich men.' He gave a hopeful smile. 'Even for you, lord.'

'I have commissioned the armoured galleys,' Vortigern said, as if he had not heard a word of it. 'There's no point in resisting it; the Picts will cut off our trade routes if we do nothing, regardless of any military designs they might have. We're using twenty of Gallus's fast merchantmen and his carpenters are standing by, waiting to turn them into fighting ships. It'll be three months before they are ready, and that will give us time to train enough men to man them. Naturally, Gallus will require to be paid for his ships and for the labour of his craftsmen. There isn't enough money in the treasury to pay for a rowing boat, so there *will* be a fleet tax, no matter who it upsets. You will sign decrees to that effect today, and they will go out to the ordines tomorrow morning.'

He folded his arms and waited for a response. Constans looked down at his slippered feet and glanced sideways at Kerin with a nervous smile. Kerin shrugged. There was nothing to add. It all made perfect sense, and in any case, nothing was going to prevent Vortigern from carrying it out one way or another.

'Lord,' Constans said timorously, 'what if the rich men refuse to pay?'

'They won't refuse to pay,' Vortigern said.

'But what if they do, lord? Won't we have a rebellion? Won't they hold it against me and try to replace me with my brother? I have to think about it, lord, and pray about it in the chapel. They could hang me for this, lord; I can't just sign these things without asking for God's guidance.'

Vortigern did not reply, but Kerin saw a darkness come over his face like a transforming cloud.

'Constans,' he said, 'please –'

'Lord King to you, Kerin Brightspear,' Constans said peevishly.

'Lord King,' Kerin said, with strained patience. 'Please, sign the decrees now. It's for the best.'

'For the best?' Constans retorted. 'Not for me, necessarily. I shall pray about it all day and night, and give you my answer tomorrow morning. May God give wisdom to us all, lords.' He flung his cloak around him and hurried off across the atrium. Two of the guards accosted him at the gate. It looked as if they were warning him not to venture alone into the dangerous world beyond the praetor's walls.

'He can't go out there on his own,' Kerin said. 'I'll tell him to wait in his chambers. Bridei and his men can escort him to the chapel and wait outside for him.'

Vortigern watched the performance by the gate. It looked as if the praetorian guardsmen were quite pre-pared to upset the king rather than their commanding officer. 'What do you make of all that?' he asked.

'Constans?' Kerin said. 'I've seen him frightened, but not like this. He wanted the crown badly enough, but he never understood the risk. I don't think he really un-derstood it until that day in the courtyard, when a few hundred raging people started shouting in front of him, and he gave you command of the armies. Why would he? He's only ever known three things. A rich Roman family, a monastery, and living in Severus Maximus's house. At the moment he's protected by the praetorian guard, the city garrison, a personal bodyguard and our warriors. Perhaps he's realised that it would only take one word from you for all that to fall away. But now he doesn't know which way to go. Whether to be more terrified of you, or of what the others might do to him if he authorises the fleet tax.'

'If he doesn't know that yet, then he's even more stupid than I thought he was,' Vortigern said. He looked hard at Kerin. 'Have they buried the girl?'

'Yes, lord.' Kerin avoided his eyes.

'Well, make sure that you do, too,' Vortigern said. 'There's no profit in remorse.'

Kerin nodded an acknowledgement and went off to summon the king's bodyguard, leaving Vortigern leaning against one of the tall pillars of the atrium, watching Constans with his predator's eyes.

22

'Oy! Lucius Arrius!' shouted the young guard on the city wall. 'Haven't you got enough bruises on your arse yet?'

He and his ten companions guffawed as Kerin and Lucius rode through the gate below them, heading for the wide open grass plain beyond the city where the patricians trained their chariot horses. It was known as the Campus Martius, after a much grander example just outside Rome. Lucius, beyond being taunted, waved gaily to the guards and pushed his horse into a trot. The snow had passed over and it was a clear blue day, although still cold enough to have frozen the ground. The horse arched his neck proudly as he trotted along, a different animal from the nervy, ill-tempered beast Kerin had purchased in the marketplace.

'I call him Diabolus, lord,' Lucius said. 'It means "devil" in Latin, as you probably know.'

'It'll do,' Kerin said. 'And for the last time, can you stop calling me lord? I'm not your lord, or anything of the sort. I'm a robber's bastard who had a stroke of luck.'

'And I'm a common soldier's orphan.' Lucius grinned. 'Let's call it quits, then.'

They had reached the fringe of the Campus Martius.

Far out on its pale surface a charioteer was putting his team through its paces.

'Go on, then,' Kerin said. 'Show me how fast he is.'

Lucius whooped, drove his heels into the horse's flanks and set off. Kerin watched as they swung out and round in a wide circle. The horse could go, alright; not as fast and fluid as the Cambrian horses, but fleet enough for an animal with a chariot horse's build.

'Good,' he said, as they trotted back. 'Now take the saddle off.' Lucius's smile became more half-hearted. 'Go on. What are you going to do if your girth bursts in the middle of a battle? Take the saddle off and do it again.'

Lucius complied. Diabolus gave him a filthy look and flattened his ears. As Lucius scrambled aboard, Kerin leaned down and slapped the horse hard across the rump. He squealed and took off like an arrow, with Lucius clinging to his mane for dear life.

'You cruel bastard,' a cheerful voice said. It was Elir, looking better for a scrub and a rest. 'I couldn't sleep,' he said. 'But I did have a chat with my father. Don't worry, I didn't tell him anything. But I managed to get him talking. He said he wouldn't let Idris in the warband because he doesn't think he knows his own mind. Do you remember when he was a lad?'

'Not really,' Kerin said. 'Rufus and I never had much to do with him.'

'Macsen neither. But Idris is the same age as me, and we used to run around together. Drank our first ale, had our first girls, you know how it is. But one day he started talking about the gods and the trees and things, and then he went off to Caradog, to ask him about becoming a druid. Well, I'm sure Caradog thought he was just a young lad having a mad moment. He sent Idris packing in a nice way, and that was that. Except that last year, just before he tried to get in the warband, Idris went to see Father Iustig, and said he wanted to give his life to god. The Christians' god, that is. So my father thought, here's a lad who can't make his mind up. And that's not much good when you've got fifty big bastards with axes coming at you, is it?'

'No, it's not,' Kerin said. He thought about the argument in the citadel, and wondered what had been in the sack which Brwyn had thrown out of his house along with his son. A voice hailed them. It was Brennius, on his elegant grey.

'Garagon's on his way,' he said. 'He's going to give that racehorse a run. What are you up to here?'

'Teaching Lucius Arrius to ride like a warrior,' Kerin said. Brennius grinned as Diabolus executed an unexpectedly tight turn, sending Lucius sailing sideways. He landed with a painful thud, but managed to keep hold of his reins, if not his dignity. The sound of trapping hooves approached. It was Garagon on his beautiful horse, accompanied unfortunately by Edlym, whom Kerin had not been this close to since the incident with the statue. Garagon looked in high spirits. The horse was twitching, dancing on its neat hooves while blood-flecked foam flew from its mouth. Elir gave a gasp of admiration. 'What do you call him, Garagon?' Kerin asked.

'He's called Ghazal,' Garagon said. 'I didn't choose the name, he already had it. It means "deer" or something where he comes from.'

'Go on, then,' Brennius said eagerly. 'Let's see what he can do.'

Garagon looked almost as excited as the horse. Lucius reined in to watch. Kerin had hoped that Edlym might be too absorbed to take much notice of him, but this proved not to be the case.

'Kerin Brightspear!' he said amiably, edging his horse over.

'Edlym, I believe,' Kerin responded with a courteous nod.

'Do you know,' Edlym fingered his clean-shaven chin, 'I have been meaning to ask you whether you have kinsmen in Londinium.'

'Kinsmen?' Kerin said brightly. 'No, I don't think so.'

'You see,' Edlym said, regarding him with intense interest, 'I know that you are of Vortigern's company and a warrior of some standing, but I could swear that I saw a man who looked just like you – your veritable double, in fact – when we had that most unfortunate mishap involving the statue of Ceres.' He spoke the last words very slowly, and ended with a thin-lipped smile. Kerin raised his hands.

'I'm sorry, Edlym. Until this year I'd never been further east than Glevum.' He smiled broadly. 'But of course, and as I'm sure you've been told, I'm a bastard. I could have a veritable double in every city from here to Cambria, if my father had a fast horse.'

Edlym snorted. 'One day the truth will out,' he said. Kerin supposed that it might, but knew that with any luck he would be safely back on his own side of the river before it did.

'Look at that!' Brennius screeched. They all looked.

The horse was galloping, or perhaps flying would have been a better description of what they saw as it thundered across their vision. Garagon, an accomplished horseman, bent low over the stallion's neck and slackened the reins. The animal responded instantly, lengthening its stride and stretching out into an effortless, floating gallop. 'Jupiter's balls!' Brennius howled. Kerin watched silently, knowing that no horse he had ever come across would have the slightest chance of matching that speed. Garagon was laughing out loud with exhilaration as he brought the stallion back.

'Well, Kerin,' he gasped, 'do you want to race me now?'

Kerin smiled. 'No, Garagon. It's the fastest horse I've ever seen.'

Garagon waited, as if expecting the compliment to be followed by some cynical afterthought. He seemed visibly disappointed when it was not. Kerin grinned. It would have been very easy to add that the horse would never last over sixty miles of mountain and bog, but it would have given him no pleasure to make the point. Lucius came trotting back, red-faced and breathless.

'That's quite a horse, Lord Garagon,' he said admiringly. Garagon ran an expert's eye over the dishevelled young guardsman and his half-bred animal.

'You'll need some more practice before you contemplate riding anything like this, I think,' he said, turning away with a condescending smile. Lucius flung on his saddle and jerked the girth tight.

'I thought I was doing rather well,' he said wistfully, watching the Kentishmen trotting away.

'You are,' Kerin said. 'Don't take any notice of

Garagon. He doesn't think we're worthy to lick his boots. Trust me, you'll soon be good enough for the cavalry.'

Lucius's eyebrows rose. 'Do you think Severus Maximus would let me go?'

'Yes,' Kerin said, and left it there. He couldn't say so, particularly in front of Elir; but he knew that what Severus wanted had ceased to matter long ago.

The road back to Londinium was busy with people of all ranks and occupations, making their way towards the city. There were numerous monks amongst them, tramping along in procession, some carrying crosses or caskets whose significance Kerin could only guess at. Near the western gate a company of druids appeared, marching in the opposite direction. Elir gave them a smile and a respectful nod.

'It's All Souls' Day,' Lucius said, noting Kerin's curious gaze. 'It's always busy in the city. Christian folk come in from the countryside to worship in the chapels here, and people of the old faith go out to light fires, because it's a holy night for them too, isn't it.'

'*Calan gaeaf*,' Kerin said, wondering what requests Caradog would be making of his gods when he lit his great fire on top of Penrhyn Fawr. Lucius nodded towards an area to the side of the road, enclosed by a low stone wall.

'That's the praetor's burial ground. That's where they put Faria's ashes.'

Kerin reined to a halt. 'I have to look,' he said.

'I'll ride back with Lucius,' Elir said, taking the hint. Kerin rode in through the open gateway and left his

374

mare to nibble the hawthorn bushes which grew along the western wall, sheltering the cemetery from the prevailing winds. A thin man in a worn grey tunic and breeches was working amongst the graves, pulling out weeds and tossing stones into a basket. He straightened up as Kerin approached.

'Lord,' he said, with a respectful nod. 'Can I be of assistance?'

'They buried some ashes here yesterday,' Kerin said, trying to sound nonchalant. 'One of the praetor's slaves.'

'Ah,' said the man. 'Haven't come to tell me to dig them up again, have you lord? We were a bit surprised, to be truthful. Thought it might have been a mistake. We don't get slaves here, as a rule. But Marcellus *magister* was quite – well, forceful. And Master Gallus. I wouldn't want to upset him in a hurry. They said they'd come on the praetor's orders, and I wasn't going to argue with that.'

'Just show me,' Kerin said. His patience was thin, and he didn't want a conversation. He simply wanted to see the place and to be left alone in it. The attendant led him to a small mound of earth below the western wall.

'There,' he said, pointing. 'That's where we put her. No-one's said anything about a memorial, or anything. The women were weeping and wailing, of course, and they scattered some dried rose petals. Blown away, I'm afraid. Give it a few months and there'll be nothing much to show for it.'

'Mark it,' Kerin said. 'When I've gone, mark it. Some of those will do for now.' He pointed to a pile of chiselled stone blocks lying beneath the wall, perhaps left over from the building of some well-to-do person's monument. He fished in the pouch at his belt, took out a denarius and gave it to the attendant. 'Here, take this. I'll be back tomorrow to check that it's been done.'

The assistant stared down at the coin glinting in the palm of his hand. 'Of course, lord.' He gave Kerin a curious look. 'May I ask – '

'No,' Kerin said. 'You may not ask. Just leave me in peace now, and do as I've said.'

The attendant went back to his work. Kerin stood and stared at the grave. He had seen a Roman mausoleum in Glevum; the tomb of some provincial governor. All black-veined marble and carved images of gods and horsemen. Perhaps the governor had been a cavalryman in his younger days. Whoever he was, the thing seemed bloated and obscene in comparison to this pitiful little pile of earth. 'You deserved better,' he said bitterly; then realised that he was talking about Faria's life and the manner of her death, not about her unmarked grave. 'There's no profit in remorse.' Vortigern's voice echoed in his head. But I'm not sure that you always practise what you preach, Kerin thought. He picked up his crucifix and examined the tiny ring which lay alongside it. He realised that he barely knew the woman who had given it to him; she was lost to him for now. And yet some instinct told him that he would find her, must find her, that he had not even touched the edge of the things she could bring to him. Whatever he had had with Faria, it was not that. The pain was real enough, though; the pain, the guilt, and the knowledge that he was not done with this yet. 'I will find him,' he said, to the anonymous little mound and the keening wind. 'I will find him, and he will pay.'

The last of the dried rose petals were clinging pathetically to the hacked-down brambles below the wall. There were of course no flowers at this time of year, but the hawthorn bushes were garlanded with red berries, untouched by the birds as yet. Kerin took his knife, sliced off a spray and thrust the pointed end into the earth where Faria's ashes lay. Then, because it was unknown for warriors to weep over slaves, he mounted up and turned for the road before the cemetery attendant was gifted another unusual event to add to his fund of gossip.

23

Along the roadside near the western gate, a string of settlements had grown up; not much more than camps, really, a chaotic mix of tents and shoddy wooden shelters, dotted with cooking fires and rough animal pens. A bunch of children spotted the good horse and well-dressed rider and came swarming out, some of them waving wooden begging bowls. An angry roar came from the nearest shack. A big, slovenly woman in a ragged dress came lumbering out, followed in short order by an aged man whom Kerin recognised instantly.

'Malan!' he exclaimed. The old man came limping over.

'Lord Kerin,' he said, getting his breath. 'We made it to the city, as you can see.'

'I saw Flora in the market a while ago,' Kerin said. 'Does she still serve Eldof's wife?'

'Yes,' Malan sighed. 'And that's no feather bed, I can tell you. But she's probably not working today. All Souls' Day, you know? Lord Eldof calls himself a Christian for appearances' sake, just to please his brother the bishop, if I'm honest. But he does let his servants go to worship on this day, if they're minded to. I couldn't care less myself, but the girl's quite devout, so she'll probably take him up on it. She said you had the job of looking after the king, is that right?'

'Yes,' Kerin said. 'He's a devout man too, as you'd expect, so he'll probably spend most of the day on his knees.'

'Flora said she was sorry for him.' Malan squinted against the setting sun. 'Said she'd seen him going about the city with that bodyguard of his, looking frightened to death. Not that he'd give her the time of day, of course, he's got his airs and graces now that he's out of the monastery.' He grimaced. 'Flora said that she thought the wrong man was king. But then she would say that, wouldn't she.'

Kerin slipped from his horse and drew Malan aside. 'What's that supposed to mean?' he asked.

'Come on, Lord Kerin, you were sitting next to me by that cooking fire,' Malan said. 'One minute Lord Eldof was rubbing his slobbery chops all over Flora's face, and the next she'd disappeared off somewhere with your Lord Vortigern. Not that he laid a finger on her, according to Flora. None of her friends believe that, of course. They all think he gave her a night to remember. Which he did, in a way, of course, but not the way those randy bitches mean. She said he did it out of kindness. And no-one's going to believe that, are they?' He chuckled. 'They'll believe it even less if he gets the crown on his head. Another reason to feel sorry for that poor monk, I suppose. Not that people like us would lose any sleep over it.'

Kerin tied his horse to a scrubby bush and led Malan away from the road. 'Is that what people are saying?' he asked. 'People in settlements like this?'

'Yes, of course,' Malan said. 'Vortigern's always had the ordinary people in his hand, hasn't he? In the West where we all come from, naturally, but now it's much the same wherever you go. People like us can't stand the powerful men, the ones whose fathers sucked up to the Romans. Lining their pockets while the rest of us get worked and whipped like galley slaves. Everyone knows that Vortigern had a go at the Roman soldiers when he was a lad, everyone knows he hammered the Irish invaders, so who do you think we'd prefer to fight the Picts for us? A man like that or a sad little bastard who's spent his life in a monastery? The answer's obvious, isn't it?'

'To you, perhaps,' Kerin said. 'But not to the men of power. Some of them don't have much idea what goes on outside the city walls. If they want a replacement for the king, it's his younger brother, Ambrosius.'

'They're even madder than I thought, then,' Malan said. 'The ordinary people in the villages and the hillforts want to see Vortigern in command, and if it doesn't happen soon, they'll be through those bloody gates over there with any weapons they can grab. There's been trouble in Calleva already. We've all heard about that meeting in the praetor's courtyard, where Vortigern climbed up a statue in the middle of a snowstorm and the king put him in charge of the army. But that's not enough, is it? It's not enough. And there's some hot-headed boys in Calleva. My daughter's husband met some of them in a smith's workshop last week. There was talk about coming down here to stir things up. And there's something about All Souls' Day, isn't there? For the old faith too. It's a holy night. Things happen on it.'

'Tonight?' Kerin said, taken aback. 'What things,

Malan? Do you know any of these men? The ones who'd rise up?'

'I know where to find them.' Malan winked. 'I might be a skinny old bastard, but I've got a loud voice. And you did save us from Bertil Redknife's butchers, didn't you. You and your friends and your Lord Vortigern.'

'We did,' Kerin said. 'And we'll save you from the invaders, too. But, Malan, if those men try to get through the city gates, there'll be a massacre. There are armed guards on the wall, you must know that. Whatever you all think about the kingship, it can't be done like that.'

'How, then?' Malan said truculently. 'By bending our knees? By asking nicely? How long is it since you were a skinny lad with no money and no weapons?'

I have never been like that, Kerin thought, understanding for the first time the power that was moving here. 'This will come,' he said. 'Vortigern must be king. We all know that. But it can't be done with blood. I'm going back to the city now. I'm responsible for the king's safety, as you know. He's gone to the chapel of St Alban to pray, but as soon as he's done there, I'll speak to him. I'm sure he realises that there are some powerful men who'd like to see him gone, but he's like most sons of high-born fathers. He has no idea about the ordinary people; what they think, what they want. If a couple of hundred men start hammering on the city gates, everyone will take notice, including the king. But if those men are armed and look as if they want trouble, even the leaders who are on our side will come after them. Good men like the Lord of Kernow and Commander Publius Luca. However much they want Vortigern to be king, they won't stand by and watch the city turned into a slaughterhouse. A lot of your young men will die, and all the patricians who think that Vortigern is a barbarian in any case will say that they've been proved right.'

There was a lengthy silence. Malan raised his hands. 'You have a point, Lord Kerin.' He grinned, showing broken teeth. 'Trouble is, I'm still a young hothead myself, inside this scrawny old body. But the years have taught me a couple of tricks. I'll find these lads. Talk to their leaders. Maybe I can hold them back for a while. But I want your word that you'll talk to the king and the Lord Vortigern. Tell them what's going on out here.'

'You have my word,' Kerin said, and held out his hand for Malan to shake.

24

Dusk was falling, and the wind was driving streams of high cloud from the north east, by the time Kerin returned to the praetor's house.

Something was going on in the courtyard. He could see a little group of people standing between the central fountain and the base of the statue of Minerva. Severus Maximus, who had been invisible for days, was one of them; Publius Luca was another, and there too were Lud, Gorlois of Kernow and Brother Padarn. They didn't appear to be doing anything much, but seeing them all together in the same place was odd enough. Lud came across the courtyard.

'What's going on over there?' Kerin asked. Lud looked gloomy and anxious.

'Constans,' he said. 'He's disappeared.'

'What?' Kerin said in horror, dismounting as Elir took his rein. 'When was he missed? He was here this morning, just before midday. He said he wanted to pray in St Alban's chapel. I told Bridei and his boys to go with him and wait outside until he'd finished.'

'He must have sneaked out this afternoon some time,' Lud said. 'He never got to the chapel. Brother Padarn came over here looking for him, and that's when we realised he'd gone.'

Kerin began to feel cold and nauseous. Whatever the opinion of people outside the city, whatever the fate of the kingship, Constans's safety was on his head. 'Where have you searched?' he asked. Lud stared up at the darkening sky.

'Where do you start? No-one's seen hide nor hair of him. That pesky Lupinus has gone too, so they're holed up together somewhere, if you ask me.'

'What about the Picts?' Kerin asked.

'Down in the mess, last time I saw them,' Lud said. 'Not their fault at all, really. They were waiting outside Constans's chambers to escort him to the chapel, but he gave them the slip. Bridei came for me. He said you'd given him his orders, but that Constans always comes out and meets them at the door. Bridei knocked but no-one answered, and he couldn't get in because the door was locked. I got the keys and went in to have a look, but I don't think anyone had been there for a while. The kitchen had sent Lupinus up with some food around midday, but it was still lying on the table.'

'Where's Vortigern?' Kerin asked.

'Up in his quarters. He's got a bunch of messengers lined up to take these fleet tax things to the ordines, and he can't move until he's got the king's bloody signature. You have to go up there. No-one's been allowed in. He's – well, I'd sooner be in my boots than yours, that's all I can say.'

They walked across the courtyard to join the others. Severus, who looked startlingly thin and white, was pleading with Publius Luca. 'There must be somewhere else you can look, commander,' he said, fiddling unhappily with his heavy gold rings. 'O Mithras, we can't just *lose* the king, when he's a guest in my own house.'

'Severus Maximus, we've been looking for hours,' Publius Luca sighed. 'You know as well as I do that it's impossible to search a city like this.'

'But suppose he's come to some harm?' the praetor said wretchedly. 'I'll hold myself responsible. The Lord Vortigern will hold me responsible, for the gods' sake. My head will go the same way as Maximian's.'

'I doubt that, sir,' Publius Luca said with a wry smile. He acknowledged Kerin with a nod.

'Commander, I'm going up to see Vortigern,' Kerin said.

'Good,' said Publius Luca. 'Do your best. And stop looking as if your head's on the block.'

'It is on the block,' Kerin said. 'I've been left in no doubt about that.'

Publius Luca sighed. 'Just get up there,' he said. 'He's not going to kill you.'

'Probably not,' Kerin said. 'But in the end, that's not enough. I owe him everything, commander. My life, everything. It's not enough, just to be tolerated. To make up the numbers. To have my life spared all over again. It's – '

'Mithras!' Publius Luca shouted. 'Is there something in the water on your side of the river? Just get up there and tell him the truth. Let him say his piece. Then come back here and tell me how you're going to find the king.'

'Alright,' Kerin said lamely. Publius Luca folded his arms.

'Good,' he said. 'Now keep a cool head. And re-member that there are some things you can't mend.'

Four soldiers were standing to attention at the door of Vortigern's apartments; members of the city garrison, rather than the usual praetorian guardsmen.

'I've been told that no-one's allowed in,' Kerin said.

'No-one but you, sir,' said the senior man, opening the door for him. Kerin stood in the antechamber and squared his shoulders as the door closed behind him. The last time he had stood here, feeling like this, was also a day when he had managed to let Constans go missing. He had feared retribution of some sort then, and it had not come. But this time was worse. The dangers were real, and the consequences unknowable. There was no point in putting things off. He walked straight into the next room without knocking. Vortigern was standing beside the table. The chest containing his writing materials was there, unopened. There was a manuscript from which he might have been reading.

'You have been told, I take it?' he asked.

'Yes, lord,' Kerin said. 'I have been told. I make no excuse. I thought I'd done enough by telling Bridei to escort Constans to the chapel, but I was wrong. I should have stayed here and done it myself.'

'Yes,' Vortigern said. 'That's an obvious truth.' His voice was distant, without expression. It didn't sound like his voice at all. 'Where have you been?' he asked.

'Out on the Campus Martius, teaching Lucius Arrius to ride,' Kerin said. There was no point in trying to dress it up.

'Ah,' Vortigern said. 'So while everyone else has been stampeding around the city trying to find Constans, you have spent a pleasant afternoon giving your friend a riding lesson.'

'Yes, lord. I could have chosen a better day. But I thought Constans was set on going to the chapel to say his prayers. It didn't occur to me that he'd do anything else. That's not an excuse. It's just the way I saw it.'

'Do you understand what this means?' Vortigern asked. 'If Constans disappears, or someone kills him?'

'Yes, I do,' Kerin said. 'It means the crown will be there for the taking, as it was before.'

'Exactly,' Vortigern said, walking towards him. 'At the moment, any power I have depends upon his good offices. I could take that power if I wanted to. You must see that. But from what I saw this morning, I think Constans was on the point of offering it to me on a plate. He's terrified of us, of his bodyguard, of Ambrosius's supporters. Not to mention Paulinus Galba. He'd abdicate and melt away into the mist without a second thought, if we gave him the right incentive. And, stupid as you are, you must see that receiving something as a gift would be preferable to taking it by force. Taking things is complicated. It's expensive. It would cost us time and blood, and we can't spare either. You know all this. And, knowing it, you left this frightened idiot on his own so that you could give Lucius Arrius a riding lesson.'

'Yes,' Kerin said. 'That's exactly what I did. Do what you like. Whatever it is, I deserve it.'

'Get out,' Vortigern said, turning away. 'I thought better of you. Get out, now.'

Kerin went. There was nothing more to be said. He could have accepted any sort of physical punishment, but not this; the door closing, the thin voice that sounded like another man's, that sounded brittle, like something which might splinter and cut him to the bone.

Publius Luca was waiting in the courtyard. 'It could be worse,' he said. 'If you find Constans alive, you'll get the credit. And if you don't, it'll move things along, don't you think?'

'Yes,' Kerin said. 'But there are better ways to do that, surely.'

'I agree,' Publius Luca said. 'And as a soldier I've always tried to keep out of politics. It's a filthy game. But we're running short of time, and that foolish monk is far less pliable than I expected.'

'There's something I must tell you,' Kerin said. 'Vortigern threw me out, so I haven't told him, but he should know. This afternoon, I spoke to an old man in one of those rough settlements outside the western gate. A camp follower of Eldof's called Malan. He keeps his ears open, and I think he has some influence with the people out there. We saved him and his granddaughter from some of Bertil Redknife's thugs back in the spring, so they think they're indebted to us. He said – well, I can do no better than repeat his exact words – that the ordinary people in the villages and the hillforts want to see Vortigern in command, and that if it doesn't happen soon, they'll be through the city gates with any weapons they can grab. Vortigern is in command already, of course, in most ways that matter. But that's not what Malan meant. It's not what those people see.'

Publius Luca met Kerin's eyes. 'I know what Malan meant,' he said. 'It's thirty years since Vortigern started calling himself the High King. Anyone who thinks he did that for nothing is deluding himself. The people of Isca took him at his word. Now, outside those gates, it's the same. It was only a matter of time. So go and find Constans – alive, if you can – and we'll go from there.' He clapped Kerin on the shoulder and went to resume his attempts to soothe Severus Maximus.

The chapel of St Alban appeared quiet. Perhaps the sick stayed at home on All Souls' Night, for fear of getting lured away by the shades of the departed. Narrow shafts of wan yellow light slanted out through the tiny windows.

'Stay here and keep watch, Elir,' Kerin said. 'Come and get me straight away if anything happens.' He eased the door open and stepped inside, trying to make as little noise as possible. Anything else would have seemed disrespectful, despite his own lack of faith. A single large candle was burning on the altar, two more in sconces on the walls. Around twenty people were kneeling on the cold stone floor, heads bowed and hands folded on the benches in front of them. Some hooded monks, recognisable by their black robes; a few guardsmen; a well-to-do couple wearing expensive fur-trimmed capes. And Flora, surely, her long dark hair tied back with a blue ribbon. Kerin wondered what she was praying for. A hand rested lightly on his arm.

'Come,' Father Giraldus murmured. Kerin followed him into a small, bare antechamber. 'No news of Constans, I suppose?' the abbot asked.

'None, Father,' Kerin said. 'I was hoping that you might have an idea where he's gone.'

'None at all, I fear,' said Giraldus. 'But here is some other news. I hope it has nothing to do with the king's disappearance. The Lord Vortimer and some of his followers have been seen in the city. A ship arrived from Armorica, bringing men and horses. The Lord Vortimer was there to meet it. Brother Servilius was told on the wharf. Your chief warrior Lud called here earlier, but for some reason I was loathe to tell him. Brother Padarn says that you and Vortimer were close friends, at least until he took up this cause of his, so I thought it might be more sensible to tell you.'

'Thank you, Father,' Kerin said. He supposed that, if he were Rufus, he might kidnap Constans and take him straight back to Abbot Paulinus. The monk would not be in peril of his life, but he would surely never wear the crown again, and what then? He wondered whether that ship from Armorica might also have brought Ambrosius. 'Father, I'm going to the wharf to see what I can find out. I know a few men down there who might help.' His eyes moved to the kneeling figure with the dark hair and the blue ribbon, just visible through the half-open door. 'That girl. Has she been here long?'

'For a few hours,' said Giraldus. 'A troubled young woman. Do you know her? She seemed unusually agitated when I asked her if she happened to have seen the king today.'

'An acquaintance,' Kerin said. 'Our paths crossed a while ago. She believes that she owes a debt to one of our company. He wouldn't see it like that. He did her a kindness once, and may well have forgotten that it ever happened. But she can't forget, unfortunately. Perhaps that's why she's praying.'

Giraldus sighed. 'I'll tell her that you asked after her.'

'No,' Kerin said, then wondered why he had said it. 'She's sorry for Constans. I'm sure she wishes him no harm. But she's quite sure that he shouldn't be king. If he was trying to get away from here, and she could see a way to help, then she might do it. A friend of mine is waiting outside. I'll ask him to follow her when she leaves.'

'And if I hear anything further?' the abbot asked.

'Come to me at the praetor's house. I'll go straight back there from the wharf.'

The abbot nodded. 'God speed,' he murmured, and slipped quietly out to join the supplicants in the chapel.

Manius was out in his boat, the man at the tavern said; him and his brother, out since first light, there was talk of a big shoal downriver, and you couldn't ignore a tipoff like that.

'They might get their arses back soon though, the way the weather's closing in,' the man said. He spat on his finger and held it up to the cold air, checking which way the wind was coming. Kerin cursed his luck. Just when you needed the man, he was out in his boat doing his job, instead of loafing around in the drinking dens listening to gossip. He ducked out through the low doorway and tramped off along the riverbank, heading for Gallus's wharf; easy enough to find now that he had got his bearings and was stone-cold sober. Most of the merchant's fleet appeared to be in port, riding at anchor out in the river. Two big galleys were tied up by the wall in front of Gallus's house, unloading their cargoes of amphorae and baled cloth. And next to them another ship; an interloper, Kerin was sure, because Gallus's vessels were distinctive, with their carved prows and beautifully painted name boards; gold on red, *Audax: Londinium, Gavia: Londinium.* He could recognise the name of the capital. The ships' names, he only knew because Vortigern had read them all out to him. He remembered, with some chagrin, that he had not made time to look for a teacher of reading. This new vessel had no markings at all, but looked robust enough to carry a substantial cargo. Some men were moving about on deck, coiling ropes and scrubbing the planks; brown-skinned like the praetor's slaves, but burnt darker by sun and wind. One of them noticed Kerin watching and stood up. 'Where are you from?' Kerin shouted. The sailor shouted back something incomprehensible. Kerin shrugged and spread his hands. The man laughed and returned the gesture.

'You won't get any sense out of them,' a voice said at Kerin's elbow, 'they're Anatolian.' Kerin turned. Gallus the merchant was smiling. 'My wife's from Byzantium,' he said. 'Those lads speak a different dialect, but we can understand each other. Come with me. They won't understand us, but my crews will.'

Kerin followed the merchant through a tall archway. Beyond lay the garden where they had celebrated the coronation of Constans. Kerin rubbed a sprig of rosemary between his fingers. The bewitching scent would always remind him of that night.

'You're looking for the king, I suppose,' said Gallus.

'I am,' Kerin said. 'And I'm also wondering what the Anatolians brought to Londinium this evening.'

'You will already have some idea of that,' Gallus said. 'There was a monk from St Alban's chapel hanging around here when the ship docked, and the religious can never keep their mouths shut.'

'I'd sooner hear it from you, though,' Kerin said.

'Because you think I'm on Vortigern's side in all this?' Gallus asked.

'Because I think you're on your own side,' Kerin said. 'And because I don't see how that side can possibly be served by having anyone other than Vortigern in power.'

Gallus grinned. 'You're a sharp one, aren't you,' he said. 'Perhaps you've needed to be, to stay alive in Vortigern's household. Very well, then. I watched them disembark, all in their fancy white tunics with big blue crosses on the front. Nine men in all. And after them came a lot of fancy white horses and some servants. The oldest son, Vortimer, was here to meet them. I've sent word to Vortigern. But no Ambrosius, in case you were worrying about that. I took some men and searched the ship to make sure. It's nothing to do with the Anatolians, they're just a hired crew. They don't know why they're here. They're leaving on the high tide at midnight. But the captain has a smattering of Latin, and that's the lingua franca amongst Vortimer and his people. The men on the ship kept mentioning Venta Belgarum and Paulinus Galba, so that's probably where they'll go.'

'Do you know if they're still in the city?' Kerin asked.

'I had them followed,' Gallus said. 'They met up with a bunch of riders outside the southern gate. Same getup, same white horses. They stopped at one of the alehouses. Do you think it's anything to do with the king's disappearance?'

'Probably not,' Kerin said. 'I know it's a tempting idea, but I think it's coincidence that these men have arrived just now. I don't think Constans has been kidnapped. I think he's hiding somewhere, probably with his servant Lupinus, because he's gone missing too. There was a showdown with Vortigern this morning. He tried to make Constans sign the fleet tax decrees, and Constans refused. He said he had to pray about it first, but that was just an excuse. He's afraid to sign the decrees, he's afraid *not* to sign the decrees –' he grinned in spite of the gravity of the situation. 'I'd hide myself, I think.'

Gallus laughed. His eyes glowed with merriment. 'I'm sure you haven't grown up with many illusions, Kerin Brightspear,' he said.

'I have not,' Kerin said. 'And Constans is my responsibility, God help me, so I need to find him alive.'

Gallus had stopped laughing. 'But surely,' he said. 'Whatever you've been told. You can't believe that this monk should be King of all the Britons.' The humour had gone out of him like a snuffed candle. In that dark, unblinking gaze, Kerin saw exactly where the magnificent house and garden, and the huge fleet of well-trimmed ships, had come from.

'What are you saying?' he asked.

'That Vortigern should be king now, not some time in the future when the monk's died of fright,' Gallus said. 'That we should untie his hands and let him raise his armies and make his own decrees. For the gods' sake, you of all people can't think that Constans was ever more than a means to an end.'

'I don't,' Kerin said, and thought of the white-faced, terrified young man who had nonetheless found the nerve to face down Maximian Galba. 'But whatever happens, I'd prefer it done without blood. If I can find Constans, we could send him to a monastery somewhere. Not to Paulinus, he'd be better off dead.' He paused, realising that Gallus was looking at him with total incomprehension. There was no doubt at all that Vortigern had chosen the most effective way to get rid of Maximian. 'In case things go wrong, I'll tell you this,' he said. 'There are thousands of ordinary men in the outlying towns and villages who'd follow Vortigern into hell. Within the city too, I'm sure. If we can't find Constans, or someone kills him, things could come to a head tonight. I've already told Publius Luca this, and he's probably the man you should speak to next. And now I'm going to look for Constans, because personally I want a redeemed monk, not a martyr.' He shook Gallus's proffered hand and marched off across the garden.

'Kerin Brightspear!' the merchant called after him. Kerin turned. 'You're right,' Gallus said. 'I do serve my own ends. I started out with one ship and a shack on the wharf. I've sweat blood to be where I am, and if Vortigern's the man to help me keep all this, I'll back him to the hilt. But he's also the closest thing I have to a friend in this city. Don't forget that.'

It was probably true. Kerin thought of his many friends, here and at home, and found that he no longer coveted the warm, opulent house or its magnificent garden, or even the fragrant sprays of rosemary. 'I won't forget it,' he said. 'And I won't forget that you looked out for me last night, or that you helped Marcellus with Faria's burial. You might have one more friend than you think.'

The praetor's courtyard was still seething. Lud and his sons had gone, but Hefin was there, patiently trying to explain something to Severus Maximus. Garagon and Brennius were listening in, adding their own few coins' worth. Eldof was haranguing a bunch of warriors and ordinary citizens, telling them where to search next. The one-armed Alberius had arrived by chariot with a troop of fancily-dressed guards. Kerin felt a hand on his arm. Gorlois of Kernow drew him aside as the arguments meandered on.

'What's really going on?' he murmured.

'I'm not sure,' Kerin said, 'but it's my guess that Constans may be hiding somewhere with Lupinus.'

Gorlois chuckled deep in his throat. 'Lupinus? That little girlie servant? Have they tried his house? He must have a family somewhere.'

'I'll bet they haven't,' Kerin said. 'Lud and the boys have only searched here, and I doubt if Publius Luca would think of it. Shall we go and look? Just the two of us, though. They'll be gone like rats down a hole if half the army comes knocking.'

They left the courtyard without a word. The streets were dark now, intermittently lit by the rising moon as the clouds came and went, sometimes with a scattering of sleet. They walked quickly past the chapel of St Alban, whose narrow windows cast a flickering yellow candlelight on the paving stones, and around the corner to the house with the tall gates and the bay laurel in the middle of the courtyard.

'Is this it?' Gorlois asked. 'It looks a bit grand for a servant's family.'

'No,' Kerin said, 'it's a merchant's house. His son's a good friend of mine. I've no idea where Lupinus comes from, but Lucius will know.' He pulled the bell-rope alongside the gate. The summons was answered by the young servant Petrus.

'Good evening, lord,' he said politely. 'No goats this time?'

'Not tonight,' Kerin said. 'Is Master Lucius in? It's important.'

'I'll call him for you, lord,' Petrus said. 'Please, come inside.'

Kerin and Gorlois followed him across the courtyard and into a small antechamber whose plain white walls and wooden benches were almost monastic in their simplicity. The servant was soon back, accompanied by Lucius.

'You see?' Petrus whispered. 'I wasn't lying.'

'Kerin!' Lucius exclaimed. 'And Lord Gorlois, I believe. We're honoured, lord!'

'Constans has disappeared,' Kerin said. 'And it's my fault, really, because we were out on the Campus Martius when he went missing. Do you know where Lupinus's family lives? We thought they might be there.'

Lucius pursed his lips. 'I know where his father lives, but Lupinus probably wouldn't go there. His mother died years ago, and I don't think the father had much time for his sons afterwards. He's a tutor to the patricians' children, so the boys were well educated, but perhaps not all that well loved.'

Gorlois stared up at the roof. 'Do you know where to find him or not, lad?' he asked. Lucius looked up at him uneasily. Confined within the antechamber, Gorlois looked rather like a large animal in a cage.

'There is one place I can think of,' he said. 'Lupinus used to be – well, friendly with a boy whose family lived down by the river. The boy died a few years ago, but after that the parents almost looked on Lupinus as another son. The father's a stonemason, and –'

'By the gods!' Gorlois roared, gritting his teeth. 'Can you take us there, or do we have to hear about the whole family tree first?'

'Yes,' Lucius said hurriedly. 'I'll get my cloak.'

Gorlois watched, shaking his woolly head as Lucius trotted away, followed by a backward-glancing Petrus.

'By the gods, Kerin Brightspear,' he said, 'does he always talk so much?'

The house was a nondescript dwelling whose single door was stoutly made and reinforced with iron straps and studs. The river lapped its wall on the far side, and there was a yard adjoining it filled with chunks of stonework in various stages of completion.

'Would you like me to knock?' Lucius asked. 'They'll be less wary of me because they know me from the praetor's house.'

'Go on, then,' Kerin said. 'Come here with me, Gorlois, and keep out of sight.'

Lucius approached the door and rapped smartly on it whilst the other two men retreated into the deep shade cast by the house on the opposite side of the street. They heard the door creak open.

'Hello, Valerius,' Lucius said, his voice clear and warm. 'You haven't seen Lupinus, have you? The praetor's looking for him, and we can't find him anywhere.'

There was a notable silence. 'No, Lucius Arrius,' a hesitant older voice eventually replied. 'I haven't seen him in weeks.'

'Well, that's a lie if ever I heard one,' Gorlois murmured. Kerin pressed his finger to his lips.

'Stay here,' he whispered. 'I'm going round the other side.'

Dodging from shadow to shadow, he gained the entrance to the stonemason's yard and slipped through the half-open gate. Lucius, who had had the presence of mind to keep Valerius talking, was enquiring after the health of the old man's wife. There was a window high up on the wall overlooking the yard, a square of glowing light. Below it was a lean-to workshop with a thatched roof. Kerin scrambled up a pile of stone blocks and onto the roof. He inched his way along it, seized the ledge and hauled himself up. There was no glass in the window. The light Kerin had seen from below was streaming through the open doorway of the adjoining room. He eased himself over the window ledge, crept towards the doorway and peered round the pillar. The room was empty now, but looked as if it had been abandoned in a hurry. There was a backgammon board, the pieces scattered about. A little amphora and two goblets, one of them tipped over, spilling a dark stain across the floor. A pile of folded garments, some of them unmistakably Constans's. The king's discarded crown was perching foolishly on top. Kerin could hear voices and footsteps drawing nearer. Valerius and

Lucius were coming up the stairs. The old man's face wore an expression of disgust as he came into the room.

'I thought I heard someone up here,' he said accusingly. 'Can't a man have peace in his own house? I've a good mind to bar the doors and keep you here.'

'Valerius, Constans is the king,' Kerin said. 'Lupinus can do what he likes, but I have to find Constans. I'm sorry to have disturbed your peace, but it'll be disturbed a great deal more if you try to stop me leaving.'

Valerius gave him a bitter smile. 'Don't worry. I'm not really stupid enough to pick a fight with a young warrior like you.'

'So where have they gone?' Kerin asked.

'You're as wise as I am,' Valerius said. 'The last time I saw them, they were sitting here in their nightshirts. Not long ago, just before it got completely dark. I heard a bit of a scuffling so I came up to see what was happening, and there they were, gone. Must have got out of that window you came in through. I ran down to the street, but there was nothing to see.'

'Do you think they were taken by force?' Kerin asked.

'No idea,' Valerius said. 'If it was someone like you or Lucius Arrius here, I'd say no, but they're not exactly musclemen, are they? If someone sneaked in quietly and grabbed them, that would be that, wouldn't it?' He hesitated as Kerin bent to pick up the crown. 'Lupinus, he's hardly been out of my sight since my son died. I know he's an annoying little runt, but I wouldn't like anything to happen to him.'

'He's in no danger unless he does something stupid,' Kerin said. Valerius sniffed.

'Youngsters these days, you might as well talk to the

wall. I don't know who you are or what influence you have, but if you find them, I'd be grateful if you could look out for him. If you get the chance, you know.'

Kerin looked at the old man, thinking that he must have been fonder of Lupinus than he admitted, to swallow his anger and lay himself on a stranger's mercy. 'I'm Kerin Brightspear,' he said. 'And I'll do my best.'

Brother Padarn met Kerin at the chapel door. 'Father Giraldus told me to look out for you,' he said. 'Elir's gone after that girl. I sent Servilius with him, in case he needs to get a message to you. And the abbot's gone somewhere with two of the brothers. I've no idea where; someone with a sick child came to ask for help.'

Kerin grimaced. 'This is for you, then,' he said, holding out the crown.

'Jesus wept,' said the monk, 'have you found him, then?'

'No,' Kerin said. 'Just this. Put it somewhere safe until I get back. Padarn, where would you go if you were Constans and you didn't want to sign the fleet tax decrees?'

The monk snorted. 'As far as I could,' he said. An idea began to crystallise in Kerin's mind.

'On the high tide at midnight,' he said under his breath. Padarn's brow creased.

'What?' he asked.

'Just a thought,' Kerin said. 'Look after the crown.' He left Padarn standing in the doorway and ran down to the corner of the street. 'Gallus's wharf,' he said, as Lucius and Gorlois fell in beside him. There was no time to explain. They ran, drawing a few curious glances from people meandering back and forth between the taverns, blithely unaware of the chaos going on in the circles above their heads. As they neared the merchant's house, Gallus's servant Hani came bolting out of the gates.

'Lords, come quick!' he panted. They followed him through the gardens and out through the archway onto the wharf. Gallus was standing there with a man's head in the crook of his arm. Swarthy, balding; it was the seaman Kerin had hailed on the deck of Rufus's transport. He gasped and retched, almost choking to death as Gallus tightened his grip. The merchant gritted his teeth.

'They're around here somewhere,' he said. 'They tried to get on that ship.' He relaxed his arm as the man passed out and slumped in a disregarded heap on the quayside. 'This fucker's the captain. I was in the garden. A girl walked up to the ship and spoke to him. Nothing unusual, it's a wharf, it happens all the time. But there was some funny sign-language going on. She kept pointing down at the water. Then he took her on board, as I'd expected. I waited to see what would happen. It didn't take long. There aren't many airs and graces when men have been at sea for weeks. But then he came ashore with her, and they went towards the steps over there. I ran out and grabbed this arsehole, the girl jumped into the water, and here we are. She'd asked him if he'd take two passengers when he sailed, he told her to show him the money, she said she didn't have any, he said come on board and spread your legs and I'll take the whole city garrison for you. And he must have been a man of his word – don't worry, Lord

Kerin, he's not dead – because that's what he was going to do. Take the king and his body servant wherever the ship was going. Ostia, I think, for olive oil, then back here for Vortimer and his cronies. We'd never have seen Constans again, if I hadn't happened to be out in my garden. I've sent a couple of lighters to search the river. The girl's probably drowned by now, but you might get your king back if you're lucky.' He winked, shouldered the unconscious body and set off for Rufus's transport.

'Jesus,' said Gorlois, short of words for once.

'Did you dream all that?' Lucius faltered.

'No!' Kerin exclaimed. 'I was here with Gallus earlier. He told me the ship was leaving on the tide at midnight, and when Padarn said – God, it doesn't matter, does it. Tell everyone I dreamed it, if you want to. All that matters now is that Constans is out there somewhere, a girl's drowned and I've lost Elir, who was supposed to be following the girl. And a monk called Servilius.' He broke off, realising that the other two men were looking at him blankly. 'It doesn't matter. None of it matters. If you were them, which way would you go?'

'Downstream,' Lucius said. 'I've been out there when the river's full, like it is now. You'd need a gladiator's muscles to pull against that current. I couldn't do it, so Constans and Lupinus wouldn't have a hope. Gallus must know that, so his men will have gone that way too.'

'Alright,' Kerin said. 'There's a tavern not far from here where the fishing boats tie up. Someone will take us out if we pay him enough.'

They kept to the riverbank. Now and again the

moon cast a vivid gleam across the broken water, but they saw no boats. Lucius looked completely baffled.

'Who's the girl?' he asked as they walked. 'Why would a girl do that to help Constans, for goodness' sake?'

'Later,' Kerin said. 'Look, some boats have come in. Gorlois and I can deal with this. Go back to the praetor's house and see if anything's happened. Then meet us here. Bring a horse each, in case we need them.'

Three heavy rowing boats had beached on the mud bank. Men were moving about, securing them to staithes and heaving nets of struggling fish clear of the river. Baskets full of the catch had already been lugged over to some long trestle tables where rows of women and children were sitting, deftly gutting the fish and tossing the innards back into the water. A big man was bending over one of the boats, doing something with a knife. Kerin recognised the broad back and balding head.

'Hey, Manius!' he shouted. The fisherman straightened up, holding a huge, headless pike. 'Good catch!' Kerin said. Manius grinned, tossed the fish back into the boat and wiped the blood and slime from his hands.

'Best for weeks,' he said. 'If this happened more often, I wouldn't have to waste my time sitting around drinking beer on your behalf.'

'Anything happening out there?' Kerin asked. Manius shrugged.

'Nothing unusual,' he said. 'Why do you ask?'

'Because the king's gone missing,' Kerin said. 'We think he's on the river somewhere with his servant. One of our warriors and a monk might be with them.'

Manius snorted with laughter. 'Well, let's think,' he said. 'Have I seen a boat with a king, a servant, a Cambrian warrior and a monk in it? No, not tonight, I don't think. You tell a good story, Lord Kerin, but nobody's going to believe that one.'

Something shoved against Kerin's back. 'Look,' said Gorlois of Kernow, looming over his shoulder, 'it isn't a story. The king's missing. Are you going to help us find him, or am I going to drown you?'

Manius cleared his throat. 'Of course I'm going to help you, lord,' he said. 'As I was about to tell Lord Kerin, here.' Kerin suppressed a smile. Because Gorlois was on his side, and didn't usually make gratuitous threats, it had never occurred to him how intimidating the Lord of Kernow could appear when annoyed. 'Wait here,' Manius said. 'I'll ask the other lads if they've seen anything.' He waded out into the water. Another rowing boat had come in and a knot of fishermen had formed around it, inspecting the catch. Someone had brought a torch and was pointing into the boat. Manius spoke to them and waved his arms above his head.

'No kings,' he said, as Kerin and Gorlois waded out to join him. 'But they fished this out of the water, look.' He leaned into the boat and yanked something from the well between the oar benches. At first sight it looked like a bundle of rags, then the flaring torch illuminated a chalk-white face.

'Flora!' Kerin exclaimed. Pushing Manius aside, he grabbed her under the armpits and hauled her out of the boat. 'Alive,' he said, as the limp bundle began to shiver violently. 'Come on, inside, quick.' Gorlois forced a path to the alehouse through the crowd which was beginning to gather around the gutting benches, necks craning to see what was going on. Kerin followed, ducking in through the low doorway. A fire was flickering in the corner as usual. Kerin dumped Flora down in front of it and tore off his cloak. The girl who served the beer was hovering. 'Please,' Kerin said, 'get all her clothes off and wrap her in this. Then bring a warm drink – anything, as long as it's warm.'

The girl did as she was asked. Gorlois gave her his heavy bearskin cloak. The landlord arrived with a steaming mug. 'Mulled ale,' he said. 'We always have it ready when the boys go out on nights like this.' He gave the mug to Kerin and pulled the serving-girl to her feet. 'Go on then, girl. You've done a good job. Tell your mother to set some more ale to heat and get the mugs lined up. All those people out there are going to be in here, any moment now.' He winked at Kerin. 'At least it'll warm the place up. Do you know this girl, then? You're going to a lot of trouble. Most men like you would just have chucked her back in the water.'

'Yes, I know her,' Kerin said, squatting down beside Flora. 'She's a servant belonging to someone I know.' There was no more he could add. An influx of customers swept the landlord away. Kerin raised Flora up and put the mug to her pallid lips. 'Come on,' he said. 'Sip it. That's right, just a little at a time.' He knew there was no point in trying to rush her, desperate though he was for her to speak. Gorlois sat down cross-legged beside them.

'Are you going to tell me what this is all about?' he asked.

'It goes right back to the spring,' Kerin said. 'When

we were on our way to the monastery to get Constans. We saved her and her grandfather from some of Bertil Redknife's cut-throats. Pure luck that we happened to be there. Then we came across them again, in a camp Eldof made on the way to Londinium. Just Vortigern and myself. He wanted to tell Eldof what we were doing, before they arrived in Londinium and heard someone else's version.'

At the mention of Vortigern's name, Flora sat bolt upright. 'Where is he?' she asked. 'The Lord Vortigern. Is he well?'

'Perfectly well, the last time I saw him,' Kerin said. 'And ready to behead me, because the king is my responsibility and he's missing. But you know where Constans is, don't you, Flora, or at least where you saw him last. Come on, for God's sake, there's no point in this.'

'There's every point!' Flora's voice caught in her throat as she tried to shout, and she coughed violently. 'There's every point,' she whispered. 'You and I both know who should be king. And Constans doesn't want it any more. He did once, but not now, because he's frightened to death, so how could it be wrong to help him get away? So that he can be rid of all this, and the right man can be king?'

'Hold your horses, girl,' said Gorlois. 'Are you telling me that you've done all this for Constans? I can see why a soft-hearted girl might be sorry for the poor little runt, but sorry enough to rip your clothes off for a baldy sailor?'

Flora gave a pitying little laugh. 'It wasn't for him,' she said. Kerin seized her arm.

'Look,' he said, 'you have to tell me. Gallus has got two boats out on the river looking for Constans, and those men would kill him as good as look at him.'

'He's not on the river,' Flora said disdainfully. 'He never was. Master Gallus thought he was, because I showed that sea-captain the steps where we were going to bring him to the ship.'

'Where, then?' Kerin asked, mad with impatience.

'Not in the city,' Flora said, staring at the fire.

'Gods!' Kerin exclaimed, letting her arm go. He felt like shaking the life out of her, but he didn't want to harm her, and violence would only set things back. 'At least tell me if you've seen Elir or Brother Servilius.'

'The dark-haired young warrior?' Flora asked vacantly. 'The one who was in the wood with you, who looks after the horses?'

'Yes. I spoke to your grandfather this afternoon. He said something which made me think. I told Elir to follow you when you left the chapel.'

'He did,' Flora said. 'But I'd spoken to Constans before that. I waited outside the chapel in the morning. I was sure he'd go there, for All Souls' Day. He never went inside. I told him to go somewhere safe, and I'd come for him when I'd found a way for him to escape from the city. His servant was with him, Lupinus, the one he sleeps with. They went – '

'I know where they went,' Kerin said. 'What about Elir?'

'He followed me, as you'd told him,' Flora said. 'Very discreetly, but I knew he was there. That was much later. I'd spent hours on my knees, trying to think of a way out. I hoped there might be a ship. I took a short cut to the wharf through Lord Eldof's house, but they wouldn't let Elir through the gates, so he had to go all the way round by the streets. When I was in the house, the other servants told me that a ship had docked, with Lord Vortimer's men. The cook saw them get out and ride away. When Elir arrived, I told him that they'd taken Constans with them, so that's where he's gone. After them. He did have a monk with him. The rest you know.'

'Not quite, my sweetheart,' Gorlois said, gently lifting Flora's chin on the tip of his forefinger. 'We went to the stonemason's house to find Constans and his chum. The old man loves Lupinus like a son, anyone could see that. But when we got there, they'd cleared off, in a hurry by the look of it, because your friend had left his crown behind. So where did you take them?'

'And if I tell you, what will you do?' Flora asked. 'Drag him back here to do your bidding?'

'Flora, you have no idea how dangerous this is,' Kerin said. 'According to your grandfather, there are men outside the city who want Vortigern to be king now. Right now. There are probably plenty more inside the walls, some that I know of. Then there are men – men with armies, and warbands – who want something quite different. All three of us here know who should be king. But it can't be done like this. If Constans surrenders the crown to Vortigern, that's one thing. But if he disappears, or gets killed, and the crown's just there to be grabbed, there could be a slaughter.' He broke off, suddenly hearing a commotion outside. Men shouting, horses whinnying and stamping the cobbles. Kerin hailed Manius, who had come in with his crew. 'Keep her here,' he said. 'Don't hurt her, just keep her here. If she tries to get away, tie her up.' He followed Gorlois, who was already in the doorway. Lucius was outside with the horses Kerin had asked for.

'You'd better come,' he said. 'There's a rumour flying round that Rufus's people have kidnapped Constans. Elir went after them, but he couldn't find them. And he's just told me that there's around a thousand men heading down the Roman road from Calleva, armed with scythes and billhooks and butchers' knives.'

'Come with me,' Kerin said. He led Lucius into the alehouse. Flora was kneeling in front of the fire with her hands tied behind her back. Manius was standing over her.

'She bit my fucking arm,' he said indignantly. Kerin pulled the girl to her feet.

'Lucius, tell her what you just told me,' he said. Lucius told Flora. Her eyes widened. 'You see?' Kerin said. 'I'm not making it up. This is happening. And Lucius, Rufus hasn't got Constans. That's just a lie Flora told Elir, to put him off the scent. So where is he, Flora? You'd better tell me now, because if you don't, a lot of people are going to die here tonight. Vortigern and ourselves amongst them, probably.'

Flora closed her eyes. 'He's at our camp,' she said. 'In my grandfather's tent with Lupinus. I told him not to leave until I came for him. My grandfather doesn't know.'

'Alright,' Kerin said. 'Manius, keep her here. I'll pay you well. And tell everyone to look out. There could be trouble in the city tonight.'

'I'm coming with you!' Flora exclaimed.

410

'You're staying here,' Kerin said, and nodded to Lucius and went out. Behind his back, above the racket of the drinkers in the alehouse, he could hear Flora shrieking.

25

'What the devil?' Gorlois asked, as the three men rode away from the river. Lucius, who was no wiser, reined close enough to hear.

'That night at Eldof's camp,' Kerin said. 'Eldof was going to bed Flora. He looked the other way for a moment, and Vortigern took her off somewhere. She says he didn't even touch her. She thinks he did it out of kindness. Perhaps he did. Or perhaps he just did it to spite Eldof. Either way, he's probably forgotten it ever happened. But Flora's thought of nothing else since. She'd die for him. Or rip her clothes off for a baldy sailor, to get Constans out of the way and help him become king.'

'Oh, Christ Almighty,' Gorlois sighed, shaking his woolly mane.

'So, where are we going?' Lucius asked. 'To the praetor's house, or the Campus?'

'The Campus,' Kerin said. 'Do you think I want to meet Vortigern before I find Constans?'

'Not for a moment,' said Lucius. 'Follow me. If we go through those alleys over there, we'll come out on a track that avoids the main road, and whoever might be on it. We won't hit it until we reach the Campus.'

There was nothing on the Roman road. It was eerier, more disturbing, than if it had been busy. One or two travellers could usually be seen, even after sunset, but not tonight. The sprawling settlements on the fringe of the Campus Martius looked all but deserted. A few lights winking from the shacks and tents, one or two smouldering fires; a handful of women shooing children off to bed. Nothing else.

'Where are all the men, then?' Gorlois asked uneasily.

'Gone to look for other men,' Kerin said. 'We need to find Constans and get him back inside the walls before they join the ones coming from Calleva.'

They dismounted and led their horses into the camp where Kerin had spotted Malan. The animals' hooves made little sound on the damp earth. Kerin handed his reins to Lucius and trod carefully towards the shack where the old man had appeared. He drew back the ragged blanket at the door. Standing in front of him, framed by the glow of a cooking fire, was the big woman who had come out of the shack with Malan. She was grasping a heavy frying pan.

'Put it down!' Kerin raised his hands. 'I mean no harm. I'm a friend of Malan. Is he your father?'

'What if he is?' the woman retorted.

'I told you,' Kerin said. 'I mean no harm. Did you see me at Eldof's camp? I'm Vortigern's warrior. We saved Malan and Flora from some trouble back in the spring. Do you know about that?'

The woman put down the pan. 'Yes. Everyone knows about that by now.'

'Are you Flora's mother?' Kerin asked.

'No,' said the woman. 'I'm Berget. Malan is my

father, but Flora's my sister's child. If she was mine, I'd have knocked some sense into her before it all got out of hand. You've come for those two lads she brought here, have you?'

'Yes,' Kerin said. 'How did you know?'

'She asked me to hide them,' said the woman. 'I told her to get lost. She said that they were in danger, and she wanted to help them get away from Londinium. Something to do with the king. I can't see why it was any of her business, even if that's true.'

'It is true,' Kerin said. 'And you're right, it's none of her business. But she's made it her business, because she wants Vortigern to be king instead of Constans the monk.'

Berget snorted. 'Well, we all want that. I go to the market by the river to sell eggs. It's all anyone talks about. My father's gone off somewhere with our men right now, because they've heard that something's going to happen tonight. But Flora should keep her nose out of it. The Lord Vortigern, she hasn't got another thought in her head. I told her, if she mentions that man's name to me again, I'm going to batter her with this pan. And those two skinny boys in their nightshirts, what's it to do with them?'

'More than you think,' Kerin said. 'I need to find them and take them back to the city, otherwise there's going to be trouble, and people are going to get killed. Where are they?'

'Probably in my father's tent,' Berget said. 'Come on, I'll show you.' Kerin followed her out of the shack. She pointed to a clump of stunted willows, a spear's throw away. Someone had pegged down the lower branches and spread animal skins across them to keep out the weather. 'Over there,' she said. 'My father's an awkward bastard. He could sleep in with us any time he liked, but he said he'd sooner be out here on his own than listen to my husband snoring. Here, take this.' She reached inside her shack and handed Kerin a rush light. She had sounded steady and forthright, but the wavering yellow flame caught the fear in her eyes. 'Please, get them out of here,' she said. 'Other men might come for them, and treat us rougher than you have.'

'I will,' Kerin said. 'Stay here. Stay inside, and don't go near the city tonight. I'll look out for your father and Flora if I can.' He raised the torch to Gorlois and Lucius. 'Over there, by those trees,' he said, keeping his voice low. 'They're probably in that shelter. Come with me, Gorlois; Lucius, go round the other side, in case they try to get away.' Lucius scampered away into the darkness. The other two men crept towards the shelter. As Kerin reached it, he dropped to his haunches and peered inside. At first he thought that there was nothing in there but a mound of rags and threadbare blankets; then came a small sound, like a puppy whimpering. He leaned forward with the rush light. Constans and Lupinus were lying on the ground under the blankets, wrapped around each other. Kerin watched them silently. He couldn't stand either of them, but all the same, he felt less than sanguine about hauling them back to the world from which they thought they had escaped. Gorlois crawled in beside him.

'Poor little sods,' he murmured. 'Let's get it over with, shall we?'

Kerin reached out and shook Constans by the

shoulder. 'Lord King,' he said. The two sleeping bodies stirred and jerked into life. Constans stared at Kerin in an agonised silence.

'How did you find us?' Lupinus said bitterly.

'It doesn't matter how,' Kerin said. 'It was nothing to do with Valerius; he lied to protect you. You have to come with me, you must know that.'

'I know,' Constans said. He gave Kerin an accusing glare. 'You could have left us here. What is it to you, all this?'

Kerin looked down at him. There was no easy answer to that. 'Come on,' he sighed. 'Get your clothes on, and let's go.'

'We haven't got any clothes,' Lupinus said petulantly. 'Just our nightshirts. We left in a hurry, didn't we.'

'Take some of those blankets, then,' Kerin said. 'You can get dressed at the praetor's house.' He didn't feel too guilty about taking Malan's bedding. Perhaps the old man would cave in and accept that his daughter's warm shack was the best place to sleep. Lucius was waiting outside. He looked at the two sorry figures and shook his head. 'Bring the horses,' Kerin said. 'They'll have to ride double with you and Gorlois. I'll meet you by the road.' He went back to Berget's shack. She was squatting beside the fire stirring a pot of something. 'We're leaving now. Are there any spears around here?' Berget grinned.

'A man like you hasn't got his own?' she asked.

'Not with me, unfortunately,' Kerin said. 'I hope we'll have no trouble on the way back, but just in case.'

'My husband's got a couple of little hunting spears,' Berget said, getting up. 'Just for sticking boar in the woods and stuff. They're under the bed here.' She got up with a grunt and went to the rear of the shack. It wasn't a bed, really; just a few planks raised clear of the floor on dressed stones pinched from somewhere. Berget delved underneath and stopped. 'They've gone. Both of them.'

'Your husband's hunting?' Kerin asked. 'On a night like this?'

'No,' Berget said. 'I told you. The men have gone somewhere with my father.'

Kerin ran out of the shack and out to the edge of the road where Gorlois and Lucius were waiting. 'Come on,' he said, swinging astride his horse. 'The men have taken their spears with them. Let's ride.'

The guards on the gate saluted and let them pass. Kerin Brightspear, Lucius Arrius and Gorlois of Kernow were too well-respected to have to justify themselves, even if two of them had shapeless, bare-legged bundles of rags clinging to their backs. Gorlois's horse clattered to a halt in the middle of the street outside the chapel of St Alban.

'Woah, woah!' Gorlois shouted to the others. 'Stop here. The king wants to pray.'

Kerin pulled the blanket clear of Constans's face. 'Now?' he asked. 'In your nightshirt?'

Constans gave a sad little smile. 'I don't think God will mind, Lord Kerin,' he said. 'And I'd really prefer not to go back to the praetor's house until I've done it. I know that the Lord Vortigern and Publius Luca are going to be furious with me, and I'd sooner face them after I've said my prayers. Father Giraldus is a kind man. I'm sure he'll lend us a habit each to keep out the cold, even if I've made a rather bad job of keeping my holy vows.'

Gorlois shook his head. 'Religion's a fine thing when it suits, little mouse,' he said, slapping Constans on the back. 'Let them stay, Kerin; we can leave someone here to keep an eye on them.'

Kerin was uneasy, but could think of no sensible reason for refusal. 'Alright,' he said. 'But I'm putting an armed guard on the door. Gorlois, can you stay here with them until it's done?'

'We're not going to run off again, you know,' Constans said plaintively.

'It's for your own protection,' Kerin said. 'Now, get inside and pray before I change my mind. Brother Padarn's looking after your crown, if you still want to look like a king.'

'Protection?' Gorlois said, as Constans and Lupinus slipped in through the side door. 'Who from?'

'I'm not sure, Gorlois. That's why it has to be done.' Kerin glanced over his shoulder as a group of men emerged from a doorway, saw them and trotted off down the alley. 'Lucius, I know you're off duty, but could you see to a guard? Just a few solid men to keep watch and make sure that those two come back to the house after they've said their prayers.'

'Of course,' Lucius said. 'I'll put Tertius in charge. He won't complain, and he won't want to know the ins and outs. If you need me later, send to our house. I want to warn my parents to stay inside and keep the gates locked.' He rode away towards the praetor's house, leaving Kerin and Gorlois in the street. The city was unnervingly quiet. It was dark now, but not late. There should have been tradesmen trudging home after a long day. There should have been drinkers, ox-drivers leading their beasts to stable, women rounding up older children.

'What now?' Gorlois asked.

'I don't know,' Kerin said. 'We need to be prepared for anything. When the guards arrive, go back to your boys and have them ready. I'm going to find Vortigern, if I can. I'm going to ask him what we're supposed to do if all those men with scythes and butchers' knives storm the city gates. The answer's not as obvious as you might expect, when you think it through.'

Gorlois had nothing to say. That in itself was proof that Kerin had not overestimated the risk.

The praetor's gates were closed and guarded. Elir stepped from the black shadow beneath the wall.

'I tried to find you,' he said. 'Gallus's wharf, the tavern where you went with Macsen —'

'It doesn't matter,' Kerin said, dismounting. 'We've found Constans. Rufus's people didn't take him, that was a lie, a distraction. He's in St Alban's chapel, saying his prayers. But you were right about one thing. Men outside the city are on the move. What's happening here?'

'I wish I knew,' Elir said, taking charge of the horse. 'Vortigern's here somewhere, I think. He was up in his quarters with Publius Luca for ages. General Publius has gone somewhere now, though. A mounted guardsman turned up leading his cavalry horse and they rode off together. My father's out with Macsen and the rest of our warriors, patrolling the city. He's been told to watch what Eldof and the Kentishmen are up to. And most of the city garrison just marched out of the castra and went down that street over there. There was a very high-up looking officer leading them.'

'Alright,' Kerin said. 'Go to the stables and get my warhorse ready. Then fetch my spears and put them in her stall. When you've done that, go and ride around the city and find out what's happening. It's like a coiled spring out there. Find your father and Macsen if you can, they may have something to report. Ride past Gallus's house and see if there's anything going on. And before you come back, go to St Alban's chapel and make sure that it's all quiet. There should be guards on the doors and a lot of people on their knees inside. Anything else, I want to know about.'

'And you?' Elir asked nervously.

'I'm going to see Vortigern,' Kerin said. 'He might forgive me, now that I've found Constans. If he decides to kill me anyway, I leave you my horse.'

26

The night was growing colder. Kerin's nerves were jangling. He was walking briskly towards his quarters when he heard rapid footsteps crossing the courtyard behind him. It was the young guard Livius, and he looked terrified.

'Livius, stop!' Kerin called after him. The young man turned, white-faced.

'Lord Kerin!' he gasped. 'Please can you do something about those Picts? Their ale's run out, and they're in the mess, threatening to burn the house down. I thought they were going to cut my throat, lord, but I told them I'd fetch ale, so they let me go.'

Kerin glanced around. 'Well, I've found the king, anyway. He's gone to say his prayers.'

Livius smiled shakily. 'Probably the best thing he could do, lord. What are we going to do about the Picts?'

Kerin weighed the options. He was as keen to fight Picts as the next man, but not in a Roman mess room over something as trivial as a jug of ale. 'Well,' he said, 'there are twelve of them and only two of us, so it would be stupid to fight them. We could just find them some ale, I suppose. Is there a lock on the mess?'

'No, lord, but the guard room's just down the tunnel.'

'Alright,' Kerin said. 'Find some ale, plenty of it, and take it to the guard room. There's bound to be some in the kitchen stores. I'll go and talk to Bridei and his friends, and once we've got them in the guard room, we'll lock them in.' He smiled cheerily, hoping that he had sounded more confident than he felt.

Livius was soon back with a gang of kitchen slaves, carrying a big wooden barrel and a box full of tankards. They brought a table and benches from the slaves' quarters and hung tallow lamps from two of the iron rings embedded in the wall of the guard room, which usually served a more sinister purpose. Kerin dismissed the slaves, left Livius tapping the barrel and hurried back to the mess. As he reached the door it was flung open from within and Bridei leapt out into the passage with his knife in his teeth. His warriors came crowding out behind him.

'Kill!' Bridei shrieked, brandishing the knife under Kerin's nose. 'We kill if there is no ale, no gold!'

Kerin took a step backwards. 'Bridei, I have ale!' he cried, raising his hands to signify his peaceful intentions. 'Good ale, enough for all.'

'I see, I believe,' Bridei spat, his mad eyes gleaming. 'The Lord Vortigern says we get ale and gold. He lies. The king, he says no ale at all for Bridei. You show, I believe.'

'I'll take you there,' Kerin said. 'But first, put your knife away.'

'No,' Bridei hissed, showing his teeth. 'I keep.'

'Put it away,' Kerin said, meeting his eyes steadily. 'Remember, I've got the ale.'

Bridei gave a grudging smile and slipped the knife

into its leather sheath. 'You are one, we are twelve. You have no ale, I slit you open like a salmon.'

Kerin raised his hands, displaying open palms. 'I'm an honest man, Bridei,' he said. 'Come on. I'll take you to the ale.'

The Picts followed him down the tunnel. Livius had opened the door of the guard room and was standing to attention against it, concealing the lock. The massive bolts were invisible on the side facing the wall. Inside the barrel was set ready on the table.

'There,' Kerin said, drawing Bridei forward. 'You see? I told the truth.'

'Good, good,' Bridei murmured. Then his lips parted in a vicious grin. 'Is good, but you drink first. Then if it is poison, you die, not Bridei.'

Kerin had fervently hoped to escape without entering the room, but there was no avoiding it. He stepped up to the table, filled a tankard from the tap and took a mouthful.

'There,' he said, holding out the tankard. 'It's good ale, Bridei. Try it for yourself.' He filled another tankard and placed it on the table. Bridei marched over, seized Kerin's tankard, and gulped down the contents.

'Is good!' he exclaimed, eyes gleaming. He turned and roared at the other Picts, who descended on the table like kites on a carcass. Bridei seized Kerin's arms. 'You do not lie!' he crowed. 'You are good man! Now, you drink with Bridei!'

Kerin's heart sank. 'I can't, Bridei,' he said. The Pict ignored him, filled a tankard and thrust it into his hands.

'You drink,' he said, face up against Kerin's. 'You do not say no to Bridei.'

'One jar,' Kerin conceded. 'But then I must go. I have to look for the king.'

'Look for him?' Bridei said, suddenly alert. 'He is lost?'

'Yes,' Kerin said. Bridei scowled.

'Is good,' he said, and leaned closer. 'I kill him for you if you like. Then you are king, and we have ale all the time. We have gold, and Bridei is your chief warrior.'

Kerin smiled and refilled the Pict's tankard. 'Well, if you're going to kill him, I'll have to find him. You stay here and enjoy your ale; I know the city better than you do.'

Bridei seized his hands. 'You find, you bring him to me!' he exclaimed.

'Yes,' Kerin said. 'I'll bring him straight here. I'll take Livius, that guard over there. He can help me.'

Bridei sniffed contemptuously. 'He is woman. But yes, you take him.' He shouted something to his companions. They roared and shook their fists and gathered round Kerin, slapping him on the back. Edging towards the door, Kerin shook as many of their hands as he could reach and ducked out into the tunnel. Inside the guard room, the Picts milled around the table, scrambling over each other to get at the ale.

'Now,' Kerin murmured to Livius, 'close the door very quietly.'

Livius eased the heavy door shut, hands shaking. Kerin slid the bolts and Livius turned the key. Inside the Picts were singing so loudly that they would not have heard a thunderstorm breaking overhead. Kerin and Livius crept away up the tunnel. As they reached the open air they broke into a run, and did not stop until they were far away on the other side of the atrium. Kerin leaned against the frescoed wall and wiped the sweat from his brow. It was a long time since he had been as frightened as that, and he could only imagine how the green young Livius was feeling.

'Give me the key,' he said. 'If I've got it, no-one can kill you for it. Is there another one?'

'Yes, lord,' Livius said, 'there's a big bunch with a key for everything in the house, but Severus Maximus keeps it in his private apartments, and I don't think he's likely to let the Picts out.'

'Alright. I'm going to find the Lord Vortigern. I want you to keep watch here. You're in no danger, they can't possibly break out of that room; but if Lud or Publius Luca comes back, I want you to tell them what's happened and that I've found the king. Do you understand all that?'

'Yes, lord,' Livius said, with a shaky salute.

'I'll come back after I've found Vortigern,' Kerin said, and hurried away, slipping the key into the pocket of his tunic. The force of the wind was rising by the minute. A gust of freezing rain drove across the court-yard, stinging his face and turning to ice as it struck walls and paving stones. For a moment he thought he had imagined the voice hailing him, but then it came again; thin but insistent, cutting through the wind like a bird's cry. A tall, thin figure came hurrying across the courtyard, black robe bellying. Abbot Giraldus was clutching something to his chest.

'Lord Kerin,' he gasped. Kerin drew him into the shelter of the covered walkway.

'Father, what's the matter?' he asked. The older man leaned against the wall, catching his breath.

'I'm sorry to come to you so late at night,' he said, 'but you should see this.' He held out the object he was carrying. Without another word said, Kerin knew what it was. A small hessian sack, secured at the neck with a red ligature. The last time he saw it Brwyn was hurling it out of his house in the citadel. 'A young man of your following gave it to me for safe keeping,' Giraldus said. 'Or at least, he was of your following. I doubt if he is any more.'

Kerin took the sack and opened it. Inside was a writing tablet, but its neat inscription looked more like the eulogy on a tomb, than the casual scribbles men dashed off to communicate with each other. 'I don't read much, Father,' he confessed. 'You'll have to explain it to me. But I do know the young man. His name is Idris. He fell out with his father over this, whatever it is.'

Giraldus sighed. 'It's a pledge. A proof of good faith. The bearer dedicates his life to Christ, and swears allegiance to a brotherhood called the Sword of God. I understand that it's led by the Lord Vortigern's son. Idris said that the Lord Vortimer is here with some of his followers, who came ashore this evening. He was on his way to join them.'

Kerin closed his eyes briefly and marshalled his thoughts. 'Why have you brought it to me?' he asked.

'You have Brother Padarn to thank for that,' Giraldus said. 'He was with me when Idris came. He calls you a man of integrity and good sense. And we were agreed that someone close to Vortigern should know. This is the last thing we need, with invaders on the march.'

Kerin looked down at the tablet, growing cold in

his hands. 'Padarn was right about my friendship with Vortimer,' he said. 'We grew up together. He's been like a brother to me. But this –' he slipped the tablet back into the sack and held it out. 'I can't keep it here. And please say nothing to anyone. Vortigern must be told, but not now. Not yet.'

'You have my word,' Giraldus said, slipping the sack inside his robe. 'You will choose your time with care. I understand. Come to me if you wish to speak of this again. But now I must go back to the chapel, to keep an eye on that silly young monk.' A pause. 'Or should I say, the king.'

'You can say either, Father,' Kerin said. 'Both are true.' A sudden anguish seized him. 'The Sword of God. What do they want?'

The abbot gave a weary smile. 'To purify the kingdom, I expect. I'm sure their new order will have no place for stupid old priests like me, who believe that God looks kindly on acts of compassion.' He nodded and turned away. Kerin watched his black form merge into the darkness. A shower of hail slapped him across the face. He ran for the nearest doorway and ducked inside. The house was uncannily calm. The long corridors were empty, and his footsteps made a hollow echo. Vortigern was not in his quarters. Even the slaves, usually ubiquitous, were absent. It was as if the fury of the night had driven everyone underground. From deep within the bowels of the house, the sound of singing and raised voices drifted up. For some obscure reason Kerin did not want to be indoors on this night. Plunging out into the bitter air he walked across the courtyard, through the lashing trees in the garden and out onto the high terrace overlooking the river. A dark shadow was visible at its far end. Kerin walked along the terrace. Sheets of spray rose from the turbulent water and froze on the balustrade. Vortigern was standing quite still, braced against the tearing wind.

'I've found him,' Kerin said. 'Constans. I've found him.'

The relief on Vortigern's face was palpable. 'Where was he?' he asked.

'Hiding with Lupinus,' Kerin said. There was no need for detail. Perhaps the need would never arise. 'They're praying in St Alban's chapel. I've put an armed guard on the door in case anything happens, or they decide to disappear again.'

'You could have saved yourself the trouble,' Vortigern said. His voice was harsh, but it had changed. This was the tone he used when reprimanding ordinary warriors. To Kerin it still sounded damning, but he was aware that something had shifted.

'I would have gone back there, but I've had trouble with the Picts,' he said.

'What kind of trouble?' Vortigern asked.

'They were raising hell because their ale had run out. Only young Livius and myself were here to deal with it. They'd already threatened to kill Livius, and they'd have done the same to me, given half a chance.'

'What did you do?' Vortigern asked.

'Found a barrel of ale and locked them in the guard room with it. They were already drunk when I saw them, so they should be senseless before long. Livius is down there keeping watch, if he hasn't died of fright by now.'

'Good,' Vortigern said; to himself rather than to Kerin. He took up the clipeum and traced its inscription with his forefinger.

'Lord, that's not the end of it,' Kerin said. 'They'd have killed me tonight if they could. And now they want to kill Constans, too, because they think we've broken the terms of our agreement. How can we let them live?'

Vortigern looked up, letting the medallion fall. 'We can't,' he said. 'But tonight, it's the least of my concerns. Publius gave me your message. And Gallus tells me that Rufus is here with a bunch of God's warriors. You've been out in the city. What do you think?'

'It's like sitting on a tinder box,' Kerin said. 'One spark, that's all it would take. You know what's happening outside the walls. The ordinary men are rising. And it'll be the same in the city. They'll have wind of it in the poor men's quarters by now, they always do. Do you remember that time I went to the market to find a horse for Lucius? The boy I bought it from told me that everyone he knew was behind you. "My father and mother, my brothers, my grandfather, all the men from the ale-house in our village, the carpenters, the weavers, the fishermen from the river." That's what he said. They're on your side, to a man. But they see the wealthy and the high-born as their enemies. Suppose Constans stands aside and names you as his successor. Then suppose that someone – Eldof, or Garagon, or even the praetor – tries to prevent it. If something starts, we may not be able to stop it.'

'That happened in Isca,' Vortigern said. The words hit Kerin like a physical shock. The place was never mentioned, ever, except in casual references to estate business. Now this.

'What happened in Isca?' he asked.

'A riot that no-one could stop,' Vortigern said. 'Things were burned. People were killed. The garrison was outnumbered by around fifty to one. In the end they just stood back and let it happen. But Publius won't do that. He's bound by honour to protect Londinium and its citizens. His men are exemplary soldiers, but there aren't many of them. They'll be overwhelmed. We can't fight with them, we can't fight against them, we can't fight the people either, but we can't let the people burn down the patricians' houses. And we have no idea what men like Gorlois and Garagon and Eldof will do, let alone the praetor, or Rufus and his crew. We have to stop this.'

'What did you do in Isca?' Kerin asked.

'Nothing,' Vortigern said. 'There's nothing you can do, when you're face down manacled to the floor of a prison cell.' He gave a brief, humourless smile. It was the closest he had ever come to an admission of what might have happened in those times. Everyone knew that Isca was a locked door. But here, now, despite all his failings, Kerin had been allowed a glimpse of what lay behind it. He was not at all sure that he wanted to look. But it could not have been said for nothing. In an odd way he felt as if he had been offered a reprieve.

'We don't have long,' he said. 'When Constans has finished saying his prayers, I'll bring him back here and lock him up. It's for the best, for him as well as ourselves. Then I'm going to find the men who are marching on the city. Malan's right in the middle of it, and he'll listen to me. I'll tell him that Constans has stood down, even if he hasn't. It'll buy us time.'

'Malan?' Vortigern said in disbelief. 'That old man we saved on the way to Caerwynt?'

'Yes. I know he looks like nobody, but some men have a way of firing others up. And he thinks he owes us his life.'

'He does owe us his life,' Vortigern said. 'But I'd almost forgotten about it.'

'Well, he won't forget about it,' Kerin said. 'If you do something for a man who has nothing, he'll have it in his gut for the rest of his life. And I should know.'

There was a silence. Kerin didn't know how to break it. Then a faint sound from the direction of the courtyard made them both turn. It could have been a door slamming, or the dull crack of stone against stone. 'What was that?' Vortigern asked, straining his ears.

'I don't know,' Kerin said. There was no sound now, except for the roaring of the wind and the slap of water below them. 'Listen!' Kerin said. Between the gusts of wind they heard the sound of footsteps running across the courtyard behind them. Voices shouted in the narrow street beyond. There were faint screams, followed by the clashing of swords.

'The chapel!' Kerin exclaimed.

They ran, battling against the wind, down from the terrace and across the courtyard. The street outside was full of people milling about with torches and sticks and clubs. Gorlois and his warriors were there on horseback, trying to force them down the street towards the river. A sword-fight had just finished in the alley beside the chapel. Publius Luca and a handful of soldiers were piling some bodies against the wall. One was a monk; the rest looked like members of the king's bodyguard. The door of the chapel was open. Kerin and Vortigern reached it, panting for breath. The corpse of Lupinus was sprawled across the doorway. His blood trickled over the flagstones to meet them. A young guardsman lay dead, his head almost hacked off. Tertius was beside him, propped against the wall, clutching an ugly wound in his side. The interior of the chapel was still lit by wavering candles and the single dim altar lamp. The monks had fled. Bridei came slowly down the narrow aisle, drunk and grinning. Impaled on the point of his long dagger was the severed head of Constans. Giraldus and Padarn burst into the chapel. Lud and his warriors came crowding in behind them, followed by Marcellus and Severus the praetor, in his night-shirt. They all stood as if frozen. Bridei laughed. The blood ran down his arms. The silver crown which he had taken from Constans's head was perched awry on his straggling red hair. On the bare stones before the altar, the surviving Picts were looting the mangled remains of the king's body. Vortigern jerked the bloody head free, seized the knife and drove it into Bridei's heart. The Pict sank to his knees with a gasp. His hands clutched impotently at the dagger's hilt. The Picts shrank from the body, pleading for mercy. Vortigern turned away, ashen-faced.

'Take them, Lud,' he said. 'Hang them at dawn in front of the curia.'

The Picts were dragged bawling from the chapel. The monks crept fearfully back. Two of them wept as they bore Constans's body away. Padarn threw a cloak over the gruesome head, gathered it up and followed them. Kerin stared at the bloody flagstones, wondering how on earth Bridei and his mob had escaped, and what had happened to poor Livius. Somewhere near the door he could hear Severus Maximus holding forth, his tremulous voice sounding both insulted and terrified. Publius Luca came up the aisle, wiping blood from his hands.

'Two guards dead, sir, and that servant,' he said matter-of-factly. 'Tertius is wounded but will live, please the gods.'

Vortigern looked up. 'The king is dead, though,' he said, with the ghost of a smile.

'Indeed,' said Publius Luca, looking particularly unmoved, Kerin thought. A knot of men had formed down by the chapel door, talking earnestly; Eldof, Garagon and Gorlois, Severus Maximus and Marcellus, some senior soldiers. Publius Luca detached himself with a polite nod and went to join them. And now here was Gallus with his green-uniformed guards, followed by a squad of lean, sun-tanned men armed with cutlasses; they had to be his ships' crewmen, but they looked like a private army, and probably they were.

'What's happened here?' the merchant asked. 'Did you find the king?'

'Yes,' Kerin said. 'I found the king. And now he's been murdered by his own bodyguard. Perhaps we should have stood back and let him go on the ship.'

'The result is the same,' Gallus said. 'We have no king.' He turned as Publius Luca came from the gathering by the door. Ignoring everyone else, the commander walked straight up to Vortigern and took him by the forearms.

'A meeting will convene in the curia within the hour,' he said. 'I have everyone's agreement on that. Whether they will agree once we get them inside is another matter. But there will be a way. This will be done tonight. Are you prepared?'

'I've been prepared for thirty years,' Vortigern said.

'As I thought,' Publius Luca said, with the trace of a smile. Kerin drew Gallus aside.

'Where are all those people who were raging around outside?' he asked.

'Down by the river,' said the merchant. 'In that open space where the markets are held. There are twice as many of them now, and more arriving all the time.'

'Keep them there, if you can,' Kerin said. 'No blood. These people are on our side. We need them outside the curia, where they were on the day Vortigern crowned Constans, but we don't need them yet. All the leading men must be inside, saying their piece. I'll send someone to you when it's time. Someone you'll know, Lucius Arrius or one of Lud's sons.'

'Done,' said Gallus. 'And you?'

'I'm going to meet the men who are coming from outside,' Kerin said. 'I have to reach them before they batter down the western gate and start setting fire to houses like yours and the praetor's. They want the same thing as the people by the river, of course. It's up to us to give it to them without blood, because if we can't, the blood might be ours.' He turned, feeling a hand on his shoulder. Publius Luca was standing there. Gallus withdrew with his armed men.

'Someone unlocked the guard room and let the Picts out,' Publius Luca said. 'Livius, the young guard, was stabbed. Marcellus has gone to attend him and Tertius. Livius had the key, I suppose.'

'No.' Kerin took the guard room key from the pocket of his tunic and held it out. 'I thought Livius would be in less danger without it. He told me that the only other key was kept in the praetor's apartments. I don't see how anyone could have got hold of it. Severus Maximus can't possibly be to blame.'

'No, no,' Publius Luca said. 'He's a weak, unprincipled man but he wouldn't get involved in anything like that. It's not my first concern, anyway. You heard what I said to Vortigern.'

'Yes,' Kerin said. 'Once again, we are going to the curia to choose a king. Will anyone oppose us?'

'Eldof of Glevum and Garagon of Kent may demand Ambrosius,' Publius Luca said. 'The Bishop of Glevum will stand with his brother, for what it's worth. And I'm told that Venta Belgarum has elected a new praetor. Between them they have enough men to make a fight of it. Some of the patricians who sit on the ordo may join them. Do you know of others?'

'Vortigern's son,' Kerin said. 'If he finds out that Constans has been killed, he'll be back in the city with every man he can raise. He's formed – I don't know what to call it. A sect? A holy brotherhood? They call themselves the Sword of God. There probably aren't many of them yet, but the power it has is greater than you'd think.'

'I've seen this sort of thing in Rome,' Publius Luca said. 'A handful of discontented young men with an idea that can fire the blood.' His eyes gleamed in the flickering light. 'But we have our fire too. We have the High King.'

'And we have the numbers,' Kerin said. 'Hold the line at the curia. I will bring them.'

27

Nothing appeared to be happening in the dark streets between the chapel and the praetor's house, but the silence was pregnant with menace. It reminded Kerin of the airless calm which sometimes hung over his home valley; the darkening sky, the distant play of light low down, the men and women driving their beasts to shelter. As he approached the gates, a sound made him turn. A quick, urgent knock. Four men came out of a dark doorway to join another in the street. They exchanged a few words and scuttled away towards the river.

Elir was standing outside the stables. His brother Macsen was with him.

'The chapel,' Elir lamented. 'Everything was alright there the last time I looked.'

'It's not your fault,' Kerin said. 'No-one could have predicted this.'

Macsen gave a wry smile. 'Not even you?' he asked.

'No,' Kerin said. 'Not even me. I locked the Picts up; someone let them out. It was the last thing I thought of. And now we have other things to think about. Where's your father?'

'Inside, with Vortigern,' Macsen said. 'He told us we're going to the curia, to crown a new king.'

'Yes. And we all know who the new king must be. Do you remember what happened, when Vortigern crowned Constans? When Maximian Galba challenged him, and he went and threw the doors open?'

'Yes,' Macsen said. 'Every living soul in the city was out there, shouting his name. It shut everyone up a treat.'

'Yes,' Kerin said. 'And it will do again. But this time it's different. Those people are angry now. They probably believe that Vortigern should have been king all along, and if anyone tries to prevent it tonight, there'll be a slaughter. Eldof and Garagon may call for Ambrosius. If they do, some of the patricians may support them. Publius Luca and the garrison are on our side, but if the people riot and start burning and killing, they're honour-bound to try to stop it. They won't be able to stop it. Elir will have told you that there are men marching towards the city gates, probably a couple of thousand by now. And there are just as many inside the walls.'

'I've seen them,' Elir said. 'Down by the river. Most of them are only armed with sticks and stones, but when there are that many of them – '

'Exactly,' Kerin said. 'I've asked Gallus to hold those men there if he can. He's a powerful man, feared in the city I'm sure, and he's got some nasty-looking armed guards with him. I've told him we need all those people outside the curia, but not until we're ready for them. Do you understand what I'm saying?'

Macsen, for all his usual bravado, looked rattled. 'Just tell me what you want me to do,' he said, as if Kerin were his battle commander.

'Go to the curia with your father and the rest of our warband. Don't let Vortigern out of your sight. You and Custennin are our best swordsmen. Protect him. That's all. Elir will have told you that Rufus and some of his followers are in the city. If they turn up at the curia and you have to fight them, fight them. I know; our friend, my blood brother. I hope it won't come to that, but if it does, don't hesitate.'

'And me?' Elir asked apprehensively.

'I've told Gallus that I'll send someone when we need the people at the curia,' Kerin said. 'He knows you, so he'll know you're telling the truth. Go the western gate, get up on the wall where the guards stand, and wait.'

Elir's eyes widened. 'Wait for what?' he asked.

'For me. I'm going to meet those men who are marching towards the city. They must be close by now, even if they're all on foot. I'm going to tell them that the only way to make sure that Vortigern becomes king is to come in peace. If they agree, I'm going to ask the guards to open the western gate for them. Then we'll join with the men from the river, and march to the curia. As soon as you see the guards move to open the gate, get your arse down to the river and explain all that to Gallus.'

Macsen looked incredulous. 'And you think they'll listen to you?' he asked. 'Two thousand armed lunatics and the guards who are supposed to be keeping the gates shut?'

'I'm depending on it,' Kerin said. 'And so are you. Elir, bring Eryr out here, but not my spears. And look after this for me.' He unbuckled his sword-belt and handed it over.

'You're going unarmed,' Elir said. It was obvious, but it seemed so mad that he still needed confirmation.

'It's the only way,' Kerin said. 'There are two thousand of them. If they want to kill me, they can. And if I want them to come in peace, I have to do the same. Now go and do as I've asked, both of you. And pray to any gods you like.'

He heard the sound long before anything became visible. At first he thought it was just the wind, blasting across the open ground west of the city. Then he realised that the sound of the gusts was underpinned by something else; a low, continuous rumble which reminded him of the way the sea sometimes roared on beautiful, benign-looking days because a storm was building out in the channel, putting its invisible shoulder behind the waves. But there was no sea within miles. Kerin reined in on the deserted road and listened. The sound was coming closer, and as it drew near enough to separate into its component parts he realised what it was and why it had confused him, because it was something he had never heard before; the steady tramp of a few thousand feet. Someone was beating out a club-footed rhythm on a skin drum. Dud-*dah*. Dud-*dah*. Dud-*dah*. Eryr stiffened under him and started to shake. The old battle-roar rumbled deep in her chest. She thinks there's a fight coming, Kerin thought. He caressed the mare's ears and stroked her arched neck, hoping that she was wrong. The corn ground here was almost flat, but just ahead lay a slight undulation. Kerin rode quickly forward and stopped on the crest. In the middle distance he saw the first of the torches, a slew of bobbing lights stretching back along the Roman road for as far as he could see. The sounds intensified; the tramping feet, the thudding drumbeat and, rolling towards him in time to it, a deep-voiced, hypnotic chant. *Vor*tigern. *Vor*tigern. *Vor*tigern. The moon broke the veil of ragged clouds, and as the mass of people drew nearer, Kerin saw Malan at the front, riding on a bony black mule. Everyone else appeared to be on foot. They were armed as Elir had said, with anything they could lay their hands on. The tools of their many trades. Axes, billhooks, hammers, gutting knives, mallets, hunting spears. Men of all ages, young lads, a few women. And druids, a whole company of them. They were the ones with the drums.

'Stand,' Kerin said to his trembling horse. 'Stand. Not today.' He looped the reins over his arm and raised both hands above his head. 'Malan!' he bellowed. 'I'm unarmed. I come in peace.' He knew that everything he said was drowning; that his only hope was for Malan to recognise him and trust his good intentions. The marchers were close enough now for him to see the rage in the eyes of the men in the front rank. Men who would see only his good clothes and his well-fed body, who would look at his beautiful horse and know that, if they worked every day for a year, they would not be able to afford one of her front legs. He chirruped to the mare and made her walk forward. If she had not been a warhorse she would have bolted in panic by now, but they trained them for this; the banging racket, the screams and shouts and the flash of blades. 'Malan!' Kerin bawled. 'I come from Vortigern!'

And this time the old man heard. A wild crow of

recognition broke from him. He turned his black mule and waved his arms about. 'Stop!' he screamed. 'This man is for us!' He had not lied about having a loud voice. That narrow, wizened chest could pump out as much noise as a roaring bull. The procession stumbled to a chaotic halt. Kerin dismounted. 'Don't kill it,' he told his horse, as Malan pushed his mule forwards and slithered to the ground. The two men faced each other in the middle of the Roman road.

'You cannot stop us,' Malan said earnestly.

'I don't want to stop you,' Kerin said. 'Constans the monk is dead. The men of power gather in the curia to choose a new king. I want you all to come to the city with me, and make sure that they choose the right one. But it cannot be done with blood. No killing. No burning.'

A dark man elbowed his way forward. A smith, probably, from the muscular shoulders and the burn scars on his forearms. 'No killing, no burning?' he howled. 'They won't listen to poor bastards like us any other way.'

'They will,' Kerin said. 'Were you in the city when Vortigern crowned Constans?'

'No!' the smith spat. 'Some of us have to work, not like you fucking high-born.' He folded his arms and planted his feet. The people behind him pushed forward.

'I'm not high-born,' Kerin said, leaning towards him. 'My mother was dirt-poor. My father was a horse-thief. I'm nobody. But I'm here, like this, because of Vortigern's good grace. And if we don't make him king tonight, the kingdom will fall, and then it won't make any difference if you're high-born or low-born, because we'll all be dying on the end of someone's spear.' He drew Malan forward. 'You were there, old one. I saw you. Tell him what it was like when the monk was crowned.'

'It was the best day of my life,' Malan said, his eyes glowing. 'All of us outside the curia, shouting for Vortigern. So many that even the praetor of Londinium, Severus bloody Maximus, had to listen.'

'Yes,' Kerin said. 'And without a sword drawn in anger.' He turned to the marchers who were crowding around him and his horse. 'There are good men on our side. Publius Luca, who commands the city garrison. Lucius Arrius, head of the praetorian guard. Gorlois of Kernow, and all the lords of the West. But if you start killing and burning, these good men will try to prevent it. Because they don't want slaughter and destruction, not because they're against you. They're not against you. We all want the same thing. And if you come to the city in peace, I will give it to you.'

'And why should we trust you to do that?' the smith shouted, to a rowdy chorus of approval. 'You could be lying, just to keep the city safe.'

'No,' Kerin said. 'I care nothing for the city.'

'Edryd, hear this man.' Malan put his thin hand on the smith's huge forearm. 'He speaks for the Lord Vortigern.'

'How can that be, if your blood is as common as ours?' the smith jeered.

'Blood means nothing to him,' Kerin said. 'He esteems what is here. The brave spirit. The quick mind and the strong voice, like Malan's. And the mighty arm.'

'The mighty arm?' The smith grinned, flexing his.

'Perhaps above all,' Kerin said, gripping the smith's shoulder. 'Edryd, will you march with us when we go north to fight the invaders?'

'You'll take me?' the smith asked, astounded.

'We'll take every man in this company strong enough to make the distance,' Kerin said. 'We'll train you in battlecraft, and arm you as warriors. But first we must crown our king. Without that, nothing happens. We will enter Londinium without force. The guards will open the western gate for me. You have my word on that. But only if you lay down any weapons you are carrying, and face them in peace. Will you do that?'

Edryd's brow puckered. 'How?' he asked. 'These things are our livelihood. I can't just throw my hammer in a bush, and hope it might be there when I come back.'

'You can all leave your tools and weapons at Malan's camp outside the western gate,' Kerin said. 'The place is full of women who will guard them well. I've met Malan's daughter, Berget, and believe me, she's as fierce as any of you.'

'Berget?' came a voice from the second rank. 'You spoke the truth there, sir. Berget's my wife, and I'm frightened to death of her.'

'She'd have you for breakfast, boy,' someone sniggered. A rumble of amusement travelled through the company. Kerin knew in his heart that he had won, but it was too soon to be complacent.

'Malan, Edryd, go to your people,' he said. 'This can't be one man's choice. If they agree to do as I ask, we march on the city.'

He stood in the middle of the Roman road with his horse and the skinny black mule and waited. Now that his two allies had gone, he felt as vulnerable as if he had been standing there naked. He was not accustomed to going unarmed anywhere, except in his own house. Now he was standing in front of this whipped up, milling crowd with not even a dagger on his belt. He knew that, at his word, Eryr would kill the first ten men who came at him before they brought her down; but for once it gave him no reassurance. The minutes crawled by. He knew that it must take forever to pass any sort of message amongst this mass of people, let alone one which most of them might not want to hear; but there was nothing to do except wait. Wait and fear and shiver as the sweat ran down his back and dried in the biting wind.

'We go!' a voice bellowed from the within the crowd. Malan's. Two big men barged forward, carrying him on their shoulders. 'We go,' gasped the old man, scrambling aboard his mule. 'To my camp first. I'll go in with our boys, and tell our women what's needed. They won't fail us. The rest is up to you.'

We go, Kerin thought. We go to possess the city, Londinium Augusta, one man on horseback, one on a rickety mule and a crowd of farmers, labourers, servants and tradesmen without a weapon between them. We go to crown the king. He glanced behind at the mass of people he was now leading. They had taken him at his word. The rest, as Malan had said, was up to him.

28

Berget stood outside her shack, hands on hips. A row of other women stood beside her, some of them with a family resemblance. Kerin wondered what Malan's wife must have looked like, for such a small, thin man to have fathered a family of bruisers like these. They watched as hammers, axes, hooks and knives of all descriptions showered onto the growing piles beside the Roman road.

'Don't worry,' Berget said. 'Most of the idiots are going to the city with you, and if any of them come sneaking back they'll have to pass me and my girls.'

'I wouldn't pass you,' Kerin said. 'And most of the time I've got a sword, two spears and a warhorse.'

'Those lads,' Berget said. 'The ones Flora brought. Is it true that one of them was the king? Constans the monk?'

'Yes,' Kerin said. 'And now he's dead.'

'Would he still be alive, if Flora had kept out of it?' Berget asked.

'Probably,' Kerin said. 'I know she had good intentions, but things went wrong. Things I didn't foresee. Constans wouldn't have been king for much longer anyway, but he might have got away with his life.'

'You wish he had, don't you,' Berget said. Kerin had

not given this a thought, but now he realised that it was true.

'Yes. I never liked him, to be truthful. But I wouldn't have wished that death on him. He was weak and harmless. It was pointless, like killing a child. Flora tried to get him aboard a ship that's due to sail at midnight. We'd never have seen him again. Perhaps I should have let her do it.'

'I saw him,' Berget said. 'A poor skinny thing that a puff of wind could have blown over. They say his father only put him in the monastery because he knew he'd never be good for anything. No wonder Flora was sorry for him. But it wasn't about him, was it? Not with her.'

'No,' Kerin said. 'It wasn't about him. But it still got him killed, in the end. Perhaps you should see to Flora when she comes back. For her own sake. Do what you said her mother should have done, before anything else happens.'

'Knock some sense into her?' Berget gave a sceptical smile. 'It's a bit late for that, lord.'

The guards were standing where they always did, on the parapet above the western gate. It was dark, there was an occasional flurry of sleet, but these men did not flinch or attempt to shield themselves from the freezing wind. Kerin would not have wavered either, if Publius Luca had been his commanding officer. He wondered what the guards would make of the thing they saw coming towards them, this huge black mass with its scatter of bobbing lights, stretching away out of sight. He supposed that he would have been petrified. There was no way of knowing, from up there, that everyone was unarmed.

'Hold the men here,' he said to Malan and Edryd, who was walking beside the mule. 'Let me speak to the guards. They don't know our intentions. They're probably filling their breeches.' The two men chuckled, turned and raised hands to halt the procession. A familiar dark head appeared above the parapet. Elir would have attempted to explain what was happening, but who knew if he had done it well, or if the guards had believed him? Kerin rode forward until he was close enough to be heard. 'I am Kerin Brightspear,' he bellowed. 'I am here for Vortigern of Glywysing, Lord of the West.'

'We know who you are,' came the shouted reply. 'But who are these?'

'We are the Britons,' Kerin shouted back, to a ripple of approval. 'And we come to crown our king. We come in peace.' He raised his arms. 'We come unarmed. But we will be heard.'

An argument had started up on the wall. The guard who had spoken, probably the leader, had been challenged by one of his companions. Elir waded in. Two more of the guards added their opinions. The disagreement fizzled out.

'Lord Kerin,' said the chief guard, 'we are sworn to defend the city until death. But our commander Publius Luca has told me that you are an honourable man. What would you have us do?'

'Open the gates,' Kerin said. 'I swear that we wish no harm upon you or your city. These men, who have all laid down their weapons, would march to the curia to crown their king. They would join with the people who are waiting within the city, led by Gallus the merchant.

All have sworn to come in peace. And I swear that they will do it, on my life and on the life of Vortigern Lord of the West, which is dearer to me than anything else on this earth. We come in peace. Receive us in peace, and open the gates.'

'And if we don't?' the dissenting guard piped up.

'If you don't, we will open them ourselves,' Kerin said. 'And all these men who have come in peace will come in blood, and the city will burn, and there will be death in its streets which you will not be able to stop, because we are thousands.'

A roar went up from behind him. The druids' skin drums began to pound. Du-*dah*. Du-*dah*. Du-*dah*. The chant began again. *Vor*tigern. *Vor*tigern. *Vor*tigern. Kerin felt the skin prickle all over his body, as it did in the last sliver of time before battle was joined. Elir vanished. With a thud and a creak, the gates swung open. Kerin turned Eryr to face his army. Malan, on his mule, did the same. Both men raised their arms, trying to damp down the noise.

'Malan, we need silence,' Kerin shouted. 'We don't need this racket until we get to the curia.'

'I know,' Malan shrieked, eyes wild in the torchlight. 'We need it there! The shock! The terror!'

Elir arrived, his face streaming sweat. 'Gallus is on the move,' he said. 'Lucius Arrius is with him. They've got thousands of people behind them. Men, women, youngsters, all sorts. They're going to hold them outside the praetor's house, if they can.'

'Alright.' Kerin glanced around and located the smith. 'Edryd, can you ride?'

'I can stay on,' Edryd said. 'Nothing fancy.'

Kerin turned to Elir. 'Get him something quiet from the praetor's stables. I need another man on horseback here. Bring it, then get over to the curia and find out what's going on. We should be outside by then. Come out and meet me, but don't make it obvious.'

'Don't make it obvious?' Elir said blankly. 'You think you can get all this to the curia without making it obvious?'

'I'm going to try,' Kerin said. Elir threw his hands in the air and rode away. The drumming and chanting had stopped, but not the shouting and high-pitched yells. 'Malan, Edryd, for God's sake, I need them quiet.' The two men sent runners down the procession, pleading for silence. Once again it took time. Kerin waited until the noise had subsided to a low muttering. 'Hear me,' he said. 'Inside the city, my friends have raised another company just like this. We march to the curia together. We go in peace. And we also go in silence. Why? Because when the moment comes to demand your king, I want you to make the same noise as you just made here, but twice as loud, because when the men of power hear that, they'll be so shocked, so terrified, that they won't dare oppose us.' He raised his hand to quell the cheers which were threatening to erupt. Elir arrived with one of the praetor's saddle horses, legged Edryd up onto her broad back and galloped off through the gateway. 'Alright,' Kerin said, 'Malan, stay here with me. Edryd, ride halfway down the line. I need you there to keep things in order.' He stretched out his hands, and the two men clasped them.

'Now we go to crown the king,' Malan said, eyes gleaming, as if the whole of his long life had been a preparation for this moment.

29

The first thing Kerin saw was Gallus, sitting on a big bay horse right outside the praetor's gates. From where he was, he could see nothing else except the narrow, empty street between them; then Lucius appeared at the merchant's shoulder, turned in the saddle and raised a hand to someone invisible. Kerin signalled to Malan. Hold them here. He rode forward, startled by the loudness of his mare's hooves striking the cobbles. Gallus was smiling.

'It's done,' he mouthed, nodding towards the street behind him. Pale faces, illuminated by torchlight, packed the space between the praetor's walls and the castra; a murmuring mass stretching far down past St Alban's chapel towards the marketplace and the river beyond. In the front ranks Kerin glimpsed a few familiar faces. Manius and his crew. The praetor's stable lads. The servant Petrus. The boy who had sold him Lucius's horse. Flora.

'I had to come,' Lucius said. 'My father's gone to the curia to stand for Vortigern. We should go there now. Most of the men who matter are inside already. Vortigern and Lud and your warriors, of course. Gorlois, Garagon, Eldof, Eldadus and some other men who look like bishops, Flavius the praetor, the company of merchants, all the patricians who sit on the ordo. Marcellus and Father Giraldus. Everyone who has warriors or guards has got them with him. Severus Maximus is trying to call it to order, but no-one's listening. Publius Luca looks as if he's about to step up. And as I came out, Elir was going in. He said he'd seen the Lord Vortimer and his men coming out of the house where Eldof and his people are staying.'

'Then it's time.' Kerin waved to Malan and Edryd, calling them forward. Gallus and Lucius moved closer. 'It's time,' he said to the four men. 'When we reach the curia, I'm going inside. Keep these people as quiet as you can. It might not be possible. Just do your best. When I need you, I'll throw the doors open like Vortigern did when he crowned Constans. That's the signal. When those doors open, I want as much noise as you can make.'

Gallus caught Kerin's eye. 'If things go wrong in there, we won't be able to hold these in the square.'

'No,' Kerin said. 'If that happens, save yourself.' He ran his eye over the street behind Gallus's back. 'Are yours armed?'

'No. We disarmed them down by the river. Kitchen knives and hammers and stuff. Some of them have probably got stones in their pockets. But my own men are armed. Yours?'

'I'm not even armed myself,' Kerin said. Gallus's brow creased – you're even madder than I thought, the look said – then he reined back to let Kerin take the lead, and the enormous, silent army of the Britons began its slow march towards the curia.

In some ways it was as if nothing had changed. The neatly clipped bay trees in their urns, flanking the entrance; the forecourt with its iron railings and tall locked gates, guarded by members of the city garrison. But last time they had come in the bright light of morning, on a wave of hope and happy delirium. Now they came in darkness, in silence, with ferocious purpose. Kerin remembered the last time he had fought the Irish, down on the shores of Dyfed; just a skirmish, he now realised, as he felt the weight of all these fierce souls bearing down upon him. He was too young to remember the great raids, or at least, to have fought in them. He remembered the consequences only too well; the wounded men, the burials, the pyres smouldering for days behind the shingle bank next to the sea. But beyond all that lay the prize, the sweet relief of knowing that the threat had lifted, that cattle could feed safely in the pastures along the river, that the cornfields would not burn. This was where he was leading these men, in all probability; to blood and reckoning and, he hoped, to the salvation of the kingdom. But only if they could crown their king.

Two guardsmen came to the gate. Kerin dismounted and handed his reins to Lucius. He saw the way the guards looked past him, the tension in their bodies, the fear in their eyes.

'I am Kerin Brightspear,' he said. 'The king is dead. We come to crown his successor.'

'We're commanded to admit you,' one of the guards said. 'But not these.'

'They don't ask to be admitted,' Kerin said. 'They'll wait here quietly, with Master Gallus and Lucius Arrius. I will speak for them.'

'He will speak for us,' shouted Malan, whose aged ears seemed as sharp as his voice was strong. The two guards exchanged uneasy glances.

'Very well, sir,' said the one who had spoken. 'Come with me.' Kerin followed him up the steps. Elir slipped from the shadow of a pillar.

'There's a new praetor of Venta Belgarum,' he said quietly. 'Maximian Galba's successor. He sounds like a proper Paulinus man. He's standing on that platform where Vortigern crowned Constans, ranting about God and Rome and the past. Gorlois got up first, calling for Vortigern to be king, and that set him off. Severus Maximus and Publius Luca are up on the dais where they were last time. Vortigern's standing halfway up the steps. My father and Macsen and Hefin are with him. He hasn't said much yet.'

'Rufus?' Kerin asked. 'Lucius said you saw him.'

'Coming out of Eldof's house, yes. He didn't look like a man who'd had an argument. Rufus could never hide it, could he?'

'No,' Kerin said. 'Perhaps he and Eldof have made an agreement. A pact of some sort. Has anyone said anything about Constans? The way he was killed?'

'Not much.' Elir looked distinctly nervous. 'Everyone agrees it was terrible, of course, but no-one's dared to make any accusations. They all seem to know that the Picts did the killing, and that you locked them up because they were drunk. But as for who let them out, no-one's saying anything. At least, not out loud, whatever they're telling each other behind their hands. Publius Luca had taken charge by the time I got back. He said that there'd be time enough to think about the killing tomorrow. That for now, settling the kingship was all that mattered.'

They had reached the outer doors. 'Stay here, Elir,' Kerin said. 'If any trouble starts, come and get me. But don't open these doors more than you need to.' He turned the ring in the door, eased it open and slipped into the vestibule where he had once waited with a shaking, terrified monk. Two members of the city garrison were standing where Publius Luca himself had stood all those months ago. It was hard to tell men apart under a Roman-style helmet, but one of these two was smiling. 'Lord Kerin,' he said respectfully, and moved aside.

The building was full, but not packed to the walls as it had been when Constans was crowned. The rows of stone benches were occupied, but the floor was clear. A large man in Roman garb was standing on the central platform. He had the angular features and penetrating gaze of Maximian Galba, but he was built like a wrestler. 'An army?' he bawled. 'You call this an army? This herd of primitives dragged down out of the western mountains? Even the Picts would laugh, and they're a bunch of animals themselves.'

Kerin trod quietly around the perimeter of the hall and mounted the steps which led up to the dais. Vortigern gave him a scarifying look.

'Another riding lesson?' he asked.

'No,' Kerin said, watching the speaker. 'I had things to attend to. You will see.' He could barely believe that he had said it, but there was little to lose. Vortigern looked as astounded as he felt. Publius Luca came down to join them.

'I am not without influence in Rome,' roared the man on the platform. 'Bring back Constantine's younger son, let them see that there's still some respect for the purple in these islands.'

'Is he a Galba?' Kerin murmured. 'He has a look of Maximian.'

'A cousin,' Publius Luca said. 'The mothers were sisters, from a large estate near Venta Belgarum. Their brother is still there, a man of some standing. This man is Marcus Tarpeius. His father served in the Victrix with Maximian's father, Titus Galba, but was higher ranking. This one's not long back from Rome. They do have a little influence there, but probably not as much as they claim. He came back when his cousin was killed, and never went away, unfortunately. The man's a windbag, as you can tell, but people who treasure their social status can't get enough of him. Look at Flavius of Eburacum, and that idiot Alberius. They look ready to burst into tears. And even Garagon of Kent, who gave certain assurances to Vortigern, and ought to know better.'

'Publius,' Vortigern interposed, 'I've kept my mouth shut, as you suggested, but if that imbecile down there doesn't –'

'Patience,' Publius Luca said, with a faint smile. 'You take it by force, they'll take it back by force soon enough. We can depend on Gorlois of Kernow, Severus Maximus and the praetorian guard, my garrison and the merchants. Possibly Eldof of Glevum. That's always an open question. And of course, every man, woman and dog from west of the River Hafren.'

'And if that's not enough?' Vortigern said, teeth set.

'It will be enough,' Kerin said. Vortigern's eyes flicked to him. Does he really believe what the others do, Kerin thought, that this open-eyed certainty has emerged, fully clothed, from the dark depths of sleep? Is that all he values in me? 'It will be enough,' he repeated, because it was time to stake everything now. 'You will see.'

And then Marcus Tarpeius's tirade stopped abruptly. Something was happening outside the great rear doors, through which Hefin and the Cambrian warriors had burst into the curia on horseback to seal the coronation of the monk. Shouting, clattering hooves.

'Stand aside, in the name of Christ the Lord!' someone shouted. The doors swung wide. Rufus rode in on a dazzling white horse, followed by six mounted warriors clothed just like him, in white tunics embroidered with a bright blue cross and an inscription Kerin could not read. He rode forward alone to the foot of the dais. Vortigern shook off Publius Luca's hand and descended the steps until he and his son were eye to eye.

'Who murdered Constans?' Rufus demanded.

'His bodyguard,' Vortigern said. 'Bridei the Pict and his men. As you surely know.'

'And who let them into the praetor's palace?' Rufus shouted. 'Who made them the king's bodyguard, against all reason and common sense?'

'I have no blood on my hands where Constans is concerned,' Vortigern said. 'I could have left him to rot, but I risked my life to make him king, as anyone in the city will tell you.'

'For one reason only,' Rufus breathed. 'To clear your way to this place. This moment. Don't suppose that I've forgotten what you said to Paulinus. That the men who sit in this room think anything from the West is the devil's spawn. That you needed Constans to make them listen to you.'

'I don't deny that for one moment,' Vortigern said. 'And I hope they're listening now, because our enemies will soon be at the gate. And when they reach it, God and a few pretty white horses aren't going to keep them out.'

'God will favour those who honour him and do his will,' Rufus retorted. 'If we turn our backs on him, we'll deserve whatever comes to us.'

Kerin knew how this argument went. He had heard it a hundred times before, at the dinner table, over wine or ale, in Vortigern's library, on hunting expeditions. He had heard it drunk and he had heard it sober, calm and angry, reasoned and plain unhinged. But at this moment, he was not really listening to it. He was thinking, they came in by the rear doors. They will have come from behind the curia, probably returning the way they left, by the southern gate. They will have no idea what is waiting outside in the square.

'I am going to lead our forces against the Picts,' Vortigern was saying. He was calm, but very pale. 'And if you and your handful of fanatics don't join us, you are every sort of traitor.'

'Of course we'll stand against the Picts,' Rufus said, bristling. 'And against any other heathen bastards who try to take this country from us.'

'Except the Romans, presumably,' came a whimsical little voice from the Cornish contingent. Marcus Tarpeius glowered up at the chortling warriors. Kerin touched Vortigern's arm.

'They know each other,' he said. 'Rufus and Marcus Tarpeius. They've met before. Look at Tarpeius. He isn't even surprised. This was planned.' He marched down the steps and planted himself in front of Rufus's horse. It was a big, handsome animal but it didn't look like a warhorse to Kerin. 'Are you going to come down from there and face me like a man?' he asked. Rufus gave him a savage glare. Refusal was impossible. As he dismounted, Kerin seized the horse's bridle, pulled its head down hard and bellowed right in its face. The horse jerked backwards in panic, eyes rolling. 'I hope you're not going to war on this,' Kerin said.

'No,' Rufus said sullenly. 'Of course not.'

Kerin grinned. 'For show then, is it?' he asked. Marcus Tarpeius came barrelling down from the platform.

'Who in God's name are you?' he shouted.

'Oh, you won't have heard of me,' Kerin said. 'I'm a man of no particular blood. A man of no consequence.' An uneasy, muttering quiet settled over the gathering. There could hardly have been anyone in the room un- aware of Kerin Brightspear, whatever they might think about his forebears or his importance. 'I'm a man of no blood,' he said, raising his voice just enough for it to reach the far corners. 'A man of no consequence. And I am here to speak for all the men of no blood and no consequence. The men whose voice is never heard, because it's drowned out by the rattle of the coins in your treasuries.' A low rumble ran around the stone benches. Uneasy in some quarters. Approving in others, no doubt, because most of the ordinary warriors and guardsmen brought along to protect their commanders were men of no blood and little consequence too. Rufus appeared to have been struck dumb. Marcus Tarpeius squared his shoulders.

'So,' he said acidly. 'You speak for the men of no consequence. The slaves and the paupers.'

'I do,' Kerin said. 'For we have come to crown the new king.'

Marcus Tarpeius laughed. He threw back his head and laughed, until his well-built body shook and tears leaked from his little grey eyes. But Eldof of Glevum was not laughing, Kerin noticed. Garagon of Kent was not laughing either. The two men were exchanging nervous comments. Eldof's face had turned crimson. Perhaps he was trying to decide which way to jump. Gorlois was standing not far from them, hands on hips. Hefydd of Carneddlas was slapping his belly, as he did when an outstanding joint of beef was brought to table. The merchants were talking earnestly amongst themselves. The priests were looking anxious.

'Who would you have for king, then?' Kerin asked, circling Marcus Tarpeius. 'This boy your cousins set so much store by?'

'Who else?' Tarpeius roared. 'The only possible successor to his brother, murdered in cold blood as Maximian was, by these barbarians who have been given the run of the praetor's house. And this is the measure of Britannia, without Rome's civilising hand. My cousin was right. Unless Imperial rule can be restored, you may as well open the gates to the Picts, because they're no worse than some of the men who are standing here now.'

From the corner of his eye, Kerin saw Vortigern step

forward and stop, restrained by Publius Luca. Thank you, Marcus Tarpeius, he thought; there can't be a man in this room who'd open the gates to the Picts, whatever he thinks of the riffraff from the West. 'No wonder you're happy to demean us, Marcus Tarpeius,' he said. 'Perish the thought that we might defeat an enemy the Romans couldn't stop.'

'Which of you will stop them, then?' Marcus Tarpeius spat, livid with rage. 'The men of no consequence?'

'Which of us will stop them?' Kerin said. 'Let's see.' He turned and walked with slow and deliberate steps towards the closed front doors of the curia. He could feel all the eyes on his back. For a single, horrifying moment, he thought: if they've all given up and gone home, I'm a dead man. His hands shook as he seized the great iron ring, raised the latch and flung the doors open. Even he was not prepared for the intensity, the volume, the sheer, deafening power of the noise which erupted from the square outside the curia. He had expected something akin to the sound which met him out on the Roman road, but there were twice as many people here now, and everything was amplified by the towering walls of the buildings surrounding the square; the roar, the chanting, the skin drums pounding like a monstrous heartbeat. Kerin stood at the top of the steps and let it envelop him. Elir ran to him. His lips were moving, but the words were lost. Someone had brought two big wagons and parked them across the gates. Gallus, Lucius, Malan and Edryd were standing on them. Lucius was shouting eagerly to the guards. Malan and Edryd were doing a crazy dance. Gallus was laughing and whipping up the crowd. As Kerin watched, Flora clambered up onto the wagon beside him. Her eyes met Kerin's and her face broke into a radiant smile, which he knew quite well was not for him. He turned back towards the curia and found himself face to face with Vortigern. Amidst the pandemonium there was suddenly a small cocoon of silence, in which they were alone.

'All this,' Vortigern began; then words seemed to fail him, and he seized Kerin by the shoulders and embraced him.

'This will keep,' Kerin said. 'Go to them now, lord. It's you they want.' He watched, filled with a joy more profound than any he had known, as Vortigern walked out onto the steps and raised his arms to his delirious people.

'This was your doing,' came a voice at his shoulder. Kerin turned. Rufus didn't look angry now, simply resigned. Hard done-by. Perhaps I'm the one who has disappointed him, Kerin thought. It wasn't likely to be God.

'It's my doing that they're all out here shouting instead of burning the city down,' he said. 'And it's my doing that they're all unarmed. Everything else is your father's doing, and if you don't believe me, ask any man out there.'

'I don't have to,' Rufus said. 'Any fool could see what's happening.'

Kerin was not sure which way to take that. The grudging acknowledgement of another man's triumph, or a damning comment on the way it was achieved? For now, he couldn't afford to waste time thinking about it. A group of men had assembled next to the platform in the centre of the floor, deep in discussion. Eldof of Glevum and his brother, the bishop. Garagon of Kent and his uncle Edlym. Gorlois of Kernow. Marcellus and Father Giraldus. There was no sign of Marcus Tarpeius, but Alberius and the young praetor Flavius were there. The uproar in the square had calmed a little. Vortigern was on his way back, flanked by Gallus and Malan. The old man was hobbling on a stick, waving gaily to the dignitaries, most of them no more than names to him until now. Gallus, smiling and dishevelled, seemed to have shed half his age. Behind them Lucius and Edryd heaved the great doors shut. The racket outside sank to a hum. Publius Luca and Severus Maximus came down from the dais. Eldof of Glevum stepped forward to meet them. He said something inaudible to Publius Luca, and the two men shook hands.

'Vortigern, this is an evil night,' Eldof said, looking shaken to the marrow. 'The murder is done now, and God knows better than I do how it came to pass. But one thing's beyond question. Our enemies will rejoice when they hear what has happened. We all ask you to be king; not out of love, for there is no love between us, but – '

'I don't want your love,' Vortigern said. 'But I'll save you from the Picts, if you like.'

'Yes,' Eldof conceded. 'I suppose you will, if any man can.'

Publius Luca moved to Vortigern's side. 'We should complete the formalities tonight, sir,' he said. 'I don't think there'll be any argument now, but I'm all for seizing the moment.'

'You're right, of course,' Vortigern said. 'As usual.' He

gave the commander a wry look which Kerin couldn't read. 'How many people do we have outside?' he asked.

'Around four thousand, probably,' Kerin said. Vortigern hailed Lucius.

'I have work for you. Any rich man's household in this city could raise a feast for a hundred people. Take the praetorian guard, visit as many of these houses as you need to, and tell them to send food, drink and cooks out to the Campus Martius. These people deserve a feast, and it'll get them out of the city. Stay to make sure it's done. Malan, pass the word around. To your own people and all the rest. Tell them that I won't forget their part in this. After the feast, they must all go back to their homes and families. But in the spring, when we march to the North, I'll be looking for able-bodied men who are ready to fight, and for craftsmen who can forge weapons and build wagons. I will send for them.'

'And for a man with a loud voice, to call them to order?' Malan asked hopefully.

'I'll look no further than you, Malan,' Vortigern said. The old man bowed from the waist, tears of pride welling in his eyes.

'We're honoured, Lord King.'

'The honour is mine,' Vortigern said. 'Now, go to your people.' He came to attention as Severus Maximus, Publius Luca and Eldof of Glevum approached.

'Lord, it's time,' said the praetor. 'Where would you be crowned? Here, in the curia?'

'No,' Vortigern said. 'In the Chapel of St Alban. In the sight of God.'

A snort of laughter came from the rear of the great

hall. Everyone turned. Rufus was standing there with Idris and two more of his white-clad acolytes. Publius Luca stepped forward.

'Lord Vortimer, your father is about to be crowned king,' he said, with barely-concealed contempt. 'Do you have no respect?'

'Not when the name of God is taken in vain,' Rufus said.

'I don't take it in vain,' Vortigern said. 'Someone has to save this country from ruin. Is it wrong to ask for God's blessing?'

'You should start at home,' Rufus said coolly. He turned to Publius Luca. 'Commander, I mean no disrespect to you, but I want no part of this.'

'You won't come to the Chapel of St Alban, then,' Vortigern said. It was not really a question. Rufus threw his head back, his eyes hurt and angry.

'I will fight the invaders with you in the spring,' he said. 'On that you have my sacred word. But I cannot be part of this tainted performance.' He turned and marched out of the curia with his followers. The sound of clattering hooves punctuated the shouts and singing drifting in from the square as Malan and Edryd got their troops on the move. The smith scrambled aboard the horse Elir had brought for him and hauled someone after him; Flora, Kerin saw, as she cast a final wistful glance towards the doors of the curia. The crowd swept them away. Lud and his warriors, taking no chances, surrounded Vortigern like an iron ring. Kerin turned to Publius Luca.

'Rufus is my dearest friend,' he said. 'But I can't fight this.'

'No-one can,' the commander said. 'Either it'll burn itself out, or there'll be civil war one day soon. Please the gods, not until we have a kingdom strong enough to take it.'

* * *

Gorlois of Kernow had taken it upon himself to guard the door of St Alban's chapel. Eldof of Glevum, somewhat ironically, had decided to help him. Kerin was out of breath. He had run to the chapel through the back streets, to make sure of getting there before Vortigern's party.

'We thought it wise to stop any undesirables getting in,' Eldof said with a condescending smile as Kerin mopped the sweat away and recovered himself.

'No slaves and paupers, then,' Kerin said, with a cheery grin. Eldof leaned towards him.

'You were lucky to get away with that tonight,' he hissed.

'Luck played no part in it,' said Gorlois, planting a large hand on the back of Eldof's neck. 'Go on, get inside and hog one of the best seats, and don't come the patrician with me. We've known each other too well for too long.' Eldof shook off Gorlois's hand, scowled and stalked off into the chapel. 'Hypocritical bastard,' Gorlois said under his breath.

'This is quite finely balanced isn't it,' mused a voice at Kerin's elbow. He didn't have to look.

'Marcellus *magister*,' he said. 'What do you make of all this?'

'It's quite a lot to digest in one evening, my young friend,' said Marcellus, surveying the rows of benches within the chapel. 'Let's speak of it tomorrow. In the meantime, I am going to join all these good Christians who have never set foot in a chapel before. It never ceases to amaze me, what men will do out of sheer self-interest. Lord Gorlois, come and help me find a place. This young man will have his hands full in a moment.'

The sound came suddenly; footsteps echoing between the high walls of the praetor's house and the castra. Lud and the warband leading; members of the city garrison bringing up the rear. And within, of course, the men who mattered. Severus Maximus, as grey and riven with anxiety as ever. Publius Luca, earnest but smiling. Gallus, eyes shining, looking as if he were embarking on the most exciting thing he had done in years. And the king-to-be; who knew what he thought? Kerin had seen him more animated at a funeral. The party reached the chapel door. Kerin stood aside to let them enter. Lud gave him a wink as he passed. The escort swept in and took their seats, leaving Vortigern behind.

'Publius told me that if I cast you off, I'd regret it for the rest of my life,' he said. 'Perhaps he was right. He usually is. If not for you, we'd be fighting in the streets by now. Some of these men would never have acquiesced.'

'I know,' Kerin said. 'I had to make the odds impossible. And I had to make amends.'

'You made some mistakes,' Vortigern said. 'It's what young men do. I should know. I've made more than you could comprehend.' He looked through the open doorway at the mass of men occupying the benches; some loyal, some of shaky allegiance, some of none at all. 'When we leave this place, I shall be king,' he said. 'God knows how it will fall out. But one thing is certain. You are my right arm. Let no man dispute that.' He gripped Kerin's shoulders tightly, then his hands fell away. Gorlois, who had come back to the door, overheard and gave Kerin a little nod of acknowledgement. He stood aside to let Vortigern pass. Kerin went into the chapel and stood at the back, his vision blurred by tears, as Vortigern walked slowly down the narrow aisle. Two men were standing beside the altar with Father Giraldus. Brother Padarn, who was holding the crown, had been joined by Marcellus. The haruspex seemed to have allied himself with the honest men rather than the Christians of convenience, whatever the gulf between their faiths.

'Father,' Vortigern said. 'Will you bless the crown?'

All eyes turned to the tall, black-robed priest.

'Very well,' Giraldus said, with unmistakable regret. Brother Padarn held out the crown, from which he had so recently rinsed the blood. The abbot made the sign of the cross over it and bowed his head in prayer. Vortigern unbuckled his sword-belt and laid it on the altar steps. Giraldus took the crown from Padarn with trembling hands. As Vortigern knelt to receive it, the feeble light on the altar flickered and went out. Kerin's eyes met Marcellus's along the length of the aisle. Giraldus raised Vortigern to his feet and turned from the altar. His eyes were rimmed with tears, which could not have been for Constans. Kerin felt a sudden stab of apprehension.

'Father!' he said, drawing the old priest aside. 'Do you think we chose the wrong king?'

Giraldus laid a gentle hand on his arm. 'You could have chosen no better,' he said. 'But it will be a crown of thorns.'

He bowed his head and went into the darkness. Outside, the wind howled like a demented beast in the empty streets as the monks of St Alban crossed themselves and crept away, white-faced and silent, to light candles for the souls of the dead.

Author's Note

I make no claim at all, in *The West Rises* or the following books in my story of Vortigern, to be writing serious history. This is historical fiction, albeit based on years of research into the period. The 5th and 6th centuries in Britain are not known as the Dark Age for nothing. Some things are known, some never will be. In many instances, it is impossible to disentangle a fragmented historical record from the myths and legends which have accumulated around it. Much of what we think we know was written centuries later, by authors who viewed the period through their own prism of religious conviction or literary convention. Countless volumes have been written about the historical value, or otherwise, of the surviving literature. The earliest-known record is the monk Gildas's *De Excidio Britanniae*, thought to date from the late 5th or early 6th century; not history but a sermon, in which the writer rails against the rulers and churchmen whom he blames for the destruction of the nation. The *Historia Brittonum* of the early 9th century, a compilation of material once attributed to the Welsh monk Nennius, purports to be a history of Britain from its foundation onwards. A synthesis of historical fact and the supernatural, it is the first known text to mention King Arthur. And it seems to have been the single most important source drawn on by Geoffrey of Monmouth, the 11th century cleric whose *History of the Kings of Britain* popularised the legends of Arthur and Merlin, shaping them, embedding them in British culture and feeding the imagination of writers down the generations.

I can still remember the shock I experienced, as a child, when I discovered that there was no King Arthur in the chronology of British monarchs. He wasn't there, and yet he was everywhere. How did that happen? When I went to Cambridge to read English, it was one of the questions which fascinated me. I specialised in medieval literature, encountering everything from the early sources to the courtly romances of Chrétien de Troyes, the alliterative poetry of *Gawain and the Green Knight,* and the chronicles of Thomas Malory. At the same time, I attempted to find out all I could about the history underlying these works. Historical detail was often elusive – sometimes the legends are all we have – but when I turned to writing historical fiction, I wanted to ground these stories in real life. To convey, if possible, an idea of what it might have been like to be alive in those times when the likelihood of death, and the destruction of home, family and way of life, was what people woke up to every single day. No-one could rely on enchantment to save them. No-one had a magic sword.

The character of Arthur was everywhere. In adult fiction, in children's books, on television, at the cinema – there he was, more often than not with his knights, magicians and a castle worthy of the Normans. I wanted to tell a different story, not least because Arthur's has been told so often, and so well. Vortigern started to agitate me. I thought that it might be interesting to write about a villain – and villain he is, throughout the Arthurian canon. Then I started digging more deeply into the history, and began to wonder. In an age where the high-born gave their sons Roman names, implying status and a privileged connection to the Empire, here was a man from the western fringe with an overtly British name – whether given or assumed – who gave his sons British names, whose enemy 'wore the purple', who at least for a while succeeded in holding back the tide of invasion. My preconceptions began to fall away. I had found my story.

Coming from Wales, I'm used to places having at least two names. Caerfyrddin is Carmarthen is Roman Maridunum. It must have been much the same in 5th century Britain. Places which had their own names before the Romans arrived were given Latin names by the occupiers. Over time, these names were sometimes conflated. Educated Romano-Britons would probably have used Latin or Latinised names; the old Brythonic names clung on in rural, less Romanised areas. My story has a mixture of Latin and British names. I don't claim consistency or historical accuracy. I've used the ancient Kernow for Cornwall, but I've stuck with Kent, not too far removed from the Latin Cantium or Welsh Ceint. My use of Cambria for Wales is an anachronism. A Latinised form of the Welsh name for the country, *Cymru*, it only emerged in medieval times, when writers coined the term to differentiate between the Celtic British and Anglo-Saxon kingdoms. But I needed a name which embraced this part of the West, and if it was good enough for Shakespeare in *Cymbeline*, it's good enough for me.

Acknowledgements

To begin at the beginning, I owe an immense debt of gratitude to the late Dr John Stevens of Magdalene College, Cambridge. Musicologist extraordinaire and my inspirational supervisor in medieval literature, he brought the whole subject to such vivid life that I felt compelled to write about it.

As for this book, I should like to thank the following people, without whose help it would not be what it is. Harry Bingham and Rebecca Horsfall of Jericho Writers, for their invaluable criticism, advice and encouragement. Jane Dixon Smith, for her brilliant covers. Debbie Young, for her expertise, enthusiasm and patience in guiding me through the self-publishing maze. And last but not least, my family. It can't be easy, living with writers and their obsessions, but they have done it with unfailing grace, support and love.

See where it all began …

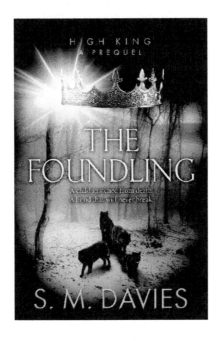

Thank you for reading *The West Rises*.

If you have enjoyed it, and would like to know more about some of the characters you have met, go to smdaviesauthor.com/the-foundling to join the High King Readers' Club and receive your free copy of *The Foundling*. This eBook is a free, no-obligation download, available exclusively to members of the Readers' Club, and will not be available elsewhere.

The Foundling is a short story about the night, many years earlier, when Vortigern saved the infant Kerin from certain death. Only the barest outline can be deduced from The West Rises and its sequels. Vortigern's story is seen through Kerin's eyes, and the young warrior was a newborn baby when these events took place – the foundling of the title.

Members of my Readers' Club will receive an occasional email about forthcoming books, my research for the series and the locations where it is set. You'll have first access to any free offers, including a link enabling you to read the first three chapters of Under The Dragon prior to publication. I care about your privacy, and it'll be easy for you to unsubscribe from the list should you ever wish to. All downloads are yours to keep regardless.

Once again, thank you for reading my books. If you have enjoyed them, and would like to tell others what you thought about them – whether by leaving a review on Amazon, Goodreads or any e-store, or on your social media – that would be great. Word of mouth matters more than anything to a writer, and any effort you make will be much appreciated.

SMD

Coming Next –
High King 2: *Under The Dragon*

Vortigern and his armies raise the dragon standard and march for Hadrian's Wall, to take on the invaders in the North. But the High King has more than one enemy to face. The breach with his oldest son threatens to become final, as Rufus condemns his father's decision to employ Saxon mercenary captain Hengist and his band of pagan adventurers. On the eve of battle, jealous rivals are already plotting to topple the king, led by old adversary Eldof of Glevum and Kerin's nemesis, his kinsman Bertil Redknife.

Kerin, now known to all as 'the king's right arm', has secured his position at Vortigern's side. Bitterly mistrustful of Hengist, but desperate to keep Vortigern's fragile coalition together, he will need all his wits and courage as the Saxons strengthen their hand and Rufus, once his closest friend, gathers fanatical allies to face down his father. Rufus is driven by faith alone, but Vortigern's enemies will soon find a way to use the idealistic young man for their own ends.

Kerin's devotion to Vortigern is beyond question, but now he has a new force to reckon with – his love for Bertil Redknife's daughter, Gael. Vortigern demands nothing less than absolute loyalty, but Kerin refuses to abandon his hope to win Gael and make her his wife. He stands to lose everything he has achieved, as battle lines are drawn and the family of the woman he loves make their play for power.

But something else is about to happen. An event which even Kerin, with all his powers of foresight and intuition, has not foreseen. An event which will rock the foundations of his life, and even make him question whose side he is on, as the kingdom slides towards civil war.

If you would like to read the first three chapters of Under The Dragon before it launches, go to smdaviesauthor.com/the-foundling to get your free eBook The Foundling, and join the High King Readers' Club. You will receive a link to the sample chapters free of charge prior to publication.

About the Author

Photography by Raul Rucarean (raphotography.org.uk)

Born in South Wales, S.M. Davies read English at Cambridge, specialising in medieval literature and exploring the history which underlies the spellbinding legends of Early Britain. After graduating she worked as a professional indexer for leading publishers, usually on historical texts – everything from Ancient Babylon to World War Two. Since then she has spent her working life on the Gower Peninsula, first as a farmer, then a hotelier, and finally as a pub and nightclub owner. During these years she continued her research and wrote the first draft of the High King series, much of it based amidst the Welsh landscapes she knows and loves. She still lives on the edge of Gower, close to her children and their families, and shares her home with two sheepdogs.

Printed in Great Britain
by Amazon

87030825R00284